ESSENTIAL
SCIENCE

Philippa Wingate, Clive Gifford and Rebecca Treays

Illustrated by Sean Wilkinson and
Robert Walster
Additional illustrations by Aziz Khan, Ian Jackson and Chris Shields

Designed by Robert Walster, Sharon Bennett
and John Russell
Additional designs by Diane Thistlethwaite
and Radhi Parekh

Consultants: John Allen, Dr Tom Petersen, Paul Bonell,
Michael White, Dr Andrew Rudge,
Kris Scheinkonig, Peter Richardson, Jonathan Cook
and Sheila Martin

Series editor: Jane Chisholm

Contents

ESSENTIAL
PHYSICS

Philippa Wingate

Illustrated by Sean Wilkinson and Robert Walster

Designed by Robert Walster

Additional designs by John Russell and Radhi Parekh

Consultants: John Allen, Dr. Tom Petersen and Paul Bonell
Series editor: Jane Chisholm

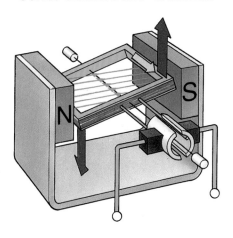

Contents

Using this section of the book

Essential Physics is a concise aid to reference and revision. It is intended to act as a companion to your studies, explaining the essential points of physics clearly and simply.

Physics is the study of matter and energy, and the way in which matter and energy interact in the world around us. This section is divided into chapters which cover the main concepts of physics.

Each chapter includes the key principles and facts for that topic, and their applications. Particularly important new words and equations are highlighted in **bold** type. If a word is explained in more detail on another page, it is printed in italic type with an asterisk, like this: *magnetism**. At the foot of the page there is a reference to the page on which the explanation can be found.

The information at the back of this section

The social, economic and environmental implications of some of the topics covered in the main part of this section are looked at in more detail in the black and white pages at the back of this section. This is followed by a variety of information, including a list of symbols used to show components in electrical circuits, and advice on number notation and graphs.

You will also find a chapter which contains some of the more difficult mathematical ideas in physics. This includes some sample examination questions and model answers, to help you become familiar with using equations and mathematical ideas.

There is a glossary that explains difficult words in the text.

Examinations

This section contains the essential information you will need when studying physics. For examinations, however, it is important to know which syllabus you are studying, because different examining

bodies require you to learn different material. You may find that there are topics in this book that you do not need to learn, or that certain topics covered by your syllabus do not appear in this book.

Equations and symbols

When studying physics it is necessary to measure certain physical quantities, such as speed, weight and distance. Each of these quantities is given its own **symbol** and **unit** of measurement. For example, time is represented by the symbol t, and is measured in seconds (s).

To find some quantities, you have to multiply or divide others. The relationship between quantities can be expressed as an **equation**, either with words or symbols. For example, the relationship between force, mass and acceleration can be expressed as:

Force = mass x acceleration or F = ma.

In this book you will find triangles beside some of the equations in the text. These triangles are a mathematical device to help you remember and rearrange equations to find unknown quantities. The triangles contain the symbols of the quantities involved in the equations.

The triangles are used as follows:
Decide which quantity you wish to calculate. Cover up the symbol for that quantity.

If the symbol you have covered is at the bottom of the triangle, you will need to divide the quantity at the top of the triangle by the one which remains uncovered at the bottom.

If the symbol you have covered is at the top of the triangle, the two quantities at the bottom must be multiplied.

For example, in an examination question you might be asked to calculate the acceleration of a mass of 2 kg, when affected by a force of 6 newtons. Cover a, and replace the symbols for force and mass with their values.

$$a = \frac{6}{2} = 3 \text{ m/s}^2$$

Structure and measurement of matter

All matter is made up of molecules. The smallest naturally occurring particle of any substance is called a **molecule**. Molecules are too small to be seen with the human eye, but their existence can be demonstrated by Brownian motion and diffusion, as described below.

Matter can exist in three physical states - as a **solid**, a **liquid** or a **gas**. The **kinetic theory** explains the structure and behaviour of substances in these states in terms of the motion of their molecules.

Solids

The molecules in a solid are packed closely together in regular structures. They do not have enough energy to break free of the forces of attraction which bind them to their neighbouring molecules. They can only vibrate. This is why solids have a fixed shape and a fixed *volume** and do not flow like liquids.

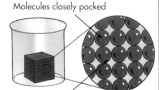

Molecules closely packed

Molecules can only vibrate.

Liquids

Molecules have just enough energy to move.

The molecules in a liquid have just enough energy to break free of the forces which bind them to their neighbours. This is why liquids are able to flow and do not have a fixed shape. However, the forces are strong enough to hold the molecules close together, giving liquids a fixed volume.

Gases

The molecules in a gas have so much energy that the force of attraction between them is negligible. They can move freely and at great speed. The molecules in a gas are much further apart than those in a liquid or a solid. This is why gases can be compressed easily.

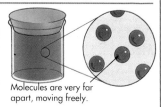

Molecules are very far apart, moving freely.

Brownian motion

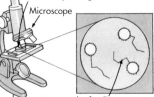

A cell of pollen grains in water

Microscope

Erratic path of pollen grains

The molecules in liquids and gases are continually moving in a completely random fashion. This is known as **Brownian motion**, after the botanist Sir Robert Brown who first studied the nature of their movement. He demonstrated that pollen grains placed in water move erratically. This motion is due to the pollen grains' unseen impact with water molecules. The tiny water molecules are able to move the much larger pollen grains because there is a large number of water molecules and they are moving very fast.

Diffusion

Diffusion is the gradual mixing of two or more different gases or liquids. Diffusion happens when the molecules of the substances collide and intermingle. For example, the scent of flowers spreads through a room because its molecules diffuse through the air. The process of diffusion supports the idea of moving molecules, since the particles must be moving in order to mix. (See page 133).

Atoms

Molecules are made up of groups of smaller particles called **atoms**. Atoms are formed of even smaller particles called **electrons**, **protons** and **neutrons**. The structure of an atom is shown here using the example of a helium atom. The central nucleus of an atom is formed of protons and neutrons. Protons have a positive *electrical charge** and neutrons have no charge. Protons and neutrons are approximately 2,000 times more massive than the electrons which orbit the nucleus. Electrons have a negative charge, equal in magnitude to the positive charge of the protons. The number of electrons in an atom is the same as the number of protons in the nucleus.

The number of protons in a nucleus is

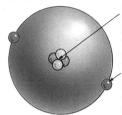

A helium atom

The nucleus is a cluster of protons and neutrons.

The electrons are held in a 'cloud-like' orbit, attracted by the positive charge of the protons.

called the **proton number** (**Z**). The total number of protons and neutrons in a nucleus is called the **nucleon number** (**A**). The nucleon and the proton number of an atom are written next to the symbol for the *element** to which the atom belongs. For example, helium is written: ${}^{4}_{2}$He

Measuring mass

The **mass** of an object is the measure of how much matter it contains. Mass is measured in **kilograms** (kg). To find the mass of an object, simple balancing scales like the ones shown are used to compare the unknown mass with a known mass.

Known mass

Unknown mass

Measuring volume

A Eureka can is filled with water.

The object displaces water into the measuring cylinder.

The object's volume is equal to the volume of the water it displaces.

The **volume** of an object is the measurement of the amount of space it occupies. It is measured in **cubic metres** (m³) or **cubic centimetres** (cm³). The volume of regular shaped solids is found using a ruler and mathematical formulae. For example, the volume of a rectangular block is found using the equation: length x breadth x height. The volume of a liquid can be found by pouring it into a measuring cylinder. The volume of an irregular shaped solid is measured by **displacement** as shown in the diagram.

Measuring density

Objects which are the same size and shape can vary greatly in mass. For example, one cubic centimetre of cork is much lighter than a cubic centimetre of lead. This is because the materials have a different **density**. Molecules of lead are heavier and more closely packed together than those of cork. This makes lead a more dense material than cork.

To find the density of a solid or a liquid its mass and volume must be measured using the methods described above. These quantities are used in the equation:

Density (d) = $\dfrac{\text{mass (m)}}{\text{volume (v)}}$

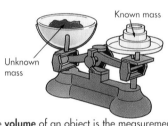

Density is measured in **kilograms per cubic metre** (kg/m³), or **grammes per cubic centimetre** (g/cm³).

Forces

A **force** is a push or a pull which can affect the motion of an object by changing its speed or direction. If two equal and opposite forces act on an object it may be squashed or stretched. Both the magnitude and direction of a force acting on an object must be stated, because both affect the way in which the object moves. If the direction in which a force is acting is known, it is possible to predict the way the object it affects may move. Forces are represented by arrowed lines whose length corresponds to the magnitude of the force. The arrow indicates the direction in which it is acting. Force is measured in **newtons** (**N**).

A man pushing a broom with 2 N force.

A man exerting a stretching force of 40 N.

The golf club exerts a 50 N force.

A man exerting a 500 N pulling force.

Magnetic and electrical forces

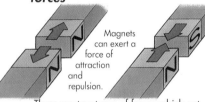

Magnets can exert a force of attraction and repulsion.

There are two types of forces which act at a distance: *magnetic** and *electrical** forces. Both types of force are described in detail later in the book. Objects which exert a magnetic or an electrical force can attract or repel objects which are brought near them. The region in which the forces act is called a **field**. The magnitude of the forces depends on the distance between the objects. The closer they are together, the stronger the force they exert.

Gravitation and weight

Gravitation is another force which acts at a distance. It is the force which exists between any two masses, attracting them toward each other. Usually it is a weak force, but if one object is massive, such as a planet, the force becomes noticeable. Gravitational force depends

A man of mass 100 kg weighs 980 N on Earth. At a distance of 10,000 km from the Earth's surface, for example, he weighs only 150 N.

Frictional forces

Friction is the force which resists the motion of two materials rubbing together. Sometimes it is a useful force - for example, it enables us to grip the ground as we walk. A vehicle is able to grip the road due to the friction between its tyres and the road surface. But friction also has unwanted effects. The friction between the moving parts of a *machine** produces heat which wastes energy. The friction between a cyclist and the air resists his or her forward movement.

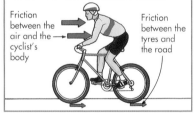

Friction between the air and the cyclist's body

Friction between the tyres and the road

on the distance between objects. The closer the objects are together, the stronger the force they exert on each other.

Weight is a measure of a planet's gravitational pull on an object. Like all forces, it is measured in newtons (N). The weight of an object depends on its distance from a planet and the planet's mass. On the Earth's surface, the force of gravity acting on a mass of 1 kg is approximately 9.8 N. The magnitude of the force diminishes as the mass moves further away from the Earth's surface. An object's mass, however, remains the same wherever it is in the Universe.

*Magnetic forces, 36; Electrical forces, 31; Machine, 15.

Elasticity

When a force is applied to an object which cannot move, the object stretches. Its molecules are pulled slightly apart and it becomes distorted. If the object remains distorted when the force is removed, its distortion is called **plastic**. If its molecules return to their original position, the distortion is called **elastic**. **Elasticity** is, therefore, a material's ability to return to its original shape. To study the elasticity of a material, such as a strip of copper, rubber or nylon, weights of increasing size are suspended from the material. The amount by which the material is stretched is found by subtracting its original length from its extended length. The size of the force is then increased and the results are used to make a graph.

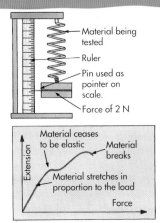

Material being tested
Ruler
Pin used as pointer on scale.
Force of 2 N

Material ceases to be elastic
Material breaks
Material stretches in proportion to the load
Extension
Force

Hooke's law

Hooke's law states that **the extension of a material is proportional to the force which is stretching it.**

There is a point, however, beyond which Hooke's law is no longer obeyed. This is called the **limit of proportionality.** If the substance is stretched further than this point, it reaches its **elastic limit.** The substance stops being elastic and remains distorted even when the stretching force is removed.

Provided a material's elastic limit is not exceeded, the principle of Hooke's law can be used in calculations to determine an unknown force or extension. For example, if a force of 10 N stretches a spring by 60 mm, the force which would produce an extension of 42 mm is calculated as follows:

60 mm extension is produced by 10 N

1 mm extension is produced by $\frac{10}{60}$

Therefore, the force which would produce a 42 mm extension is calculated as follows:

$$\frac{10 \times 42}{60} = 7 \text{ N}$$

A spring balance

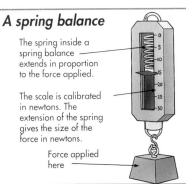

The spring inside a spring balance extends in proportion to the force applied.

The scale is calibrated in newtons. The extension of the spring gives the size of the force in newtons.

Force applied here

The easiest way of measuring forces is to use a **spring balance**, often called a **Newton balance.** This is a device containing a spring. The spring obeys Hooke's law. This means that it stretches in direct proportion to the force applied to it. For example, if the force applied to the spring is doubled, its extension doubles. The spring balance will measure forces accurately until it is stretched beyond its elastic limit and it becomes permanently distorted.

Scalar and vector quantities

Quantities in physics are described as either scalar or vector quantities.

A **scalar** quantity is one which has magnitude only. For example, mass and temperature are scalar quantities.

A **vector** quantity is one which has both direction and magnitude. Force is a vector quantity. The magnitude and direction of a vector must always be stated. Vectors can be represented with arrowed lines.

Turning forces

If an object is fixed at a point around which it may rotate, the point is called the **fulcrum**. If a force is applied to it, at a distance from the fulcrum, the object may rotate. This turning effect is called a

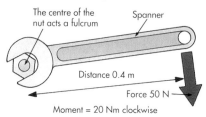

The centre of the nut acts a fulcrum

Spanner

Distance 0.4 m

Force 50 N

Moment = 20 Nm clockwise

moment. A moment is exerted if a door is opened, if a crowbar is used to lift a load and when a spanner turns a nut.

The moment which tries to rotate an object in a anticlockwise direction is called an **anticlockwise moment**. The moment which tries to turn the object clockwise is called a **clockwise moment**.

A turning moment is equal to the magnitude of the force, multiplied by the distance of the point where the force is acting from the fulcrum. This is written:

Moment = force x distance from fulcrum.
Turning moments are measured in **newton metres (Nm)**.

The principle of moments

If an object is in **equilibrium** (or balanced), the sum of the clockwise moments about any point is equal to the sum of the anticlockwise moments about the same point. This is the principle of moments and, when two moments are exerted, this is written as follows:

Weight $_1$ x distance $_1$ = Weight $_2$ x distance $_2$

If an object is in equilibrium it is possible to calculate an unknown weight, or the unknown distance between a weight and the fulcrum. For example, the seesaw shown here is 2 m long. It is balanced. Child A weighs 200 N and sits 0.75 m

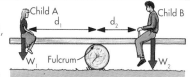

Child A
d_1

d_2
Child B

W_1 Fulcrum W_2

from the fulcrum, or point of balance. Child B, of unknown weight, sits 0.5 m from the fulcrum. The weight of child B can be calculated as follows:

$$W_1 \times d_1 = W_2 \times d_2$$
$$200 \times 0.75 = W_2 \times 0.5$$
$$W_2 = \frac{200 \times 0.75}{0.5}$$
$$W_2 = 300 \text{ N}$$

The centre of gravity

An object's **centre of gravity** is the point through which its total weight is considered to act. The centre of gravity of a regular shaped object is its geometrical centre. For example, the centre of gravity of a square is the point at which lines bisecting each of its angles cross.

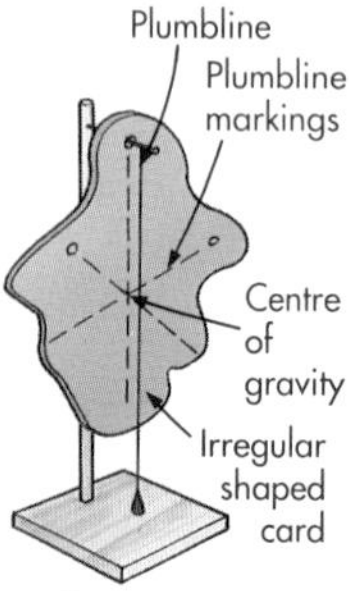

Plumbline

Plumbline markings

Centre of gravity

Irregular shaped card

The centre of gravity of an irregular shaped flat object is found by suspending it from a pin fixed in a clamp and hanging a plumbline from the pin. The position of the plumbline is marked. This is repeated with the pin at different places on the shape's edge. The centre of gravity lies where all the plumbline markings intersect.

Stability

The **stability** of an object is its ability to return to its original position when tilted. Stability is governed by the position of an object's centre of gravity and the surface area of its base.

Stable objects have a low centre of gravity and a large base.

Centre of gravity

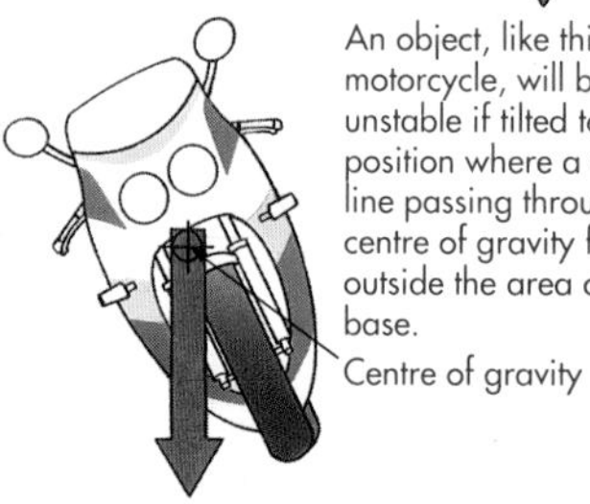

An object, like this motorcycle, will become unstable if tilted to a position where a vertical line passing through its centre of gravity falls outside the area of its base.

Centre of gravity

Pressure

Pressure is affected by the magnitude of a force and the area over which the force acts. It is calculated with the equation:

Pressure (P) = $\frac{\text{force (F)}}{\text{area (A)}}$

Pressure is measured in **newtons per metre² (N/m²)** or **Pascals (Pa)**.

A woman with high-heeled shoes exerts a greater pressure on the ground than if she wears flat-soled boots. Her weight

The boots exert a smaller pressure.

The high-heeled shoes exert a larger pressure.

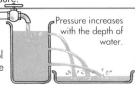

acting on a small area produces a large pressure. Her weight acting over the larger area of the boot produces a smaller pressure.

Pressure in liquids

Pressure in a liquid depends on its depth and *density**. For example, as a swimmer dives to the bottom of a pool the pressure acting on him or her increases. The pressure is produced by the weight of the water above the swimmer. The more water there is, the greater the pressure it exerts. If the pure water is replaced by a denser liquid, such as sea water, the pressure exerted on the swimmer is greater.

Pressure increases with the depth of water.

Pressure in liquid = depth of the liquid (h) x the density of the liquid (d) x *acceleration due to gravity (g)**

Hydraulic machines

A hydraulic press

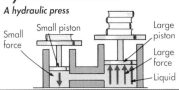

Small force

Small piston

Large piston

Large force

Liquid

Hydraulic machines use liquids to function. Pressure acts equally in all directions throughout liquids and changes in pressure are transmitted instantly. In a hydraulic press, a small force applied to a small piston is magnified as it is transferred to a second piston with a larger surface area.

Atmospheric pressure

Atmospheric pressure is the pressure exerted by the weight of air particles. It varies with height above the ground. A long column of air exerts a greater pressure than a short one. Atmospheric

pressure is smaller on a mountain top because the air column above is shorter and the air itself is less dense. The mercury barometer and aneroid barometer measure atmospheric pressure.

A mercury barometer

The column of mercury in a **mercury barometer** is pushed up the glass tube by air pressure. The height of the mercury column is directly affected by the magnitude of atmospheric pressure.

Atmospheric pressure can be expressed as the height of the mercury column (h).

Atmospheric pressure

Vacuum

Mercury

Glass tube

h

An aneroid barometer

An **aneroid barometer** measures the effect of pressure on a metal box which has had some of the air removed from inside it.

If air pressure increases, the case is slightly squashed, moving the spring.

The levers translate the movement of the spring to move a pointer against a scale.

Partial vacuum

Thin metal case

Spring

Scale

Pointer

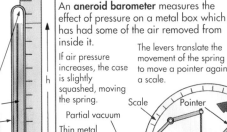

*Density, 5; Acceleration due to gravity, 11.

Linear motion

Any change in an object's position is called **motion**. When a force acts on an object which is able to move, the object will begin to move in the direction in which the force is acting. If the object moves in a straight line, its motion is said to be linear.

Speed

The **speed** of an object is defined as the distance it travels in one second. For example, the speed of a train might be 5 metres per second. If an object's speed does not change from the beginning of its journey to the end, it is moving at **constant** or **uniform speed**. If its speed constantly changes, the object's average speed can be calculated with the following equation:

Average speed = distance travelled / time taken

Speed is measured in **metres per second** (**m/s**). It is a *scalar** quantity.

A ticker-timer

Motion can be studied using a ticker-timer. A moving object pulls a paper tape through the timer which prints a dot on the tape every $\frac{1}{50}$th of a second.

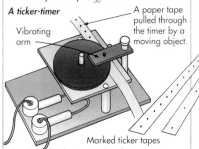

A ticker-timer

Vibrating arm

A paper tape pulled through the timer by a moving object.

Marked ticker tapes

The distance between the dots on a tape depends on how fast the object travels. A slow-moving object produces dots printed close together. A faster moving object produces more widely spaced dots.

Distance/time graphs

The ticker-timer tapes produced by a moving trolley can be used to construct distance/time graphs. One dot on the tape is chosen as a starting point and the distance between this dot and successive dots is measured. This gives the distance travelled by the trolley in $\frac{1}{50}$th, $\frac{2}{50}$ths and $\frac{3}{50}$ths of a second and so on. When a distance/time graph is drawn, the trolley's speed at any moment is equal to the *gradient** at that point.

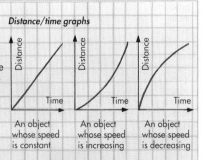

Distance/time graphs

An object whose speed is constant

An object whose speed is increasing

An object whose speed is decreasing

Velocity

An object's **velocity** is a measure of how fast it travels in a given direction. Velocity is a *vector** quantity. For example, the velocity of a car might be 10 m/s north. An object whose velocity does not change is said to have a **constant velocity**. If an object's velocity is constantly changing, its **average velocity** can be calculated with the equation:

Average velocity
= distance travelled in a given direction / time taken

Velocity is measured in **metres per second** (**m/s**) in a given direction.

Acceleration

An object is accelerating when its velocity increases. If its velocity decreases, it is decelerating. An object whose velocity is changing by the same amount in equal periods of time is said to be moving with **uniform acceleration**. Acceleration is a vector quantity and includes an indication of direction. The average acceleration of an object is calculated with the following equation:

Acceleration = change in velocity / time taken for change

Acceleration is measured in **metres per second per second** (**m/s²**).

*Gradient , 55; Scalar, Vector, 7.

Velocity/time graphs

A velocity/time graph can be constructed using ticker-tapes as shown in this diagram. The tapes are cut into strips showing 5 time intervals between them. The length of each strip is a measure of the trolley's average velocity over a $\frac{5}{50}$ ths of a second period (0.1 s). The trolley's acceleration at any moment is equal to the gradient of the graph at that point. The distance the trolley travels is equal to the area under the speed/time *graph* * it produces.

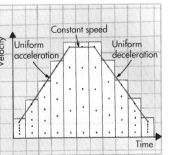

Force, mass and acceleration

The relationship between force, mass and acceleration can be studied with the equipment shown in this diagram.

A trolley is pulled down a ramp by a fixed pulling force. This fixed force is applied by one elastic band which is stretched by a fixed amount. To calculate the trolley's acceleration, a velocity/time graph is constructed from the tape produced. The force exerted on the trolley is then doubled by using two elastic bands and the trolley's acceleration is calculated again.

The results of the experiment show that the trolley's acceleration doubles when the force doubles. This means that, if the trolley's mass remains constant, that acceleration is *directly proportional** to force.

The experiment is repeated with the force applied to the trolley kept constant, but the trolley's mass is increased by stacking another trolley on top of the first. Acceleration is calculated.

This experiment shows that, when the trolley's mass is doubled, its acceleration is halved. This means that, if the force remains constant, acceleration is *inversely proportional** to mass.

The results produced by the experiments prove the following equation:

Force (F) = mass (m) x acceleration (a)
(in newtons) (in kg)   (in m/s²)

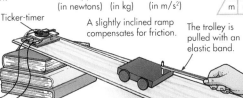

Ticker-timer

A slightly inclined ramp compensates for friction.

The trolley is pulled with an elastic band.

The acceleration of a free-falling object

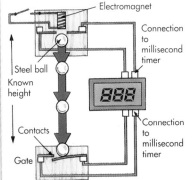

Electromagnet

Connection to millisecond timer

Steel ball

Known height

Contacts

Connection to millisecond timer

Gate

An object falling toward the ground accelerates as it falls, because of the pull of *gravity**. The value of **acceleration due to gravity (g)** can be determined using the equipment shown in the diagram. A steel ball is held by an electromagnet. A switch turns off the magnet and turns on the millisecond timer simultaneously. The ball falls a known distance, hitting a gate which turns off the timer.

The results show that the value of g at the Earth's surface is 9.8 m/s². This means that for each second an object is falling, its velocity increases by 9.8 m/s.

*Graph calculations, 55; Directly proportional, Inversely proportional, 61; Gravity, 6.

11

Dynamics

Dynamics is the study of the effect of a force on the motion of an object. Newton described this relationship in three laws.

Newton's first law

When the forces acting on an object are equal and opposite, they cancel each other out. If the object on which they act is at rest, it will stay at rest; if it is moving, it will move at _constant velocity_*.

For example, if a parachutist jumps from a plane, there is a period before his parachute opens, when the drag force between his body and the air balances his

A spacecraft out of reach of the Earth's gravitational pull, no forces are acting on it.

weight, and his velocity remains constant. This law also explains why a spacecraft deep in space moves at a constant velocity until a force acts on it. This force could come from having its engines fired, or from entering the _gravitational field_* of a planet.

Newton's second law

If an unbalanced force acts on an object, it accelerates in the direction in which the force acts. The object's acceleration is directly proportional to the force, if its mass remains constant.

For example, the constant force produced by the rocket engines of a spacecraft makes it _accelerate_*. The acceleration doubles if the force of the

engines doubles. Newton's second law is also demonstrated by the ticker-timer and trolley experiment (page 11) which proved the equation:

Force = mass x acceleration.

This is an important statement of Newton's second law. It produces the definition of a newton as the force which gives a mass of 1 kg an acceleration of 1 m/s².

Newton's third law

The force of the football on the ground

The upward force of the ground on the football

For every force there is an equal and opposite force called a reaction force.

Newton's third law shows that forces always occur in pairs. When one object (A) exerts a force on another object (B), object B exerts an equal but opposite force on A. For example, if a person on roller skates pushes someone else on roller skates, both skaters will move away from each other in opposite directions. The equal and opposite forces do not cancel each other out, because each force is acting on a different object.

Momentum

The **momentum** of an object is its mass multiplied by its velocity. Momentum is a _vector_* quantity. A car of mass 1,500 kg travelling at a velocity of 10 m/s has a momentum of 15,000 kg m/s.

When two objects collide they apply equal and opposite forces to each other. One object may gain an amount of momentum equal to the amount the other object loses, but their total momentum remains the same before and after the collision. This is a statement of the **principle of conservation of momentum.**

Before collision the cars' total momentum $= m_1u_1 + m_2u_2$

The moving car has a velocity u_1.

The stationary car has a velocity u_2.

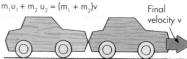

m_1 m_2

After the collision the cars move together, their total momentum $= (m_1+m_2)v$. Then by the law of conservation of momentum:

$m_1u_1 + m_2u_2 = (m_1 + m_2)v$

Final velocity v

*Constant velocity, Acceleration, 10; Gravitational field, 6; Vectors, 7.

Energy

Everything needs **energy** to function. Creatures need the energy stored in food to carry out their vital functions. Machines need the energy stored in chemical fuels to perform tasks. All forms of energy are measured in **joules (J)**.

Different forms of energy

Energy exists in many forms. *Heat**, *sound**, *nuclear energy**, *electromagnetic radiation** and *electrical energy** are all forms of energy and each is looked at in detail later in this book.

Potential energy is the energy an object has because of its position. It is energy which has been stored.

Gravitational potential energy is an example of potential energy. It is the energy an object has because of its position above the Earth. The further above the Earth it is, the more gravitational potential energy it stores up. For example, a diver on a high board has more gravitational potential energy than she has when standing on the ground. When she dives and returns to ground level, she loses her gravitational potential energy.

Elastic energy is the potential energy some materials have when they are squashed or stretched. They have the potential energy to spring back to their normal shape. For example, a spring has elastic energy when it is squashed.

Chemical energy is stored energy which is released during some chemical reactions. Coal and wood contain chemical energy and produce heat when burnt. Cells contain chemical energy which is used to produce electrical energy.

Kinetic energy is the energy possessed by any object because it is moving. For example, a swing has kinetic energy when it is moving.

As the swing moves, energy is continually converted from potential energy, at the top of its swinging motion, to kinetic energy at the bottom of its swinging motion.

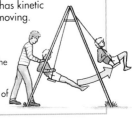

Energy conversion

When energy changes from one form to another it is called **energy conversion**. For example, the diver's potential energy is converted into kinetic energy as she dives. If a number of energy changes take place, an energy chain is produced.

The source of most of the energy on Earth is the Sun. In most energy chains the last form of the energy is heat. The diagram below shows the chain of energy conversions which take place in a coal-fired power station.

Fossil fuels store chemical energy.

Furnace - Fuel is burnt to produce heat energy.

Steam driven turbines produce kinetic energy.

Dynamo - Kinetic energy is used to produce electrical energy.

Appliances - Electricity produces heat, light and sound.

The law of conservation of energy

The law of conservation of energy states that **energy cannot be created or destroyed, only converted from one form to another.** At any stage in a chain of energy conversion the number of joules of energy present is the same, because the total amount of energy in existence cannot alter.

Heat, 26; Sound, 18; Nuclear energy, 44; Electromagnetic radiation, 45; Electrical energy, 32. **13**

Work, energy and machines

Work is done when a force is applied to an object and the object moves in the direction the force is acting. For example, work is done when a crate is lifted or a car is pushed. However, if a crate is too heavy to be lifted, or if the person pushing the car is unable to get the car moving, no work is done.

To calculate the amount of work done when a force moves an object, the magnitude of the force is multiplied by the distance the object is moved. This is written as follows:

Work (W) = force (F) x distance object moves in direction of force (d)

Work is measured in **joules (J)**. 1 J of work is done when a force of 1 N moves an object a distance of 1 m.

Work and energy

Energy is needed for work to be done. For example, if an object A exerts a force on another object B, and B moves, then work has been done by A on B and energy has been transferred from A to B. The amount of energy transferred is equal to the amount of work done.

Lifting

Work is done when an object is lifted off the ground against the force of gravity. The object which is lifted gains *potential energy** as the work is done. The amount of potential energy the object gains is calculated with the equation:

Potential energy (P.E.) = weight (mg) x height raised (h)

This can also be written as follows:

P.E. = mgh

Mass (m)

Force of gravity (g)

Height (h)

Pushing and pulling

Work is done when an object is pushed or pulled and it moves. For example, when the man below pushes the car, the car starts to move, gaining *kinetic energy**. The amount of kinetic energy it gains is calculated with the following equation:

Kinetic energy (K.E.) = ½ mass (m) x velocity² (v²)

This can also be written as follows:

K.E. = ½ mv²

The man must do work to overcome the force of friction between the car's tyres and the ground.

Non-renewable sources of energy

*Electrical energy** is essential to many aspects of human activity. A variety of fuel sources are used to generate electrical energy. Fossil fuels, such as coal, oil and natural gas, are called **non-renewable energy sources**. They were laid down under the Earth's surface millions of years ago.

At present these resources are in plentiful supply, but once used up, they cannot be replaced. Energy-saving measures, ranging from increasing the efficiency of machines to insulating homes to reduce heat loss, will help preserve non-renewable resources.

Renewable sources of energy

Some sources of energy, such as the Sun, are virtually inexhaustible. These are called **renewable energy sources**. Solar power can be converted into electrical energy in solar furnaces or solar powered homes. Other renewable energy sources include geothermal power (heat energy from the centre of the Earth), wind and wave power. Renewable energy soruces will become more and more important in the future.

Windmills gain kinetic energy from the wind.

*Potential energy, Kinetic energy, Electrical energy, 13.

Machines

The force applied to a machine is called the **effort**. The force moved by an effort is called the **load**. Machines are used in many different situations to make work easier. They achieve this by magnifying the effect of an effort. In this way, a small effort can be used to overcome a much greater load.

A pulley

A **pulley** is a machine made up of one or more wheels and a rope, belt or chain. A small effort applied to a pulley system can lift a heavy load. However, in order to do this, the effort has to move a

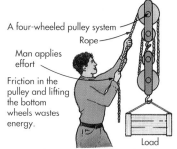

A four-wheeled pulley system

Rope

Man applies effort

Friction in the pulley and lifting the bottom wheels wastes energy.

Load

greater distance than the load. In the pulley system shown above, the effort must move far enough to shorten all four strings of the lower part of the pulley before it lifts the load.

Power

The **power** of a person or a machine is a measure of how quickly they do work or the rate at which they change one form of energy into another. Power is calculated with the following equation:

Power (P) = $\frac{\text{work done (W)}}{\text{time taken (t)}}$

Power is measured in **watts (W)**. 1 W is equal to 1 joule of work done in 1 second. Large quantities of power are measured in kilowatts (1,000 watts) and megawatts (1,000,000 watts).

The power output of a system like the

human body can be calculated with the following equation:

Power output = $\frac{\text{force x distance moved}}{\text{time taken}}$

For example, if a boy weighing 600 N runs up a flight of stairs (vertical height of 3 m) in 6 seconds, his power output is calculated as follows:

Power output
$= \frac{600 \times 3}{6}$
$= 300$ watts

Height

Efficiency of a machine

Efficiency is a measure of how good a machine is at doing its job. Machines are never perfectly efficient. When they convert one form of energy to another form, some of the energy supplied by the effort is not changed into the required form. This means for all machines, the work output is less than the work input. For example, the man lifting a crate (shown at the top of this page) not only lifts the weight of the crate, he also lifts the weight of the lower wheels and the rope of the pulley. In addition he does work to overcome the frictional forces which exist between the moving parts of the pulley system. This wasted energy reduces the efficiency of the pulley.

Efficiency is usually expressed as a percentage. A 'perfect machine' which

did not waste any energy would be 100% efficient. Efficiency is calculated with any of the following equations:

Efficiency = $\frac{\text{work output}}{\text{work input}}$ x 100

or = $\frac{\text{energy output}}{\text{energy input}}$ x 100

or = $\frac{\text{power output}}{\text{power input}}$ x 100

For example, if the man using the pulley system exerts a 200 N effort through a distance of 2 m, to lift a 600 N load a height of 0.5 m, his work input is 400 J (200 x 2). The machine's work output is 300 J (600 x 0.5).

The pulley system's efficiency
$= \frac{300}{400}$ x 100
$= 75\%$

*Friction, 6.

Waves

When an object disturbs the *medium** around it, the disturbance travels away from the source in the form of **waves.** Waves which transport energy away from a source are called **progressive waves**. A wave does not permanently disturb the medium through which it travels. For example, as a wave passes along the surface of water, the water particles vibrate up and down. They do not travel with the wave; they eventually return to their original positions. Waves are either **longitudinal** or **transverse**, depending on the vibrations which cause them.

Transverse waves

In a transverse wave the vibrations which form the wave move at right angles to the direction in which the wave is travelling. Water waves have a transverse motion.

The rope is vibrated up and down

Rope

Direction the wave is travelling

Longitudinal waves

A longitudinal wave is one in which the particles vibrate in the same direction as the wave is travelling. As a vibrating object moves forwards, it squashes the particles of a medium together to form **compressions**. When the object moves backwards, the particles of the medium become widely spaced, forming **rarefactions**. The compressions and rarefactions produced both travel away from the object. *Sound waves** have a longitudinal wave motion.

Compression   Rarefaction

Direction the wave is travelling

The coil is vibrated backwards and forwards.

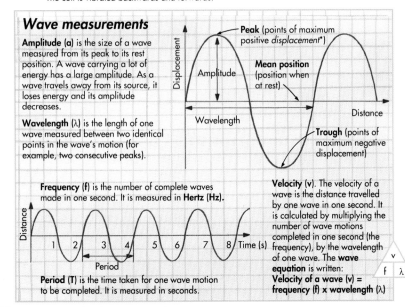

Wave measurements

Amplitude (a) is the size of a wave measured from its peak to its rest position. A wave carrying a lot of energy has a large amplitude. As a wave travels away from its source, it loses energy and its amplitude decreases.

Wavelength (λ) is the length of one wave measured between two identical points in the wave's motion (for example, two consecutive peaks).

Peak (points of maximum positive *displacement**)

Mean position (position when at rest)

Amplitude

Displacement

Distance

Wavelength

Trough (points of maximum negative displacement)

Frequency (f) is the number of complete waves made in one second. It is measured in **Hertz (Hz)**.

Distance

1 2 3 4 5 6 7 8 Time (s)

Period

Period (T) is the time taken for one wave motion to be completed. It is measured in seconds.

Velocity (v). The velocity of a wave is the distance travelled by one wave in one second. It is calculated by multiplying the number of wave motions completed in one second (the frequency), by the wavelength of one wave. The **wave equation** is written:

Velocity of a wave (v) = frequency (f) x wavelength (λ)

$$\frac{v}{f \quad \lambda}$$

*Medium, 61; Sound waves, 18; Displacement, 61.

The behaviour of waves

The behaviour of waves is studied using a **ripple tank**. This is a shallow tank of water, with a lamp above which casts shadows on to a piece of paper below the tank. A bar in the tank produces the straight-fronted waves shown below.

Reflection

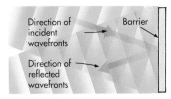

Direction of incident wavefronts

Barrier

Direction of reflected wavefronts

A wave is **reflected** when it bounces off a barrier. Before reflection the waves are called incident waves and, after reflection, reflected waves. The angle at which incident waves hit a barrier is equal to the angle at which they are reflected. All waves experience reflection, including light and sound waves.

Refraction

Refraction is the change in the direction of a wave as it passes from one medium to another. Refraction is caused by the wave changing speed as it passes into the new medium. If, for example, water waves in a ripple tank pass from deep water into shallow water they change speed and direction as shown in the diagram. Light waves are also refracted when they pass between different media.

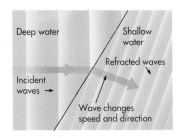

Deep water

Shallow water

Refracted waves

Incident waves →

Wave changes speed and direction

Diffraction

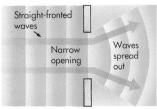

Straight-fronted waves

Narrow opening

Waves spread out

Diffraction occurs when waves bend around a barrier or spread out after passing through a gap. Waves are diffracted most when the gap through which they pass is about the same size as their wavelength. For example, sound waves have a long wavelength and are diffracted by large gaps. Light waves have a short wavelength, and are diffracted by a very tiny gap.

Wave interference

Wave interference occurs when two waves combine with each other. When the waves have the same frequency and direction, and peak and trough at the same time, they are said to be 'in phase'. The combined amplitude of two in phase waves is larger than a single wave. This is called **constructive interference**.

Destructive interference occurs when 'out of phase' waves meet. They peak and trough at different times. The amplitude of their resultant wave is smaller than that of the waves before they meet. Constructive interference of light waves causes patches of bright light, and destructive interference produces patches of darkness.

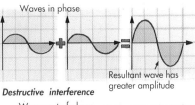

Constructive interference

Waves in phase

Resultant wave has greater amplitude

Destructive interference

Waves out of phase

Waves cancel each other out

Sound

Sound is produced by vibrating objects such as musical instruments and the vocal cords which produce a human voice. Sound waves are *longitudinal waves** which carry vibrations from a sound source. A vibrating object disturbs the medium which surrounds it by moving backwards and forwards producing compressions and rarefactions in the particles of the medium.

Sound waves need the particles of a medium to travel through. For example,

The tuning fork's prongs vibrate.

Compression Rarefaction Human ear

a bell ringing in a jar from which the air has been removed cannot be heard. It is silent on the Moon because there is no atmosphere and, therefore, no medium.

The speed of sound

Sound waves travel at different speeds through different media. They travel fastest through solids, and faster through liquids than gases. When a sound wave hits an obstruction it may be reflected. This is called an **echo**. The speed of sound in air can be measured by a simple method using echoes.

To calculate the speed of sound in air, stand 100 m away from a wall which has no other walls or trees nearby. Clap your hands and listen for the echo. Practice clapping rhythmically until the echo cannot be heard because it coincides exactly with the next clap. Time how long it takes to clap 20 times.

Experiment to calculate the speed of sound

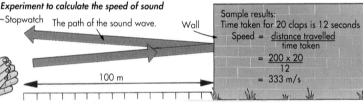

Stopwatch The path of the sound wave. Wall

100 m

Sample results:
Time taken for 20 claps is 12 seconds

$$\text{Speed} = \frac{\text{distance travelled}}{\text{time taken}}$$

$$= \frac{200 \times 20}{12}$$

$$= 333 \text{ m/s}$$

The shape of sound

The shapes of different sound waves can be compared by feeding them into a microphone and displaying them on the screen of a *cathode ray oscilloscope**.

Loudness and amplitude

Large amplitude   Small amplitude

Loud note   Soft note

A sound can be loud or soft depending on the *amplitude** of its wave. A sound with a large amplitude is carrying a lot of energy and will be loud. A sound with a small amplitude will be soft.

Pitch and frequency

High frequency   Low frequency

High pitch   Low pitch

If a musical note has a sound wave with a high *frequency**, it will have a high pitch. Many musical instruments can produce similar pitches, but they sound very different from one another. This is because each instrument produces other frequencies called **overtones** which change the shape of a sound wave. Overtones vary according to the size, shape and construction of an instrument.

*Longitudinal waves, 16; Cathode ray oscilloscope, 48; Amplitude, Frequency, 16.

Light

Light is a form of energy emitted by luminous objects such as the Sun or candles. An object which emits light is called a **source**. A few living creatures, such as fireflies, glow worms and some deep-water fish, produce their own light.

Most objects are non-luminous and can only be seen because light from another source bounces off them into the eye. For example, you can see this page because daylight or lamplight is bouncing off it into your eyes. Light energy is carried from a source by waves. Light waves are part of the *electromagnetic spectrum**. They travel in straight lines away from their source. This is called **rectilinear propagation**. In diagrams light is represented by straight lines called rays. An arrow on a ray indicates the direction in which the light is travelling.

Shadows

If light rays from a small source hit an object in their path, a sharp edged shadow or **umbra** is formed. The umbra appears behind the object in the area that no light has reached.

If the source of light is large, a shadow with blurred edges, called a **penumbra**, is formed around the umbra. A penumbra is an area of less sharp shadow, which a small amount of light has reached.

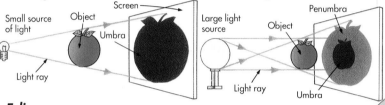

Small source of light • Object • Umbra • Screen • Light ray

Large light source • Object • Penumbra • Light ray • Umbra

Eclipses

When the Moon moves to a position directly between the Sun and the Earth, it casts a circular shadow on the Earth's surface. This is called a **solar eclipse**. This diagram is not drawn to scale.

Viewed from the umbra, no light from the Sun can be seen. This is called a **total eclipse**.

Viewed from the penumbra, some light from the Sun is seen. This is called a **partial eclipse**.

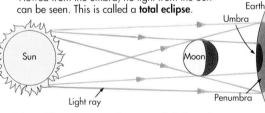

Sun • Light ray • Moon • Earth • Umbra • Penumbra

A pinhole camera

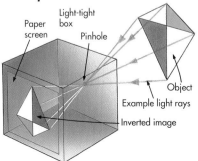

Paper screen • Light-tight box • Pinhole • Object • Example light rays • Inverted image

A pinhole camera is the simplest form of camera. It can be made from an ordinary box with a tracing paper screen. Light rays from an object enter the box, crossing over as they pass through a pinhole in the side of the box. This produces an upside down *image** on a screen. If the object is moved nearer to the camera, the image becomes larger. If the screen is replaced with photographic paper, a permanent picture of the object will be formed.

*Electromagnetic spectrum, 45; Image, 20.

The reflection of light

Reflection of light occurs when a light ray hits a surface and bounces off, changing direction. Mirrors are usually used to demonstrate the reflection of light because their shiny surfaces reflect more light than dull, rough surfaces.

Reflected light always obeys two laws, called the **laws of reflection**. These state:
1. The incident ray, the reflected ray and the normal are all in the same plane.
2. The angle of incidence is equal to the angle of reflection.
The diagram shows light being reflected and identifies the terms used above.

The **incident ray** is the light ray before reflection.

The **angle of incidence** is the angle between the incident ray and the normal.

The **normal** is a line at right angles to the mirror's surface at the point where the light ray hits the mirror.

The **reflected ray** is the light ray after reflection.

The **angle of reflection** is the angle between the reflected ray and the normal.

Real and virtual images

There are two types of image; real and virtual. A **virtual** image is formed when, for example, light rays from an object placed in front of a mirror are reflected into the human eye. The eye sees an image of the object behind the surface of the mirror. The image is called a virtual image, because the light rays only appear to come from it.

A **real** image is formed when rays from an object actually pass through the image, as in the *pinhole camera**. A real image produces a photographic image if film is placed where the image forms. The image projected onto the screen at the cinema is a real image.

Reflection in a plane mirror

The image formed by reflection in a plane mirror is always virtual and erect (the same way up as the object). It is the same distance behind the mirror as the object is in front. The image is laterally inverted, which means that the left side is interchanged with the right.

It is possible to construct a ray diagram to find the position of the virtual image formed by an object in front of a mirror. The steps below should be followed carefully to produce an accurate diagram.

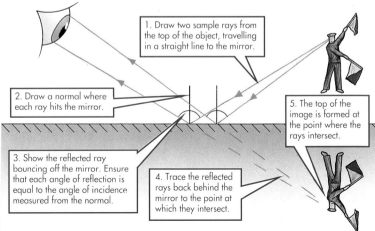

1. Draw two sample rays from the top of the object, travelling in a straight line to the mirror.

2. Draw a normal where each ray hits the mirror.

3. Show the reflected ray bouncing off the mirror. Ensure that each angle of reflection is equal to the angle of incidence measured from the normal.

4. Trace the reflected rays back behind the mirror to the point at which they intersect.

5. The top of the image is formed at the point where the rays intersect.

*Pinhole camera, 19.

The refraction of light

When a light ray passes from one *medium** to another it changes direction. This is called **refraction**. Refraction is caused by the light wave changing speed as it passes into the new medium.

For example, a ray passing from one medium into an optically more dense medium (such as from air into glass), slows down and bends toward the normal. A ray passing into an optically less dense medium speeds up, bending away from the normal.

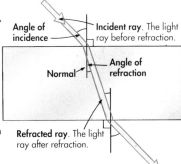

Angle of incidence

Incident ray. The light ray before refraction.

Angle of refraction

Normal

Refracted ray. The light ray after refraction.

The critical angle

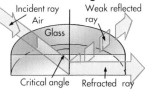

Incident ray
Air
Glass
Weak reflected ray
Critical angle
Refracted ray

If a light ray emerging from glass into air skims along the surface of the glass, its angle of incidence is called the **critical angle**. The ray is refracted at 90° to the normal. A small amount of light is reflected at the boundary and passes back into the glass. A light ray passing into any optically less dense medium will behave in this way.

Total internal reflection

If a light ray which hits the boundary between glass and air has an angle of incidence greater than the critical angle it is not refracted. All the light is reflected back inside the denser medium. This is called **total internal reflection**.

Total internal reflection Air
Glass
Incident ray
Angle $i°$ is greater than the critical angle.
Total internal reflected ray

Right angled prisms

Ray turned 90°
Ray turned 180°

Right angled prisms use total internal reflection to alter the path of light, turning it through 90° or 180°. These prisms are used in periscopes, binoculars and cameras.

Optical fibres use total internal reflection to transmit light along a glass or plastic tube. They are used in medicine and telecommunications.

An optical fibre

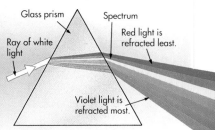

Glass fibres
Path of light ray

Colour and the spectrum

White light is made up of different colours of light. When a ray of white light is shone through a glass prism it splits into a rainbow of colours called the **spectrum**. The splitting of light in this way is called **dispersion**. Dispersion is caused by the different colours of light travelling at slightly different speeds in glass or water. Each of the colours is refracted by slightly different amounts.

Glass prism
Spectrum
Ray of white light
Red light is refracted least.
Violet light is refracted most.

*Medium, 61.

Lenses and optical instruments

A **lens** is a piece of glass with curved surfaces. When light is refracted by a lens an image is formed. There are two main types of lens: **converging** lenses which have outward curving surfaces, and **diverging** lenses which have inward curving surfaces. Lenses are used in a variety of optical instruments.

A converging lens

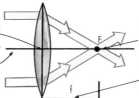

The **optical centre** is the centre of the lens. Rays travelling through the optical centre pass straight through the lens.

The **principal axis** is an imaginary line through the optical centre of the lens at right angles to the lens.

The **principal focus (F)** is the point at which all rays travelling parallel to the principal axis intersect after refraction.

The **focal length (f)** is the distance from the optical centre to the principal focus.

Measuring the focal length of a converging lens

A converging lens is held between a screen and a distant light source, such as a window. The distance between lens and screen is adjusted until a clear image of the window forms on the screen. Because the window is distant, the light rays from a point on it are almost parallel to each other when they reach the lens. This means that the image is formed roughly at the principal focus of the lens. The focal length is the distance between the lens's optical centre and the image.

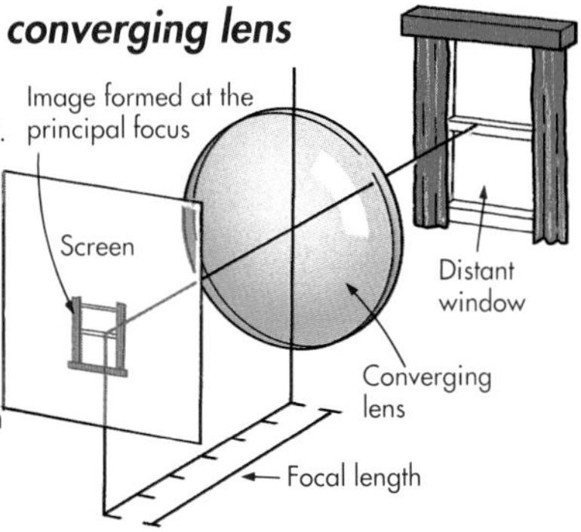

Image formed at the principal focus

Screen

Distant window

Converging lens

Focal length

Image formation with a lens

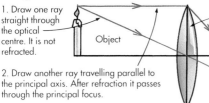

1. Draw one ray straight through the optical centre. It is not refracted.

Object

2. Draw another ray travelling parallel to the principal axis. After refraction it passes through the principal focus.

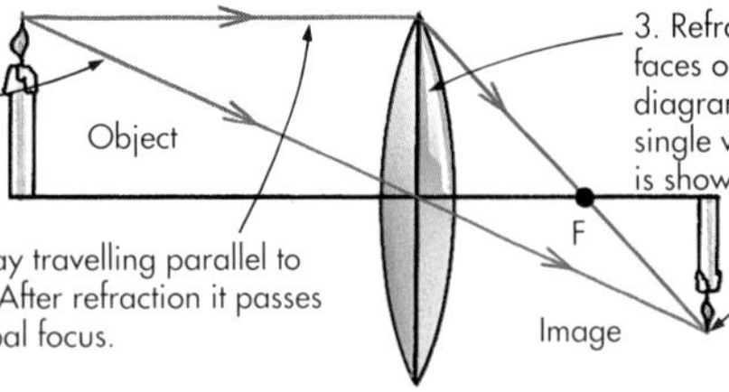

Image

3. Refraction takes place at both faces of the lens, but on a ray diagram the lens is replaced by a single vertical line and refraction is shown at this line only.

4. The top of the image is formed where the two rays intersect.

Optical instruments

Optical instruments contain one or more lenses to produce a specific type of image. For example, a camera uses a converging lens to form a real, diminished (smaller than the object), inverted image on photographic film.

A slide projector uses converging lenses to form a real, magnified, inverted image of a photographic slide on a screen. A magnifying glass is a converging lens which produces a magnified, erect, virtual image as shown in the ray diagram below.

A page of text viewed through a magnifying glass.

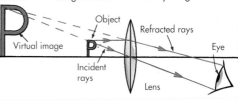

Object

Virtual image

Refracted rays

Eye

Incident rays

Lens

The eye and the ear

The human eye

The eye is a highly developed optical instrument. Light rays are refracted by the **cornea** and the **lens** to form an image on the **retina.** The retina, made of light sensitive cells, changes light into electric signals which are sent to the brain by the **optic nerve**. The *focal length** of the lens depends on its shape. The lens's shape is controlled by a ring of muscle called the **ciliary muscle**. When the eye looks at distant objects, the muscle relaxes. The ring becomes larger, tightening the **fibres of the suspensory ligament**. This flattens the lens, giving it a long focal length. When viewing close objects, the muscle contracts, the fibres relax and the lens becomes fatter, with a short focal length.

A **short-sighted** person has difficulty focusing on distant objects because the light rays are focused in front of the retina. In glasses and contact lenses, a

The coloured **iris** contains a hole called the **pupil**. In bright light, the iris expands to reduce the pupil's size and let in less light. In dim light it contracts to increase the pupil's size and let in more light.

The lens is the fine focusing component of the eye.

The transparent cornea is one of the focusing components of the eye.

Fibres of the suspensory ligament Ciliary muscle Retina Optic nerve

diverging lens is used to correct this. A **long-sighted** person has difficulty focusing on close objects because the light rays are focused behind the retina. A converging lens is used to correct this.

Short sight

Image formed in front of retina

Rays from a distant object

Diverging lens corrects short sight

Long sight

Image formed behind retina

Rays from a close object

Converging lens corrects long sight

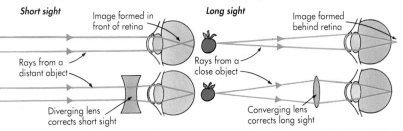

The human ear

Sound waves travel down the **ear canal** to the **ear drum**. The ear drum vibrates at the same *frequency** as the sound waves. The vibrations are then transferred by a chain of three bones in the **middle ear**, called the **ossicles**, to the **oval window**. The ossicles and the oval window increase

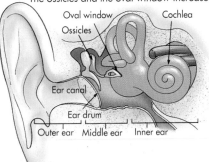

Oval window Cochlea
Ossicles

Ear canal

Ear drum

Outer ear Middle ear Inner ear

the amplitude of the vibrations. In the **inner ear** the vibrations pass along the **cochlea** where sound waves of different frequencies stimulate different nerves. The nerves change sound waves into electrical signals, which are sent to the brain.

Humans can hear frequencies ranging from 20 Hz to 20,000 Hz. Sounds above 20,000 Hz are called **ultrasound** and can be heard by some animals, such as bats.

Old age leads to an inability to hear high frequency sounds. Listening to loud sounds can damage the sensory cells in the cochlea and result in an inability to hear certain frequencies.

Poor hearing can be improved with a hearing aid, which increases the *amplitude** of sound waves.

Focal length, 22; Frequency, Amplitude, 16.

The Earth in space

Developments in science and technology have led to space travel, advanced communication systems and the chance to study the Earth from space.

Astronomers think the **Universe** began about 15,000 million years ago with a huge explosion, called the **Big Bang**. Before the Big Bang all the matter in the Universe is thought to have been concentrated into a very small volume.

The explosion sent matter flying out in all directions. This matter later formed **stars** and **planets**. The **galaxies**, which are huge collections of stars, are still moving away from each other today as a result of the explosion. No one knows whether the Universe will continue to expand forever, or whether *gravitational forces of attraction** will start to pull the galaxies back towards each other.

The Milky Way

The Milky Way is the galaxy in which the Earth lies. It is just one of millions of galaxies that make up the Universe. On a clear night the other stars of the Milky Way can be seen as a faint band of light in the sky.

The Sun is a star like the millions of other stars in the Milky Way.

The Milky Way is spiral shaped and formed from an estimated 100,000 million stars.

The Solar System

The Sun lies at the centre of our Solar System which is made up of nine known major planets, including the Earth.

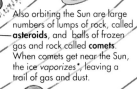

A **satellite** is an object in space, such as a moon, which orbits another larger object like a planet. Many planets have their own natural satellites.

Also orbiting the Sun are large numbers of lumps of rock, called **asteroids**, and balls of frozen gas and rock called **comets**. When comets get near the Sun, the ice *vaporizes**, leaving a trail of gas and dust.

The Earth's motion

The Earth takes 365.26 days to travel once around the Sun. The shape of its orbit is 'elliptical', which is like a slightly squashed circle. As the Earth orbits the Sun, it spins on its **axis** once every twenty-four hours. The axis is an imaginary line which runs through the Earth from the North Pole to the South Pole. As it orbits the Sun, the Earth is not completely upright. Its axis is tilted at an angle of approximately 23° to the plane of its orbit.

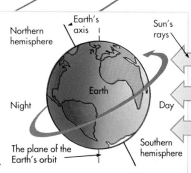

Earth's axis

Northern hemisphere

Sun's rays

Earth

Night

Day

The plane of the Earth's orbit

Southern hemisphere

*Gravitational forces, 6; Vaporizes, 61.

Seasonal changes

The inclination of the Earth's axis causes seasonal changes and a variation in the number of daylight hours in a day. Summer is the period during which the land is inclined towards the Sun and the Sun's rays hit the ground almost perpendicularly. When it is summer in the northern hemisphere, it is winter in the southern hemisphere and vice versa. In winter, the Sun's rays slant across the Earth's surface. Their heat is spread over a larger area, weakening their intensity.

The length of a day is governed by the Sun's position in the sky. Due to the inclination of the land during summer, the Sun gets higher in the sky and is visible longer. In winter it is lower in the sky, rising above the horizon later in the day and disappearing earlier.

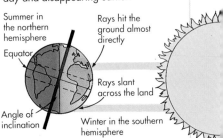

Summer in the northern hemisphere

Equator

Angle of inclination

Rays hit the ground almost directly

Rays slant across the land

Winter in the southern hemisphere

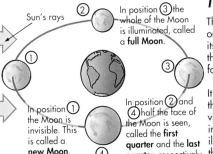

Sun's rays

In position ③ the whole of the Moon is illuminated, called a **full Moon**.

In position ① the Moon is invisible. This is called a **new Moon**.

In position ② and ④ half the face of the Moon is seen, called the **first quarter** and the **last quarter**, respectively.

The Moon's motion

The Earth has one moon which orbits it once every 27.3 days. The Moon spins on its axis once during this orbit. This means that the same half of the Moon is always facing the Earth.

The Moon does not produce its own light. It is visible because it *reflects** light from the Sun. The part of the Moon which is visible from Earth depends on its position in relation to the Sun. The different illuminated sections of the Moon shown in the diagram are called its **phases**.

The effects of gravity

There is a strong force of gravitational attraction which exists between two objects the size of planets and stars. Gravity keeps the planets in orbit around the Sun, and the Moon in orbit around the Earth.

The Moon is constantly moving forward in a straight line. It would move further away into space if the Earth did not exert a gravitational force which pulls it back in the direction of the Earth's centre. The effect of this gravitational pull acting at right angles to the Moon's motion produces the circular orbit of the Moon.

Gravity also affects the seas and oceans on Earth. The gravitational force exerted by the Moon on the Earth attracts the water on the side of the Earth it faces. This causes a bulge in the water's surface

called a **high tide**. There are two high tides and two **low tides** every twenty-four hours. When the Sun is in line with the Moon, the combined gravitational force on the water is greater, producing higher tides called **spring tides**.

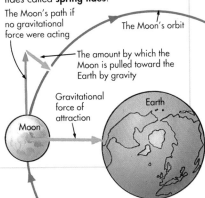

The Moon's path if no gravitational force were acting

The Moon's orbit

The amount by which the Moon is pulled toward the Earth by gravity

Gravitational force of attraction

Moon

Earth

*Reflection, 20.

Heat and temperature

Heat is a form of energy. When a substance is supplied with heat energy, its molecules gain *kinetic energy** from the heat source and move at a greater speed. The faster they move, the hotter the substance becomes. The substance is said to have gained **internal energy**.

Temperature is a measurement of how hot or cold a substance is. It does not mean the same thing as 'heat'. It depends on the average speed of the molecules in a substance. For example, a hot spark of magnesium has a higher temperature than a mug of boiling water, because its molecules are moving faster. However, the water has more heat energy than the spark because it has more molecules and their total energy is greater.

Thermometers

Temperature is measured using a **thermometer**. Thermometers contain substances which change when heated. Some contain liquids which expand when heated. For example, if a 'liquid-in-glass' thermometer is placed in a hot substance, the liquid inside it will expand and rise up the tube. Alcohol and mercury are commonly used in these thermometers. Alcohol freezes at a lower temperature than mercury and is used to measure very low temperatures, for instance at the North and South Poles. Other thermometers include the resistance thermometer, which contains a wire whose *resistance** to electric current changes if its temperature changes.

A clinical thermometer

A clinical thermometer is used to measure the small variations in the temperature of the human body.

The triangular glass acts as a magnifying glass.

A constriction in the tube prevents mercury returning to the bulb before a reading can be taken. The thermometer must be shaken to force the mercury back into the bulb.

The scale is calibrated in degrees Celsius, between 35 °C and 42 °C

A narrow tube ensures the mercury moves a visible distance even for very small changes in temperature.

The Celsius temperature scale

The **Celsius scale** has two fixed points. The lower one (0 °C), called the ice point, is the melting point of pure ice. The upper one (100 °C), called the steam point, is the temperature of the steam above water, which is boiling at normal atmospheric pressure. One hundred divisions are made between these points, called **degrees Celsius (°C)**.

Finding the fixed points to calibrate a Celsius scale on a thermometer

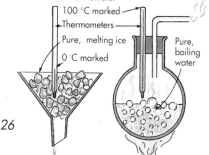

100 °C marked
Thermometers
Pure, melting ice
0 °C marked
Pure, boiling water

The absolute temperature scale

The **absolute temperature** scale starts at a point called **absolute zero**. This is the lowest temperature theoretically achievable. It is the point at which no more heat energy can be removed from a substance. Measured in degrees Celsius, absolute zero is −273 °C. The absolute scale uses units called **kelvins (K)**. Kelvins are the same size as degrees Celsius.

How to convert between degrees Celsius and kelvins

To convert a temperature from degrees Celsius to kelvins, add 273 to the Celsius temperature. For example, 0 °C is 273 K, 50 °C is 323 K and 100 °C is 373 K. To convert a temperature from kelvins to degrees Celsius, subtract 273 from the temperature in kelvins. For example, 200 K is −73 °C, 300 K is 27 °C.

*Kinetic energy, 13; Resistance, 34.

Heat and expansion

Most substances increase in size when heated. This is called **expansion**. The molecules in the substance gain kinetic energy and begin to move faster. They are able to make larger vibrations and push each other further and further apart, causing the substance to enlarge.

The expansion of solids and liquids

Solids will only expand by a very small amount. This is because their molecules are held together by strong forces of attraction. Most liquids expand more than solids because their molecules have more energy to break free of the forces which attract them to their neighbours.

A bimetallic strip

Different solids expand at different rates. This is demonstrated in the behaviour of a **bimetallic strip**, which is used in thermostats to regulate temperature in central heating systems.

A bimetallic strip is a strip of copper and iron fixed firmly together.

When heated, copper expands more than iron. This causes the strip to bend outwards breaking the electrical circuit and turning off the heater. When it cools the strip bends back and the heater is switched on.

The expansion of gases

The volume of a gas is affected both by heating and by the pressure exerted on it. Therefore, when studying the expansion of gases, three variables must be considered: temperature, volume and pressure.

Gas at constant temperature

If the volume of a gas is decreased, its pressure increases. The pressure in a gas depends on the rate at which its molecules hit the sides of the container. As volume decreases, the gas molecules are pushed closer together. Although they are moving at the same speed, they hit the container's walls more often, increasing the gas's internal pressure.

Gas at constant volume

If a gas is heated, but not allowed to expand, its internal pressure increases. This means the gas molecules gain kinetic energy from the heat source and hit the walls of their container more violently and more often.

Gas at constant pressure

A gas at constant pressure expands when heated because its molecules gain kinetic energy. The internal pressure of the gas remains constant because the molecules hit the walls of their container at the same rate because they have more space to move in.

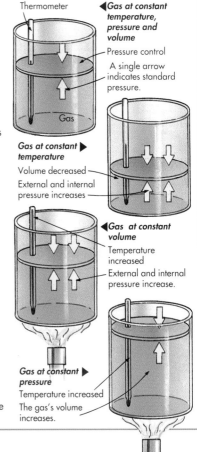

◄ **Gas at constant temperature, pressure and volume**

Pressure control

A single arrow indicates standard pressure.

Gas at constant ▶ temperature

Volume decreased

External and internal pressure increases

◄ **Gas at constant volume**

Temperature increased

External and internal pressure increase.

Gas at constant ▶ pressure

Temperature increased

The gas's volume increases.

Heat transfer

If a temperature difference exists between two places, heat energy is transferred from the hotter to the cooler place. This heat transfer continues until the temperature is the same in both places.

Heat can travel in three ways: by **conduction**, **convection** and **radiation**. It is important to be able to recognize which of these three processes is taking place in any given situation.

Conduction

Conduction is the transfer of heat, from *molecule** to molecule, throughout a material. The molecules inside the material which are nearest to a heat source gain *kinetic energy**. They vibrate vigorously, and their movement affects the molecules immediately next to them. They pass on some of their energy, spreading heat through the material. Conduction is chiefly associated with solids, because the closely packed molecular structure of a solid is most suited to it.

Metals are very good conductors of heat. They conduct heat rapidly, because they contain *'free' electrons**. The free

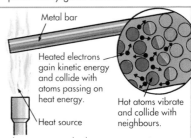

Metal bar

Heated electrons gain kinetic energy and collide with atoms passing on heat energy.

Heat source

Hot atoms vibrate and collide with neighbours.

electrons near the heat source gain energy and move rapidly throughout the metal. They collide with atoms, passing on their kinetic energy. Saucepans, radiators and central heating pipes are made of metallic materials to ensure rapid heat conduction.

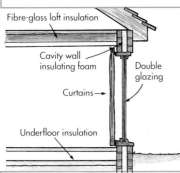

Fibre-glass loft insulation

Cavity wall insulating foam

Double glazing

Curtains →

Underfloor insulation

Insulation

Substances which conduct heat slowly, such as wood and water, are called **insulators**. Air is one of the best insulators of heat. Therefore materials which trap air inside them, such as cork, polystyrene and wool, are good insulators. Insulating materials have a variety of uses. Wrapping an object with insulation can keep heat in or out. Fibre-glass and polystyrene are used for loft insulation. Woollen clothing prevents heat leaving the human body.

Convection

The most efficient way of transferring heat in liquids and gases is by convection. Convection is the upward movement of a warm liquid or gas. When a liquid (or gas) is heated, the part nearest the heat source expands, becomes less dense and rises. The cooler, denser liquid then sinks towards the heat source. The upward currents of hot liquid or gas are called **convection currents**. Some water heating systems work on the principle of convection. Water rises to the hot water tank when it is hot, and sinks to the boiler when it cools.

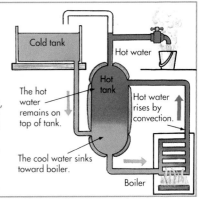

Cold tank

Hot water

The hot water remains on top of tank.

Hot tank

Hot water rises by convection.

The cool water sinks toward boiler.

Boiler

*Molecule, 4; Kinetic energy, 13; 'Free' electrons, 31.

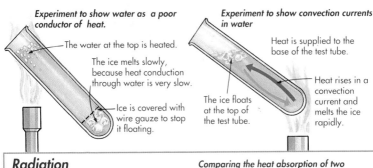

Experiment to show water as a poor conductor of heat.

The water at the top is heated.

The ice melts slowly, because heat conduction through water is very slow.

Ice is covered with wire gauze to stop it floating.

Experiment to show convection currents in water

Heat is supplied to the base of the test tube.

The ice floats at the top of the test tube.

Heat rises in a convection current and melts the ice rapidly.

Radiation

Radiation is the method by which heat is transferred through empty spaces. Warm objects emit heat waves which can travel through a *vacuum**. These waves are called *infra-red waves**, and are part of the *electromagnetic spectrum**. Infra-red waves travel away from their source at the speed of light, until they hit an object in their path. The object absorbs the heat energy and its temperature rises. The surfaces of some objects absorb more heat than others. Darkly coloured, dull surfaces absorb more radiation than shiny or light coloured ones. This is because shiny, light objects reflect back more heat energy than they absorb.

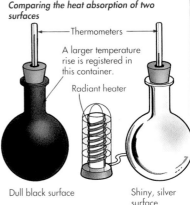

Comparing the heat absorption of two surfaces

Thermometers

A larger temperature rise is registered in this container.

Radiant heater

Dull black surface

Shiny, silver surface

The greenhouse effect

A greenhouse traps the Sun's heat. High energy, short wavelength radiation from the Sun passes through its glass. The radiation is absorbed by the plants and soil inside, which in turn emit their own radiation. The radiation they emit is low energy, long wavelength, which is unable to pass through the glass and is reflected back into the greenhouse.

The warming effect produced when radiation cannot escape the atmosphere is called the **greenhouse effect** (see page 111). It is caused when carbon dioxide in the atmosphere forms an insulating layer around the Earth and behaves like the glass in a greenhouse. Industrial pollution is constantly adding to carbon dioxide levels. If this continues, experts predict an increase in global temperatures, which may have a damaging effect on agriculture and human livelihood.

A vacuum flask

A vacuum flask is designed to reduce heat transfer in any form. It is made of glass, which is a bad conductor of heat. A vacuum surrounding the liquid eliminates convection and conduction. A shiny, silvered inside surface minimizes radiation by reflecting the heat energy back into the flask.

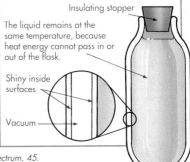

Insulating stopper

The liquid remains at the same temperature, because heat energy cannot pass in or out of the flask.

Shiny inside surfaces

Vacuum

*Vacuum 61; Infra-red waves, Electromagnetic spectrum, 45.

Changes in state

The physical state of a substance can change if heat is added or removed from it. For example, if water is supplied with enough heat it will change to steam. If water is made cold enough it changes to ice. Changes in state are caused by the *molecules** in a substance gaining or losing their *kinetic energy**.

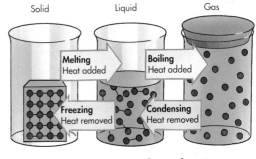

Melting and boiling

The change from a solid to a liquid is called **melting**. When a substance melts, its molecules use the kinetic energy they gain from the heat source to break the forces which hold them in a solid form. The change from a liquid to a gas is called **boiling**. The molecules of the liquid use heat energy to escape the attractive forces of other molecules and move independently and freely as a gas.

Freezing and condensing

The change from a gas to a liquid is called **condensing** and the change from a liquid to a solid is called **freezing**. These changes in state are the reverse processes of melting and boiling. Condensing and freezing involve the removal of heat energy. As a substance freezes or condenses, its molecules lose kinetic energy and reform their bonds with neighbouring molecules.

Latent heat

While a substance is changing state its temperature does not change. For example, when water begins to boil its temperature remains constant even though heating continues. The heat supplied is used to enable the water molecules to escape the attractive forces of their neighbours. This heat is called **latent heat**

No temperature change is observed at the condensing and freezing points of a substance. In the process of reforming

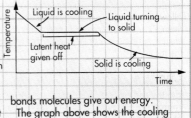

bonds molecules give out energy. The graph above shows the cooling curve which is produced by a liquid from which heat is removed until the liquid freezes.

Evaporation

When a liquid changes into a *vapour** it is said to have **evaporated**. Some of the molecules in a liquid have greater energy than others and manage to escape from the surface of the liquid, even when the

liquid is not boiling. The average kinetic energy of the molecules left in the liquid is then lower. This means the temperature of the liquid has become lower. This process is called cooling by evaporation.

When human beings sweat, they produce water which evaporates from the surface of their skin. Energy is needed to give the water molecules enough energy to change into a vapour. The molecules absorb heat energy from the skin. This has the effect of cooling the body down.

Vapour — The energetic molecules escape, carrying away heat energy.

The slower molecules remain in the liquid.

Liquid — The average energy of molecules left is lower.

*Molecule, 4; Kinetic energy, 13; Vapour, 61.

Electricity

Electricity is the phenomenon caused by the production of electrically charged particles. There are two types of charged particle: positive and negative. These charged particles are called **ions**. Ions are produced when an electrically neutral atom loses or gains *electrons** in a process called **ionization**. An object which has a surplus of electrons is said to be **negatively charged** and an object which has a deficiency of electrons is **positively charged**. The magnitude of the electric charge on an object is measured in **coulombs (C)**.

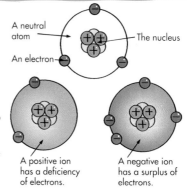

A neutral atom — The nucleus
An electron

A positive ion has a deficiency of electrons.

A negative ion has a surplus of electrons.

Static electricity

An object is said to be charged with **static electricity** if electrically charged particles are 'held' on its surface. The charges are unable to move through the material of which the object is made. There are many everyday examples of the effects of static electricity, such as the tiny electric shock produced by touching a metal object after walking across a nylon carpet, or the way in which dust clings to a record.

Charged objects exert an **electrical force**. **Objects which carry like charges repel each other. Objects which carry opposite charges attract each other**.

Conductors and insulators

Most materials fall into two groups: conductors and insulators. **Conductors** allow electric charges to move through them. The atoms of metals have some electrons which are free to move through the material. Metals such as silver and copper have a large number of these 'free' electrons and are very good conductors of electricity. **Insulators** are materials, such as acetate and polythene, which do not allow charges to flow through them. They hold the electric charge on their surface.

Charging objects

The two main ways of producing electric charge are by **friction** and **induction**. If a plastic pen is rubbed with a cloth, the friction causes a transfer of charge between the pen and the cloth. Both the pen and cloth are insulators and hold the charge on their surface. When charged, the pen will attract small pieces of paper.

Static charge can be induced on a conductor by bringing a charged object close to it, but without the two touching.

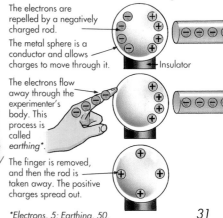

The electrons are repelled by a negatively charged rod.

The metal sphere is a conductor and allows charges to move through it.

Insulator

The electrons flow away through the experimenter's body. This process is called *earthing**.

The finger is removed, and then the rod is taken away. The positive charges spread out.

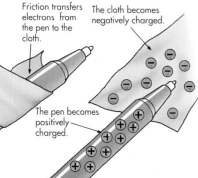

Friction transfers electrons from the pen to the cloth.

The cloth becomes negatively charged.

The pen becomes positively charged.

*Electrons, 5; Earthing, 50.

31

Current electricity

Electricity is a form of energy which can be converted into different forms of energy, such as heat, light and mechanical energy. It has a wide variety of uses ranging from light bulbs and calculators to high speed trains.

An electric current is a flow of electrically charged particles. In wires this current is a stream of electrons. The size of a current depends on the rate at which electric charges flow through a conductor. It is calculated with the following equation:

$$\text{Current (I)} = \frac{\text{charge (Q)}}{\text{time (t)}}$$

Electric current is measured in **amperes (A)**. One ampere is equal to one *coulomb** of charge passing any point in the conductor in one second.

Electric circuits

To maintain the flow of a current, a continuous conducting path is needed, called a **circuit**. A break in a circuit stops current flowing. Circuits contain components, such as lamps and ammeters (see opposite). Components convert the electrical energy carried by a current into other forms of energy, such as light and heat. They do not use up the current itself. The size of the current at the end of the circuit is the same as at the beginning.

This circuit can be drawn as a diagram using circuit symbols.

Wire — Battery
Light bulb
Switch

Conventional current

Source of electrical energy
Conductor wire
Electrons travel in this direction
Direction of conventional current

Scientists decided that current would always be shown travelling from a positively charged area to a negatively charged area. This is called **conventional current** and is indicated with an arrow on circuit diagrams. This convention was decided before it was known that the current in wires consists of electrons travelling in the opposite direction.

Potential difference

Charged objects have *electrical potential energy**. The amount of potential energy they have depends on the size of their charge. When there is a difference in the electrical potential energy between two areas, a current will flow if a conducting path is placed between them. Energy is carried from an area of higher electrical potential to an area of lower electrical potential. A **potential difference (p.d.)** is said to exist between the two areas.

Potential difference is measured in **volts (V)** and is often called **voltage**. The p.d. between the ends of a conductor is equal to the amount of electrical energy (in joules) which is converted into different forms for every coulomb of electric charge which passes through the conductor. P.d. is calculated with the following equation:

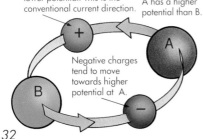

Positive charges move toward lower potential. This is the conventional current direction.

A has a higher potential than B.

Negative charges tend to move towards higher potential at A.

$$\text{Potential difference (V)} = \frac{\text{electrical energy (E)}}{\text{charge (Q)}}$$

*Coulomb, 31; Electrical potential energy, 13.

Creating a potential difference

A potential difference is produced by an electrical energy source. An electric cell is a source of electrical energy. It contains two metal terminals. Chemical reactions in the cell give one terminal a higher electrical potential than the other. When the terminals are joined by a conductor a current will flow. The size of the p.d. between the ends of the conductor can be increased by increasing the number of cells included in a circuit. A number of cells joined together is called a **battery**.

A selection of batteries and cells

Electromotive force

An **electromotive force (e.m.f.)** is the energy which a cell or *dynamo** produces to get electric charges moving. It is a source of electrical energy because it maintains a p.d. between two terminals. An e.m.f. is measured in volts (V).

Series and parallel circuits

Components can be arranged in a circuit in two ways: in series and in parallel. A **series** circuit has a single path for the current. The current passes through components one after another. The voltage across the cell in the circuit equals the sum of the voltages across each of the components. One disadvantage of a series circuit is that if one component stops working it breaks the circuit and the current will not flow.

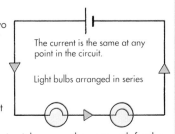
The current is the same at any point in the circuit.

Light bulbs arranged in series

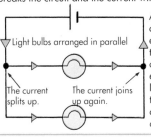
Light bulbs arranged in parallel

The current splits up. The current joins up again.

A **parallel** circuit has more than one path for the current. The current splits up and passes through each branch at once. The voltage across each of the components is equal, and equal to the voltage across the cell. The total current in the circuit is equal to the sum of the currents in all its branches. In the circuit shown, the total current is the sum of the current through both bulbs. If a component in one branch of a parallel circuit breaks, the current continues to flow through the other branches.

Ammeters and voltmeters

An **ammeter** is a device used to measure the amount of electric current flowing through a particular point in a circuit. An ammeter must be connected in series at the point in the circuit where the current is to be measured.

A **voltmeter** is a device which is used to measure the potential difference between any two points in a circuit. It must be connected in parallel across these points. To measure the potential difference across a circuit component, a voltmeter must be connected in parallel across the component, as shown below.

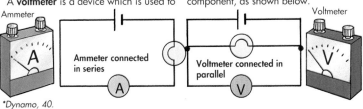
Ammeter

Ammeter connected in series

Voltmeter connected in parallel

Voltmeter

Controlling current

It is important to be able to control the amount of current flowing through a circuit. The size of the current flowing through a component can be controlled by varying the *potential difference** across the component. The current is also affected by the type of components in the circuit. Different components use different amounts of electrical energy provided by the energy source. Some components can be used to limit the current flowing through parts of a circuit.

Current and potential difference

A current will flow through a component only if there is a potential difference across it. The size of the potential difference directly affects the amount of current which will flow.

The circuit shown below can be used to demonstrate the relationship between current and p.d. The current in the circuit and the p.d. across the component is recorded. The p.d. is then increased by adding batteries into the circuit one by one. The current is recorded each time.

The experiment shows that, for the circuit and the particular component shown, the current is directly proportional to the potential difference. This means that when the potential difference in the circuit is doubled, the current doubles. When the p.d. is trebled, the current trebles.

If the results of the experiment are plotted on a graph showing current against voltage, the gradient produced is a straight line.

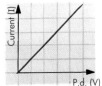

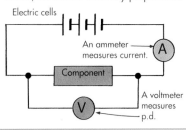

Electric cells

An ammeter measures current.

Component

A voltmeter measures p.d.

Ohm's law

Ohm's law states that **the current flowing through a conductor is directly proportional to the p.d. across its ends, provided the temperature remains constant.**

The p.d. across a conductor divided by the current through it produces a quantity called the conductor's **resistance**. If the conductor obeys Ohm's law, this ratio always gives a constant value.

Resistance

Resistance is the ability of a substance to resist, or oppose, the flow of an electric current in a conductor. All the components in a circuit have a certain resistance to current. This resistance makes the electrons in the current flowing through the component give up some of the electrical energy they carry. If the component is a lamp, for example, it converts the electrical energy into heat and light energy. The element in a kettle is a resistor which converts electrical energy into heat energy.

A conductor's resistance decreases if the area of its cross-section is increased. Its resistance increases if its length increases.

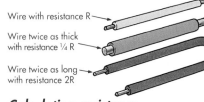

Wire with resistance R

Wire twice as thick with resistance ¼ R

Wire twice as long with resistance 2R

Calculating resistance

To calculate the resistance of a conductor the p.d. across its ends is divided by the current passing through it.

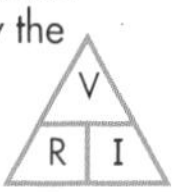

Resistance (R) = p.d. (V)
              current (I)

Resistance is measured in **ohms** (Ω). One ohm is the resistance of a conductor through which a current of 1 amp passes when the p.d. between its ends is 1 volt.

Non-ohmic conductors

Conductors which obey Ohm's law are called **ohmic.** Some conductors, such as a filament bulb, do not obey Ohm's law. These are called **non-ohmic.** The resistance of the bulb's tungsten filament increases as its temperature increases. It produces a current/voltage graph like the one shown. A *thermistor* is also made of non-ohmic material. Its resistance decreases as its temperature increases.

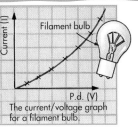

The current/voltage graph for a filament bulb.

Resistors

Resistors control the current flowing in a circuit. When included in a circuit, resistors limit the current passing through components, reducing the danger of damage caused by over-heating.

There are two main types of resistor: **fixed resistors** and **variable resistors.** Fixed resistors are available at different resistance values. Variable resistors are called **rheostats.** By adjusting a rheostat the amount of current flowing through a circuit can be controlled. A device called a **potential divider** (or voltage divider) can be used in a circuit to produce a required p.d. from another higher p.d. A potential divider divides the voltage

supplied by the battery, enabling different sized currents to flow through different parts of a circuit.

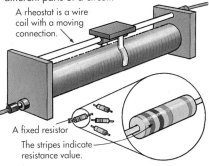

A rheostat is a wire coil with a moving connection.

A fixed resistor

The stripes indicate resistance value.

Resistors in series

If the resistors in a circuit are arranged *in series** the total resistance in the circuit is equal to the sum of the resistance of all the resistors. This is written:

Total circuit resistance (R) = $R_1 + R_2 + R_3$

For example, the total resistance in the circuit below is calculated:

Total resistance (R) = 3 + 5 + 2
= 10 ohms

The magnitude of the current in this circuit is calculated using Ohm's law:

$$\text{Current (I)} = \frac{\text{p.d. (V)}}{\text{resistance (R)}}$$
$$= \frac{20}{10}$$
$$= 2 \text{ amps}$$

Resistors in parallel

The total resistance in a circuit where the resistors are arranged *in parallel** is calculated with the equation:

$$\frac{1}{R} = \frac{1}{R_1} + \frac{1}{R_2} + \frac{1}{R_3}$$

For example, the total resistance in the circuit below is calculated:

$$\frac{1}{R} = \frac{1}{6} + \frac{1}{12} + \frac{1}{4} = \frac{6}{12}$$
$$R = \frac{12}{6} = 2 \text{ ohms}$$

The total current in the circuit is calculated:

$$I = \frac{V}{R} = \frac{20}{2} = 10 \text{ amps}$$

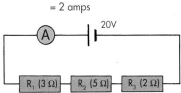

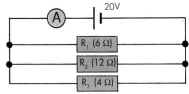

Magnetism

The ability to attract iron and steel is called **magnetism** and materials which have this property are called **magnetic**. Knowledge of magnetism goes back to the Ancient Greeks who realized that a rock called magnetite attracted pieces of iron. If a bar magnet is hung by a thread, it will rotate until it is pointing in a north-south direction. The regions near the ends of a magnet are called its **poles**.

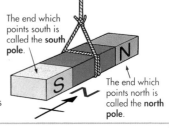

The end which points south is called the **south pole**.

The end which points north is called the **north pole**.

Repulsion and attraction

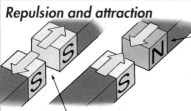

If two north or two south poles are brought towards each other, they will push away, or repel, each other.

If one north pole and one south pole of two magnets are brought together, they will pull towards, or attract, each other.

The law of magnetism

The behaviour of the *magnetic forces** exerted by the two bar magnets shown demonstrates the law of magnetism. This law states that **the like poles of two magnets repel each other, and the unlike poles attract each other.**

Magnetic materials

If materials such as cobalt, nickel or iron are put near a magnet they begin to act like magnets. This is called **magnetic induction**. Materials which react in this way are called **ferromagnetic**.

Iron is a 'soft' ferromagnetic material. This means it will become magnetized very easily, but quickly loses its magnetic properties if the magnetizing force is removed. Steel is more difficult to magnetize, but once it is magnetized, it retains its magnetic properties for a long time. Steel is called a 'hard' ferromagnetic material.

How to make a magnet

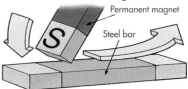

Permanent magnet

Steel bar

A steel bar will become magnetized if it is stroked repeatedly with one pole of a permanent magnet. The magnet should be lifted high above the bar between each stroke. This **'single touch'** method produces a weak magnet.

What happens when something is magnetized.

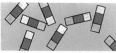

The domains are jumbled in a non-magnetized state

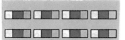

The domains line up in a magnetized state

In magnetic materials there are groups of *molecules**, called **domains**, which behave like tiny magnets. When a piece of magnetic material is in a non-magnetized state, these domains are jumbled up. When it is magnetized, the domains line up, with all their north poles pointing north and their south poles pointing south. Most materials (including some metals) cannot be magnetized. This is because the molecules in these substances do not behave like domains.

Magnetism can be destroyed by extreme heat. Heat makes the domains in a magnetized material vibrate and break out of their ordered pattern. They return to a jumbled, non-magnetized state.

*Magnetic force, 8; Molecules, 4.

Magnetic fields

A magnet is surrounded by an area called its **magnetic field**. Magnetic objects entering this field are affected by the magnet's forces of attraction and repulsion. The pattern of a magnetic field can be plotted on a sheet of paper using a plotting compass. The position of the compass's needle is marked as shown in the diagram. The north pole of the compass is attracted toward the south pole of the magnet.

The strength and direction of a magnetic field is shown by **magnetic field lines** (sometimes called **magnetic flux lines**). These lines have arrows which indicate the direction in which a plotting compass's north pole would point if placed in the field. Magnetic force is strongest near a magnet's poles, and so the magnetic field lines are drawn very close together.

If the like poles of two magnets are

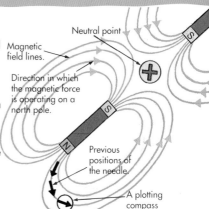

Neutral point

Magnetic field lines.

Direction in which the magnetic force is operating on a north pole.

Previous positions of the needle.

A plotting compass

placed close together, as shown in the diagram, their magnetic fields combine to produce **neutral points**. These are areas where the magnetic forces are equal but opposite and cancel each other out.

Creating a permanent magnet with a solenoid

The most efficient and effective way of creating magnets is by an electrical method using a *solenoid coil**. An electric current flowing through the wire coil of a solenoid produces a magnetic field which is similar in shape to that produced by a bar magnet. If a bar of ferromagnetic material is placed inside the solenoid, the magnetic force makes the domains in the metal line up in a north-south direction, and the bar begins to act like a magnet.

To create a permanent magnet, a strong magnetic force is needed. The solenoid

must have a large number of turns of wire per unit length and must be supplied with a large *direct current**. A steel bar placed in this magnetic field will become magnetized, retaining its magnetism even when the current is switched off.

The position of the new magnet's poles depends on the direction of the current in the solenoid. The memory aid below is a useful means of working out which end of the magnet is a north pole and which end a south pole. These will be reversed if the current direction is reversed.

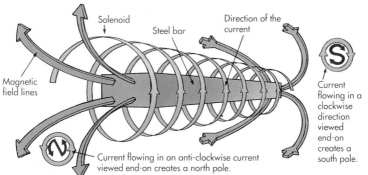

Solenoid

Steel bar

Direction of the current

Magnetic field lines

Current flowing in a clockwise direction viewed end-on creates a south pole.

Current flowing in an anti-clockwise current viewed end-on creates a north pole.

*Solenoid coil, 38; Direct current, 40.

Electromagnetism

When an electric current flows in a conductor it produces a *magnetic field**. This effect is called **electromagnetism**. The field is circular and can be plotted with a small compass. The direction of the magnetic field around a wire depends on the direction the current is flowing through the wire. The **right-hand grip rule** (shown in the diagram), is a useful method of working out the direction of the field. If the right hand is held as if gripping the wire, with the thumb pointing in the direction of the current, the fingers are pointing in the direction of the magnetic field lines.

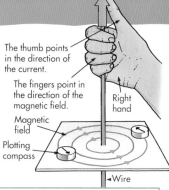

The thumb points in the direction of the current.

The fingers point in the direction of the magnetic field.

Right hand

Magnetic field

Plotting compass

Wire

A solenoid

A solenoid coil

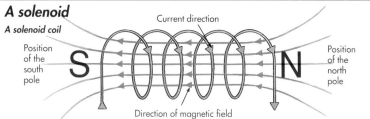

Current direction

Position of the south pole

S

N

Position of the north pole

Direction of magnetic field

A **solenoid** is a cylindrical coil of insulated wire. When a current flows through it, the magnetic fields produced by each part of the wire combine to produce a strong magnetic force inside the solenoid. The shape of the field outside the coil is like that of a *bar magnet**. The position of the poles can be found using the memory aid shown on page 37. The strength of the magnetic field in the solenoid will increase if the size of the current increases, or if the length of the wire on the solenoid is increased, by wrapping it more closely along the length of the solenoid.

Electromagnets

The electromagnetic effect is used to make powerful magnets called **electromagnets**. If a piece of 'soft' iron* is placed inside a solenoid coil and the current is switched on, the iron becomes magnetized. The combined magnetism of the solenoid and the magnetized iron core is very strong. 'Soft' iron is used because it only acts as a magnet when the current is on. So the magnetism of an electromagnet can be switched on and off with the current. Electromagnets which are the shape of the one shown here, with unlike poles next to each other, produce a very strong magnetic field.

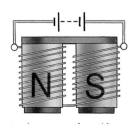

N   S

An electromagnet formed from two solenoids with iron cores.

A relay switch

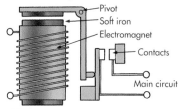

Pivot
Soft iron
Electromagnet
Contacts
Main circuit

When electromagnets are switched on they attract *ferromagnetic** materials towards them. For example, in a **relay** switch, an electromagnet operated by a small current is used to close a pair of metal contacts, which completes a main circuit. This means that a small current in the electromagnet's coil can switch on a large current without the circuits being electrically linked.

**Magnetic field, Bar magnet, Soft iron, Ferromagnetic, 36.*

The motor effect

When a current-carrying wire is brought into a magnetic field, a force acts on it producing an effect called the **motor effect**. The wire may be thrust out of the magnet's field. The motion of the wire is always at right angles to both the magnetic field and the current direction. If there is an increase in the size of the current through the wire, or the strength of the magnetic field, the motor effect becomes stronger.

The direction of the motor effect can be worked out using **Fleming's left-hand rule**, which is a useful memory aid. The thumb and first two fingers of the left hand are held at right angles to each other, as shown in the diagram. If the first finger points in the direction of the magnetic field and the second finger points in the direction of the current, the thumb will be pointing in the direction of the thrust force or the motor effect.

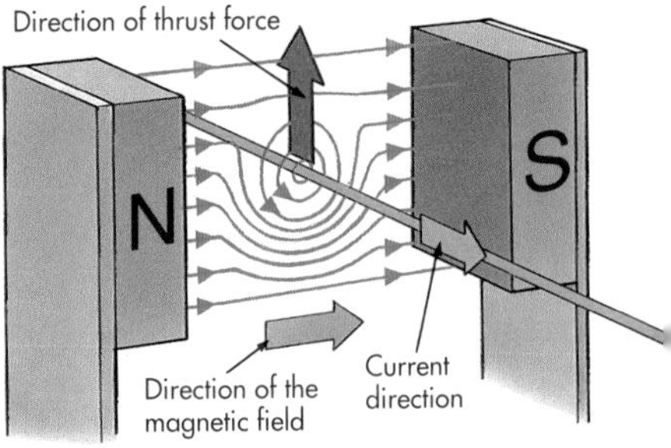

Direction of thrust force

Direction of the magnetic field

Current direction

The magnetic field of the current and the magnet combine below the wire, producing an upward force.

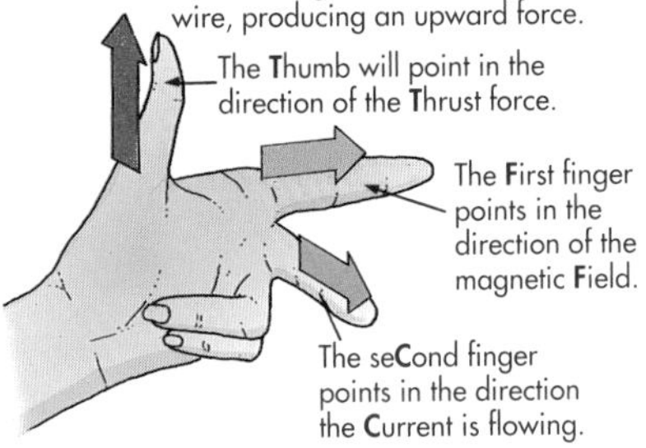

The **T**humb will point in the direction of the **T**hrust force.

The **F**irst finger points in the direction of the magnetic **F**ield.

The se**C**ond finger points in the direction the **C**urrent is flowing.

A simple d.c. electric motor

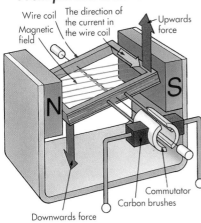

Wire coil
Magnetic field
The direction of the current in the wire coil
Upwards force
Commutator
Carbon brushes
Downwards force

A **simple *direct current** electric motor** uses the motor effect to convert electrical energy into *kinetic energy**. A flat coil of current-carrying wire is placed in a magnetic field. One side of the wire coil experiences an upwards force, while the other side experiences a downward force. This makes the coil rotate until it is vertical. At this point the coil stops moving, unless the direction of the current through the coil is reversed. A **commutator**, formed of a metal ring split into two halves, is used to reverse the current direction in the coil every half turn, making the motion of the coil continuous. The current enters and leaves the commutator through two carbon brushes.

A galvanometer

Galvanometers measure electric current. They contain a moving coil which turns when a current flows through it. The greater the current, the more the coil turns, tightening a return spring. This moves a pointer across a scale, indicating the size of the current.

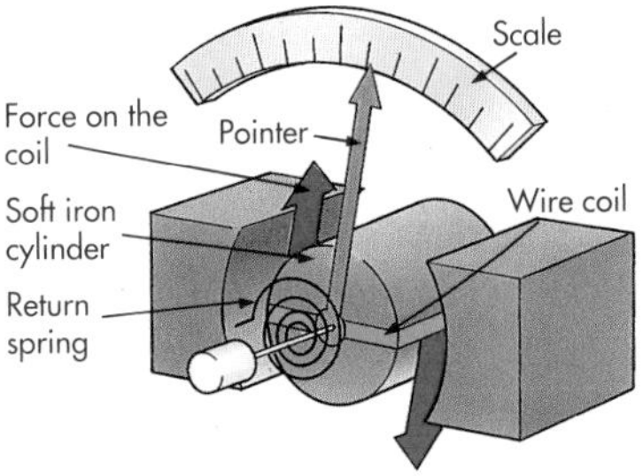

Scale
Force on the coil
Pointer
Soft iron cylinder
Return spring
Wire coil

*Direct current, 40; Kinetic energy, 13.

39

Electromagnetic induction

If a conductor wire is moved in a magnetic field so that it cuts through the magnetic field lines, an **electromotive force (e.m.f.)** is induced in the wire. If the wire forms a circuit, the e.m.f. causes a current to flow. This effect is called **electromagnetic induction.** It happens whenever a conductor cuts through magnetic field lines or if it is placed in a changing magnetic field.

The size of the e.m.f. induced in the wire is affected by three factors: the length of wire moving in the magnetic field; the speed of the wire's movement; and the strength of the magnetic field. If any of these three quantities is increased, the size of the e.m.f. induced in the wire increases.

The current only flows while the wire is cutting through magnetic field lines. The maximum e.m.f. is produced when the wire's movement is at right angles to field lines. When the wire is stationary or moving parallel to the field lines without cutting them, the current does not flow.

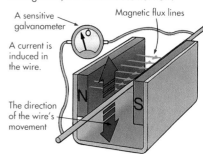

A sensitive galvanometer

Magnetic flux lines

A current is induced in the wire.

The direction of the wire's movement

N   S

Simple dynamos

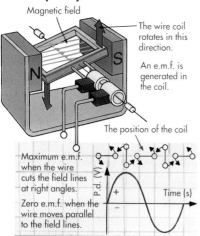

Magnetic field

The wire coil rotates in this direction.

An e.m.f. is generated in the coil.

The position of the coil

Maximum e.m.f. when the wire cuts the field lines at right angles.

Zero e.m.f. when the wire moves parallel to the field lines.

P.d. (V)   Time (s)

The principle of electromagnetic induction is used in a **simple dynamo** to convert *kinetic energy** into electrical energy. A flat coil of conducting wire is rotated in a magnetic field. This induces an e.m.f. in the wire and a current flows.

In the alternating current dynamo, shown here, an alternating e.m.f. is induced in the coil as it rotates. This means the direction of the induced e.m.f. changes at regular intervals, which produces an alternating current in the coil.

Another simple dynamo called the direct current dynamo has a commutator, similar to the one on the electric motor shown on page 39. The commutator rings ensure that the current always flows in one direction only.

Direct and alternating current

Direct current (d.c.) is usually supplied by a *cell** or *battery**. It flows in one direction only.

The electricity which is supplied to houses by power stations is called **alternating current (a.c.).** The direction of this current changes many times a second. This means the electrons in the current flow alternately one way and then the other, as the ends of the circuit change rapidly from positive to negative and back again.

If d.c. and a.c. voltages are displayed on the screen of a *cathode ray oscilloscope** they produce the voltage/time graphs shown here.

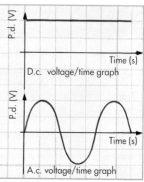

P.d. (V)   Time (s)

D.c. voltage/time graph

P.d. (V)   Time (s)

A.c. voltage/time graph

*Kinetic energy, 13; Cell, Battery, 33; Cathode ray oscilloscope, 48.

Transformers

Transformers are used to change the size of a voltage. A transformer consists of two coils of wire wound on to a soft iron core. An alternating voltage is supplied to one coil (the primary coil). The changing direction of the alternating current produces an alternating magnetic field in the iron core. This has the same effect on the other coil (the secondary coil) as moving a wire through a magnetic field. The changing magnetic field induces a voltage in the secondary coil. Therefore, by using a transformer, electrical energy can be transferred from the primary coil to the secondary coil without the coils being electrically connected.

The size of the voltage induced in the secondary coil depends on the size of the voltage applied to the primary coil.

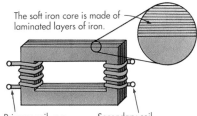

The soft iron core is made of laminated layers of iron.

Primary coil, a.c. voltage supplied here

Secondary coil, voltage induced here

The circuit symbol for the transformer

Primary coil

Secondary coil

The size of the voltage in the secondary coil also depends on the number of turns of wire on the two coils. It is calculated with the following equation, known as the **turns ratio**:

$$\frac{\text{Primary turns (Np)}}{\text{Secondary turns (Ns)}} = \frac{\text{Primary voltage (Vp)}}{\text{Secondary voltage (Vs)}}$$

Step-up transformers

A **step-up transformer** is one in which the number of turns of wire on the secondary coil is larger than those on the primary coil. When a voltage is applied to a primary coil, a voltage of greater magnitude is produced in the secondary coil. As the number of turns of wire on a secondary coil increases, the total voltage produced increases. Step-up transformers are used to produce the high voltage at which electricity is transmitted by the *grid system**.

Step-up transformer

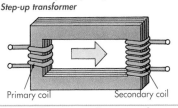

Primary coil   Secondary coil

Step-down transformers

A **step-down transformer** is one in which the number of turns of wire on the secondary coil is smaller than those on the primary coil. When a voltage is applied to the primary coil, a voltage of smaller magnitude is produced in the secondary coil. Many electrical appliances require a voltage much lower than that supplied by the grid system. These appliances often contain step-down transformers to change, or transform, the mains voltage to the lower voltages they require.

Step-down transformer

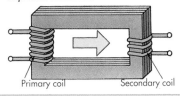

Primary coil   Secondary coil

The efficiency of a transformer

Transformers are very efficient devices. Two circuits linked by a well-designed transformer lose very little electrical energy. A current flowing through a material produces heat which wastes energy. Therefore, low resistance copper wire is used on a transformer to minimize the amount of heat produced. The iron core of a transformer is made of varnished sheets of iron, which have been glued together. These insulated sheets reduce the waste of energy in the form of heat by minimizing the currents induced in the core by electromagnetic induction.

*Grid system, 50.

Radioactivity

Some substances, like uranium and radium, are **radioactive**. This means the nuclei of their atoms are unstable. They break up, and emit particles or rays known as **radiation**. This process is called **radioactive decay**. Some substances only emit radiation in controlled conditions.

Some atoms belonging to the same element have a different number of neutrons in their nucleus. These atoms are called **isotopes**. All the isotopes of a particular element have the same *proton*

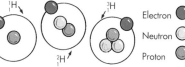

Three isotopes of hydrogen

Electron
Neutron
Proton

number*, but a different *nucleon number** Some atoms have a much larger number of neutrons than protons in their nuclei. It is thought that this causes atoms to be unstable and prone to radioactive decay.

Radiation

Three types of radiation can be emitted by radioactive materials: alpha (α) particles, beta (β) particles and gamma (γ) rays. When a nucleus decays, energy is released. If alpha or beta particles are

emitted, a new nucleus is formed. This change in a nucleus can be written as an equation. The equations vary according to the type of radiation emitted and some examples are shown below.

Alpha particles

An **alpha particle** is a helium nucleus, which consist of two protons and two neutrons. It is emitted from an atom's nucleus in a process called **alpha decay**. The diagram shows alpha decay taking place. If a thorium–232 nucleus undergoes alpha decay, its original proton number is reduced by two and its nucleon number is reduced by four. This can be written: $^{232}_{90}\text{Th} \rightarrow ^{228}_{88}\text{Ra} + ^{4}_{2}\text{He}$

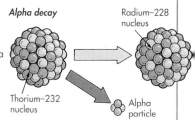

Alpha decay

Radium–228 nucleus

Thorium–232 nucleus

Alpha particle

Beta particles

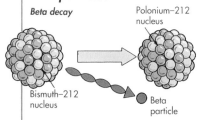

Beta decay

Polonium–212 nucleus

Bismuth–212 nucleus

Beta particle

A **beta particle** is an electron formed in an atom's nucleus when a neutron decays, splitting into a proton and an electron. The electron is emitted in a process called **beta decay**. The diagram shows beta decay. If a bismuth–212 nucleus undergoes beta decay, its original proton number increases by one. Its nucleon number remains the same, because a neutron has formed a proton. This is written: $^{212}_{83}\text{Bi} \rightarrow ^{212}_{84}\text{Po} + ^{0}_{-1}\text{e}$

Gamma rays

After an atom has undergone alpha or beta decay, it may be left with excess energy. The atom becomes more stable by emitting this excess energy in the form of gamma radiation. Gamma rays are part of the *electromagnetic spectrum**. The rays are not particles, so the atom's nucleon and proton number remain unchanged. This is written: $^{228}_{88}\text{Ra} \rightarrow ^{228}_{88}\text{Ra} + \gamma$

Gamma radiation

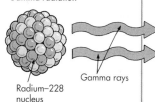

Gamma rays

Radium–228 nucleus

Proton, Nucleon number, 5; Electromagnetic spectrum, 45.

Ionization

Alpha particles, beta particles and gamma rays *ionize** the substances through which they pass. However, producing ions reduces the energy of the radiation. Alpha particles cause a great deal of ionization, which quickly reduces their energy and limits the distance they can travel. Beta particles are more penetrating because they cause less ionization. Gamma rays travel the greatest distance because they cause only minimal ionization in the substances through which they pass.

Alpha particles travel a few centimetres in air. They can be stopped by a sheet of paper.

Beta particles travel a few metres in air. They can be stopped by about 1 mm of copper.

The intensity of gamma rays can only be halved by 10 mm of lead.

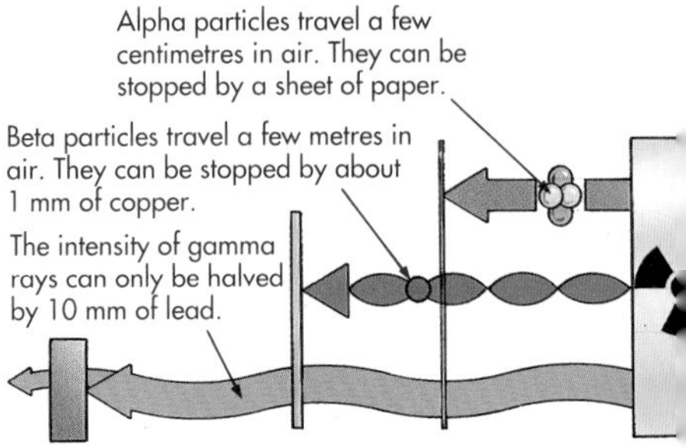

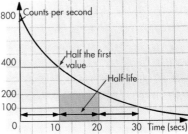

A Geiger counter

A **Geiger counter** is used to detect radioactivity. It consists of a **Geiger–Müller tube**, a **scaler** and/or a **ratemeter**. Radiation produces ionization in the gas-filled tube. This causes electrical pulses to pass between the positively charged central wire and the negatively charged metal wall. The scaler then counts each of the pulses and the ratemeter measures the average rate of pulses in counts per second. A high **count-rate** indicates a high level of ionizing radiation in the test sample. The tube can also be connected to an amplifier and loudspeaker, so that a click is heard every time a pulse passes between the wire and the wall.

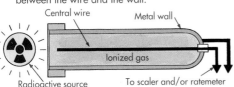

Central wire

Metal wall

Ionized gas

Radioactive source

To scaler and/or ratemeter

Background radiation

Background radiation is the radiation which is continually present on Earth. It has a variety of sources including the following: radioactive materials in the Earth; cosmic radiation from outer space; radioactive waste (from both the nuclear power industry and the use of radioactive isotopes in medicine - see page 44); and the nuclear weapons industry. There are even some radioactive elements which occur naturally in the human body. Background radiation can easily be measured with a Geiger counter, which produces a **background count**.

Radioactive half-life

The process of radioactive decay is completely random. This means it is impossible to say when any particular atom of a radioactive sample will decay. Physicists can measure how long it takes, on average, for the radioactivity of a test sample to fall by half. This is called a **half-life**. Each type of isotope has a different half-life. It varies from a fraction of a second to millions of years.

If the count-rate of an isotope is plotted against time, a graph is produced. It can be used to calculate an isotope's half-life and predict the count-rate of a sample at any given moment.

The graph below shows the decreasing count-rate of a substance whose half-life is ten seconds. This means that for every ten second period that passes the count-rate of the sample will be halved.

800 Counts per second

Half the first value

Half-life

400

200
100

0   10   20   30   Time (secs)

Using radiation and nuclear energy

The radiation emitted by some isotopes can be put to a variety of uses in medicine and industry.

Radiocarbon dating is a method used by archaeologists to calculate the age of preserved, organic materials such as leather, parchment or textiles. All living things contain carbon–14 which emits radiation. After death, carbon–14 is not replenished and its emission decreases. The age of remains can be calculated from the strength of the emission, using carbon–14's half-life (6,000 years).

Radiotherapy is the use of carefully controlled doses of high level radiation to destroy cancerous cells.

Radioactive tracing uses the movement and concentration of radioactive isotopes in the body to study the functions of organs and to diagnose disorders. For example, radioactive iodine is used to study the thyroid gland. A high concentration of the isotope in the gland may indicate the presence of cancer.

Radiography is used in industrial quality control. Faults in materials can be detected using a beta radiation source and a Geiger counter. For example, to ensure a roll of paper is of even thickness, a scalar is used to alert machine operators. When the count-rate goes down the paper is too thick; if it goes up the paper is too thin.

Radioactivity and safety

Exposure to radiation must be minimized because it can seriously damage living cells. In laboratories and schools radioactive sources are stored in lead containers. When in use they are handled with forceps and kept at a distance from people behind lead shields. In nuclear power stations, people working with larger radioactive sources must wear special clothing and devices.

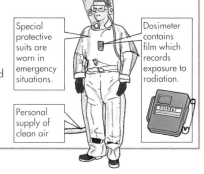

Special protective suits are worn in emergency situations.

Dosimeter contains film which records exposure to radiation.

Personal supply of clean air

The nuclear power industry

A vast amount of energy is stored in the nucleus of an atom which can be released by a process called **fission**. During this process uranium nuclei are bombarded with neutrons. They become unstable and split, releasing energy. Each nucleus also emits two or three neutrons which hit other atoms, causing more fission. This is called a **chain reaction**. An uncontrolled reaction would cause an atomic explosion. In a

Nuclear fission causing a chain reaction

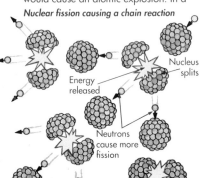

Energy released

Nucleus splits

Neutrons cause more fission

nuclear *reactor**, the fission process is slowed down using control rods which absorb some of the neutrons. Fission produces heat which is used to generate electricity using steam driven *turbines**.

Nuclear power stations generate more energy per unit mass of fuel than any other type of power station. Nuclear power is clean to produce, compared with the burning of fossil fuels which causes environmental problems like the *greenhouse effect**. However, building reactors is expensive. The waste materials are radioactive, and great care must be taken when transporting and disposing of them. They are sealed in concrete and buried deep in vaults underground or dropped into the sea. The consequences of a nuclear accident are catastrophic. In 1986 an accident at Chernobyl, USSR, left many dead and vast areas of land were contaminated with radiation.

*Reactor, Turbines, 61; Greenhouse effect, 29.

The electromagnetic spectrum

The **electromagnetic spectrum** is made up of a huge range of energy-carrying waves called **electromagnetic waves**. The waves are produced in different ways, by different sources and have different *wavelengths** and *frequencies**. However, they do have common properties which link them. They are all *transverse waves** and are made up of oscillating electric and magnetic fields. All the waves carry energy from one place to another. They can pass through a *vacuum**, as they do not need the particles of a medium to travel. All the waves travel at the same speed (approximately 300,000,000 m/s in a vacuum). This is very much faster than the speed of sound (330 m/s). It is important to remember where each group of electromagnetic waves appears in the spectrum. In the sequence below the wavelength of the waves becomes shorter as you go down the page.

Type	Sources	Detection	Uses	
Radio waves Microwaves	Electrical circuits and transmitters	Radio waves can be detected by radio aerials and television.	Radio waves are used in communication systems. Microwaves are used in radar detection and satellite communications. They are also used for cooking in microwave ovens.	
Infra-red radiation	Warm and hot objects	Infra-red is strongly absorbed by objects and causes a rise in temperature.	With heat-seeking equipment, hot objects can be identified at night by the infra-red radiation they emit. Infra-red sensitive cameras are used in medicine to detect disease.	
Visible light	Hot objects, such as fire or lamps	Light is visible to human eye and photographic film.	Apart from enabling us to see objects, light is used in optical fibres for medicine and communications. Plants need visible light to grow.	
Ultra-violet radiation	Very hot objects such as the Sun and mercury vapour lamps	UV rays are detected by photographic film. Fluorescent materials absorb UV rays and radiate visible light, called fluorescence.	Some washing powders use fluorescent chemicals to make washing look whiter. UV rays causes the human skin to tan. High energy UV waves can damage the cells of plants and can cause skin cancer in humans. Most UV rays from the Sun are absorbed by the *ozone layer**. If the ozone layer continues to be destroyed cases of skin cancer may increase.	
X-rays	X-ray tubes	X-rays are detected by special types of photographic film.	Low energy X-rays are used in medicine for studying broken bone and detecting cracks in metal objects. X-rays are harmful to living cells. Repeated exposure to X-rays can cause cancer.	
Gamma rays	*Radioactive** materials	Gamma rays are detected by *Geiger–Müller tubes**.	Gamma rays are used in medicine to kill cancerous growths, to kill bacteria when sterilizing instruments and to study the function of organs. Large doses of gamma rays can damage living cells.	

*Wavelength, Frequency, Transverse waves, 16; Vacuum, Ozone layer, 61;
Radioactivity 42, Geiger–Müller tube, 43.

Electronics is the careful and precise control of tiny *electric currents** and *voltages**. Electronic components are built into circuits which perform specific tasks. Digital watches, calculators and computers all work by electronic means.

Electronic components are made from substances called **semiconductors** whose ability to conduct electricity lies between that of *conductors** and *insulators**.

Semiconductor materials, such as silicon, are mixed with a small amount of impurity in a process called **doping**. Depending on the type and quantity of impurity used, the semiconductor produced has different current-carrying properties.

Electronic components are used as 'switches' in circuits, because their ability to conduct electricity is affected by factors such as heat, light and current direction.

Diodes

Diodes can be used as 'one way' switches. They allow an electric current to flow through them in one direction only. A diode is said to be '**forward biased**' when current flows through it. However, if the diode is reversed in the circuit, it will not conduct current and is said to be '**reverse biased**'. Diodes can be used to change *a.c.** to *d.c.** in a process called **rectification**. If a circuit which includes a diode is supplied by an a.c. voltage, the diode acts as a valve, because it allows the current to flow in one direction only. A diode used like this is called a **half-wave rectifier**, because half of the a.c. is cut out. A.c. which has undergone half-wave rectification will produce the time/voltage graph shown.

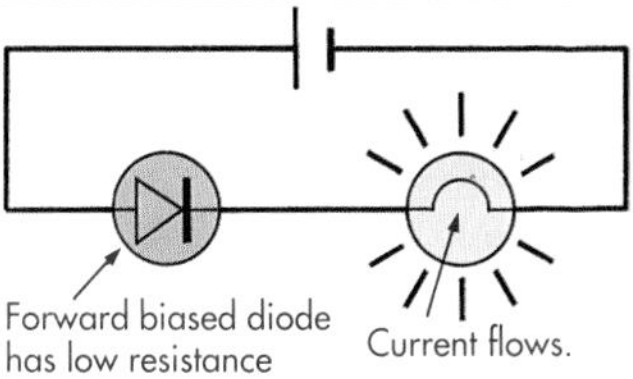

Forward biased diode has low resistance

Current flows.

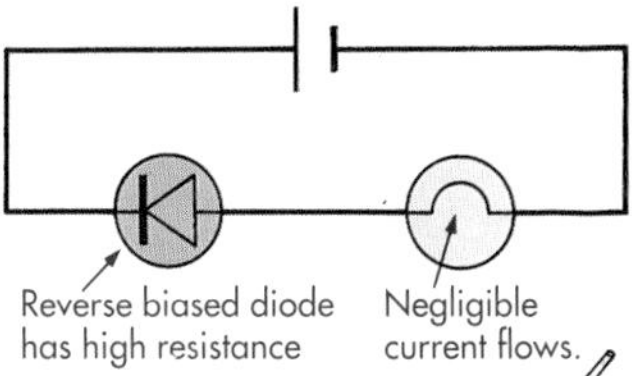

Reverse biased diode has high resistance

Negligible current flows.

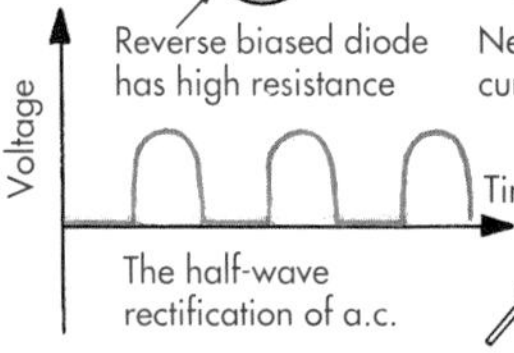

Voltage

Time

The half-wave rectification of a.c.

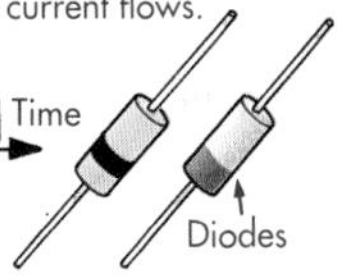

Diodes

Light emitting diodes (LEDs)

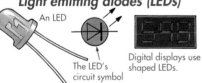

An LED

The LED's circuit symbol

Digital displays use shaped LEDs.

Light emitting diodes emit light, glowing like tiny bulbs, when they are forward biased. LEDs and diodes can be damaged by large currents, so a *resistor** must be included in the circuit.

Light dependent resistors (LDRs)

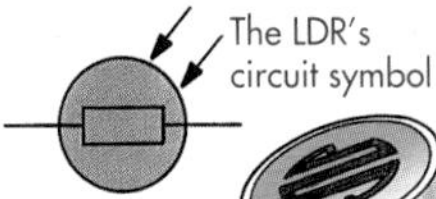

The LDR's circuit symbol

The resistance of a **light dependent resistor** depends on the amount of light it is exposed to. In the dark, its resistance is very high and it allows only a very tiny current to flow through it. However, in the light, the LDR's resistance is very low and a much larger current can flow through it. LDRs are used in alarm systems to detect light.

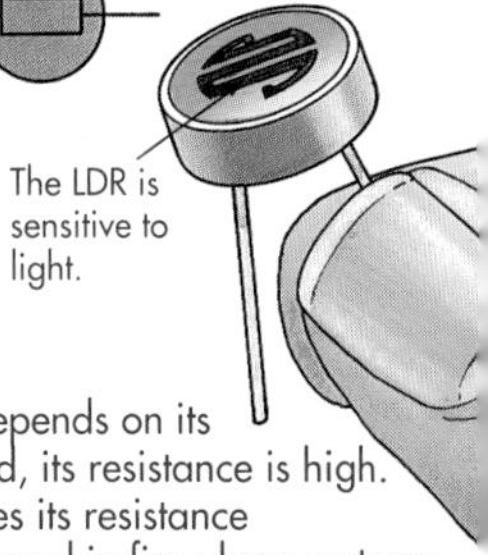

The LDR is sensitive to light.

Thermistors

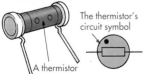

The thermistor's circuit symbol

A thermistor

A **thermistor**'s resistance depends on its temperature. When it is cold, its resistance is high. As the temperature increases its resistance decreases. Thermistors are used in fire alarm systems and thermostat systems to regulate temperature.

Transistors

A **transistor** is a component which is used as an electronic switch. It is connected into a circuit at three points called the **base**, the **collector** and the **emitter**. When a small current flows into the base, the resistance between the collector and the emitter changes from very high to very low and a current flows. Therefore, by controlling the size of the base current, the much larger collector/emitter current can be switched on and off. The voltage between base and emitter must exceed 0.6 V before the base current can switch on the collector current.

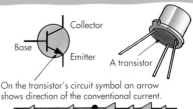

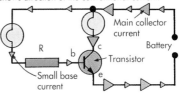

On the transistor's circuit symbol an arrow shows direction of the conventional current.

Main collector current

Battery

R b c Transistor

Small base current

Electronic switches

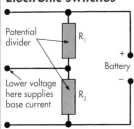

Potential divider

R_1

Lower voltage here supplies base current

R_2

Battery + −

Electronic components can be combined to make switches which turn on and off in response to different conditions. In a switch circuit which includes a transistor, a *potential divider** is used to vary the voltage between the base and the emitter. Resistors R_1 and R_2 (shown in the diagram) form a potential divider. They divide the voltage supplied by the battery. This creates a lower voltage between them which can be used to supply a small base current to the transistor.

A light sensitive switch

When light falls on the LDR in this circuit, its resistance becomes low. The p.d. between the base and emitter is very low. The transistor is switched off and no current flows between the collector and emitter. In the dark the LDR's resistance is much higher. The p.d. between the base and emitter becomes large enough for a current to flow and to switch on the transistor.

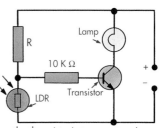

R

Lamp

10 K Ω

Transistor

LDR

+ −

A heat sensitive switch

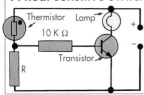

Thermistor   Lamp

10 K Ω

Transistor

R

+ −

In this circuit, when the thermistor's temperature is low, its resistance is high. The p.d. between the base and the emitter is too low to switch on the transistor. When the thermistor's temperature rises, its resistance becomes low. The p.d. between the base and emitter of the transistor becomes large enough to switch the transistor on and the warning lamp light up.

The uses of electronic devices

The miniaturization of electronic equipment and the cheap cost of components has lead to the widespread use of electronic systems - in industry, offices, schools, hospitals and communication systems. Complex circuits are built to perform particular tasks. Devices ranging from calculators to word processors contain electronic circuits.

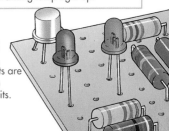

*Potential divider, 35.

The cathode ray oscilloscope

The **cathode ray oscilloscope (CRO)** is used to study wave *frequencies** and *waveforms**, and to measure *voltage**.

The CRO contains a **cathode ray tube** which produces a beam of electrons called a **cathode ray**. This ray hits a **fluorescent screen** and produces a spot of light. The spot is swept repeatedly across the screen at a preselected speed. This produces a trace across the screen. If a voltage signal is fed into the CRO's signal inputs, the spot's position on the screen is affected. The trace produced shows how the voltage changes with time.

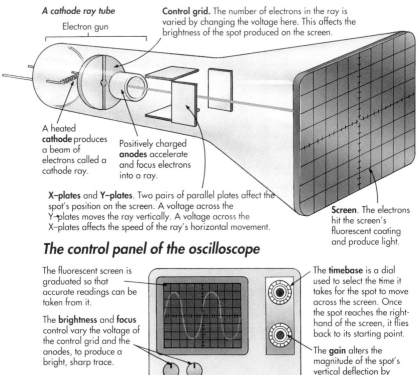

A cathode ray tube

Electron gun

Control grid. The number of electrons in the ray is varied by changing the voltage here. This affects the brightness of the spot produced on the screen.

A heated **cathode** produces a beam of electrons called a cathode ray.

Positively charged **anodes** accelerate and focus electrons into a ray.

X–plates and **Y–plates**. Two pairs of parallel plates affect the spot's position on the screen. A voltage across the Y–plates moves the ray vertically. A voltage across the X–plates affects the speed of the ray's horizontal movement.

Screen. The electrons hit the screen's fluorescent coating and produce light.

The control panel of the oscilloscope

The fluorescent screen is graduated so that accurate readings can be taken from it.

The **brightness** and **focus** control vary the voltage of the control grid and the anodes, to produce a bright, sharp trace.

The **X-shift** and **Y-shift** alter the position of the spot on the screen, vertically and horizontally.

The **timebase** is a dial used to select the time it takes for the spot to move across the screen. Once the spot reaches the right-hand of the screen, it flies back to its starting point.

The **gain** alters the magnitude of the spot's vertical deflection by varying the voltage across the Y-plates.

Signal inputs

Displaying waveforms on the CRO screen

When the CRO's timebase is switched on and the spot is moving across the screen at a constant speed, the screen's horizontal axis becomes a time-scale. If a voltage is then applied across the Y-plates, the trace displays a waveform which shows how the size of this voltage varies with time.

Trace produced by a 4 V a.c. voltage source.

Trace produced by a 4 V d.c. voltage source.

Frequencies, 16; Waveforms, 18; Voltage, 32.

Logic gates

A **logic gate** is an electronic component which can be used as a switch in a circuit. Logic gates have one or two **input** connections and one **output** connection. They are called gates because they are either 'open', which means their output is at a high *voltage**, or 'closed', which means that their output is at a low voltage. The gates can only be opened if a certain combination of information is fed into them. This information takes the form of voltages.

Voltages are applied across the inputs of a logic gate. These voltages can be either high or low. When the right combination of high and low voltages is fed into the inputs, the gate opens which means its output is high. For example, the symbol below is for a logic gate called an AND gate. The output of an AND gate (C) will only be at a high voltage when both its input voltages (A and B) are high.

An AND gate

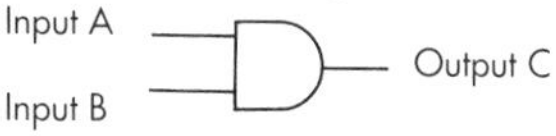

Input A
Input B
Output C

Truth tables

There are five basic logic gates. The combinations of high and low voltages which will open these gates can be represented in the form of a **truth table**. In these truth tables high voltages are coded '1' and low voltages are coded '0'.

AND gate

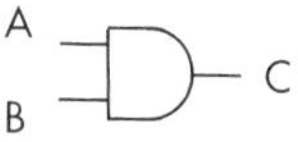

A
B — C

Input	Input	Output
A	B	C
0	0	0
0	1	0
1	0	0
1	1	1

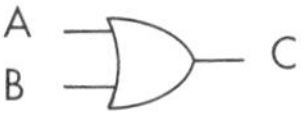

NAND gate

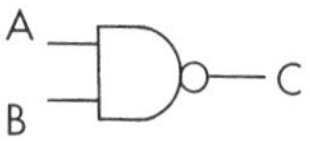

A
B — C

Input	Input	Output
A	B	C
0	0	1
0	1	1
1	0	1
1	1	0

OR gate

A
B — C

Input	Input	Output
A	B	C
0	0	0
0	1	1
1	0	1
1	1	1

NOR gate

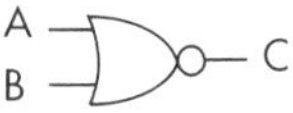

A
B — C

Input	Input	Output
A	B	C
0	0	1
0	1	0
1	0	0
1	1	0

NOT gate

Input   Output

Input	Output
0	1
1	0

Combining gates

Logic gates can be linked together as shown below. A truth table can be produced to determine the final output.

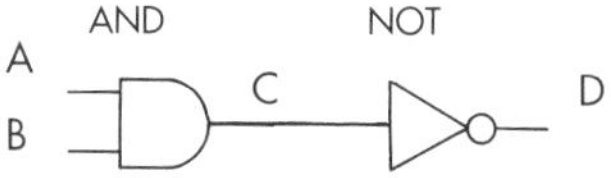

AND   NOT

A
B — C — D

Input A	Input B	C	Output D
0	0	0	1
0	1	0	1
1	0	0	1
1	1	1	0

In most electronic devices, many logic gates are linked together to form complex circuits. These circuits can be used to perform all sorts of functions. For example, the central processing unit of a computer contains thousands of linked logic gates.

These complex circuits are called **integrated circuits** when they are put on to an electronic component called a **microchip**. Each microchip is made from a tiny slice of silicon.

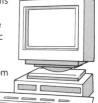

*Voltage, 32.

49

Household electricity

Electricity for domestic and industrial use is mostly produced in power stations using large *generators**. These generators are powered by the heat energy produced by burning fossil fuels, or from the heat energy produced by *nuclear fission**.

Electricity is transmitted around the country by a network of overhead cables known as a **grid system**. This grid system supplies *alternating current**. A.c. is used because *transformers**, which are used to reduce or increase *voltage**, only function if they are supplied with an alternating voltage. The electricity is transmitted at very high voltage. It is cheaper to transmit electricity at high voltage because less energy is wasted as heat in the cables.

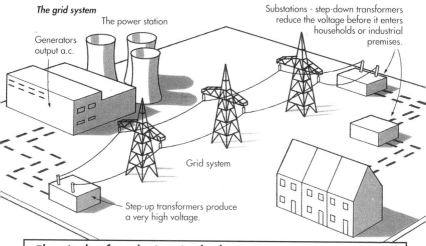

The grid system

The power station

Generators output a.c.

Substations - step-down transformers reduce the voltage before it enters households or industrial premises.

Grid system

Step-up transformers produce a very high voltage.

Electrical safety devices in the home

When an electric current flows through a wire it produces heat. If wires overheat, appliances can be damaged and fires may start. **Fuses** are fitted in circuits to reduce the possibility of overheating by limiting the size of the current which can flow through a wire.

Fuses have current **ratings**, which specify the maximum current they will allow through them. If a current exceeds the number of amps specified, the wire inside the fuse melts and cuts off the electricity supply. The fuse is said to have 'blown'.

It is possible to calculate the fuse rating required to protect an appliance. For example, the current required by a 2,400 watt electric fire supplied with 240

volts, is calculated as follows:

Current (I) = $\dfrac{\text{power rating (P)}}{\text{voltage (V)}}$

$= \dfrac{2400}{240}$

= 10 amps maximum

A 13 A fuse should be used in the kettle.

The cable bringing electricity into a house contains three wires, the **live**, the **neutral** and the **earth** wire. The live and neutral wires carry the current. The earth wire is a safety device. It provides a very low resistance path between the casing of an appliance and ground through which an electric current can escape into the Earth. This reduces the danger of electric shocks which may occur if the insulation around the wires inside an appliance or a plug becomes worn and the live wire touches the casing. The electricity supply may then begin to flow through the casing and through anybody touching the appliance.

Fuses

There is a fine wire inside the fuse case.

*Generator, 61; Nuclear fission, 44; Alternating current, 40; Transformers, 41; Voltage, 32.

Household electrical circuits

Electricity is carried around a house by **circuits**. There are three main types of circuit: **ring mains**, **lighting circuits** and the **cooker circuit**. Appliances are arranged in these circuits in *parallel**. This ensures that if one appliance breaks or is switched off the others in the circuit still function.

The electricity cable enters the house through a **fuse box** containing a fuse which limits the current in the cable. It also contains fuses to protect each of the electrical circuits in the house. Fuses and switches used in the circuits are placed in the live wire of an electricity cable. This means that if a fuse blows or a switch is turned off, the current does not continue to flow. The appliances are connected into the circuit by three-pin or two-pin plugs as shown below.

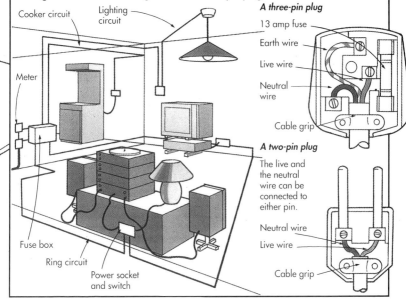

Cooker circuit
Lighting circuit
Meter
Fuse box
Ring circuit
Power socket and switch

A three-pin plug

13 amp fuse
Earth wire
Live wire
Neutral wire
Cable grip

A two-pin plug

The live and the neutral wire can be connected to either pin.

Neutral wire
Live wire
Cable grip

Electrical energy and power

The amount of **electrical energy** converted by an appliance into other forms such as heat or light is calculated with the following equation:

Energy (E) = **p.d. (V) x current (I) x time (t)**
(in joules)   (in volts) (in amps) (in seconds)

Electrical power is the rate at which electrical energy is converted. Power is calculated with the following equation:

Power (P) = energy (V x I x t) = V x I
                      time (t)
(in watts)   (in joules/in seconds)

Electrical power is measured in watts (W). Larger quantities of power are measured in kilowatts (1,000 watts).

Paying for electricity

As an electricity cable enters a house it passes through a meter box. The meter measures how much electrical energy a household uses in **kilowatt-hours (kW hr)**. One kilowatt-hour is the amount of electrical energy used by a 1 k W device in one hour and is called one **unit**. The amount of energy an appliance uses depends on its power rating and the time for which it is used. It is calculated using the following equation:

Energy used = **power (P) x time (t)**
(in units)   (in kW)   (in hours)

For example, an appliance rated at 5 kW, used for 2 hours, uses 10 units of energy.

Energy, power and the environment

Energy is needed to generate the electrical energy that provides light, heat and transport all over the world. Careful management of fuel resources and investment in new technology will ensure we have enough energy in the future.

Comparing energy sources

The different sources of energy used worldwide have different benefits and costs. Some resources produce more energy than others, some are expensive to exploit and others are difficult to transport. Economic and political considerations usually determine why governments and companies chose a particular source of energy. However, as evidence of the damaging effects of pollution increases, environmental issues are becoming more and more important.

Hydro-electricity

More than 20% of the world's power comes from **hydro-electricity**. The water that is held high up in the lakes behind hydro-electric dams has 'stored' *potential energy** and is at high pressure. It is used to drive *turbines**, which produce electricity in *generators**. Although the initial building costs are high, the dams go on to provide a limitless supply of electricity at little cost. Hydro-electric power produces no waste or pollution.

Building the large dams, however, can cause political, social and environmental problems. Often when dams are constructed large areas of fertile land must be cleared of people and animals before flooding. 'Water wars' may develop when dams are built on rivers which run through several countries. For example, if Turkey built a dam across the River Euphrates, downstream the people of Syria would have no river water while the lake behind the dam filled up. The Iraqis, even further downstream, would also be deprived of water.

The lakes behind dams can become blocked by silt (soil carried by rivers). For example, the Sanmenxia Dam on the Huang Ho River in China, built in 1960, was taken out of action after just four years when its lake filled with silt. In hot countries the lakes can cause an increase in diseases, such as bilharzia, caused by tiny organisms in still water.

Nuclear power

Almost 20% of the world's electricity is provided by nuclear power. Initially it seemed cheap. Vast amounts of energy can be produced from small amounts of fuel. For example, two pellets of nuclear fuel the size of sugar lumps can produce the same amount of energy as two and a half tonnes of coal.

Today, however, many countries are cutting back on nuclear power. Although experts predicted the huge cost of building nuclear power stations, they failed to consider the massive cost of research, of incorporating rigorous safety features, and of reprocessing the nuclear waste produced by the power stations.

Public fears about nuclear power have been aroused by nuclear catastrophes such as those at 'Three Mile Island' in the USA and Chernobyl in USSR. On a smaller scale, the increased number of cases of leukaemia (cancer of the blood), in people working in and living near nuclear power stations, has caused concern.

This sign warns of the presence of radioactive substances.

*Potential energy, 13; Turbines, Generators, 61.

Oil

Oil and **natural gas**, which are *fossil fuels**, provide over 60% of the world's energy requirements. They can be stored and transported easily and, at present, resources are plentiful. However, if energy consumption continues at its current rate, in 20 to 40 years new reserves will be increasingly difficult to locate and extract.

The price and availability of oil is controlled by the oil producing countries in the Middle East. This can cause problems for other countries which become dependent on imported fuel. For example, in 1976 the USA suffered from its dependency on imported oil when prices increased by 400%.

The burning of oil and gas contributes to major environmental problems such as the *greenhouse effect** and acid rain (see below). Oil accidentally spilled on land is messy, poisonous and a fire hazard. It can make soil infertile for

More areas undersea are drilled for oil as resources on land are being used up.

many years. At sea, oil spilled from tankers or oil rigs can kill sea birds and fish, destroying the livelihoods of fishermen (see page 95). In March 1989 an oil tanker called the Exxon Valdez caused a slick of up to 2,400 square kilometres. Experts predict the damage could take over ten years to clear up. Oil companies are often unwilling to spend the money and time necessary to repair the damage oil spillage causes.

Acid rain

Acid rain is a damaging mixture of rain or snow with polluting chemicals, such as sulphuric acid and nitric acid, which are produced by the burning of fossil fuels (see page 110). The acid can kill trees, people and animals, pollute soil and damage the outside of buildings.

Acid rain can now be prevented by the installation of new anti-pollution technology in power stations. However, many countries say they cannot afford the expensive equipment needed.

Energy efficiency

As the world population increases and third world countries develop, the demand for energy will increase. Knowledge and technology must be shared between developed countries and the third world, to enable the third world to develop their own efficient and appropriate ways of producing energy.

Greater energy conservation and efficiency is needed in order not to use up the world's energy resources. More money must be provided for research into cleaner, safer, renewable energy sources. Examples of these are solar power, wind power, wave power, tidal power, geothermal power and the burning of biomass (the energy stored in living or dead plant and animal matter,

such as wood and dung).

Money must be invested to develop appliances which require less energy to function. For example, light bulbs have been developed recently which use less than half the amount of electricity used by standard light bulbs. Refrigerators are being produced which use only a fifth of the electricity used by other refrigerators of the same size.

A collection of wind generators on a 'wind farm' in Altamont Pass, California

*Fossil fuels, 14; Greenhouse effect, 29.

53

Circuit symbols and number notation

This table shows the main symbols used to represent the various components used in electric circuits.

There are many more circuit symbols, but the table includes all the components that appear in this book.

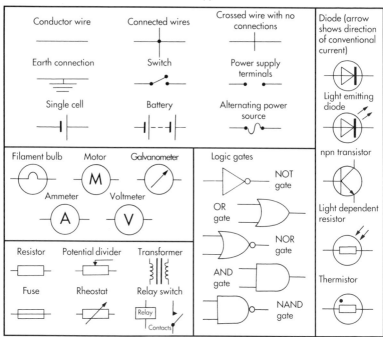

Number notation

Very large or very small numbers (e.g. 10,000,000 or 0.000001) take a long time to write out and are difficult to read. For this reason a method called **index notation** is used instead. This notation indicates the position of the decimal point in a number by showing what power of ten the number should be raised to.

1,000,000	is written 10^6
100,000	is written 10^5
10,000	is written 10^4
1,000	is written 10^3
100	is written 10^2
10	is written 10^1
1	is written 10^0
0.1	is written 10^{-1}
0.01	is written 10^{-2}
0.001	is written 10^{-3}
0.0001	is written 10^{-4}
0.00001	is written 10^{-5}
0.000001	is written 10^{-6}

If you have a large or small number, move the decimal point until it is after the first numeral. Write 10 to the power of the number of places you have moved the decimal point. If you move the decimal point to the left the index is positive, e.g. 10^9. If you move the point to the right the index is negative, e.g. 10^{-2}.

For example:

32,874	is written 3.2874×10^4
3,000	is written 3×10^3
45.7	is written 4.57×10^1
0.98	is written 9.8×10^{-1}
0.00287	is written 2.87×10^{-3}

When multiplying numbers, their indices are added together. For example:
$$10^6 \times 10^{-4} = 10^2.$$
When dividing one number by another, the indices are subtracted as follows :
$$10^8 \div 10^{-5} = 10^3$$

Graphs

A **graph** is a visual representation of how one quantity changes in relation to another. Graphs can be used to show the information gained from an experiment.

Constructing a graph

1. Draw two axes. Along the **x-axis** plot the quantity which is varied during an experiment. This is called the **independent variable**. Along the **y-axis** plot the quantity which changes as a result. This is called the **dependent variable**.

Label each axis with the quantity which is plotted along it and the quantity's unit, e.g. distance (m) or time (s).

2. Mark the **scale** of each quantity along its axis. (The scales do not have to be the same on both axes.) When choosing scales, use the squares on your graph paper to represent values which make plotting the points easy (e.g. avoid the squares representing multiples of three).

3. Plot the points on your graph, marking each one with a cross **X** or a dot within a circle ⊙.

Draw a smooth curve or straight line which best fits the points. This is called the **line of best fit**. The points may be scattered about this line. One or two may be a long way from the line due to experimental error.

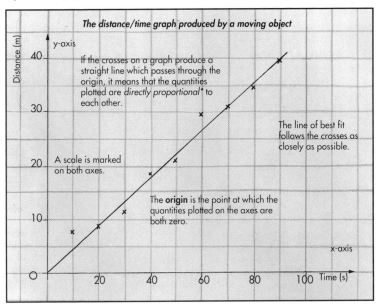

The distance/time graph produced by a moving object

y-axis

If the crosses on a graph produce a straight line which passes through the origin, it means that the quantities plotted are *directly proportional** to each other.

The line of best fit follows the crosses as closely as possible.

A scale is marked on both axes.

The **origin** is the point at which the quantities plotted on the axes are both zero.

Distance (m) — 40, 30, 20, 10

Time (s) — 20, 40, 60, 80, 100

Calculating the gradient of a graph

The **gradient** shows the rate of change of the quantity plotted on the y-axis with that plotted on the x-axis. The gradient of a straight line graph is value Δy divided by Δx (where Δ means 'change in').

The unit of the gradient is the unit of the quantity y/x. For example, the unit of the gradient of the graph shown here is m/s (distance/time).

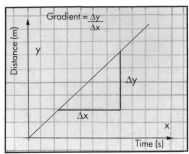

Gradient = $\frac{\Delta y}{\Delta x}$

Distance (m)

Time (s)

*Directly proportional, 61.

Sample questions and answers

This section contains some of the more difficult mathematical ideas used in physics. It includes examples of how to use some of the equations which appear in the coloured section of this book, and some new and more complex equations are introduced. There are sample examination questions and model answers to show you how to tackle certain types of question.

The mathematical ideas and examples appear under the heading of the topic to which they relate. The page number which follows each heading indicates where you can find the topic in this book.

Pressure (page 9)

The pressure at a certain depth in a fluid can be calculated with the following equation:

**Pressure in a fluid (P)
= depth of liquid (h) x density of fluid (d) x acceleration due to gravity (g)**

This equation can only be used when the density throughout the fluid is constant.

Example A : What is the pressure due to the water at the bottom of a lake which is 20 m deep. (The density of the water is 1,000 kg/m^3.)

Answer A : P = hdg
$$= 20 \times 1,000 \times 9.81$$
$$= \textbf{1.96} \times \textbf{10}^5 \, \textbf{N/m}^2$$

In the atmosphere the density of air is not constant with height. A *mercury barometer** can be used to measure atmospheric pressure.

Example B : What is the value of the atmospheric pressure which supports a column of mercury of height 76 cm (76 cm = 0.76 m) in a mercury barometer. (The density of mercury is 13,600 kg/m^3.)

Answer B : P = hdg
$$= 0.76 \times 13,600 \times 9.81$$
$$= 101,000$$
$$= \textbf{1.01} \times \textbf{10}^5 \, \textbf{N/m}^2$$

To calculate the total pressure at the bottom of a 20 m deep lake, the atmospheric pressure and the pressure of

the water must be added together.
Pressure = 1.01 x 10^5 + 1.96 x 10^5
$$= \textbf{2.97} \times \textbf{10}^5 \, \textbf{N/m}^2$$

Linear motion (page 10)

The following equations relate to moving objects:

Average velocity = $\dfrac{\text{change in } \textit{displacement}^* \text{ (d)}}{\text{time taken (t)}}$

and

Acceleration (a) = $\dfrac{\text{change in velocity (v-u)}}{\text{time taken for change (t)}}$

(where v is the final velocity and u is the original velocity).

These equations are usually used on their own, but occasionally you may need to use them together, as shown in the example below.

Example C : Calculate the value of acceleration due to gravity using the following results gained from the experiment described on page 11. A steel ball falls a distance of 1 m in 0.45 s.

Answer C : If the steel ball's initial velocity (u) is 0, and its final velocity is v, its

average velocity $= \dfrac{v}{2} = \dfrac{d}{t}$

this can be rearranged as v $= \dfrac{2d}{t}$

If its acceleration (a) $= \dfrac{v - u}{t} = \dfrac{v}{t}$

then, a $= \dfrac{2d}{t^2}$

$$= \dfrac{2 \times 1}{0.45^2}$$
$$= \textbf{9.9 m/s}^2$$

Velocity/time graphs (page 11)

The velocity/time graph produced by a moving object can be used to calculate the object's acceleration and the distance it travels in a given time.

Example D : A car accelerates uniformly from rest to a velocity of 20 m/s in 15 s. It then travels at constant velocity for 20 s before decelerating uniformly to rest in 10 s.
From the following velocity/time graph below calculate a) the object's acceleration, b) its deceleration and c) the total distance it has travelled.

*Mercury barometer, 9; Displacement, 61.

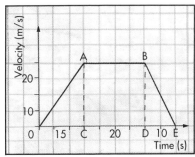

Answer D : An object's acceleration or deceleration is equal to the gradient of the velocity/time graph it produces.

a) Acceleration = $\dfrac{AC}{OC}$ = $\dfrac{20}{15}$

= **1.33 m/s²**

b) Deceleration = $\dfrac{BD}{DE}$ = $\dfrac{20}{10}$

= **2 m/s²**

c) The distance travelled by the object is equal to the area under the velocity/time graph. This is calculated as follows:
Distance = area OAC + area ABDC + area BED

= ($\frac{1}{2}$ x 15 x 20) + (20 x 20) + ($\frac{1}{2}$ x 10 x 20)

= 150 + 400 + 100

= **650 m**

Momentum (page 12)

According to the principle of the conservation of momentum, when objects collide, their total momentum is the same before and after the collision (as long as no outside forces act). For two objects in collision, this principle can be written:

Momentum before = momentum after

$m_1u_1 + m_2u_2 = m_1v_1 + m_2v_2$

(where m_1 and m_2 are the masses of two objects, u_1 and u_2 are their velocities before impact and v_1 and v_2 to their velocities after impact).

Example E : A car of mass 2,000 kg, moving at 3 m/s, collides with a stationary car of mass 1,000 kg. After the impact they move together. Calculate the final velocity of the cars after the impact.

Answer E : From the principle of conservation of momentum:

$m_1u_1 + m_2u_2 = (m_1+m_2) \times v$

(2,000 x 3) + 0 = (2,000 + 1,000) x v

6,000 = 3,000v

v = **2 m/s**

The principle of conservation of momentum applies to all interactions, including explosions (as long as no external forces act). This is demonstrated in the following example.

Example F : A bullet of mass 0.01 kg is fired from a rifle of mass 4 kg. If the rifle recoils with a velocity of 2.5 m/s, find the velocity of the bullet.

Answer F : The total momentum of the rifle and bullet before the explosion is zero. Therefore, the total momentum afterwards is zero too. The velocity of the rifle must be considered to be a negative quantity as it is moving in the opposite direction to the bullet.

0 = (0.01 x v_1) - (4 x 2.5)

0.01 x v_1 = 10

v_1 = **1,000 m/s**

The expansion of gases (page 27)

When considering the expansion of a fixed mass of gas, three quantities must be considered: pressure, temperature and volume. If any of these quantities changes, it is possible to work out how the other quantities are affected by the change using the following equation which is called the **general gas equation**:

$$\frac{p_1V_1}{T_1} = \frac{p_2V_2}{T_2}$$

(where p_1, V_1 and T_1, refer to the pressure, volume and temperature in kelvins of a gas before it undergoes a change, and p_2, V_2 and T_2 to the values afterwards).

It is important to remember that the temperature must always be in kelvins. The pressure of a gas is often measured in **atmospheres**. One atmosphere is the pressure considered to be normal atmospheric pressure. A pressure of one atmosphere would support a mercury column of height 76cm.

Sample questions and answers continued

The general gas equation can often be simplified. For example, if the temperature of a gas remains constant ($T_1 = T_2$), then, $p_1V_1 = p_2V_2$

If its volume remains constant ($V_1 = V_2$), then, $\dfrac{p_1}{T_1} = \dfrac{p_2}{T_2}$

If its pressure remains constant ($p_1 = p_2$), then, $\dfrac{V_1}{T_1} = \dfrac{V_2}{T_2}$

Example G : If 2m³ of a gas at 1 atmosphere pressure is compressed to 0.25m³ at constant temperature, what is its new pressure?

Answer G : As temperature is constant,
then, $p_1V_1 = p_2V_2$
$1 \times 2 = p_2 \times 0.25$
$p_2 = \textbf{8 atmospheres}$

Example H : A gas at 27 °C (300 K) is heated at constant pressure until its volume has doubled. What is the new temperature of the gas?

Answer H : As pressure is constant,
then, $\dfrac{V_1}{T_1} = \dfrac{V_2}{T_2}$
$\dfrac{V_1}{300} = \dfrac{2 \times V_1}{T_2}$
$T_2 = 2 \times 300$
$= \textbf{600 K (327 °C)}$

Ohm's law (page 34-35)

Ohm's law produces the equation:
Resistance (R) $= \dfrac{\textbf{p.d. (V)}}{\textbf{current (I)}}$

This relationship can apply to single components or any group of components in an electrical circuit.

Example I : For the circuit below, calculate: a) the current through each of the resistors in the circuit, and b) the total current flowing.

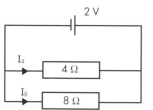

Answer I : a) The resistors are in parallel, therefore, the p.d. across each resistor is 2 V.

If Ohm's law is applied to the 4 Ω resistor, then $I_4 = \dfrac{V}{R}$
$= \dfrac{2}{4}$
$= \textbf{0.5 amps}$

If Ohm's law is applied to the 8 Ω resistor, then $I_8 = \dfrac{2}{8}$
$= \textbf{0.25 amps}$

b) Total current $= I_4 + I_8$
$= 0.5 + 0.25$
$= \textbf{0.75 amps}$

Example J : For the circuit below calculate: a) the current flowing, and b) the p.d. across each of the resistors.

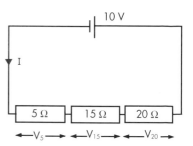

Answer J :
a) Total resistance $= 5 + 15 + 20$
$= 40\ \Omega$

If Ohm's law is applied to the whole circuit, then $I = \dfrac{V}{R} = \dfrac{10}{40}$
$= \textbf{0.25 amps}$

b) If Ohm's law is applied to each of the resistors in turn, then:
P.d. across 5 Ω resistor (V_5) $= 0.25 \times 5$
$= \textbf{1.25 V}$
P.d. across 15 Ω resistor (V_{15}) $= 0.25 \times 15$
$= \textbf{3.75 V}$
P.d. across 20 Ω resistor (V_{20}) $= 0.25 \times 20$
$= \textbf{5 V}$

Example K: Calculate the current through each of the three resistors in the following circuit diagram.

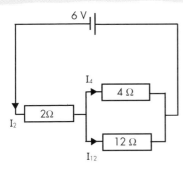

6 V

I_4

4 Ω

2Ω

I_2

12 Ω

I_{12}

Answer K : The combined resistance of the 4 Ω and 12 Ω resistor in parallel is calculated as follows:

$$\frac{1}{R} = \frac{1}{4} + \frac{1}{12}$$

$$= \frac{3 + 1}{12}$$

$$= \frac{4}{12}$$

$$\frac{1}{R} = \frac{1}{3}$$

$$R = 3 \ \Omega$$

The total resistance in the circuit (R)

$$R = 2 + 3 = 5 \ \Omega$$

If Ohm's law is applied to the whole circuit, then the total current through the circuit $I_2 = \frac{6}{5}$

$$= \textbf{1.2 amps}$$

If Ohm's law is applied to the 2 Ω resistor, the p.d. across it is:

P.d. = 1.2 x 2

= 2.4 V

Therefore, the p.d. across the 4 Ω and 12 Ω resistors = 6 - 2.4

= 3.6 V

If Ohm's law is applied to the 4 Ω resistor and 12 Ω resistor in turn then, the current through the 4 Ω resistor is calculated as follows:

$$I_4 = \frac{3.6}{4}$$

$$= \textbf{0.9 amps}$$

and the current through 12 Ω resistor,

$$I_{12} = \frac{3.6}{12}$$

$$= \textbf{0.3 amps}$$

(Note: $I_2 = I_4 + I_{12}$)

Transformers (page 41)

The turns ratio shows the relationship between the number of turns of conductor wire on the primary and secondary coils of a transformer and the p.d.s produced in both coils.

$$\frac{\text{No. primary turns (}N_p\text{)}}{\text{No. secondary turns (}N_s\text{)}} = \frac{\text{primary p.d. (}V_p\text{)}}{\text{secondary p.d. (}V_s\text{)}}$$

Example L : If an alternating p.d. of 240 V is applied to the primary coil of a transformer which has 200 turns of wire, what will be the p.d. produced in the secondary coil which has 10 turns?

Answer L : $\frac{N_p}{N_s} = \frac{V_p}{V_s}$

$$\frac{200}{10} = \frac{240}{V_s}$$

$$20 = \frac{240}{V_s}$$

$$20 \times V_s = 240$$

$$V_s = \frac{240}{20}$$

$$= \textbf{12 V}$$

Electrical power is calculated with the equation:

$$\textbf{P = VI}$$

(where P is power, V is voltage and I is current).

In a perfectly efficient transformer the electrical power supplied by the primary coil would be equal to the power delivered to the secondary coil. This relationship can be written as follows:

$$V_p\, I_p = V_s\, I_s$$

(where I_p and I_s are the currents in the primary and secondary coils).

Example M : Using the same transformer as in example L, calculate the current in the secondary coil (I_s) if the current in the primary coil (I_p) is 0.1 amp.

Answer M : $240 \times 0.1 = 12 \times I_s$

$$24 = 12 \times I_s$$

$$I_s = \frac{24}{12}$$

$$= \textbf{2 amps}$$

Summary of equations

The following table as acts a summary of some of the important equations in this book. The table contains **derived quantities** which are worked out by dividing or multiplying two or more other quantities. The unit of a derived quantity (called a **derived unit**) is found from its defining equation. Some derived units are given special names. These are shown in the table.

Derived quantity	Symbol	Defining equation	Derived unit	Name of unit	Abbreviation
Density	d	$d = \dfrac{mass}{volume}$	kg/m^3		
Moment		Moment = force × perpendicular distance	N m	Newton metre	N m
Pressure	P	$P = \dfrac{force}{area}$	N/m^2	Pascal	Pa
Velocity	v	$v = \dfrac{distance\ moved}{time}$	m/s		
Acceleration	a	$a = \dfrac{change\ in\ velocity}{time}$	m/s^2		
Force	F	F = mass × acceleration	$kg\ m/s^2$	Newton	N
Momentum		Momentum = mass × velocity	$kg\ m/s$		
Energy	E	Capacity to do work	Nm	Joule	J
Work	W	W = force × distance	Nm	Joule	J
Power	P	$P = \dfrac{work\ done}{time}$	J/s	Watt	W
Frequency	f	Number of waves per second	1/s	Hertz	Hz
Electric charge	Q	Q = current × time	A s	Coulomb	C
Potential difference	V	$V = \dfrac{energy\ transferred}{charge}$	J/C	Volt	V
Resistance	R	$R = \dfrac{potential\ difference}{current}$	V/A	Ohm	Ω

Glossary

The glossary explains some of the more difficult terms used in this book. The terms defined appear in **bold**, as do other related words which are used in the definition. Words within the explanations which have their own entries in this list are followed by a †.

Directly proportional. When applied to two quantities, if one quantity changes by a certain proportion, then the other changes by the same proportion. For example, if one quantity is doubled, the other quantity is doubled too.

Displacement. A measurement of the distance and direction of an object at any time from a chosen fixed point. Displacemant is a *vector** quantity.

Earth potential. The *electrical potential** of the planet Earth. The Earth is able to supply or absorb electrical charge without changing its own potential. It is considered to be at zero electrical potential.

Element. A substance which cannot be split into simpler substances by a chemical reaction. Atoms of the same element have the same number of protons in their nucleus. There are over one hundred known elements.

Generator. A machine which converts kinetic energy into electrical energy. The kinetic energy may be provided by an engine or a turbine†.The *simple dynamo** is an example of a generator.

Inversely proportional. When applied to two quantities, this means that one quantity is directly proportional† to the reciprocal† of the other. For example, if one quantity is doubled, the other quantity is halved.

Medium. The substance or space in which objects exist and phenomena take place. For example, glass is described as a medium when light travels through it.

Ozone layer. A layer of gas which forms part of the Earth's upper atmosphere. It absorbs some of the harmful ultra-violet radiation from the Sun (see page 111).

The ozone layer is being destroyed by man-made chemicals. If the ozone layer continues to be destroyed and more UV radiation is allowed to reach the Earth, it may lead to an increase in the number of cases of skin cancer and be harmful to crop production.

Rate. The amount by which one quantity changes in relation to another. For example, acceleration is the rate of change of velocity in relation to time. (Note that the second quantity is not time in all cases.)

Reactor. The container in a nuclear power plant in which atoms are split to release a vast amount of energy.

Reciprocal. The value obtained from a number when one is divided by that number. The reciprocal of any number x would be $1/x$. For example, the reciprocal of 10 is $1/10$ which is 0.1).

Spectrum. A particular range of wavelengths or frequencies. For example, the wavelength of the waves which make up the visible spectrum of light range from 4×10^{-7} m to 7.5×10^{-7} m.

Turbine. A device with rotating blades. The blades are turned by a force. For example, jets of steam turn the turbines in a coal-fired power station. The kinetic energy of a moving turbine can be converted into electricity in a generator†.

A turbine

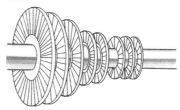

Vacuum. A space which is completely empty of matter. A **partial vacuum** is created in a container from which some air or gas has been removed, so that the pressure inside the container is much less than the atmospheric pressure outside it.

Vaporization. The change of state from liquid to **vapour**. A liquid will **vaporize** at a temperature called its **boiling point**.

*Vector, 7; Electrical potential, 32; Simple dynamo, 40.

Practical work in science

When studying a science subject it is important to carry out practical experiments. Experiments can be used to prove whether a scientific 'fact' is correct or not. Some examination boards consider practical work when assessing a candidate's final examination grade. A successful experiment can also demonstrate a student's ability to understand and follow instructions correctly. Practical work can help you to understand and remember scientific ideas.

The purpose of an experiment

Experiments can be used to prove whether a statement is true or false, or to find out how one factor is affected by another. For example, you might be asked to perform an experiment to test whether the following statement is true: 'a long column of plasticine is stronger than a short one'. The strength of a column of plasticine can be tested by measuring the size of the force required to make the column buckle. The force which causes the column to buckle can be called the **buckling force**.

Planning

The amount of planning needed before beginning an experiment depends on the complexity of the experiment. First check you have all the equipment you require for the experiment. If you are given instructions to follow, ensure you understand them before starting. If there are no instructions, a careful plan of action is needed.

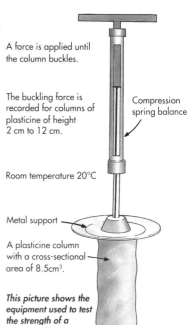

A force is applied until the column buckles.

The buckling force is recorded for columns of plasticine of height 2 cm to 12 cm.

Compression spring balance

Room temperature 20°C

Metal support

A plasticine column with a cross-sectional area of 8.5cm³.

This picture shows the equipment used to test the strength of a plasticine column.

Variables in an experiment

There are always factors which will affect the results of an experiment. These factors are called **variables**. For example, in the sample experiment there are factors which will affect the strength of a plasticine column. These include its height, the area of its cross-section and the type and temperature of the plasticine.

To make the results of an experiment accurate, only one of the variables should be changed at a time. In the sample experiment the height of the plasticine is the variable changed; the others are kept the same. The **independent variable** is the quantity the experimenter changes during the experiment. In this experiment it is the height of the plasticine column. The **dependent variable** is the quantity which changes during the experiment as a result of the independent variable being altered. In this experiment it is the force required to buckle the column.

Measurement

The instruments used to measure the results of an experiment must be chosen carefully. In the sample experiment, for example, a ruler can be used to measure the height of the column, and a compression spring balance to measure the buckling force. If a compression spring balance is not available, weights can be used instead.

Decide how many measurements you are going to record. To obtain useful results a minimum of six readings is required. The range over which the measurements are taken must also be considered. For example, in the sample experiment the range of heights of the plasticine column must be chosen.

Units of measurement

The units of measurement used should be suitable for the quantities involved in an experiment. For example, if an experiment involves measuring small distances centimetres can be used. For large distances metres should be used. However, it is important to remember that if measurements gained from an experiment are used in an equation they will have to be converted into the appropriate **SI units**. (An SI unit is the unit chosen for a quantity by an international committee.) For example, the SI unit for force is the newton (N) and for distance the SI unit is the metre (m).

Writing a report on practical work

When writing a report on practical work the following details must be included: details of the equipment used; a diagram of how the equipment was arranged; a step by step account of how the experiment was set up and performed; details of any special precautions taken to ensure the accuracy of the results; the results of the experiment and any conclusions.

The results or data gained from the experiment should be displayed as clearly as possible. Data can be put into a chart. The relationship between two variables can be visually represented by plotting points on a graph. (For help drawing graphs see page 55.)

When thinking about how to write a report, it helps to imagine that the person who will read the report is a scientist and understands scientific terms, but that they have not seen the experiment performed.

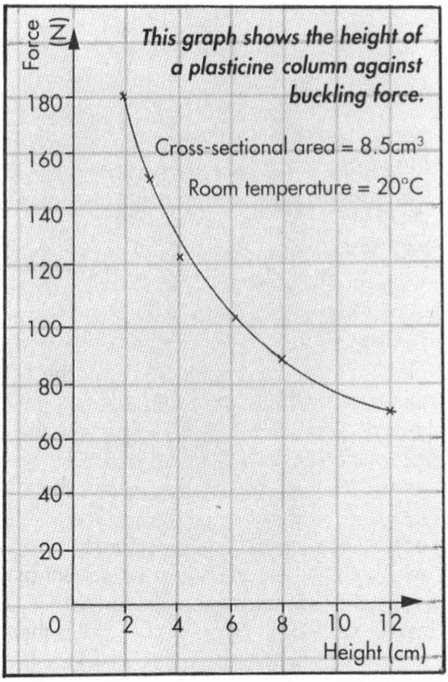

This graph shows the height of a plasticine column against buckling force.

Cross-sectional area = 8.5cm³
Room temperature = 20°C

Force (N) — vertical axis: 180, 160, 140, 120, 100, 80, 60, 40, 20
Height (cm) — horizontal axis: 0, 2, 4, 6, 8, 10, 12

Drawing conclusions

The results of practical work should be used to draw conclusions at the end of a report. The type of conclusion will depend on the nature of the experiment. A conclusion may take the form of a statement of fact. An experiment may prove that a given statement is true or false. For example, the statement investigated by the sample experiment is proved false. The results show that a short column of plasticine is stronger than a long column of plasticine.

Famous scientists

Below are details of the lives and achievements of a selection of scientists who contributed to the theories and discoveries discussed in this section of the book. Scientists discussed later in this book are listed with a reference to the page on which you will find them.

Ampère, André Marie (1775-1836). French physicist and mathematician. He studied the motor effect produced when a current-carrying wire is placed in a magnetic field. He developed the solenoid and laid the foundations for the development of the galvanometer.

Becquerel, Antoine Henri (1852-1908) French physicist. See page 120.

Brown, Robert (1773-1858). Scottish botanist. He was the first scientist to notice the continuous random motion of pollen grains in water. Scientists later deduced that this movement was due to the impact of moving water molecules.

Celsius, Anders (1701-1744). Swedish astronomer. He devised a temperature scale based on the freezing and boiling points of pure water.

Curie, Marie (1867-1934). Polish-French scientist. See page 120.

Dalton, John (1766-1844). English chemist. See page 120.

Faraday, Michael (1791-1867). English chemist and physicist. He believed that a magnetic field would produce a current. Eventually he discovered electromagnetic induction, when he demonstrated how an electric current could be induced by moving a conductor through a magnetic field. He went on to produce the first dynamo and the first electric motor.

Gilbert, William (1544-1603). English physician and physicist. He is best known for his study of magnetism. He discovered the method of making a magnet by stroking an iron bar with a permanent magnet (descibed on page 36). He introduced the word 'pole' to describe the different areas of a magnet.

Hertz, Heinrich Rudolph (1857-1894). German physicist. He studied electromagnetic waves and discovered radio waves.

Maxwell, James Clerk (1831-1879). Scottish physicist. He proved that electromagnetic waves were made up of electric and magnetic fields oscillating at right angles to each other. He contributed to the kinetic theory of gases, showing that the velocity of the molecules in a gas depends on the temperature of the gas.

Newton, Isaac (1642-1727). English mathematician and physicist. He produced the first experimental spectrum, proving that white light is made up of different colours. In 1665-66 he investigated and formulated the universal law of gravitation. In 1685 he published his three laws of motion.

Oersted, Hans Christian (1777-1851). He discovered that an electric current in a wire produces a magnetic field around it.

Ohm, Georg Simon (1789-1854). German physicist. He formulated Ohm's law which describes the relationship between potential difference and current.

Pascal, Blaise (1623-1662). French physicist and philosopher. Pascal studied fluid pressure and hydraulics. He showed that pressure in a liquid acts equally in all directions, and that changes in pressure are transmitted instantly.

Rutherford, Ernest (1871-1937). New Zealand physicist. See page 121.

Snel, Willebrord (1580-1626). Dutch physicist. He discovered the relationship between the angles a light ray makes with a surface when it is refracted as it passes from one medium to another.

Thomson, William (Baron Kelvin of Largs) (1824-1907). English physicist. His study of the nature of heat led him to propose the 'absolute' scale of temperature. The scale's starting point is the temperature at which, in theory, molecules would not have enough energy to move and would remain stationary.

ESSENTIAL
CHEMISTRY

Clive Gifford

Illustrated by Sean Wilkinson and
Robert Walster

Designed by Sharon Bennett and John Russell
Additional designs by Diane Thistlethwaite

Consultants: Michael White, Dr Andrew Rudge
Series editor: Jane Chisholm

With thanks to Steve Mersereau

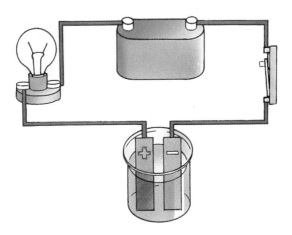

Contents

Using this section of the book

Essential Chemistry is a concise aid to reference and revision. It is intended to act as a companion to your studies, explaining the essential points of chemistry clearly and simply.

This section is divided into chapters which cover the main concepts of chemistry. Each chapter includes the key principles and facts for that topic. Important new words are highlighted in **bold** type. If a word is explained in more detail elsewhere, it is printed in italic type with an asterisk, like this: *bonding**. At the foot of the page there is a reference to the page on which the explanation can be found.

The black and white pages at the back of this section offer a variety of reference material, from tables of valencies and densities to details of common experiments. It finishes with a glossary that explains difficult words in the text, and a detailed index.

Examinations

This section contains the essential information you will need when studying chemistry. For examinations, however, it is important to know which syllabus you are studying because different examining bodies require you to learn different material.

Atoms: the building blocks of chemistry

Chemists study the behaviour and characteristics of substances. These are called the **properties** of a substance. All substances are made up of tiny particles called **atoms**. A substance the size of a pinhead contains billions of atoms.

An atom is the smallest unit of a substance that can exist and retain the properties of that substance. There are over 100 different types of atom, known as *elements**. Each element has its own chemical name and a shortened name known as a **chemical symbol**. Most symbols are abbreviations of the chemical name, like H for hydrogen. However, some symbols come from other languages. For example, the chemical symbol for gold, Au, comes from its Latin name, *aurum*.

Molecules

Atoms are rarely found on their own. They tend to group together into particles called **molecules**. A molecule is a particle of a substance which contains two or more atoms *bonded** together. A molecule that consists of two atoms is known as a **diatomic molecule**. Hydrogen, oxygen, and chlorine are all examples of diatomic molecules.

formula. This shows what atoms are contained in the molecule and in what proportions. A chemical formula can also be shown in two other ways. You can use a diagram, like the hydrogen molecule above, or you can use a **structural formula** which shows how the atoms in a molecule are bonded together.

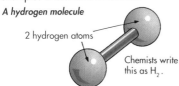

A hydrogen molecule

2 hydrogen atoms

Chemists write this as H_2.

It is possible for atoms and molecules to combine with different types of atoms and molecules to create a huge variety of different substances. Chemists give each type of molecule a **chemical**

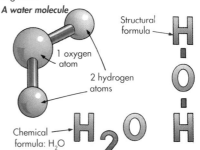

A water molecule

1 oxygen atom

2 hydrogen atoms

Structural formula

Chemical formula: H_2O

*Elements, 68; Bonded, 76.

Elements, mixtures and compounds

Chemists classify substances as elements, mixtures or compounds.

An **element** is a substance which consists of one type of atom. It cannot be broken down into a simpler substance.

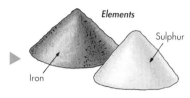

Elements

Iron

Sulphur

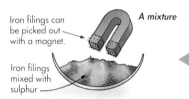

A mixture

Iron filings can be picked out with a magnet.

Iron filings mixed with sulphur

A **mixture** is a substance containing two or more different elements mixed together. It can be physically separated with ease.

A **compound** is a substance which contains two or more different elements joined or *bonded** together. This bonding is caused by a *chemical reaction**. A compound cannot be broken down into its individual elements by physical means.

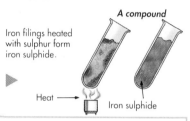

A compound

Iron filings heated with sulphur form iron sulphide.

Heat → Iron sulphide

The states of matter

All substances can be divided into **solids**, **liquids** or **gases**. These are known as the **states of matter**. It is possible for a substance to move from one state to another. This is known as a **change of state**. It normally occurs because of a change in the energy of a substance as a result of heating or cooling.

Many substances can exist in more than one state. In a chemical reaction it is important to know in which state the various chemicals are being used. This is done by placing the symbol (s) for solid, (l) for liquid, and (g) for gas after the name of the substances. A glass of water would be written $H_2O(l)$, whereas ice would be written $H_2O(s)$.

Kinetic theory

All substances are made of particles of matter. **Kinetic theory** explains the changes of state in terms of the positioning and movement of particles.
   Particles in a solid are tightly packed and cannot break free from their neighbours. They cannot move; they can only vibrate.

Particles in a solid

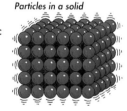

Particles in a liquid

When heated, a solid's particles vibrate more and more quickly. Eventually they are able to move around each other, although they can only move within the confines of the liquid.

Further heat gives the particles the energy to escape from the surface of the liquid to form a gas. The particles in a gas are far apart. A gas has no fixed volume; it can expand or be compressed. There is little force holding the particles together, so they are free to move in any direction.

Particles in a gas

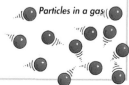

Evidence of molecules

The molecules in liquids and gases are continually moving in a completely random way. This can be seen when smoke molecules are viewed under a microscope. They move in a random zig-zag fashion because they are being hit by invisible air molecules. This movement is known as **Brownian motion**.

The gradual mixing of two or more different gases or liquids is called **diffusion** (see page 133). This mixing is caused by molecules of the different substances colliding and intermingling. Perfumes can be smelled at a distance because their molecules diffuse through the air.

Air

Bromine gas

15 minutes later

Gas and air mixed

Boiling and melting

The process by which a solid changes to a liquid is known as **melting**, and the temperature at which the change takes place is called the **melting point**. The process by which a liquid changes into a gas is called **boiling**, and the temperature at which this change occurs is called the **boiling point**. A substance is classified by the state in which it exists at 25°C (known to chemists as **room temperature**). However, two other factors can affect the state of a substance: pressure and purity.

Pressure

The air in the atmosphere exerts pressure on the earth which decreases with altitude. Pressure is measured in **atmospheres**; one atmosphere is the standard pressure at sea level. Boiling points are affected by pressure. The lighter the pressure, the easier it is for particles in a liquid to escape into the air. For this reason, water boils at a lower temperature on a high mountain (where the pressure is lower) than at sea level.

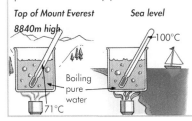

Top of Mount Everest 8840m high

Sea level

100°C

Boiling pure water

71°C

Purity

A substance is **pure** if it contains no trace of any other substance. An impure substance will not have the same melting or boiling point as the pure material. Measuring boiling and melting points is an important way of assessing the purity of a sample.

Freezing and condensing

Unlike melting and boiling, there are some changes of state that require a decrease in energy. **Freezing** is the change of state from liquid to solid. The **freezing point** of a substance is the same as its melting point. **Condensation** is the change of state from gas to liquid caused by cooling. Water vapour in warm air condenses into liquid when cooled.

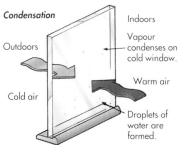

Condensation

Outdoors

Cold air

Indoors

Vapour condenses on cold window.

Warm air

Droplets of water are formed.

Atomic structure

Atoms are made up of particles of matter known as **subatomic** or **fundamental particles**. The three main subatomic particles are called protons, neutrons and electrons. An atom mostly consists of empty space. Almost all of an atom's mass is concentrated in a structure at its centre called the **nucleus**. This consists of protons and neutrons grouped together. Electrons orbit the nucleus.

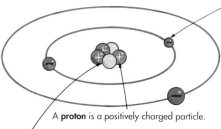

An **electron** is a negatively charged particle. It is kept in orbit round the nucleus because it is attracted to the positively charged protons. This attraction holds the atom together. An electron is more than 1800 times smaller than a neutron or proton.

An atom usually contains an equal number of positively charged protons and negatively charged electrons. This makes it **electrically neutral**.

A **proton** is a positively charged particle.

A **neutron** has no electrical charge.

Atomic number and mass

The number of protons in the nucleus of an atom is called the **atomic number**. This number determines which element the atom belongs to. The total number of protons and neutrons in the nucleus of an atom is called the **atomic mass** or **mass number**. Chemists write the atomic mass and the atomic number in front of the chemical symbol for an element as shown on the right.

15 protons + 16 neutrons = mass number 31

Phosphorus has 15 protons and 16 neutrons.

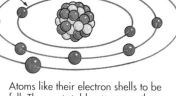

15 protons = atomic number

Electrons and electron shells

The **chemical properties** of an atom (the way in which it reacts with other atoms) are determined by the electrons. In some cases electrons are passed from one atom to another; in others, electrons are shared between the combining atoms. The electrons in an atom exist in layers called **shells**, or **energy levels**. Electrons are arranged in the shells according to certain rules.

The first shell outside the nucleus holds up to **two** electrons.

The second shell holds up to **eight** electrons.

The third shell holds up to **eight** electrons.

When a shell is full, a new one is started.

The atomic number of an element tells you how many electrons that element has. An atom has as many shells as it needs to arrange its electrons. The number of electrons in the outer shell determines how *reactive** an atom is.

Atoms like their electron shells to be full. The most stable atoms are those with full outer shells, like helium. The most reactive atoms, like sodium, are those which only need to lose or gain one electron to obtain a full outer shell.

*Reactive, 78.

Placing electrons

You can use the rules described on page 6 to determine how electrons are distributed in their shells. For example, the element calcium (Ca) has 20 electrons. Two go into the first shell, while eight go into each of the second and third shells. With the third shell full, the remaining two electrons go into the fourth shell. This information can be written as 2.8.8.2. This is called the **electron structure** or **configuration**.

A calcium atom

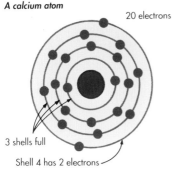

20 electrons

3 shells full

Shell 4 has 2 electrons

Electron structure: 2.8.8.2

Relative atomic mass

An individual atom of an element cannot be weighed, but its mass can be compared to that of another atom chosen as a standard. One twelfth of the mass of a *carbon-12** atom is used; this comparison is known as **relative atomic mass**, or **A_r**. The A_r number is very similar to the mass number. However, A_r is a measure of the mass of an 'average' atom of an element. It takes into account the proportions of all the isotopes of an element.

Average atom

$1/12$th mass of carbon-12

For example, chlorine has two isotopes. One has a relative atomic mass of 35 and in a typical sample of chlorine will make up 75% of the atoms. The other

Isotopes

Isotopes are atoms of the same element which have different numbers of neutrons. All the isotopes of an element have the same atomic number, but different mass numbers. For example, hydrogen has three isotopes. These are:

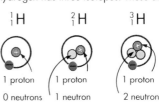

^1_1H ^2_1H ^3_1H

1 proton   1 proton   1 proton

0 neutrons   1 neutron   2 neutrons

The isotopes of an element have different *physical properties** but, because they all have the same number of electrons, their chemical properties are identical. A typical sample of an element usually has one common isotope and smaller percentages of other isotopes. A typical sample of hydrogen contains 99.9% ^1_1H, under 0.1% ^2_1H and a tiny amount of ^3_1H. The smaller quantities are known as **isotopic impurities**.

isotope has a relative atomic mass of 37 and occurs a quarter of the time. The relative atomic mass of chlorine is therefore calculated as follows:

$$A_r \text{ (Cl)} = \frac{(3 \times 35) + (1 \times 37)}{4} = 35.5$$

With the exception of chlorine, chemists often round the relative atomic mass of an element to the nearest whole number. Relative atomic masses are used to find the relative mass of a molecule. **Relative molecular mass** (written M_r) is the sum of the relative atomic masses of all the atoms in a molecule. For example, the relative molecular mass of a molecule of magnesium chloride ($MgCl_2$) is calculated as:

$$
\begin{array}{lll}
A_r \text{ of magnesium} & = & 24.3 \\
2 \times A_r \text{ of chlorine} & = & 2 \times 35.5 \\
M_r \text{ of } MgCl_2 & = & 95.3
\end{array}
$$

The periodic table

The **periodic table** is a structured list of all known elements, arranged in order of their *atomic numbers**. It is based on the work of the Russian scientist Mendeleev, who published his table in 1869. Each element is represented by a block in the table containing its chemical symbol, atomic number and approximate *relative atomic mass**. (A list of symbols with each element's full name can be found on page 119)

Elements in the table can be classified as metals, non-metals, or metalloids. **Metals** have certain properties which distinguish them from **non-metals**. These include generally high melting points, a shiny appearance, and good *malleability**, *ductility** and *conductivity** of electricity and heat. Some elements, such as silicon (Si), have both metallic and non-metallic properties. These elements are known as **metalloids**.

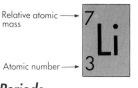

Relative atomic mass →

Atomic number →

Periods

The horizontal rows are called **periods**. All elements in a period have the same number of shells of electrons. As you move down the table, the next period contains elements with one more shell than the last.

As you move from left to right across a period, you find that each element has one more electron in its outer shell than the element before. Lithium (Li), for example, has one electron in its outer shell, while its neighbour beryllium (Be) has two. The change in the number of electrons in the outer shell produces changes in the properties of elements. For example, as you move from left to right across period 2 you find that the melting and boiling points of the solid elements (lithium, beryllium, boron and carbon) increase. The position of an element in the periodic table gives you an idea of its properties.

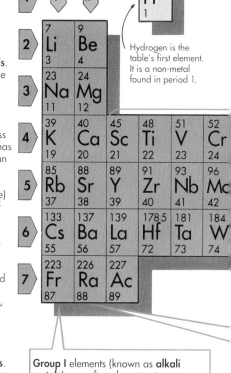

Hydrogen is the table's first element. It is a non-metal found in period 1.

Groups

The vertical columns are called **groups**. Elements within the same group all have the same number of electrons in their outer shell. They therefore tend to have similar chemical properties. For example, group I elements, with one electron in their outer shells, tend to be very *reactive**.

Group I elements (known as **alkali metals**) are soft and create strong *alkaline** solutions when reacted with water. Their softness and reactivity increase down the group. Sodium (Na) is a group I element found in many compounds, such as sodium chloride (salt).

*Atomic number, 70; Relative atomic mass, 71; Malleability, 78; Ductility, 78; Conductivity, 78; Reactive, 78; Alkaline, 89.

Transition metals are found between groups II and III. They are hard, tough and shiny. They are less reactive and have greater densities than group I or II elements. Some transition metals, such as tungsten (W), copper (Cu) and iron (Fe), have a number of different uses. For example, tungsten, is used to make tools and filaments in light bulbs.

Group 0 (once known as group VIII) contains the **noble** or **inert gases**. Their outer electron shells are full, which makes it difficult for them to gain or lose electrons. They are therefore almost totally unreactive. Helium (He) is a very light group 0 element. Being unreactive and *non-flammable**, it is used to inflate hot air balloons.

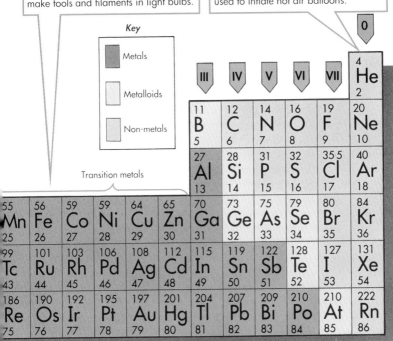

Key

Metals

Metalloids

Non-metals

Transition metals

Group II elements have one more electron in their outer shells than group I elements. Although they are reactive, the extra electron makes them less reactive than group I elements. All group II elements, except beryllium, have similar chemical properties. Their reactivity increases as you move down the group. Group II elements are found in compounds which form important rocks in the earth's crust. This gives rise to the group's alternative name, the **alkaline earth metals**.

Group VII elements are known as the **halogens**. They are non-metals and are too reactive to occur on their own in nature. They are usually found combined with other elements in a *salt**. They become less reactive, and their melting points increase further down the group. For example, fluorine (F) is a yellow gas at room temperature, whereas bromine (Br) is a liquid, and iodine (I) is a black solid. Iodine dissolved in *ethanol** is used as an antiseptic.

*Non-flammable (flammable), 122; Salt, 90; Ethanol, 109.

The air

Air consists of a mixture of gases (see right), the most common of which is nitrogen. It is possible to turn the gases in air into liquids by cooling them under high pressure. The different gases can then be separated by the process of *fractional distillation**. Many of the *noble gases** found in air are used in different forms of lighting. Argon is used in ordinary light bulbs, xenon in some lighthouse bulbs, and krypton in powerful bulbs used in miners' lamps.

The level of water vapour in the air is known as **humidity**. It varies from day to day and from place to place around the world.

The gases in air

Nitrogen 78%

Oxygen 21%

Other 1% (argon, carbon dioxide, water vapour, noble gases)

Oxygen

Test for oxygen

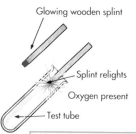

Glowing wooden splint

Splint relights

Oxygen present

Test tube

Oxygen is essential to life. Without it animals could not breathe and there could be no fire. It is the most abundant element in the earth's crust. Oxygen has a boiling point of -186°C. It is used in many industries, from the burning off of impurities in steel-making, to the provision of emergency breathing units in hospitals.

The gases in air are slightly *soluble**. Nitrogen is less soluble in water than oxygen. Only about 33% of the air in water is nitrogen; the rest is oxygen. If water is warmed it contains less air. The escaping air can be seen leaving the water as bubbles.

Combustion and energy from fuels

Combustion, or burning, a chemical reaction in which a fuel is *ignited** in the presence of oxygen. When a substance burns it uses up oxygen and forms *oxides**. Energy, usually in the form of heat and light, is also given out. A slow form of combustion is also an essential part of the *respiration** process. Combustion of fuels such as

coal and natural gas provide us with energy. Below is the equation for the combustion of the gas methane. Energy is also produced in the reaction but is not shown in the equation.

$$CH_4 + 2O_2 \rightarrow CO_2 + 2H_2O$$

Methane + Oxygen → Carbon dioxide + Water

Firefighting

The fire triangle

Fuel

Heat

Oxygen

Three essential ingredients are needed to make something burn: **fuel**, **oxygen** and **heat**. These appear in the fire triangle. Heat is present usually in the form of a spark. Firefighters stop fires burning by removing at least one of these three things. For example, special foams are used by fire services to suffocate a fire by removing its oxygen source. Forest rangers use fire breaks (a corridor cleared of trees) to cut off a fire's supply of fuel. A fire can be made worse if the firefighter does not use the correct method of extinguishing the fire. For example, using water on a *flammable** liquid fire could spread the fire further.

*Fractional distillation, 105; Noble gases, 73; Soluble, 114; Ignite, 122; Oxides, 123; Respiration, 104; Flammable, 122.

Air pollution

Main causes of air pollution		
Pollutant	Effects	Method of control
Soot and smoke	Dirties buildings	Use smokeless fuel. Improve air supply.
Carbon monoxide	Poisonous	Adjust/tune engines. Use catalytic convertors.
Lead compounds	Poisonous	Use unleaded petrol. Reduce lead additives.
Carbon dioxide	Greenhouse effect*	Burn less fossil fuel*. Replant rainforests.
CFCs*	Ozone* depletion	Limit use of CFCs. Develop alternative
	Greenhouse effect	chemicals.
Sulphur dioxide	Acid rain*	Burn less coal and oil. Remove sulphur dioxide from waste gases.
Nitrogen oxides	Acid rain	Adjust/tune engines. Fit catalytic converters.

Ozone depletion, acid rain and the greenhouse effect are looked at on pages 110-111.

When a substance burns in excess oxygen, **complete combustion** is said to be taking place. **Incomplete combustion** is when combustion occurs in the presence of insufficient oxygen. The burning of *hydrocarbon (HC)**-based fuels can result in incomplete combustion. Smoke and soot (both unburned forms of carbon) and carbon monoxide (CO) are formed. Carbon monoxide is a highly poisonous gas that prevents the blood from carrying oxygen.

Many cities like Los Angeles, suffer from serious air pollution. In some cases, a mixture of fog and polluted air forms a **photochemical smog**. This may contain a combination of toxic smoke, soot, ozone and carbon monoxide.

Vehicle exhausts create most of the carbon monoxide released into the air. They also release nitrogen oxides (NO$_x$), a major cause of acid rain, and lead compounds. Lead compounds are added to gasoline to make its combustion more efficient. However, lead is a very toxic chemical and has been linked with an increased incidence of brain damage in children. Lead is known as a **cumulative poison** because it builds up in the body and cannot be removed.

Pollution control

Most of the air pollution discussed above is caused by vehicles burning fuels.

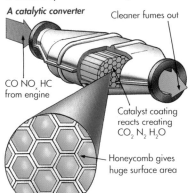

A catalytic converter

Cleaner fumes out

CO NO$_x$ HC from engine

Catalyst coating reacts creating CO$_2$ N$_2$ H$_2$O

Honeycomb gives huge surface area

One solution is to cut down the amount of travelling in motor vehicles. This can be done in practical ways such as car-sharing, living closer to work, using public transport more, and increasing the efficiency of engines.

Most new cars are now capable of using lead-free petrol and many can be fitted with a device called a **catalytic converter**. This contains a *catalyst** which heavily reduces carbon monoxide emissions and can cut down soot, smoke and nitrogen oxides. A catalytic converter can only work with lead-free petrol, as lead prevents metals in the catalyst (palladium, platinum and rhodium) from working properly.

*Greenhouse effect, 111; Fossil fuels, 104; CFC's, 111; Ozone, 111; Acid rain, 110; Hydrocarbons, 104; Catalyst, 99.

Bonding

Atoms with a full outer shell are more stable than atoms with an incomplete one. In order to become stable, atoms with an incomplete outer shell attempt to join chemically with other atoms. This is called **bonding**. The three main types of bonding are ionic (where a metal and non-metal combine), metallic (where atoms of one metal combine) and covalent (where two non-metals bond).

In order to bond with other atoms in a chemical reaction, atoms lose, gain or share electrons. The number of electrons involved is called an atom's **combining power**, or **valency**. For example, sodium needs to lose one electron to obtain a full outer shell, while chlorine needs to gain one. Both have a valency of one. Valencies tend to be related to an element's position in the periodic table. For example, all group I elements have a valency of one. Some elements have more than one valency. The relevant valency is written in Roman numerals after the element. You can find the valencies of elements on page 118.

Ionic bonding

When an atom loses or gains electrons it becomes electrically charged and is known as an **ion**. A positive ion is called a **cation**; a negative ion is called an **anion**. The joining together of ions is called **ionic bonding**. Ions with opposite charges are pulled towards each other, this is known as **electrostatic attraction**. This is shown opposite.

For example, a sodium atom can lose an electron to form a positive ion (Na^+). A chlorine atom can accept an electron to become a negative ion (Cl^-). Each ion now has a complete outer shell of electrons. The sodium

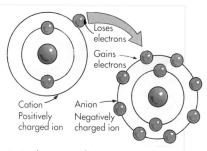

Loses electrons

Gains electrons

Cation
Positively charged ion

Anion
Negatively charged ion

ion's electron configuration is 2.8; the chlorine ion's configuration is 2.8.8. The ions are drawn together and bond, forming a molecule of sodium chloride (NaCl). This is shown below.

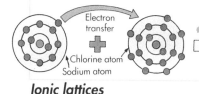

Electron transfer

Chlorine atom
Sodium atom

Full outer shell

Attraction between 2 ions

Sodium ion Na+   Chloride ion Cl-

Ionic lattices

Ionic compounds are formed from positive metal ions and negative non-metal ions. When a number of these ions all react together they form an **ionic lattice**. The forces which hold an ionic lattice together are very strong.

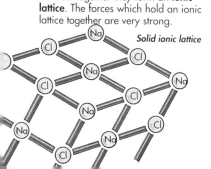

Solid ionic lattice

Ionic equations

An **ionic equation** shows the transfer of electrons, written as e^-. An ion is written with its charge shown after its chemical symbol. For example, magnesium has a valency of 2. When it loses two electrons to form an ion, it is written as Mg^{2+}. Here is an ionic equation showing the formation of magnesium oxide.

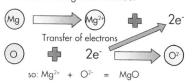

Transfer of electrons

so: $Mg^{2+} + O^{2-} = MgO$

Covalent bonding

The atoms of some elements, such as those in the middle of the periodic table, do not lose or gain electrons easily. Instead atoms of such elements form bonds by sharing electrons. This is called **covalent bonding**. For example, a hydrogen molecule consists of two hydrogen atoms each sharing its one electron with the other, giving both a stable outer shell. The atoms in carbon dioxide are also covalently bonded. Each of the oxygen atoms shares two

pairs of electrons with the carbon atom. This is called a **double bond**.

Hydrogen molecule H$_2$

2 hydrogen atoms

Carbon dioxide molecule CO$_2$

Carbon   Oxygen

Shared electrons

Oxygen

Double bond

Properties of ionic and covalent compounds

Ionic	Covalent
Formed by swapping electrons	Formed by sharing electrons
High melting and boiling points	Often lower melting and boiling points
Form lattices	No lattices, except diamond and graphite
Dissolve in water	Do not dissolve in water
Do not dissolve in organic solvents	Dissolve in organic solvents
Conduct electricity when melted or dissolved in water	Do not conduct electricity (graphite is the only exception)
Strong forces holding whole compound together	Atoms in molecule held by strong forces but forces between molecules weak

Metallic bonding

Atoms of a metal can form a lattice similar to that found in ionic compounds. The lattice of a metal is formed when the atoms share their outer electrons to create what is called a **sea of electrons**, or **delocalized electrons**. These electrons can move through the lattice; this enables metals to conduct heat and electricity. The forces holding the lattice

together are very strong, which is why metals tend to have high melting and boiling points.

Metallic lattice

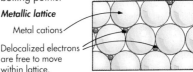

Metal cations

Delocalized electrons are free to move within lattice.

Giant molecular lattices

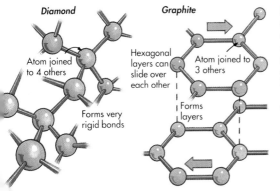

Diamond

Atom joined to 4 others

Forms very rigid bonds

Graphite

Hexagonal layers can slide over each other

Atom joined to 3 others

Forms layers

Some non-metals form a sort of lattice in which atoms of the same type are held together with covalent bonds. This is called a **giant molecular lattice**. A good example is carbon which forms two different lattices: diamond (which is hard and tough) and graphite (which is smooth and flaky).

Metals

More than three-quarters of all elements are metals. Some metals, such as gold, can be found in a pure state in nature. These metals are relatively unreactive and do not combine easily with other substances. Most metals, however, are found combined with other elements in compounds known as **ores**. For instance, aluminium, a very common metal, is only found in ores. Ores are mined and the metal is then extracted and purified.

The most common aluminium ore is bauxite (Al_2O_3).

The properties of metals

Mercury, used in thermometers, is the only metal which is a liquid at room temperature; the rest are all solids. Metals conduct heat and electricity because of the way their atoms are *bonded** together. The harder metals produce a ringing sound when they are hit. Here are some other properties of metals.

Most metals are shiny and silvery grey. They have what chemists call a **metallic lustre**.

Copper is unusual in having an orange-red colour.

Metals can be drawn into wires. This property is called **ductility**.

Metals can be beaten flat into sheets. This property is called **malleability**.

Transition metals

Many of the most commonly used metals, such as iron and silver, belong to a group called **transition metals**, found in the middle of the periodic table. Transition metals have more than one *valency**. For instance, copper can have a valency of +1 or +2. The compounds that they form are often brightly coloured, like potassium dichromate ($K_2Cr_2O_7$), the orange compound of chromium (Cr). Transition metals make good *catalysts**.

The reactivity series

Many metals react with water, with dilute acids and with the oxygen in the air. Metals can be listed in order of how reactive they are. This is known as the **reactivity series**. (A complete reactivity series can be found on page 113). The position of a metal in the series determines the ease with which it can be extracted from its ore. The more reactive the metal, the more difficult it is to extract.

Here is a general reactivity series for some common metals. Hydrogen, although a non-metal, is usually included because it can behave like a metal.

Most reactive
Potassium
Sodium
Calcium
Magnesium
Aluminium
Zinc
Iron
Hydrogen
Copper
Silver
Gold
Platinum
Least reactive

The most reactive metals, like sodium and potassium, have to be stored in oil as they react rapidly with air and water.

Sodium
Covered by oil

Copper is the least reactive metal that can be produced at a reasonable cost. It is much more common than gold and so is cheaper. It is used for water tanks, pipes and electrical wiring.

Copper

Silver, gold and platinum are the least reactive metals. However they are rare, which makes them expensive and highly prized.

*Bonded, 76; Valency, 76; Catalysts, 99.

Alloys

Metals can be combined by being heated until they are in a liquid state, then mixed together. This forms a substance called an **alloy**. One important alloy is *steel**, which is a mixture of a metal (iron) and a non-metal (carbon). Alloys can be created with properties that make them more useful for specific purposes than pure metals. For example, solder, made from tin and lead, has a very low melting point and is used to join electrical components.

Brass is an alloy of copper mixed with up to 20% zinc. It is harder than copper, does not corrode and is easily worked. It is often used, for ornaments and picture frames.

Reactions with water

When reacted with water, group I metals produce hydrogen and a metal *hydroxide**. The metal hydroxide is water-soluble and produces an *alkaline** solution. As you move down group I of the periodic table, the metals become increasingly reactive towards water. For example, sodium, in the middle of group I, reacts vigorously. This is shown in the following equation:

$$Na + H_2O \longrightarrow NaOH + \tfrac{1}{2}H_2$$
Sodium   Water   Sodium   Hydrogen
                 hydroxide

Caesium, at the bottom of group I, reacts explosively in cold water.

Group II metals react less vigorously with water. Magnesium, for example,

reacts very slowly with cold water but much faster when reacted with heated steam. In both cases the reaction produces hydrogen and magnesium oxide:

$$Mg + H_2O \longrightarrow MgO + H_2$$

Zinc reacts in a very similar way to magnesium, producing zinc oxide which is found in many skin creams.

Some transition metals, such as gold and silver, barely react with water, even over a long period of time.

Old gold coins recovered from the sea still look new.

Reactions with air

Calcium reacts with air giving off a bright red light. It is used in fireworks.

Gold and silver do not react when exposed to the gases in the air, nor do they burn. Copper reacts very slowly. It may take years before a green coloured *oxide** covers its surface. However when copper is burned fiercely, black copper oxide (CuO) is produced. A number of other metals, including magnesium and sodium, burn in air to form metal oxides.

Reactions with dilute acids

Many metals react with dilute acids (except nitric acid) to produce a metallic *salt** and hydrogen. For example:

$$Zn + 2HCl \longrightarrow ZnCl_2 + H_2$$

Zinc + Hydrochloric → Zinc + Hydrogen
         acid   chloride

When dilute sulphuric acid is reacted with a metal, it will produce hydrogen and a metallic sulphate. As you move down the reactivity series, the reactions become slower, until you reach copper at the bottom which does not react at all.

---

* Steel, 84; Hydroxide, 122; Alkaline, 89; Oxide, 123; Salt, 90.

Chemical reactions

In a physical change the substance may change its shape or its *state*, but it is still the same substance. Water boiling to steam is an example of a physical change. However in a **chemical change**, or **chemical reaction**, a substance is converted into one or more different substances. When sodium and chlorine react to produce sodium chloride, a chemical reaction has taken place.

Equations

Any chemical reaction can be written in an abbreviated form, called an **equation**. An equation shows the **reactants** or **reagents** (the substances that take part in the reaction) and the **products** (the substances produced by the reaction), separated by an arrow. If a *catalyst* is involved, it is shown above the arrow. An equation in which each substance is given its full name is known as a **word equation** and is shown below.

A word equation

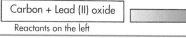

| Carbon + Lead (II) oxide | | Carbon dioxide + Lead |
| Reactants on the left | | Products on the right |

Law of conservation of mass

A basic law of chemistry is that you cannot create or destroy matter in a chemical reaction. This is called the **law of conservation of mass**. This means that although substances change into other substances in a chemical reaction, the actual number of atoms remains the same. The number of atoms of products after a reaction will always equal the number of atoms of reactants before the reaction took place. For example:

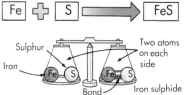

Balancing equations

In an exam you may be given an equation like this one for water.

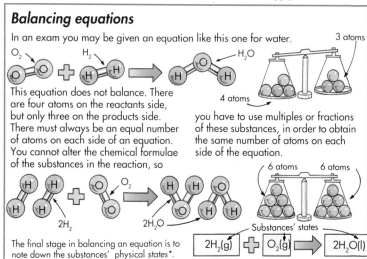

This equation does not balance. There are four atoms on the reactants side, but only three on the products side. There must always be an equal number of atoms on each side of an equation. You cannot alter the chemical formulae of the substances in the reaction, so you have to use multiples or fractions of these substances, in order to obtain the same number of atoms on each side of the equation.

The final stage in balancing an equation is to note down the substances' physical *states*.

$$2H_2(g) + O_2(g) \longrightarrow 2H_2O(l)$$

Types of chemical reaction

There are three main types of chemical reaction: thermal decomposition, displacement, and redox reactions (see page 82). These three types account for nearly all the chemical reactions that can take place.

Thermal decomposition

Thermal decomposition is a reaction in which a substance breaks down when it is heated, and the products do not recombine on cooling. Compounds formed from less reactive elements have weaker bonds between their atoms. They are more readily decomposed by this method than those formed by more reactive elements.

Two examples of thermal decomposition are the reactions of sodium nitrate and calcium nitrate when heated (see opposite).

$$NaNO_3 \implies NaNO_2 + \tfrac{1}{2}O_2$$

Sodium nitrate — Sodium nitrite — Oxygen

You can test for oxygen with a glowing splint. If it relights it shows that oxygen is present.

$$2Ca(NO_3)_2 \implies 2CaO + O_2 + 4NO_2$$

Calcium nitrate — Calcium oxide — Oxygen — Nitrogen dioxide

Nitrogen dioxide is a brown, acidic gas which can be easily identified.

Displacement reactions

A reaction in which one element replaces another in a compound is called a **displacement reaction**. An element will only displace another element lower than itself in the reactivity series. The reaction opposite ▶ occurs if iron is put in copper sulphate solution. Iron is higher than copper in the series so it pushes the copper out of the solution.

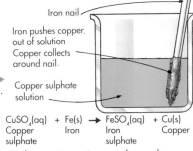

Iron nail

Iron pushes copper out of solution

Copper collects around nail.

Copper sulphate solution

$$CuSO_4(aq) + Fe(s) \rightarrow FeSO_4(aq) + Cu(s)$$

Copper sulphate — Iron — Iron sulphate — Copper

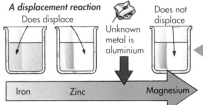

A displacement reaction

Does displace   Does not displace

Unknown metal is aluminium

Iron   Zinc   Magnesium

Displacement reactions can be used to identify an unknown metal by finding its place in the reactivity series. The metal is placed in a series of known metal ion* solutions. Those the metal displaces are below it in the reactivity series; those it does not displace are above it.

Reversible reactions

A reaction that does not convert all of its reagent into product is known as a reversible reaction. The symbol ⇌ is used to show a reversible reaction.

For example, the thermal decomposition of ammonium chloride involves a **reversible reaction**. When heated, the substance produces two gases, hydrogen chloride (HCl) and ammonia (NH_3). These two gases react together to produce ammonium chloride. This reaction can go forwards or backwards. Some of each substance will always remain.

$$NH_4Cl(s) \rightleftharpoons NH_3(g) + HCl(g)$$

Reversible reaction symbol

*Ion, 76.

Reduction and oxidation

Reduction and oxidation are reactions which involve electrons moving from one atom to another. One or more of the actions in the table opposite occur during such a reaction.

Oxidation and reduction take place simultaneously; this is known as a **redox reaction**. If one substance loses electrons, or atoms of oxygen or hydrogen, then another substance must gain them. There is an example of this in the equation opposite.

Oxidation	Reduction
Electrons lost	Electrons gained
Hydrogen lost	Hydrogen gained
Oxygen gained	Oxygen lost

Carbon reduces copper(II) oxide.

Copper(II) oxide loses oxygen.

$$2CuO + C \Rightarrow CO_2 + 2Cu$$

Copper(II) oxide oxidizes carbon.

Carbon gains oxygen.

Electron swapping

Redox reactions always involve the swapping of electrons. The electrons are either on their own, or within hydrogen or oxygen atoms which are exchanged between substances in a reaction. The reduction and oxidation reactions can each be shown as half of an *ionic equation**. These are called **half equations**. In the example below, magnesium and chlorine undergo a redox reaction to form magnesium chloride.

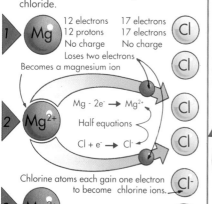

1 Mg 12 electrons / 12 protons / No charge   Cl 17 electrons / 17 electrons / No charge
Loses two electrons
Becomes a magnesium ion

2 Mg^{2+} $Mg - 2e^- \rightarrow Mg^{2+}$
Half equations
$Cl + e^- \rightarrow Cl^-$

Chlorine atoms each gain one electron to become chlorine ions.

3 Mg^{2+} 10 electrons / 12 protons / Charge +2 Cl^- 18 electrons / 17 protons / Charge -1

Oxidation numbers

All elements in compounds have an **oxidation number**. This is the number of electrons that have been added or taken away from the neutral atom to create the positively or negatively charged ion. The oxidation number increases (it becomes more positive or less negative) during oxidation and decreases (it becomes less positive or more negative) during reduction. The oxidation number is the same as the *valency** of an element. (See page 119 for a list of oxidation numbers).

The oxidation number of an element in its neutral state, such as fluorine gas or solid copper, is zero. The sum of the oxidation states of all the atoms in a compound will also equal zero.

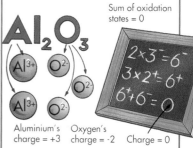

Sum of oxidation states = 0

Al_2O_3

Al^{3+} O^{2-}
O^{2-}
Al^{3+} O^{2-}

Aluminium's charge = +3   Oxygen's charge = -2   Charge = 0

$2 \times 3 = 6^-$
$3 \times 2 = 6^+$
$6 + 6 = 0$

Oxidizing and reducing agents

A substance that oxidizes another substance is called an **oxidizing agent**. Common oxidizing agents are hydrogen peroxide, oxygen and chlorine. A **reducing agent** is a substance which reduces another. Reducing agents are used in industry to reduce metal oxides to pure metal. For example, carbon, in coke form, is used to reduce zinc and iron oxides to their pure metals.

*Ionic equations, 76; Valency, 76.

Resources

The substances found in nature which can be processed to provide the things we need and use in life are known as **resources**. There are many different resource types, but they come from the four main sources shown here.

From water
(the hydrosphere)

From air
(the atmosphere)

From rocks
(the lithosphere)

From living things
(the biosphere)

Renewable and non-renewable resources

Renewable resources, such as plants and wave power, are those which can be replaced as they are used. However these will run out if they are not replaced fast enough. For example, forests will be exhausted if new trees are not planted. **Non-renewable resources** such as gold or tin are not replaceable and will run out. Also see pages 52-53.

The amount of a resource worth extracting is called its reserve. The reserve depends on the cost of extraction and the price at which it can be sold. For example, there is still tin in mines in South West England but its price is not high enough to make extraction worthwhile.

Conserving resources

It is important to conserve all our resources. This can be done in several ways, as shown below.

One way is to avoid waste and use materials more carefully. New techniques and designs can help to reduce the amount of a resource used. For example, cars are now being designed to be more efficient.

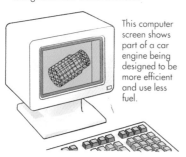

This computer screen shows part of a car engine being designed to be more efficient and use less fuel.

Another way of conserving resources is to adapt common resources to take the place of less plentiful ones. For example, plastic pipes and guttering are replacing pipes made from less common resources such as copper and lead.

Recycling

Instead of being disposed of after first use, some materials are now being reused. This is known as **recycling**. Paper, glass, iron and aluminium are all being increasingly recycled.

Recycled paper products

Old paper is collected and processed back into all kinds of paper products.

Recycling means that less new material is being used, so there is less waste to dispose of. It also means that energy normally used in extracting the material is saved. It is estimated that for every tonne (1.016 tons) of recycled glass used, the equivalent of 136.5 litres (36 US gallons) of oil is saved.

Bottle banks are now popular in many countries. The collected glass is sorted, melted and then re-used.

Iron and steel

Iron is the most important metal in industry. It is extracted through *reduction** by carbon. This reaction takes place in a **blast furnace** using iron ore, coke and limestone (calcium carbonate $CaCO_3$).

Iron is found in iron oxide called **haematite**.

It has the chemical formula, Fe_2O_3.

A blast furnace

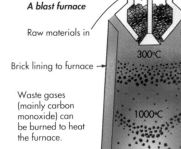

Raw materials in

300°C

Brick lining to furnace

Waste gases (mainly carbon monoxide) can be burned to heat the furnace.

1000°C

Molten slag

Blasts of hot air

2000°C

Molten iron

Melting zone*

Slag and molten iron run off from different taps.

Stages in the extraction of iron

1. Hot coke burns to form carbon dioxide: $C(s) + O_2(g) \rightarrow CO_2(g)$

2. Carbon dioxide is reduced to carbon monoxide: $CO_2(g) + C(s) \rightarrow 2CO(g)$

3. Carbon monoxide reduces iron oxide: $Fe_2O_3(s) + 3CO(g) \rightarrow 2Fe(s) + 3CO_2(g)$

4. The calcium carbonate is decomposed by the intense heat of the furnace: $CaCO_3(s) \rightarrow CaO(s) + CO_2(g)$

5. The calcium oxide (CaO) reacts with sand and clay-like impurities in the ore (such as calcium silicate): $CaO(s) + SiO_2(s) \rightarrow CaSiO_3(l)$ The reaction removes some of the

impurities from iron forming a waste product called **slag**.

The iron produced from the blast furnace is called **pig** or **cast iron**. It contains a number of impurities such as carbon, sulphur and silicon.

Steel

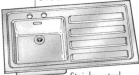

Stainless steel contains nickel and chromium and does not corrode.

Steel, an *alloy** of iron and carbon, is the most commonly used alloy in industry. It is made by blowing oxygen onto molten scrap and pig iron at high pressure. This process removes impurities from the metal in the form of slag and gases. The gases are burned off at high temperature. Various other materials are then added to the iron in order to make different types of steel. For example, mild steel, which contains 0.3% carbon and is very *malleable**, is used in making vehicle bodies.

Aluminium

Aluminium[†] is the most abundant metal in the world, but it is never found in its pure state. It is always combined with other elements in *ores**: Aluminium cannot be extracted by simple reduction in the way that iron can. This is because it is very reactive and forms very strong bonds with oxygen. Instead it has to be extracted by *electrolysis**.

Aluminium is quite high in the reactivity

series but, due to the limited way it *corrodes**, it is stable enough to be used in the manufacture of many household goods.

Aluminium is now used for most of the world's drinks cans.

*Reduction, 82; Alloy, 79; Malleable, 78; Ores, 78; Electrolysis, 86; Corrodes, 88.
[†](Aluminum in US)

Limestone

Limestone is mainly calcium carbonate ($CaCO_3$). It is a solid found in nature as hard rock and has a number of uses in industry, as shown below.

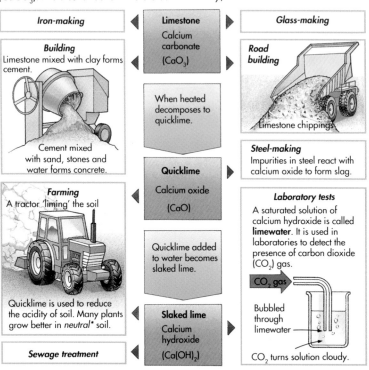

Iron-making

Limestone
Calcium carbonate (CaO_3)

Glass-making

Building
Limestone mixed with clay forms cement.

Cement mixed with sand, stones and water forms concrete.

When heated decomposes to quicklime.

Road building

Limestone chippings

Quicklime
Calcium oxide (CaO)

Steel-making
Impurities in steel react with calcium oxide to form slag.

Farming
A tractor 'liming' the soil

Quicklime is used to reduce the acidity of soil. Many plants grow better in *neutral** soil.

Quicklime added to water becomes slaked lime.

Laboratory tests
A saturated solution of calcium hydroxide is called **limewater**. It is used in laboratories to detect the presence of carbon dioxide (CO_2) gas.

CO_2 gas

Bubbled through limewater

Slaked lime
Calcium hydroxide ($Ca(OH)_2$)

CO_2 turns solution cloudy.

Sewage treatment

Percentage composition calculations

Resources are often extracted from ores. In industry, it is important to know how much ore is needed to obtain a certain amount of a resource. The method used involves finding what percentage of the ore is made up by the resource. It is called a **percentage composition calculation** and has three stages.

1. Find the relative atomic or molecular mass of the resource.

2. Find the relative molecular mass of the ore and the percentage of ore that is made up of the resource.

3. Divide 100 by the percentage of the resource and then multiply this figure by the amount of the resource required.

This example shows how much iron ore (Fe_2O_3) is needed to make 150 tonnes of iron. The relative atomic mass of iron is 56, and that of oxygen is 16.

The composition of Fe_2O_3 ← 2 iron atoms
← 3 oxygen atoms

$(2 \times 56) + (3 \times 16) = 170$
Relative molecular mass = 170

112 parts out of 170 are iron
$112/170 \times 100 = 65.9\%$
65.9% of haematite is iron

150 tonnes of iron required

$\dfrac{100}{65.9} \times 150 = 227.6$ tonnes of ore

*Neutral, 89; Relative molecular mass, 71.

Electrolysis

All metals conduct electricity because their structures contain *a sea of electrons** which can move through the metal. If a power supply is connected it acts like a pump causing electrons to flow through the metal. No chemical change occurs when this happens.

Some substances do not conduct electricity when they are in a solid state, but do so when they are melted or dissolved. These substances are called **electrolytes**. When electricity is passed through an electrolyte, a chemical change occurs. The electrolyte breaks up into *ions** which conduct the electric current. When an electrolyte conducts electricity, the process is known as **electrolysis**.

*Covalent** substances are not made up of ions; they cannot conduct electricity.

Electrolytic cells

The apparatus used in electrolysis is called an **electrolytic cell**. It consists of an electrolyte, a power supply and two electrically conductive pieces of metal or graphite called **electrodes**. The electrodes are connected to the power supply and are dipped into the electrolyte. Some electrodes used in industry (see opposite page) change chemically during electrolysis. Electrodes that do not change are called **inert electrodes**.

An electrolytic cell

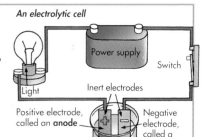

The electric circuit is complete if the bulb in an electrolytic cell lights up when connected to the power supply. Electricity is flowing between the annode and the cathode, which means the liquid can conduct electricity and is therefore an electrolyte.

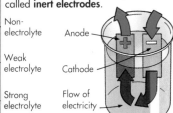

Non-electrolyte
Weak electrolyte
Strong electrolyte

Anode
Cathode
Flow of electricity

The electrolysis of copper chloride

When a current from a power supply is passed through a solution of copper chloride ($CuCl_2$), chlorine gas and copper are produced. The copper is deposited on one of the electrodes. This happens because copper chloride is an electrolyte which breaks up into copper ions (Cu^{2+}) and chloride ions (Cl^-).

Opposite charges attract, so the positively-charged Cu^{2+} ion is attracted to the negatively-charged cathode, while the negatively-charged Cl^- ion is attracted to the positively-charged anode. When each Cl^- ion arrives at the anode, it gives up one electron. When each Cu^{2+} ion arrives at the cathode, it receives two electrons. These processes can be shown by *ionic equations** like the ones below:

$$Cu^{2+}(aq) + 2e^- \longrightarrow Cu(s)$$
$$2Cl^-(aq) \longrightarrow 2Cl(g) + 2e^-$$

Single chlorine atoms combine in pairs whenever possible, each producing a molecule of chlorine gas (Cl_2).

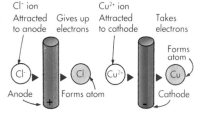

Cl⁻ ion
Attracted to anode | Gives up electrons | Forms atom

Cu²⁺ ion
Attracted to cathode | Takes electrons | Forms atom

Anode | Forms atom | Cathode

*Sea of electrons, 77; Ions, 76; Covalent, 77; Ionic equations, 76.

Electrolysis of aqueous solutions

Water always contains some molecules which have split into *hydroxide** (OH⁻) and hydrogen (H⁺) ions. These ions undergo changes during the electrolysis of an *aqueous solution**. The OH⁻ ions move to the anode where oxygen gas is produced. The H⁺ ions move to the cathode where hydrogen gas is produced. This is shown in the following equation.

$$2H^+(aq) + 2e^- \longrightarrow H_2(g)$$
$$2OH^-(aq) \longrightarrow H_2O(l) + \tfrac{1}{2}O_2(g) + 2e^-$$

These gases are produced along with the products from the electrolyte.

Electrolysis and its products

Substance electrolysed	At anode	At cathode
Hydrochloric acid	Chlorine	Hydrogen
Sodium chloride	Chlorine	Hydrogen
Molten lead bromide	Bromine	Lead
Aqueous potassium iodide	Iodine	Hydrogen
Copper(II) sulphate (inert electrodes)	Oxygen	Copper
Copper(II) sulphate (copper electrodes)	Anode dissolves	Copper
Aluminium oxide	Oxygen	Aluminium

The table shows the products created by the electrolysis of certain compounds. As a general rule, metals and/or hydrogen are discharged at the cathode and non-metals and/or oxygen are discharged at the anode.

Industrial uses of electrolysis

Electrolysis is used in a number of industrial processes involving metals.

Many metals can be industrially extracted from their *ores** by electrolysis. Aluminium's main ore, bauxite, consists mainly of aluminium oxide. The extraction of aluminium uses large amounts of electricity. For this reason aluminium plants are often close to a source of cheap electricity, such as a hydro-electric dam.

Aluminium oxide has a very high melting point (over 2000°C) but it can be dissolved in a solution containing molten *cryolite** at a much lower temperature. Electrolysis is then performed in a special tank with a carbon lining that acts as a cathode.

At the cathode: $Al^{3+} + 3e^- \longrightarrow Al$
At the anode: $2O^- - 4e^- \longrightarrow O_2$

Electrolysis can be used to *purify** metals. For example, if impure copper is used as an anode and placed in a solution of copper sulphate ($CuSO_4$), the copper dissolves and is deposited on the cathode, leaving behind the impurities.

The purification of copper

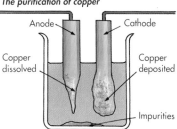

Anode — Cathode
Copper dissolved — Copper deposited
— Impurities

Copper sulphate solution

Electroplating is a technique used for plating objects in metal. The object is used as a non-inert electrode and coated with a thin layer of a substance from the electrolyte. For example, if a nail is suspended in copper(II) sulphate solution, it will become plated in copper. In industry, chromium-plated iron is used to make bicycle and car parts.

Aluminium extraction

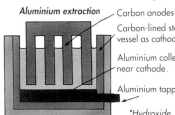

Carbon anodes
Carbon-lined steel vessel as cathode
Aluminium collects near cathode.
Aluminium tapped off.

*Hydroxide, 122; Aqueous solution, 122 ; Ores, 78; Cryolite, 122; Purify (purity), 69.

87

Corrosion

When a metal reacts with the oxygen in air (usually in the presence of water), it is undergoing **corrosion**. First, the metal loses its lustre or shine, then the structure of the metal breaks down. Corrosion is a slow process. Metals high in the reactivity series, such as sodium, magnesium and calcium, corrode more easily. Lead, which is near the bottom of the reactivity series, is resistant to corrosion and was once used for roofing. Metals at the bottom of the reactivity series, such as gold and silver, hardly corrode at all.

Corrosion can be very serious as it makes metal objects unusable.

Rusting of iron and steel

The corrosion of iron and steel is known as **rusting**. Rusting involves a reaction between the metal, oxygen in the air and water. This can be shown in the following experiment in which iron nails are put into three test tubes. The first test tube contains air and water, the second only water, and the third, air but no water.

Air — Oil prevents any air entering.

No air

No water, Dry air — Anhydrous calcium chloride. Cotton wool stops water entering test tube.

Water — Nail rusts

Water containing no air — Nail does not rust.

Nail does not rust.

Protection of iron and steel

Iron and steel can be protected from corrosion in a number of different ways.

Greasing is used for moving parts but the grease has to be renewed regularly.

Tin-plating is used on cans to prevent corrosion. However, tin is less reactive than steel and if the outer surface of tin is scratched through, the steel underneath will corrode.

Painting is used for large objects but needs to be reapplied when the paint surface is broken.

Chromium-plating is performed by electrolysis and forms a brightly shining surface. It is used for decoration as well as protection.

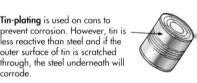

Galvanizing involves coating steel with a layer of zinc, which is more reactive than steel. If the surface is scratched, the oxygen reacts with the zinc rather than the steel.

The iron hulls of ships can be protected by attaching bars of a more reactive metal such as zinc, to the iron. This metal corrodes first and is called a **sacrificial metal**.

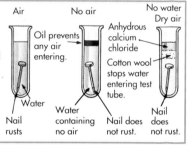

Zinc bars

Corrosion of aluminium

Aluminium reacts rapidly with the oxygen in air to create aluminium oxide. This forms a tough layer on the metal's outer surface, preventing any further reaction with air and water. This explains why household products made from aluminium, such as saucepans and kitchen foil, can come into regular contact with water and air without corroding.

The aluminium oxide layer can be thickened by being used as the *anode** in a form of *electrolysis** known as anodizing. This protects the aluminium further and allows the outer surface to be painted and decorated.

*Anode, 86; Electrolysis, 86.

Acids, bases and salts

Acids are compounds which contain the hydrogen *ion** H⁺ and dissolve in water. Examples of acids include hydrochloric acid (HCl), sulphuric acid (H_2SO_4) and ethanoic acid (CH_3COOH). Acids are *electrolytes** and the acids found in foodstuffs (like the citric acid in lemons) taste sour and sharp. Many acids are highly *corrosive** and have warning labels on their containers. A list of hazard labels can be found on page 111.

Hazard label for corrosive substances

Bases and alkalis

Bases are substances which can accept acids' hydrogen ions. The oxide ion in metal oxides (O^{2-}) and the hydroxide ion in metal hydroxides (OH⁻) are both able to combine with the H⁺ ion. Therefore all metal oxides and hydroxides, such as sodium hydroxide (NaOH) and magnesium oxide (MgO), are bases. Many bases have a soapy feel. A base that is soluble in water is called an **alkali**.

There are three common alkalis.

Sodium hydroxide (NaOH)

Potassium hydroxide (KOH)

Ammonia solution (NH₃(aq))

Ammonia gas bubbled through water creates a solution of positive ammonium ions and negative hydroxide ions.
$$NH_3(g) + H_2O(l) \longrightarrow NH_4^+(aq) + OH^-(aq)$$

Proton donors and acceptors

Acids
Vinegar
Citrus fruits

A hydrogen ion is a hydrogen atom which has lost its electron and now consists of just one proton. An acid contains many protons, and seeks to lose them in reactions. Acids, therefore, are said to be **proton donors**. A base, on the other hand will accept hydrogen ions. Bases are referred to as **proton acceptors**.

Bases
Household cleaner
Bicarbonate of soda
Indigestion tablets

Indicators and the pH number

The **pH number** of a substance tells you how acidic or alkaline the substance is. It stands for the 'power of hydrogen' and is a measure of the concentration of hydrogen ions in a solution. pH values are found on a scale generally between 0 and 14. The lower the pH number, the greater the concentration of hydrogen ions and the more acidic the substance. pH 7 is neutral. A substance with a pH value of above 7 is a base. For example, lemon juice has a pH of 2.1 and is acidic, whereas household ammonia, an alkali, has a pH value of 11.9.

The pH number is determined by an **indicator**, a substance whose colour changes when the pH changes. There are a number of different indicators. **Litmus indicator** distinguishes solely between an acid (which turns it red) and an alkali (which turns it blue). With **universal indicators** the colour varies according to the pH scale.

pH scale

acidic   neutral   alkaline

| 1 | 2 | 3 | 4 | 5 | 6 | 7 | 8 | 9 | 10 | 11 | 12 |

Ion, 76; Electrolytes, 86; Corrosive, 88.

Strong and weak acids and bases

The concentration of an acidic or basic solution may vary, but the strength of the acid or base is constant. The strength of an acid or base is determined by its ability to *ionize**, that is, the ability of its *cations** and *anions** to split up. For example, hydrochloric acid, which is strong, can completely ionize all its hydrogen atoms in water. Similarly, a strong base, such as sodium hydroxide, can ionize all its hydroxide atoms.

Weak acids, like ethanoic acid, can only partially ionize; only a small number of their molecules split to form hydrogen ions. Similarly, only a small number of molecules of weak bases, such as calcium hydroxide, split up to produce hydroxide ions.

Strong acid

$HCl(aq) \rightleftharpoons H^+(aq) + Cl^-(aq)$

Weak acid

$CH_3COOH(aq) \rightleftharpoons CH_3COO^-(aq) + H^+(aq)$

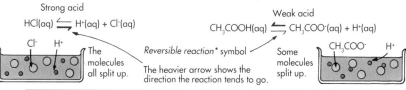

The molecules all split up.

Reversible reaction* symbol
The heavier arrow shows the direction the reaction tends to go.

Some molecules split up.

Neutralization

When an acid and a base are mixed together they form an ionic compound called a **salt**. If excess acid or base is added, the final solution will contain water, a salt and some of the excess acid or base. A chemical reaction between an acid and a base, in which all of the acid and base are completely used up, is called **neutralizaton**. A salt and water are produced and the

resulting solution is usually neutral.

Neutralization reactions occur frequently in everyday life, for example in *liming** the soil and in relieving indigestion caused by too much stomach acid.

Bee stings are acidic. Acid can be neutralized and the sting soothed by applying an alkali.

Reactions of acids and bases

 Acids react with metals above copper in the *reactivity series**, to form salts and hydrogen. For example:

$2HCl + Mg \longrightarrow MgCl_2 + H_2$
Hydrochloric acid, Magnesium, Magnesium chloride

 Metal hydroxides and metal oxides, such as copper oxide, react in the same way as metals, producing a salt and water.

$CuO + 2HCl \longrightarrow CuCl_2 + H_2O$
Copper oxide, Hydrochloric acid, Copper chloride, Water

 Metal carbonates and metal hydrogen carbonates are similar to bases. They react with acids to form a salt and water, but they also produce carbon dioxide.

$Na_2CO_3 + 2HNO_3 \longrightarrow 2NaNO_3 + CO_2 + H_2O$
Sodium carbonate, Nitric acid, Sodium nitrate, Carbon dioxide

 When in solution, the salts of some metals, such as magnesium, often react

with the hydroxide (OH^-) ions in an alkali to form an insoluble metal hydroxide.

 When a base is warmed with an ammonium compound, ammonia gas is produced. For example, ammonium chloride and calcium hydroxide produce

calcium chloride and ammonia. This reaction is used to make ammonia gas, and as a test to see whether a substance is an ammonium compound.

Preparation of salts

There are a number of ways in which salts can be prepared in the laboratory. Direct combination is one method, but it can only be used when the salt consists of two elements. For example, the salt iron sulphide is made by direct combination when iron and sulphur are heated together.

Making a soluble salt

A soluble salt can be made by the reaction between an acid and an insoluble metal or an insoluble base.

For example, copper sulphate can be made from sulphuric acid and copper as shown below.

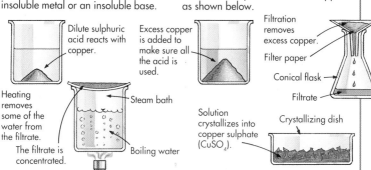

Dilute sulphuric acid reacts with copper.

Excess copper is added to make sure all the acid is used.

Filtration removes excess copper.

Filter paper

Conical flask

Filtrate

Heating removes some of the water from the filtrate.

The filtrate is concentrated.

Steam bath

Boiling water

Solution crystallizes into copper sulphate ($CuSO_4$).

Crystallizing dish

Titration

An alkali will neutralize an acid but, because the salt produced is soluble, it cannot be separated by filtration. A *titration** will determine the exact volumes needed for neutralization without the use of an indicator. The process can then be repeated and the salt can then be isolated by evaporation. For example, if a titration is used to combine the correct quantities of sodium hydroxide and hydrochloric acid, it will produce the salt sodium chloride.

Making insoluble salts

Two soluble substances are needed to form an insoluble salt. For example, to form the insoluble salt lead chloride, you need a soluble compound of lead (lead nitrate, for instance) and a soluble chloride (such as sodium chloride).

$$Pb(NO_3)_2 + 2NaCl \rightarrow PbCl_2 + 2NaNO_3$$
Lead nitrate + Sodium chloride → Lead chloride + Sodium nitrate

Lead chloride is the one insoluble product. It forms a *precipitate** which can be isolated by *filtration**.

Choosing a method of making a salt

It is important to know which method of preparation is correct for each type of salt. Instead of learning a long list of salts and appropriate methods, it is easier to ask a series of questions about the salt and its components. These questions are shown in the diagram opposite.

Analysis of salts can be found on page 52.

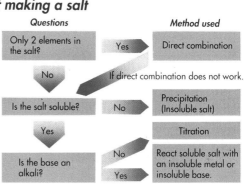

Questions   **Method used**

Only 2 elements in the salt? — Yes → Direct combination

No ↓   If direct combination does not work.

Is the salt soluble? — No → Precipitation (Insoluble salt)

Yes ↓ → Titration

Is the base an alkali? — No → React soluble salt with an insoluble metal or insoluble base. — Yes

The mole

Although atoms are too small to count individually, chemists need to know how many are present in a sample. To do this, they use a set number of particles as a base unit of measurement. This unit is called a **mole**. The number of atoms in a mole is the number of atoms found in 12g of carbon-12, which is 6×10^{23} (600,000 billion billion[†]). This is called the **Avogadro number**.

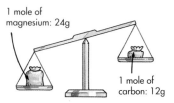

The mass, in grammes, of a mole of any element is equal to that element's *relative atomic mass**. The mass, in grammes, of a mole of a compound is that compound's *relative molecular mass**. A mole of two different substances will have the same number of particles but, as they have different relative atomic masses, they will weigh different amounts.

1 mole of magnesium: 24g

1 mole of carbon: 12g

6×10^{23} This equals 23 zeros following the 6.

$$= 600,000,000,000$$
$$000,000,000,000$$

Calculations of reacting mass

A calculation to determine how much of a substance is used in a reaction is called a calculation of **reacting mass**.

All substances in a reaction are in ratio to one another. For example, the ratio of hydrogen and oxygen atoms in water is 2:1. Knowing the ratios and the amount

of a product or reagent used, you can calculate in three stages how much of the other substances is used and created. In the example below, the amounts of the other substances can be found if you know that 10g of sodium hydroxide is used.

Sodium hydroxide	Sulphuric acid		Sodium sulphate	Water	Reactant's ratio 2:1
$2NaOH$	H_2SO_4	$\Rightarrow$	Na_2SO_4	$2H_2O$	Product's ratio 1:2
2 moles	1 mole		1 mole	2 moles	

To determine how many grammes there are in a mole of each substance, find the relative molecular mass of each substance. This figure is equal to the number of grammes in a mole.

Substance	Relative molecular mass
Sodium hydroxide	40
Sulphuric acid	98
Sodium sulphate	142
Water	18

Find out how many moles of the substance of known weight are used in the reaction. In the example, a mole of sodium hydroxide has a mass of 40g, so 10g equals $1/4$ mole. Using the ratios

between the products and reactants you can then calculate how many moles of the other substance are involved in the reaction. In the example, the amounts of the other substances are shown below.

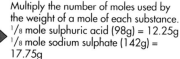

| $2NaOH$ | H_2SO_4 | $\Rightarrow$ | Na_2SO_4 | $2H_2O$ |
| $1/4$ mole | $1/8$ mole | | $1/8$ mole | $1/4$ mole |

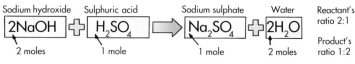

Multiply the number of moles used by the weight of a mole of each substance.
$1/8$ mole sulphuric acid (98g) = 12.25g
$1/8$ mole sodium sulphate (142g) = 17.75g

$1/4$ mole water (18g) = 4.5g
There should be an equal mass of substances on each side of the equation. In the example, there are 22.5g of both reactants and products.

*Relative atomic mass, 71; Relative molecular mass, 71.
[†]Billion = thousand million.

Calculating the formula of a compound

Chemists can calculate the formula of a compound if they know how much of each substance is used to create it. The unknown substance in the example below is made from 2.34g of Potassium (K) and 0.96g of Sulphur (S). Its formula can be determined by finding the mass of a mole of each substance and then finding the number of moles of each substance in the compound.

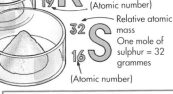

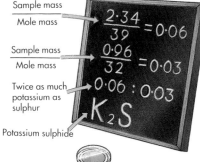

Relative atomic mass
One mole of potassium = 39 grammes

(Atomic number)

Relative atomic mass
One mole of sulphur = 32 grammes

(Atomic number)

Sample mass / Mole mass

Sample mass / Mole mass

Twice as much potassium as sulphur

Potassium sulphide

$$\frac{2\cdot34}{39}=0\cdot06$$

$$\frac{0\cdot96}{32}=0\cdot03$$

$$0\cdot06 : 0\cdot03$$

K_2S

Molar volume and gases

The volume occupied by one mole of a substance is called its **molar volume**. It is expressed in cubic decimetres ($1000cm^3$). A cubic decimetre is equal to one litre. The molar volumes of solids and liquids vary. All gases, however, have the same molar volume at a given temperature and pressure. At *room temperature** and *atmospheric pressure** (known as RTP), the molar volume of any gas is 24 dm^3. This is called **Avogadro's law**.

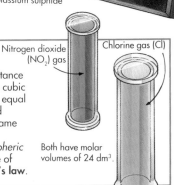

Nitrogen dioxide (NO_2) gas

Chlorine gas (Cl)

Both have molar volumes of 24 dm^3.

Using Avogadro's law

Avogadro's law is useful for finding out how much of a gas is used in an equation. The reaction below shows the decomposition of potassium hydrogencarbonate, which produces carbon dioxide gas. If you know how many grammes of potassium hydrogencarbonate are used (in this case, 20g), you can find the volume of carbon dioxide produced.

1. Find the mass of one mole of potassium hydrogencarbonate (This is the same as its relative molecular mass: 100g.) Then calculate the ratio in moles between the substances involved in the reaction.

$2KHCO_3 \Rightarrow K_2CO_3 \;+\; H_2O \;+\; CO_2$

2 moles   1 mole

Two moles (200g) of potassium hydrogencarbonate produce one mole of carbon dioxide.

2. Calculate how many moles of carbon dixoide are produced when 20g of potassium hydrogencarbonate are used: 20g/200g = $^1/_{10}$. This means that a reaction involving 20g of potassium hydrogencarbonate produces $^1/_{10}$ mole of carbon dioxide. As one mole of CO_2 occupies 24 litres at RTP, this reaction produces 2.4 litres of carbon dioxide.

*Room temperature, 69; Atmospheric pressure, 69.

93

Water

Water is essential to life. Your body needs approximately two litres of liquids each day but each person uses many times that. Flushing the toilet uses 10 litres of water, and a bath can take as much as 70 litres.

In industry, millions of litres are used for cooling, washing and as a *solvent**. For example, it takes 10 litres of water to make 1 litre of lemonade, 50,000 litres to make one car, and 5 million litres to cool a power station each day.

Water is sometimes known as the **universal solvent**. This is because a large number of substances can be dissolved to some extent in water. Because of its solvent properties, natural supplies of water contain many impurities. Water free of impurities is called **distilled water**.

The water cycle

Water in the atmosphere *condenses** in the air and falls to earth as rain or snow. Warmed by the sun, water evaporates back into the atmosphere. This process is called the **water cycle**.

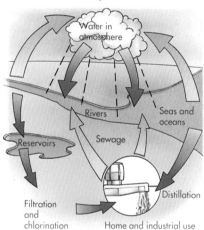

Water in atmosphere

Rivers

Seas and oceans

Reservoirs

Sewage

Filtration and chlorination

Distillation

Home and industrial use

Water purification

Clean water is essential for healthy living. Certain impurities in water can be harmful to animals and humans and can spread diseases such as cholera. In order to prevent this, the water that reaches your tap has been through two processes. The first, **filtration**, is designed to remove solid particles from the water. Screens remove pieces of rubbish and settling tanks remove smaller particles. In the second process, **chlorination**, chlorine is added to the water to kill bacteria. In some countries, fluoride is also added to protect teeth from decay.

Waste water and materials are called **sewage**. At one time, all sewage was piped back into rivers and seas, causing a lot of disease. In some places this is still done, but in most the sewage is treated first. It is mixed with air and decomposed by bacteria into harmless products.

Settling tank

Solid particles drop to bottom.

Detergents

Detergents are substances which when added to water enable it to remove dirt. Detergents do this in three ways. They lower the water's *surface tension**, they enable grease molecules to dissolve in water, and they keep the removed dirt in *suspension** in the water. Soaps are one type of detergent, but there are many soapless detergents as well. The head of a detergent molecule is attracted to water; it is described as **hydrophillic**. The tail of the molecule is **hydrophobic**; it is repelled by water.

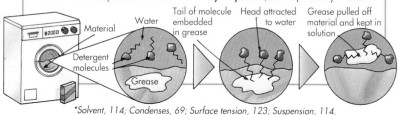

Material

Detergent molecules

Grease

Water

Tail of molecule embedded in grease

Head attracted to water

Grease pulled off material and kept in solution

*Solvent, 114; Condenses, 69; Surface tension, 123; Suspension, 114.

Water pollution

Polluted water contains either too little oxygen or too many toxic substances and can support little or no life.

Untreated sewage, fertilizers, oil, detergents and industrial waste are the most common causes of water pollution.

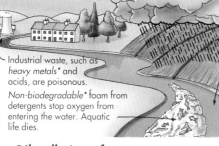

Rain washes fertilizers from fields into rivers and lakes.

Fertilizers contain substances called *nitrates** and *phosphates**. These stimulate excessive growth of bacteria and water plants, which use up all the oxygen in the water and die. Oxygen dissolved in water is vital to aquatic life. Once the oxygen is gone, fish and other aquatic creatures die too. This process is called **eutrophication**.

Industrial waste, such as *heavy metals** and acids, are poisonous.

*Non-biodegradable** foam from detergents stop oxygen from entering the water. Aquatic life dies.

Oil pollution of water

Detergent is used to break up oil slicks.

Oil forms a film on the surface of water restricting the entry of sunlight. This prevents the *oxidizing** bacteria and small organisms from breeding and living. The creatures die and this adversely affects the *food web**.

Most oil pollution occurs at sea, partly from oil tanker accidents, but mainly from the dumping of waste oil from tankers and refineries. This oil pollutes beaches and kills birds and fish.

Hard water

Water containing a lot of calcium and magnesium *salts** is called **permanent hard water**. Water containing a lot of the salt calcium hydrogencarbonate is called **temporary hard water**. These salts have some benefits. For example, calcium helps maintain healthy teeth and gums. However, hard water is considered a nuisance. It does not easily produce a lather. The calcium *ions** in hard water react with soap forming an insoluble solid called **scum**.

Hard water leaves insoluble deposits.

Deposits clog kettles, pipes and boilers.

Water softening

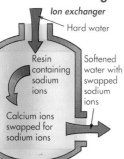

Ion exchanger

Hard water

Resin containing sodium ions

Softened water with swapped sodium ions

Calcium ions swapped for sodium ions

Temporary hard water can be softened by boiling. Permanent hard water can be softened in four ways. The first method, *distilling**, uses a lot of energy and is too expensive for household use. Another way is to use enough soap to react with all the calcium ions, but this wastes soap and creates a lot of scum.

However, there are two more practical methods. Sodium carbonate (known as washing soda) can be added to remove calcium ions by forming calcium carbonate: $(Ca^{2+}(aq) + CO_3^{2-}(aq) \longrightarrow CaCO_3(s))$. The second method swaps the damaging calcium ions for sodium ions which do not form scum. This is known as **ion exchange**.

*Heavy metals, 122; Non-biodegradable, 108; Nitrates, 101; Phosphates, 123; Oxidizing, 82; Food web, 122; Salts, 90; Ions, 76; Distilling (Distillation), 114.

95

Energy changes

The capacity to work is called **energy**. Heat, light, electricity and chemical energy are all different types of energy. In most chemical reactions, energy (usually in the form of heat) is either given out or taken in. If a chemical reaction produces heat, it is said to be an **exothermic** reaction. If heat is taken in from the surroundings, it is called an **endothermic** reaction.

Exothermic reactions

Respiration*, *neutralization** and many reactions which involve the formation of bonds between atoms and molecules are all exothermic.

Combustion* is also exothermic. This can be seen in the following experiment. Ethanol is burned in a spirit burner with a beaker of water placed on a tripod above the burner. The temperature of the water can be observed to rise. This is due to the heat given out by the combustion reaction.

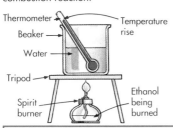

Endothermic reactions

Most reactions which result in the breaking of bonds between atoms and molecules draw in heat energy and are therefore endothermic. Endothermic reactions include *photosynthesis** and *electrolysis**.

Another type of endothermic reaction occurs when ammonium chloride crystals are dissolved in water. This is shown in the experiment below.

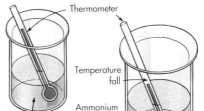

Measuring energy changes

Energy is measured in units called **joules**. 1000 joules equals a **kilojoule** (or **kJ** for short). It can be important to know how much energy is required to raise the temperature of a substance. The amount of energy in joules needed to raise the temperature of one gram of a substance by one *Kelvin** (or K) is known as the **specific heat capacity**. This figure varies according to the substance. The specific heat capacity of water, for example, is 4.2 joules per gram per K. (A Kelvin is equal to one degree Celsius).

Diagrams which show energy changes in terms of the energy levels of the *reagents** and *products** in a reaction are called **energy level diagrams**. The difference in energy between the reagents and the products is known as the **enthalpy change**. The enthalpy change is measured in units of kilojoules per *mole**, or **kJmol^{-1}** for short. The symbol for enthalpy change is a triangle followed by a capital H: ΔH or delta H. The example below shows the energy level diagram for the formation of the gas methane:

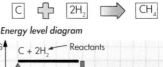

Energy level diagram

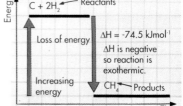

For every mole of methane produced, 74.5 kilojoules of energy is given off.

*Respiration, 104; Neutralization, 90; Combustion, 74; Photosynthesis, 104; Electrolysis, 86; Kelvin, 123; Reagents, 80; Products, 80; Mole, 92.

Direction of energy change

If a chemical reaction is exothermic in one direction, then the reverse reaction will be endothermic. This is shown on an energy level diagram by the direction of the arrow representing the enthalpy change ΔH. For example, when carbon is oxidized to form carbon dioxide (C + $O_2 \longrightarrow CO_2$), the enthalpy change is negative (the energy level decreases). For the reverse reaction, it is positive.

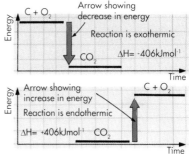

Arrow showing decrease in energy

Reaction is exothermic

$C + O_2$

CO_2 ΔH= -406kJmol⁻¹

Arrow showing increase in energy

Reaction is endothermic

ΔH= +406kJmol⁻¹ CO_2

$C + O_2$

Calculating energy changes

It is possible to calculate the energy changes in a reaction. You need to know the amounts of substances involved in the reaction and the rise or fall in temperature. For example, from the experiment opposite showing the burning of ethanol, it is found that 0.1g of ethanol raises the temperature of 50g of water by 11K. The specific heat capacity of 50g of water is:

50 × 4.2 = 210

Amount of ✕ Specific   = Joules
water   heat
             capacity

If 210 joules of energy are needed to raise 50g of water by 1K, raising the temperature by 11K requires:
210 x 11 = 2310J or 2.31kJ.

As energy change is measured in kJmol⁻¹ units, you need to know the equivalent of 0.1g of ethanol in moles. A mole of ethanol has a mass of 46g, so 0.1g of ethanol (0.1 divided by 46) equals 0.0022 moles.

If 0.0022 moles of ethanol produces 2.31kJ of heat energy, then one mole of ethanol will produce:

$$\frac{1}{0.0022} \times 2.31 \text{ kJ} = 1050 \text{ kJmol}^{-1}$$

Activation energy

For a reaction to take place reagent molecules must collide with one another. When they do so they must possess enough energy to cause or initiate a reaction. The level of energy needed to start a reaction is called its **energy barrier**. The actual energy required to start the reaction is called the **activation energy**.

Activation energy is essential to the start of a reaction. For example, in the process of combustion, the activation energy is usually provided by a spark or a flame. This is why a spark from, for example, a lit splint is needed to light a bunsen burner. If no activation energy was needed to start combustion, the gas from the bunsen burner would burn as soon as the gas tap was opened.

Energy level diagram showing activation energy

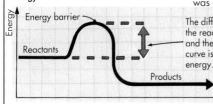

Energy barrier

Reactants

Products

The difference between the reactant's energy and the peak of the curve is the activation energy.

Bunsen burner

Rates of reaction

The **rate of reaction** is the rate at which products* are formed or reactants* used up in a chemical reaction. The rate of reaction varies greatly. Some chemical reactions, such as explosions, happen very rapidly. Others, like rusting*, occur very slowly. The rate of a reaction can be affected by a number of factors: temperature, concentration and pressure, catalyst*, surface area/particle size and light. These are considered below.

Many reaction rates can be measured using the formula:

$$\text{Rate} = \frac{\text{change in amount of a substance}}{\text{time taken}}$$

Readings can be taken and the results plotted to form a **rate curve**. The rate of reaction measured at any one point on the rate curve is called an **instantaneous rate**. In the experiment below, calcium carbonate and hydrochloric acid are reacted together to produce calcium chloride, water and carbon dioxide.

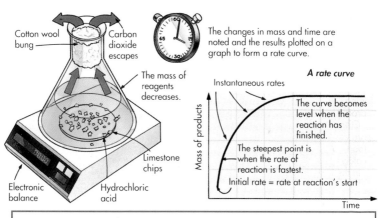

Cotton wool bung

Carbon dioxide escapes

The changes in mass and time are noted and the results plotted on a graph to form a rate curve.

The mass of reagents decreases.

Limestone chips

Electronic balance

Hydrochloric acid

A rate curve

Instantaneous rates

The curve becomes level when the reaction has finished.

The steepest point is when the rate of reaction is fastest.

Initial rate = rate at reaction's start

Mass of products

Time

Temperature and reaction rates

The rate of reaction can be affected by temperature. For example, if the above reaction was repeated, but with the reactants heated, the rate curve would be different from the previous one. The change occurs because an increase in temperature increases the speed of most reactions.

The higher the temperature, the more rapidly the particles move. They collide together more frequently and with greater energy.

Particles in a reaction

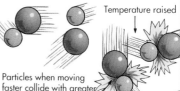

Temperature raised

Particles when moving faster collide with greater power. The reaction therefore becomes faster.

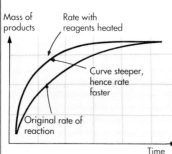

Mass of products

Rate with reagents heated

Curve steeper, hence rate faster

Original rate of reaction

Time

Lowering the temperature slows down reactions. This is why fridges are used to store food. The cold air slows down the reactions which cause food decay.

*Products, 80; Reactants, 80; Rusting, 88; Catalyst, 99.

Concentration and pressure

The number of reactant particles dissolved in a certain volume of *solvent** is called the **concentration** of a solution. The greater the concentration, the faster the rate of reaction. This is because the particles are closer together and therefore collide more frequently.

With a gas, the rate of reaction is affected by pressure in the same way that, in a solution, it is affected by concentration. At higher pressures, the reagent gas molecules are forced closer together. This means they are more likely to collide and bring about a reaction. The technique of compressing or concentrating gas is used, for example, in the *Haber Process** for making ammonia.

Catalysts

Catalysts are substances which are added to change the rate of reaction, but are not themselves chemically changed. Many catalysts are used in industry to speed up reactions and lower the cost of the eventual products. For example, a compound of vanadium is used as a catalyst in the production of sulphuric acid.

Catalysts which slow down reactions, are called **inhibitors**. The *oxidizing** of food, for example, is slowed down by catalysts called antioxidants.

In the laboratory the decomposition of hydrogen peroxide is used to prepare oxygen. The decomposition would be very slow, but for the presence of the catalyst manganese(IV) oxide (MnO_2).

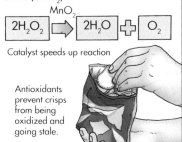

$$2H_2O_2 \xrightarrow{MnO_2} 2H_2O + O_2$$

Catalyst speeds up reaction

Antioxidants prevent crisps from being oxidized and going stale.

Surface area/particle size

A solid will react faster both physically and chemically, if it is broken up into smaller pieces. This is because a reaction can only take place at the surface of a solid. Breaking an object into more pieces increases its surface area, allowing more collisions with other reactants. For example, hydrochloric acid will react faster with powdered limestone than with limestone chippings. Sugar undergoes a physical reaction when dissolved in tea. Granulated sugar will dissolve quicker than sugar lumps.

10g of sugar grains have a greater surface area than a 10g sugar cube.

More collisions per second with boiling water

Light

Some reactions and their rates are affected by light. These reactions are called **photosensitive**. The most common reaction of this type is *photosynthesis**, which takes place in green plants. It is the process by which carbon dioxide is converted into glucose, oxygen and energy. Light also plays a vital part in photography. It darkens the silver bromide coating on the film in the camera, to form a negative picture.

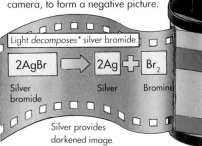

Light *decomposes** silver bromide.

$$2AgBr \Rightarrow 2Ag + Br_2$$

Silver bromide

Silver

Bromine

Silver provides darkened image.

*Solvent, 114; Haber process, 100; Oxidizing, 82; Photosynthesis, 104; Decomposes, 81.

Nitrogen

Nitrogen is a colourless, odourless gas which makes up 78% of air. It can be isolated from the other gases in air by *fractional distillation**. Nitrogen is used as an unreactive atmosphere for the storage of foods such as crisps and bacon. Ordinary air would *oxidize** the food, turning it stale a lot quicker. Nitrogen does not normally burn and so is used to flush out oil tanks and pipe lines. Liquid nitrogen, with a very low boiling point of -196°C, is used to preserve human organs prior to surgery. It is also used to freeze foods.

The nitrogen cycle

Nitrogen is present in a wide range of compounds in nature. It is an essential element in the making of *proteins** which are needed for growth. Nitrogen is constantly recycled in nature in a process called the **nitrogen cycle**.

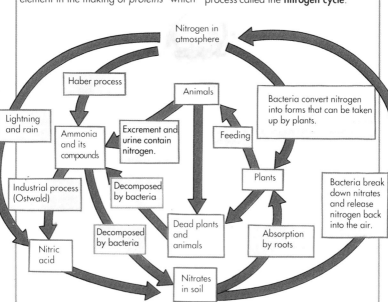

Nitrogen in atmosphere

Haber process

Animals

Bacteria convert nitrogen into forms that can be taken up by plants.

Lightning and rain

Ammonia and its compounds

Excrement and urine contain nitrogen.

Feeding

Industrial process (Ostwald)

Decomposed by bacteria

Plants

Bacteria break down nitrates and release nitrogen back into the air.

Nitric acid

Decomposed by bacteria

Dead plants and animals

Absorption by roots

Nitrates in soil

Ammonia

Nitrogen and hydrogen are the elements used to make ammonia (NH_3), a poisonous, colourless gas which has a pungent odour. The method used in industry to make ammonia is called the **Haber Process**. It was invented in 1909 by the German chemist, Fritz Haber. The process operates at a high temperature (approx 450°C) and pressure (*up to 1000 atmospheres**), with iron as a catalyst.

$$N_2(g) + 3H_2(g) \rightleftharpoons 2NH_3(g)$$
Nitrogen   Hydrogen   Ammonia

The Haber process is a *reversible reaction**. The gases are cooled and the ammonia is separated. Only about 15% of the mixture is converted to ammonia. The unreacted substances are recycled.

Ammonia forms an *alkaline** solution in water called ammonium hydroxide, or aqueous ammonia.

Aqueous ammonia is a degreasing agent. Household cleaners contain ammonia to cut through grease.

*Fractional distillation, 105; Oxidise, 82; Proteins, 123; Atmospheres, 69; Reversible reaction, 81; Alkaline, 89.

Nitric acid

Nitric acid (HNO_3) is manufactured in a three-stage process called the **Ostwald process**. First, ammonia is oxidized, with the help of a high temperature ($900°C$) and a platinum-rhodium catalyst, to form nitrogen monoxide:

$$4NH_3(g) + 5O_2(g) \longrightarrow 4NO(g) + 6H_2O(l)$$

The nitrogen monoxide cools and reacts with oxygen to produce nitrogen dioxide:

$$2NO(g) + O_2(g) \longrightarrow 2NO_2(g)$$

Finally, nitrogen dioxide reacts with water and oxygen to produce nitric acid:

$$4NO_2(g) + O_2(g) + 2H_2O(l) \longrightarrow 4HNO_3(l)$$

Nitric acid is used to make many common fertilizers, including ammonium nitrate (NH_4NO_3) as well as other products such as dyes and synthetic fibres. It is a very powerful oxidizing agent. Salts of nitric acid which contain the ion NO_3^- are called **nitrates**. Nitrates are used mainly in the making of fertilizers.

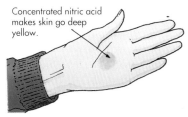

Concentrated nitric acid makes skin go deep yellow.

Fertilizers

Massive increases in population this century have made it necessary to grow more and more crops to keep

World population

1900 1.6 billion

1950 2.5 billion

1992 5.5 billion

people alive. This increase has upset the balance of nitrogen and other elements in the soil, which has been maintained for thousands of years. Soils which are continually sown with crops do not get the chance to replace the missing nitrogen. So farmers use chemical fertilizers made from ammonia to replace it. Other elements that have been depleted can also be replaced artificially. However, the overuse of fertilizers can have damaging effects (see below).

Damaging effects of fertilizer overuse	
The effect	Resulting damage
Changes the soil pH	Plants die, *food web** affected
Unwanted elements accumulate in soil	Eventually poisons soil, plants die
Fertilizer compounds washed into rivers	Causes *eutrophication**
Harms plants and animals in soil	Breaks down food web

NPK values

Most fertilizers are a mixture of compounds containing nitrogen, phosphorous and potassium (the three elements which most need replacement in the soil). These fertilizers are assigned a series of numbers showing the percentage of nitrogen, phosphorous(V) oxide (P_2O_5) and potassium oxide (K_2O) contained in the fertilizer. This number is called the **NPK value**.

NPK Fertilizer

18% N

12% P_2O_5

15% K_2O

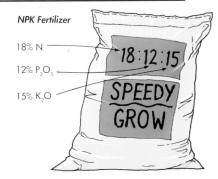

18:12:15

SPEEDY GROW

*Food web, 122, 173; Eutrophication, 95.

Sulphur and chlorine

Sulphur occurs naturally in volcanic regions in underground deposits known as **sulphur beds**. It is also found in fossil fuels and combined in ores such as copper sulphide (CuS).

Sulphur is a non-metallic, brittle solid which can be powdered. It does not conduct electricity and does not dissolve in water. It is coloured a bright yellow.

Sulphur's most important use is in the making of sulphuric acid (see below). It is also used in a process called **vulcanization** to make rubber harder and tougher for use in

Sulphur crystal

products like tyres and hoses.

When sulphur burns it produces a blue flame and is converted to sulphur dioxide (SO_2). Sulphur dioxide is a poisonous gas. It is a common air pollutant because it is frequently found as an impurity in fossil fuels. However sulphur dioxide also has important uses. It can be used as a *reducing agent**, as a *bleach**, and as a good preservative for food products containing fruit.

Sulphur dioxide is used to kill insects such as cockroaches. This process is called **fumigation**.

Sulphuric acid

The process used to manufacture sulphuric acid (H_2SO_4) is called the **contact process**. First, sulphur is *combusted** to make sulphur dioxide.

$$S(s) \; + \; O_2(g) \implies SO_2(g)$$

Then, more oxygen is reacted with the sulphur dioxide to make sulphur trioxide (SO_3). Heat (450°C) and a vanadium(V) oxide (V_2O_5) *catalyst** are used to speed up the process.

$$2SO_2(g) \; + \; O_2(g) \implies 2SO_3(g)$$

Finally, sulphur trioxide is passed into concentrated sulphuric acid to form fuming sulphuric acid, called **oleum**.

$$SO_3(g) \; + \; H_2SO_4(l) \implies H_2S_2O_7(l)$$

Oleum $H_2S_2O_7(l)$ is diluted into concentrated sulphuric acid (H_2SO_4).

Sulphuric acid is known as a **dibasic** acid because it contains two hydrogen atoms which become hydrogen *ions** when dissolved in water. It is very reactive and highly corrosive. Much care needs to be taken in its transportation, handling and storage.

Sulphuric acid produces a large amount of heat when dissolved in water. The acid must always be added to the water and not the other way round. This way, the acid is rapidly diluted and the heat safely absorbed by the water.

Sulphuric acid is stored in special containers.

Hazard signs — Harmful

Corrosive

Sulphuric acid as a dehydrating agent

Concentrated sulphuric acid is described as a good **dehydrating agent**, which means that it absorbs moisture from a number of other substances. For example, a beaker of the acid left open will gradually increase in volume because it absorbs water from the air. When sulphuric acid is added to sugar, it absorbs the water from sugar, leaving carbon as a hot, black mass.

$$C_{12}H_{22}O_{11}(s) \longrightarrow 12C(s) \; + \; 11H_2O(l)$$

H_2SO_4
Sulphuric acid acts as a catalyst.

Sugar

Carbon   Water

Uses of sulphuric acid

Sulphuric acid is very important industrially. It is commonly used as a raw material in the manufacture of many products, some of which are shown opposite.

Detergents

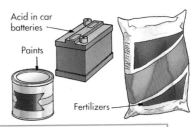
Acid in car batteries

Paints

Fertilizers

Chlorine

Chlorine is a *halogen** found in Group VII of the periodic table. At room temperature it is a greenish-yellow gas which is very poisonous. Chlorine is used to kill bacteria in the water supply. It is also important in the manufacture of paints, aerosol propellants, bleach, disinfectants, insecticides and plastics.

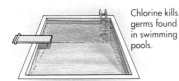
Chlorine kills germs found in swimming pools.

Most compounds formed when chlorine combines with another element are called **chlorides**. Chlorides of non-metals, such as hydrogen chloride, are usually *covalent** compounds. Chlorides of metals, such as magnesium chloride, are usually water soluble *ionic** compounds.

Hydrogen chloride is a colourless gas made by burning hydrogen in chlorine. It reacts with ammonia and dissolves in water to form hydrochloric acid.

Hydrochloric acid

Hydrochloric acid is used in industry for cleaning metals in a process called **pickling**. It is also used in electronics to make printed circuit boards. In the laboratory hydrochloric acid is used with barium chloride to detect the presence of sulphate (SO_4^{2-}) ions in a substance.

Test for sulphate ions using hydrochloric acid

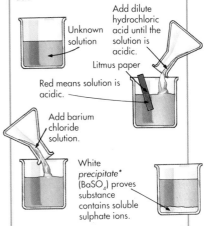

Add dilute hydrochloric acid until the solution is acidic.

Unknown solution

Litmus paper

Red means solution is acidic.

Add barium chloride solution.

White *precipitate** ($BaSO_4$) proves substance contains soluble sulphate ions.

Sodium chloride

Sodium chloride (NaCl) is an ionic compound which readily dissolves in water. It is better known as **common salt**. It can be extracted from sea water and is found in solid form as **rock salt**. Salt is used to flavour and preserve food. It is essential to animal life, although too much in your regular diet can be harmful. Salt is sprinkled on roads in winter to lower the *freezing point** of water and prevent ice forming.

Sodium chloride is also used as a raw material for a number of other important substances. A heavily concentrated solution of sodium chloride is called **brine**. When brine undergoes *electrolysis**, chlorine, hydrogen and sodium hydroxide (a base used in making soaps, detergents and bleaches) can all be extracted.

*Halogen, 73; Covalent, 77; Ionic, 76; Precipitate, 123; Freezing point, 69; Electrolysis, 86.

Organic chemistry

Organic chemistry is the study of compounds containing carbon. It is called organic because chemists used to think that these compounds could only be found in living things. Today we know that they are also to be found in many man-made substances, such as *plastics**. Organic molecules are found in medicines, plastics, fuels and food. **Biotechnology**, the exploitation of plant and animal organic material (known as the **biomass**), is increasing in importance and producing many useful new substances.

Organic molecules are made up of carbon atoms bonded together by *covalent bonds**. The simplest organic molecules contain only hydrogen and carbon atoms and are called **hydrocarbons** (HC).

The carbon cycle

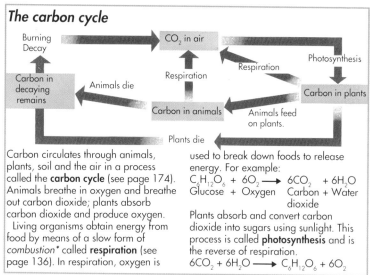

Carbon circulates through animals, plants, soil and the air in a process called the **carbon cycle** (see page 174). Animals breathe in oxygen and breathe out carbon dioxide; plants absorb carbon dioxide and produce oxygen.

Living organisms obtain energy from food by means of a slow form of *combustion** called **respiration** (see page 136). In respiration, oxygen is used to break down foods to release energy. For example:

$$C_6H_{12}O_6 + 6O_2 \longrightarrow 6CO_2 + 6H_2O$$
Glucose + Oxygen → Carbon + Water
dioxide

Plants absorb and convert carbon dioxide into sugars using sunlight. This process is called **photosynthesis** and is the reverse of respiration.

$$6CO_2 + 6H_2O \longrightarrow C_6H_{12}O_6 + 6O_2$$

Fossil fuels

Gas, coal and oil are all called **fossil fuels**. They are formed from decaying animal and plant matter over many millions of years. They are called fossil fuels because they are formed under pressure in a similar way to fossil formation. When a fossil fuel burns, it releases a lot of heat energy which can then be harnessed to propel vehicles, produce electricity and provide heating for home and industry. However, it may release waste products which cause pollution (see pages 74-75).

Fossil fuels satisfy most of the world's energy needs but they are *non-renewable resources**. Estimates suggest that our coal supply will last for 200-300 years but our oil and gas reserves may only last 50-60 years. In order to conserve fossil fuels, more use should be made of renewable, non-fossil fuels, such as hydro-electric (see page 52) and solar power. These are called **alternative energies**.

Windmills can harness wind power.

Solar cells convert heat from the sun into electricity.

Tidal barrages exploit energy generated by waves and tides.

 *Plastics, 108; Covalent bonds, 77; Combustion, 74; Non-renewable resources, 83.

Oil

Crude oil is a mixture of different organic compounds most of which are hydrocarbons. These hydrocarbons are all different sizes. The smaller ones are lighter and have lower boiling points than the larger molecules. This is because smaller hydrocarbons do not stick together as well as bigger ones.

The hydrocarbons are separated in a process called **refining**. Hydrocarbons which have boiling points within a certain range are grouped together into **fractions**. These fractions are separated from each other in a **fractional distillation column** (also known as a **fractionating tower**). The process starts with the crude oil heated to a temperature of about 350°C. As it boils, the oil vapour passes up the column, losing heat as it rises. The different fractions cool and condense at different places in the column according to their boiling points. Each fraction is separated off and distilled again to make it purer.

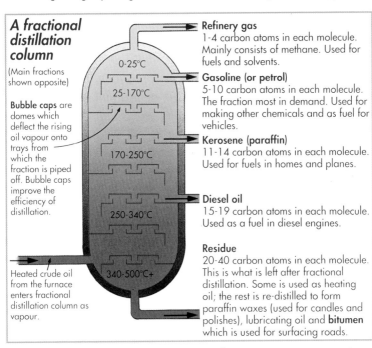

A fractional distillation column

(Main fractions shown opposite)

Bubble caps are domes which deflect the rising oil vapour onto trays from which the fraction is piped off. Bubble caps improve the efficiency of distillation.

Heated crude oil from the furnace enters fractional distillation column as vapour.

0-25°C
25-170°C
170-250°C
250-340°C
340-500°C+

Refinery gas
1-4 carbon atoms in each molecule. Mainly consists of methane. Used for fuels and solvents.

Gasoline (or petrol)
5-10 carbon atoms in each molecule. The fraction most in demand. Used for making other chemicals and as fuel for vehicles.

Kerosene (paraffin)
11-14 carbon atoms in each molecule. Used for fuels in homes and planes.

Diesel oil
15-19 carbon atoms in each molecule. Used as a fuel in diesel engines.

Residue
20-40 carbon atoms in each molecule. This is what is left after fractional distillation. Some is used as heating oil; the rest is re-distilled to form paraffin waxes (used for candles and polishes), lubricating oil and **bitumen** which is used for surfacing roads.

Fuels and feedstocks

When oil is combusted, an *exothermic** reaction occurs producing heat energy. Most crude oil (about 90%) is used as fuel. The remaining 10% is used as a raw material in the chemical industry and is known as **chemical feedstocks**. Refinery gas and naptha (a part of the gasoline fraction) are the main fractions found in chemical feedstocks.

Cracking

There is far more demand for the lighter fractions of oil, such as gasoline, than for the heavier fractions. To satisfy demand, the heavy fractions, with their larger molecules, are broken down into smaller molecules in a process called **cracking**. Cracking is carried out at very high temperatures. A *catalyst** is sometimes used.

*Exothermic, 96; Catalyst, 99.

Alkanes and alkenes

Organic molecules consist of carbon atoms each with four covalent bonds*. These bonds enable carbon-based molecules to form long chains with other atoms. Organic molecules with the same atoms, bonded in the same way to carbon atoms, are grouped into families called **homologous series**. Alkanes, alkenes and alcohols are all examples of homologous series.

Within each series, the only difference in structure between each type of molecule is the number of carbon atoms present. Members of a homologous series share the same chemical properties, but their physical properties change gradually as you descend the series.

Organic molecules are given names based on the homologous series they belong to and the number of carbon atoms they contain.

No. of carbon atoms	Homologous series		
	Alkane -ane	Alkene -ene	Alcohol -anol
1 Meth-	CH_4 Meth-ane	———	CH_3OH Meth-anol
2 Eth-	C_2H_6 Eth-ane	C_2H_4 Eth-ene	CH_3CH_2OH Eth-anol
3 Prop-	C_3H_8 Prop-ane	C_3H_6 Prop-ene	$CH_3CH_2CH_2OH$ Prop-anol

Alkanes

An ethane molecule

Alkanes are the simplest type of hydrocarbon. They all contain carbon atoms with each one bonded to four other atoms. For example, methane, has one carbon atom which forms bonds with four hydrogen atoms. Each alkane in the series has one more carbon atom, and two more hydrogen atoms, than the one before. Alkanes therefore have the *general formula** C_nH_{2n+2}.

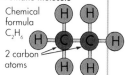

Chemical formula C_2H_6

2 carbon atoms

n=2, therefore 2n+2=6

The first three alkane molecules

Name	Structural formulae*	Formula	A_r*	No. carbon atoms	Boiling point	Energy of combustion*
Methane	H–C–H (with H above and below)	CH_4	16	1	-161°C	-890kJmol⁻¹
Ethane	H–C–C–H (with H H above and H H below)	C_2H_6	30	2	-89°C	-1560kJmol⁻¹
Propane	H–C–C–C–H (with H H H above and H H H below)	C_3H_8	44	3	-42°C	-2220kJmol⁻¹

Alkanes are called **saturated** molecules because no more atoms can be added to them. As a result, alkanes do not react easily with other atoms or molecules. They are insoluble in water, but dissolve in organic *solvents** such as benzene. Alkanes are very important fuels. They burn cleanly, producing much energy.

Alkanes can undergo reactions in which one atom swaps places with another. This is called a **substitution reaction**. For example, one of methane's hydrogen atoms can swap places with a chlorine atom, creating chloromethane and hydrogen chloride.

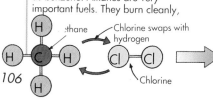

:thane
Chlorine swaps with hydrogen
Chlorine

Chloromethane
Hydrogen chloride

Alkenes

Alkenes, like alkanes, are made up of both carbon and hydrogen atoms. Their structures differ from alkanes in that they have a double bond between two of their carbon atoms. This double bond enables atoms to be added to alkenes during a chemical reaction. Alkenes are therefore called **unsaturated** molecules and are more reactive than alkanes. Alkenes can also be used as fuels by being burned in excess oxygen. They produce a smoky, yellow flame.

Ethene, an important alkene, is produced on a large scale by *cracking**the heavier fractions of crude oil. Ethene can also be prepared in the laboratory by passing *ethanol** vapour over a *dehydrating agent** such as aluminium oxide (Al_2O_3).

Laboratory preparation of ethene

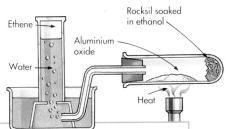

Ethene

Water

Rocksil soaked in ethanol

Aluminium oxide

Heat

Reactions of alkenes

When alkenes react, the double bond between the two carbon atoms is broken. The atoms in the other *reagent** are added to the alkene. This is called an **addition reaction**. For example, in the diagram, the bromine molecules bond with ethene to form 1,2-dibromoethane, an important additive in petrol. This reaction results in bromine losing its brown colour. All alkenes decolourize both bromine and acidified potassium permanganate (which is a purple solution). This decolourizing can be used to distinguish between alkenes and alkanes.

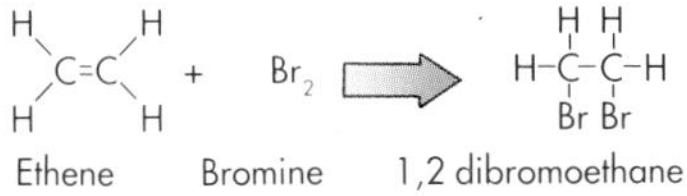

Ethene   Bromine   1,2 dibromoethane

Hydrogenation and hydration

When hydrogen is heated with an alkene in the presence of a nickel *catalyst**, the hydrogen atoms in the hydrogen molecule combine with the alkene molecule to form an alkane. This is called **hydrogenation**.

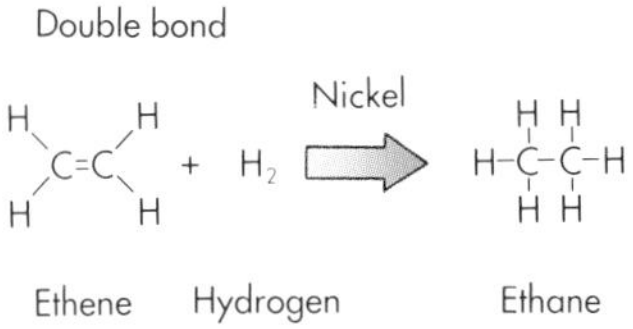

Double bond

Nickel

Ethene   Hydrogen   Ethane

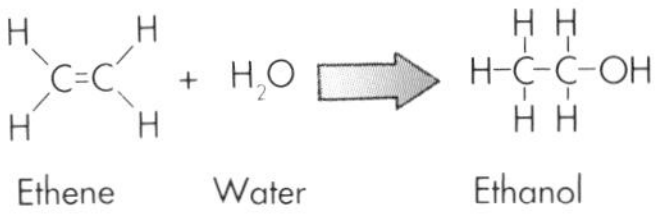

Ethene   Water   Ethanol

Water reacts with alkenes in the presence of the catalyst sulphuric acid to form alcohols. The addition of water is called **hydration**.

Isomers

Both alkanes and alkenes can form compounds called **isomers**, which have the same set of atoms, but are joined in different ways. They have the same chemical formula but different structural formulae. For example, butane (C_4H_{10}) has two isomers:

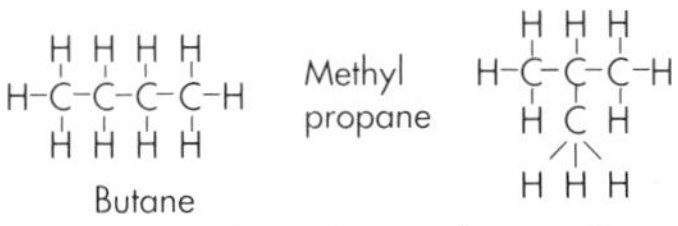

Butane

Methyl propane

Both isomers have four carbon and 10 hydrogen atoms, but they are arranged in different ways.

*Covalent bonds, 77; General formula, 122; Solvents, 114; A_r, 71; Structural formulae, 67; Energy of Combustion, 122; Cracking, 105; Ethanol, 109; Dehydrating agent, 102; Reagent, 80.

Polymers

Polymers are organic compounds which contain enormously long chains of atoms. These chains are made up of small repeating units of molecules called **monomers**. Some polymers, such as starch, occur naturally. Others, such as nylon, are man-made and are called **synthetic polymers**. Chemists can make a vast range of synthetic polymers to serve particular purposes.

Plastics

Plastics are a large group of synthetic polymers which have had a tremendous impact on our everyday lives. All plastics have a number of useful qualities in common. They are strong as well as being light and flexible, easily coloured and moulded into shape. In addition, they are good heat insulators and are rot and corrosion-proof.

The alkene, ethene, forms the basis of many important plastics. For example, under the right conditions, ethene molecules will react with each other, opening up their double bonds and joining together to form the polymer **(poly)ethene**, or **polythene**. This process is known as **addition polymerization**.

Addition polymerization

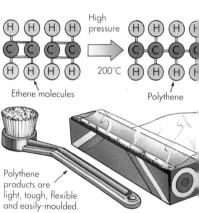

High pressure

200°C

Ethene molecules

Polythene

Polythene products are light, tough, flexible and easily-moulded.

Thermosoftening and thermosetting plastics

Plastics which soften and melt when heated, but do not change their structure, are called **thermosoftening** plastics. They are flexible and can be remoulded and used again, but are not very heat resistant. PVC, nylon, polystyrene and polythene are all thermosoftening plastics.

Plastics which can be heated, melted and moulded once only are called **thermosetting** plastics. Their molecules are fixed rigidly in place which makes them hard and heat-resistant. Bakelite is a thermosetting plastic. It was one of the first plastics invented and is still used for light fittings. Melamine is also a thermosetting plastic. It is used for kitchen worktops.

Problems with plastics

Plastics in rubbish can give off methane gas which can be explosive.

Rainwater seeps through the rubbish forming a toxic slime called **leachate**.

Leachate is harmful if it leaks into underground water supplies.

Water supply

Most plastics are made from raw materials derived from crude oil. They are difficult to recycle, so many of the resources used to create them cannot be reclaimed. Most plastics cannot be burned as they release toxic fumes. They do not decay naturally and so are called **non-biodegradable**.

Most non-biodegradable rubbish is buried in huge holes dug deep into the ground. These are called **landfill sites**. In addition to the large amount of land they take up, landfill sites have a number of serious drawbacks.

Alcohols

Alcohols form a *homologous series**. The first four in the series are:

Name	Formula	Structural formulae*
Methanol	CH$_3$OH	H–C–OH (with H above and H below)
Ethanol	C$_2$H$_5$OH	H–C–C–OH
Propan-1-ol	C$_3$H$_7$OH	H–C–C–C–H
Propan-2-ol	C$_3$H$_7$OH	H–C–C–C–H

Propan-1-ol and propan-2-ol are *isomers**.

Ethanol

Alcohols are an important group of organic compounds. They are different from *alkanes** and *alkenes** in that their structure does not consist exclusively of carbon and hydrogen atoms. Ethanol is the most important of the alcohols. It is a clear, sweet-smelling, water-soluble liquid which evaporates quickly.

Ethanol is widely used in industry as a *solvent** for many substances, including paints, dyes and perfumes. It burns with a clean blue flame, produces a lot of heat and doesn't give off pollutants such as sulphur and nitrous oxides. It is occasionally used as a fuel in some countries and may become more important in the future.

Alcoholic fermentation

Ethanol is the potent substance found in alcoholic drinks. Alcohol in drinks can give people pleasure, but it can cause serious damage when consumed in excess.

Ethanol can be made by adding yeast to a sugar, in a process called **alcoholic fermentation**. This process has been used for thousands of years to make beer and wine. The equation for fermentation using glucose as the sugar is shown below.

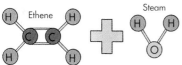

| C$_6$H$_{12}$O$_6$ | → | 2C$_2$H$_5$OH | + | 2CO$_2$ |
| Glucose | Yeast → | Ethanol | + | Carbon dioxide |

Substances in yeast, called **enzymes**, act as *catalysts** in the process during which sugar is broken down into ethanol. After a time the ethanol produced during fermentation will kill the yeast. To obtain pure ethanol, the mixture left is separated by *fractional distillation**.

Laboratory fermentation

Bung — Flask — Sugar is broken down and ethanol is produced. — Escaping carbon dioxide — Glass tube — Beaker

Fermentation mixture: yeast, sugar and water (ideal temperature: 37°C)

Oxygen must not be allowed to enter the reaction vessel as it could oxidize the ethanol and produce **ethanoic acid** (CH$_3$COOH). Vinegar is a weak solution of ethanoic acid.

Industrial production of ethanol

Most of the ethanol used in industry is made, not by alcoholic fermentation, but by an *addition reaction** between ethene and steam. This is shown below.

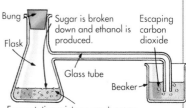

Ethene + Steam → (Very high pressure, 300°C) → Ethanol

*Homologous series, 106; Structural formulae, 67; Isomers, 107; Alkanes, 106; Alkenes, 107; Solvent, 114; Catalysts, 99; Fractional distillation, 115; Addition reaction, 107.

The problems of the chemical industry

The chemical industry has provided people with enormous benefits, from increased food production to new drugs to fight diseases. It employs many people and is a major factor in the growth of modern industry. However, in addition to the benefits, there are problems. Many of these are related to aspects of pollution which have been discussed earlier in this section (see air pollution, pages 74-75, water pollution, pages 94-95, and landfill sites, page 108).

Siting industrial plants

Many factors, apart from pollution, influence the siting of a chemical plant. These can be split into two groups: technical and financial issues, and social and ecological factors.

The issues considered by the organization responsible for building and running the plant tend to be technical and financial ones. Examples of such considerations are the need for raw materials, land, transport links and a suitable workforce nearby. All these factors need to be available at an affordable price, making the site as profitable as possible.

The social and environmental factors are ones which affect the local community and its surroundings. These give rise to questions concerning potential waste, pollution and noise generated by the plant, as well as safety risks associated with the particular substance manufactured. There is also the question of whether the plant will overburden the community, or benefit the area by bringing money and employment.

Both types of factor have been considered in the example below.

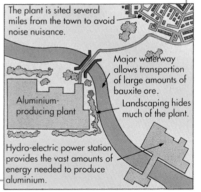

The plant is sited several miles from the town to avoid noise nuisance.

Major waterway allows transportion of large amounts of bauxite ore.

Aluminium-producing plant

Landscaping hides much of the plant.

Hydro-electric power station provides the vast amounts of energy needed to produce aluminium.

Acid rain

When *fossil fuels** containing sulphur are burned, they produce sulphur dioxide. Nitrogen in the air is normally unreactive but it reacts at high temperatures (such as inside a car engine) to form nitrogen oxides. Sulphur dioxide and nitrogen oxides are toxic acidic gases which can cause chest and lung diseases. They react with rain water to form sulphurous, nitric and nitrous acids which give rain a far greater acidity than normal. This is known as **acid rain**.

Acid rain *corrodes** metals and the stonework of buildings. It also frees some metal *ions** which were previously 'locked' safely in soil particles. These can cause harm by, for example, changing the *pH** of water in rivers and lakes. This, in turn, kills aquatic life.

The level of acid rain can be reduced by burning fewer fossil fuels, removing sulphur and nitrogen from fuels, and refining engines to cut down harmful emissions.

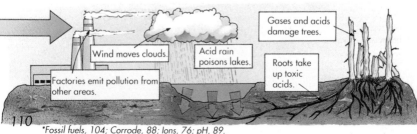

Gases and acids damage trees.

Wind moves clouds.

Acid rain poisons lakes.

Roots take up toxic acids.

Factories emit pollution from other areas.

*Fossil fuels, 104; Corrode, 88; Ions, 76; pH, 89.

Ozone depletion

Dangerous ultra-violet rays from the sun can cause skin cancer. The earth is protected from these rays by a layer of ozone (O_3) molecules found in the atmosphere. However, substances called **chlorofluorocarbons** (CFCs), used in aerosols, fridges and the manufacture of polystyrene, are attacking and destroying this layer. International action has been taken to reduce CFC emissions, but many scientists would like to see more done.

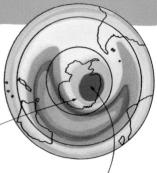

A Total Ozone Map

There is a shortage of ozone over the Antarctic. This was discovered in 1985.

Purple indicates lowest amount of ozone.

The greenhouse effect

Carbon dioxide plays an important role in warming the earth by trapping the sun's heat. This is called the **greenhouse effect**. For millions of years the *carbon cycle** maintained a balance between the processes that add and those that take away carbon dioxide from the air.

In modern times, people have upset this balance by burning vast amounts of fossil fuels, and so releasing excess carbon dioxide into the atmosphere. A lot of tropical rainforest has been destroyed, which in turn has reduced the amount of carbon dioxide used up by green plants during *photosynthesis**. This has resulted in an increase in carbon dioxide (CO_2) in the air.

As the concentration of carbon dioxide in the air increases, more heat energy is trapped. Less can escape out of the atmosphere and the average temperature of the earth's surface gradually increases. It is believed that other gases, such as methane and the ozone-destroying CFC's, act in a similar way to carbon dioxide. Scientists are in doubt as to precisely how much temperatures will rise as a result of the continued emission of these gases. However, they argue that it could possibly cause severe changes in climate.

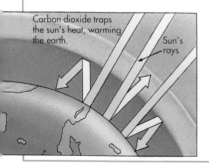

Carbon dioxide traps the sun's heat, warming the earth.

Sun's rays

Chemicals in the home and laboratory

Some household chemicals, such as bleach and glue, are dangerous if inhaled or drunk. They should always be kept out of the reach of small children.

Substances in the laboratory can be dangerous in a number of ways. They can, for example, be *radioactive**, harmful if inhaled, or corrosive to the skin and worksurfaces. To handle chemicals with care, you need to know in what way they may be hazardous. Chemical hazard symbols (see below) act as warnings telling you what to beware of. They are found as labels on containers of substances and at entrances to dangerous areas.

Toxic	Toxic (USA)	Harmful	Flammable	Oxidizing	Explosive

*Carbon cycle, 104, 174; Photosynthesis, 104; Radioactive, 112.

Nuclear power and radiation

In a chemical reaction it is only the number of electrons in the outer shell that change. A **nuclear reaction** is one which involves changes to the nucleus itself. The nuclei of some types of atom are unstable, which causes them to break up. When they do, they emit waves and particles called **radiation**, in a process called **radioactive decay**. There are three types of radiation: **alpha particles** (helium nuclei), **beta particles** (streams of electrons) and **gamma rays** (high energy *waves**). They can be identified by the distance they can travel.

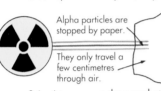

Alpha particles are stopped by paper.

They only travel a few centimetres through air.

Beta particles are stopped by a few millimetres of lead.

They can travel a few metres through air.

Gamma rays

are stopped by 2-3 cm of lead.

Scientists measure the speed at which radioactive decay occurs (known as the **rate of decay**) in half-lives. A **half-life** is the time it takes for half of a radioactive substance (known as a **radioisotope**) to disintegrate. This rate varies from substance to substance. For example, carbon-14 has a half life of 5500 years, whereas radium-221's half life measures just 30 seconds. The longer the half life, the slower the rate of decay and the more stable the radioisotope.

Uses and problems of radiation

Radioactive materials are used to treat certain types of cancer. Some radioisotopes, such as cobalt-60, are used to detect flaws in metals and to measure the thickness of paper and plastics.

Carbon-14 is a radioisotope found in all living things. It starts to decay after the organism dies. As carbon-14's half-life is known, the age of a sample can be calculated by measuring how much carbon-14 is left in it. This process is called **radiocarbon dating**.

Although radiation can be of use, it is extremely dangerous and is lethal in large doses. It can destroy or damage living tissue and can cause skin burns, sickness, sterility and various forms of cancer. Scientists, doctors and energy personnel who work with radioactive materials must take many safety precautions. These include working behind lead shields and wearing protective clothing.

Archeologists use carbon-dating to establish the age of ancient artefacts.

Radiation hazard sign

Special badge indicates level of radiation encountered.

Nuclear power

Nuclear power produces cheap electricity without the pollution problems associated with burning fossil fuels. However, it does have a number of serious problems. Leaks from faulty power stations (such as Chernobyl in 1986) have resulted in many deaths both directly and through cancers. Many people worry about the likelihood of a nuclear power station explosion, which would result in massive devastation.

Disposal of nuclear waste is a major concern. Some waste materials remain radioactive for hundreds of years and must be left undisturbed in sealed containers. These containers are often buried deep underground or dropped onto the sea-bed. (Also see page 52.)

The reactivity series

Metal	Reaction with air	Reaction with water — Cold	Reaction with water — Steam	Reaction with dilute acids	Reaction of metal's oxides — With hydrogen	Reaction of metal's oxides — With carbon	Solubility*	Reaction of heat and hydroxides*
Potassium	Burn readily to form oxide	Explosive H_2 evolved*	Explosive H_2 evolved	Explosive H_2 evolved	No reaction	No reaction	Very soluble	No reaction
Sodium	Burn readily to form oxide	Violent H_2 evolved	Violent H_2 evolved	Violent H_2 evolved	No reaction	No reaction	Very soluble	No reaction
Calcium	Burn readily to form oxide	Quiet H_2 evolved	Strong H_2 evolved	Strong H_2 evolved	No reaction	No reaction	Slightly soluble	No reaction
Magnesium	Form oxide when heated	No reaction	Quiet H_2 evolved	Normal H_2 evolved	No reaction	No reaction	Sparingly soluble	Decomposed* by heat to form oxide
Aluminium	Form oxide when heated	No reaction	Reversible reaction	Normal H_2 evolved	No reaction	No reaction	Insoluble	Decomposed* by heat to form oxide
Zinc	Form oxide when heated	No reaction	Reversible reaction	Normal H_2 evolved	Reversible reaction	Reduced to metal Carbon dioxide formed	Insoluble	Decomposed* by heat to form oxide
Iron	Form oxide when heated	No reaction	Reversible reaction	Weak H_2 evolved	Reduced* to metal Water formed	Reduced to metal Carbon dioxide formed	Insoluble	Decomposed* by heat to form oxide
Tin	Form oxide when heated	No reaction	No reaction	Weak H_2 evolved	Reduced* to metal Water formed	Reduced to metal Carbon dioxide formed	Insoluble	Decomposed* by heat to form oxide
Lead	Form oxide when heated	No reaction	No reaction	Weak H_2 evolved	Reduced* to metal Water formed	Reduced to metal Carbon dioxide formed	Insoluble	Decomposed* by heat to form oxide
Copper	Form oxide when heated	No reaction	No reaction	No reaction	Oxides reduced to metal by heat only	Oxides reduced to metal by heat only	Insoluble	Decomposed* by heat to form oxide
Mercury	Reversible reaction	No reaction	No reaction	No reaction	Oxides reduced to metal by heat only	Oxides reduced to metal by heat only	Insoluble	Decomposed* by heat to form oxide
Silver	No reaction	No reaction	No reaction	No reaction	Oxides reduced to metal by heat only	Oxides reduced to metal by heat only	Insoluble	Unstable or not formed
Gold	No reaction	No reaction	No reaction	No reaction	Oxides reduced to metal by heat only	Oxides reduced to metal by heat only	Insoluble	Unstable or not formed

*Evolved, 122; Oxides, 123; Reduced, 82; Solubility, 114; Hydroxide, 122; Decomposed, 114.

Solubilities and separation

A solid that dissolves in a liquid is called a **solute** and is said to be **soluble**. The liquid that dissolves the solid is called a **solvent** and the resulting mixture is called a **solution**. For example, sodium chloride is soluble. It dissolves readily in water forming a colourless solution. Sand, on the other hand, is insoluble; it does not dissolve in water at all.

Most insoluble solids settle to the bottom of a liquid, but some split into tiny particles which spread throughout the liquid. This type of mixture is called a **suspension**. For example, milk is a suspension of fat particles in water.

The mass of a substance that dissolves in 100g of solvent is described as the **solubility** of that substance. Solubility can vary with temperature; plotted against temperature, it produces a **solubility curve**. When no more of a substance can be dissolved, the solution is said to be **saturated**.

Methods of separation

There are a number of methods of separating substances from each other. Some of the most commonly used techniques are shown below.

Simple distillation is similar to evaporation (see below), except that the evaporated liquid is collected after cooling. It is used for liquids with greatly differing boiling points and for obtaining pure solvent from a solution containing a dissolved solid.

A **Liebig condenser** speeds up the cooling and condensing process. The vapour passes through the condenser's centre and is cooled by water flowing round the condenser's outer wall.

Simple distillation

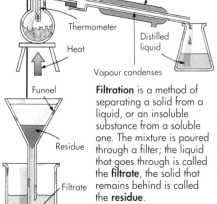

Vapour rises out of flask. Liebig condenser

Thermometer

Heat

Distilled liquid

Vapour condenses

Funnel

Filtration is a method of separating a solid from a liquid, or an insoluble substance from a soluble one. The mixture is poured through a filter; the liquid that goes through is called the **filtrate**, the solid that remains behind is called the **residue**.

Residue

Filtrate

Separating funnel
When two liquids completely mix with each other, such as water and ethanol, they are said to be **miscible**. Liquids which do not mix, such as oil and water, are **immiscible**. Two immiscible liquids can be split using a **separating funnel**.

A separating funnel

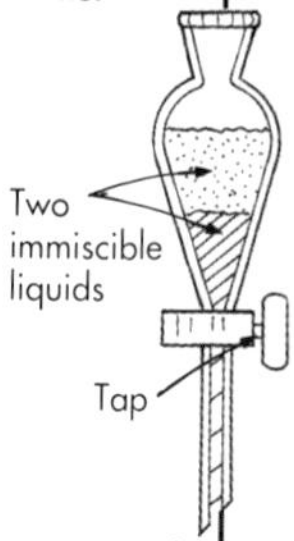

Two immiscible liquids

Tap

In the laboratory, *evaporation** is used to separate a solid dissolved in a liquid. The solution is boiled, which releases the liquid as a gas. This leaves the solid in the evaporating dish.

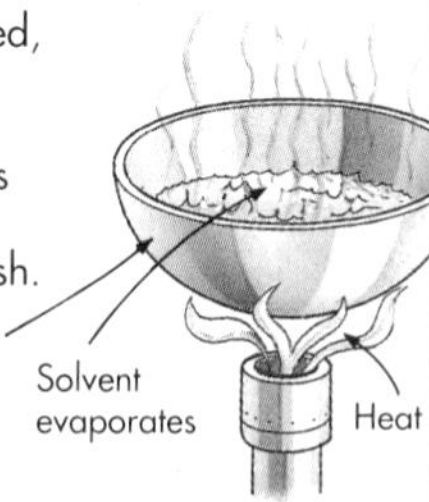

Evaporating basin

Solvent evaporates

Heat

Centrifuging is a method in which a suspension is spun very quickly in a machine called a **centrifuge**. This forces the solid particles to the bottom of the container. The liquid can then be poured off. This method is used in hospitals to separate the red cells from the blood.

A laboratory centrifuge

Fractional distillation

Fractional distillation is similar to simple distillation but uses an additional piece of apparatus called a **fractionating column**. A fractionating column contains glass rings or balls which provide a large surface area for condensation and re-evaporation. The vapour of the liquid with the lowest boiling point reaches the top of the column first. Fractional distillation is used to separate liquids with close boiling points.

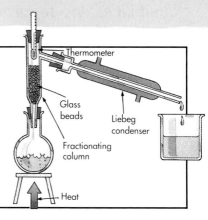

Thermometer

Glass beads

Liebeg condenser

Fractionating column

Heat

Chromatography

Chromatography is the method used to separate several substances dissolved in a solvent. A spot of the mixture to be separated is placed near the bottom of some filter paper and solvent added. The different components in the solution move up the paper with the solvent, but at different speeds. Eventually, the substances are separated out and remain as distinct spots or bands on the paper. This is called a **chromatogram**.

Chromatography is only suitable for separating very small quantities. It is mainly used as a purity test, but also to determine what a substance consists of.

A chromatogram can be made of some known pure substances and one unknown. The positions of the different components of the unknown substance are compared to those of the known substances. This method is used, for example, to determine the different dyes in ink.

A, an unknown substance, breaks up into two substances. These must be the known substances, C and D because of their matching positions on the filter paper.

B   C   D   E

Titration

The **concentration** of a solution is the number of *moles** of a substance dissolved in $1dm^3$ of solvent. Finding the concentration of a solution is called **volumetric analysis**. Two solutions, one of known and one of unknown concentration, are mixed together using a measuring vessel called a **burette**. This technique is known as a **titration**.

A measure of one solution is placed in the burette. It is gradually added to the second solution until the two solutions have finished their reaction. The solution remaining in the burette is measured. This is called the **end point**. The original amount in the burette, minus the end point, gives you the amount of solution used. From this, calculations can be made to assess the concentration of the unknown solution.

The most common type of titration is an **acid-base titration**. An acid solution of known concentration is added to a base solution of unknown concentration. An *indicator** is used to find the end point.

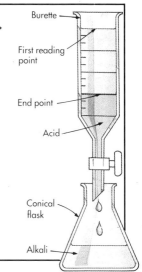

Burette

First reading point

End point

Acid

Conical flask

Alkali

*Moles, 92; Indicator, 90.

Practical experiments

Analysis of salts

The *cation** present in a salt can usually be identified by a **flame test**. A tiny sample of the unknown salt is added to concentrated hydrochloric acid. This is placed on the end of a clean piece of platinum wire and ignited in a bunsen flame. Different cations produce different colours in the bunsen flame.

A bright yellow colour — sodium
A lilac colour — potassium
A brick-red colour — calcium
A blue-green colour — copper

The ammonium cation (NH_4^+) does not have a distinctive flame colour, but can be detected because it gives off ammonia gas when sodium hydroxide is added to it. Ammonia has a pungent smell and turns damp red litmus paper blue.

There are a number of tests for the different types of *anion** found in a salt. Carbonates, which contain the CO_3^{2-} ion, give off carbon dioxide when an acid is added. Sulphates, which contain the SO_4^{2-} ion, produce a white *precipitate** when barium chloride and hydrochloric acid are added. Chlorides, which contain the Cl^- ion, produce a white precipitate when silver nitrate and dilute nitric acid are added.

Salts that react with both acids and bases are called **amphoteric salts**. If an excess of sodium hydroxide is added, for example, to zinc hydroxide it will react and the precipitate will dissolve.

Testing for purity

Pure substances all have fixed melting and boiling points at a set *pressure**. An impure solid has a lower melting point than a pure solid. An impure liquid has a higher boiling point than a pure one.

For example, 10 cm³ of pure water has 1g measures of salt added to it at regular intervals. In between each extra addition, the solution is heated and its boiling point taken. A graph can then be plotted. This shows that the more salt in the water, the higher the solution's boiling point.

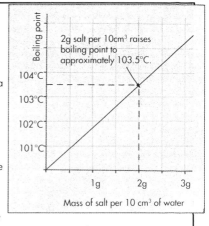

2g salt per 10cm³ raises boiling point to approximately 103.5°C.

Mass of salt per 10 cm³ of water

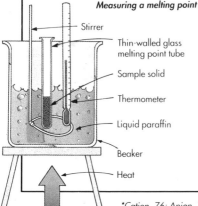

Measuring a melting point

- Stirrer
- Thin-walled glass melting point tube
- Sample solid
- Thermometer
- Liquid paraffin
- Beaker
- Heat

Measuring a melting point requires more *apparatus** than measuring a typical boiling point. A sample of the substance is placed in a thin walled glass tube. The tube and a thermometer are then suspended in a bath of liquid paraffin. The bath is slowly heated and an even temperature is maintained by constant stirring. When the sample melts (turns from solid to liquid), the temperature can be recorded. This temperature can be compared against the melting point of the pure substance.

*Cation, 76; Anion, 76; Precipitate, 123; Pressure, 69; Apparatus, 124.

Gases in the laboratory

Preparation of nitrogen

Impure nitrogen is produced by removing oxygen and carbon dioxide from air. This leaves nitrogen with some residue of water vapour and *noble gases**. The oxygen is removed by passing the air over heated copper. The carbon dioxide is removed by passing air through sodium hydroxide solution.

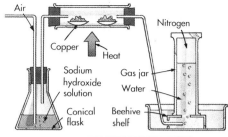

Air
Copper
Heat
Sodium hydroxide solution
Conical flask
Nitrogen
Gas jar
Water
Beehive shelf

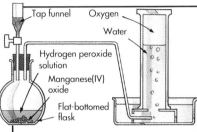

Tap funnel
Oxygen
Water
Hydrogen peroxide solution
Manganese(IV) oxide
Flat-bottomed flask

Preparation of oxygen

In the laboratory, oxygen is produced when hydrogen peroxide decomposes. Manganese (IV) oxide (MnO_2) is used as a catalyst to speed up the reaction.

$$2H_2O_2(aq) \xrightarrow{MnO_2} 2H_2O(l) + O_2(g)$$

Hydrogen peroxide   Water   Oxygen

Preparation of hydrogen

Hydrogen can be made by adding dilute hydrochloric acid to granulated zinc. To speed up the reaction, copper sulphate solution can be added.

$$Zn(s) + 2HCl(aq) \longrightarrow ZnCl_2(aq) + H_2(g)$$

Zinc   Hydrochloric acid   Zinc chloride   Hydrogen

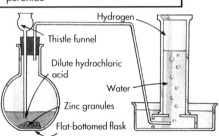

Hydrogen
Thistle funnel
Dilute hydrochloric acid
Water
Zinc granules
Flat-bottomed flask

Preparation of chlorine

Chlorine is prepared through the oxidation of concentrated hydrochloric acid by manganese(IV) oxide. The gas produced contains some hydrogen chloride which is water soluble, and so can be removed by bubbling the gas through water. The chlorine gas is then dried using concentrated sulphuric acid. As chlorine is heavier than air it can be collected in a gas jar. The heavier chlorine settles at the bottom of the jar and pushes the lighter air out. This is called **upward displacement**.

Hydrochloric acid   Chlorine   Water

$$MnO_2 + 4HCl \longrightarrow MnCl_2 + Cl_2 + H_2O$$

Manganese(IV) oxide   Manganese(IV) chloride

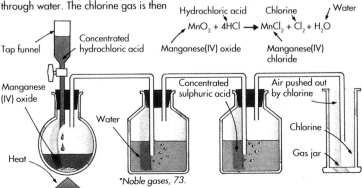

Tap funnel
Concentrated hydrochloric acid
Manganese (IV) oxide
Water
Heat
Concentrated sulphuric acid
Air pushed out by chlorine
Chlorine
Gas jar

*Noble gases, 73.

117

Percentage of oxygen in the air

The amount of oxygen in the air can be found by using the *apparatus** below. A specified amount of air is passed from the left hand gas syringe over heated copper in a glass tube. The heated copper combines with the oxygen in the air to form black copper oxide. The remaining elements of air enter the previously empty right hand gas syringe.

The air is repeatedly passed from the left to the right syringe over the heated copper and back again. This continues until all of the oxygen has reacted with the copper. (This is when there is no further change in the volumes of air found in the gas syringes.) The

apparatus is left to cool and then a reading of the volume of air (minus the oxygen) is taken from one of the syringes. The percentage of oxygen in air is calculated using the following formula:

$$\frac{\text{% oxygen}}{\text{in air}} = \frac{\text{decrease in volume of air}}{\text{initial volume of air}}$$

In the example below, $200 \ cm^3$ of air is used in the apparatus. The decrease in the volume of air is $42 \ cm^3$. Using the calculation above, the precentage of oxygen in air is found to be 21%.

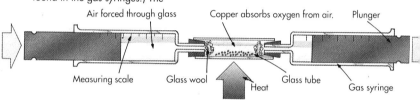

Air forced through glass — Copper absorbs oxygen from air. — Plunger

Measuring scale — Glass wool — Glass tube — Gas syringe — Heat

Identifying gases

Measuring the amount of a substance in a reaction is called **quantitative analysis**. Identifying a particular substance in a reaction is called **qualitative analysis**. Tests to identify gases are forms of qualitative analysis. Testing for carbon dioxide is described on page 21, and for oxygen on page 10.

The table below shows the methods used to identify a number of other gases.

Name	Formula	Colour	Test
Ammonia	NH_3	Colourless	Red litmus paper is turned blue.
Bromine	Br_2	Red/brown	Forms a yellow solution in water.
Hydrogen	H_2	Colourless	Burns with a pop forming water.
Nitrogen monoxide	NO	Colourless	Forms brown fumes when in air.
Sulphur dioxide	SO_2	Colourless	Turns potassium dichromate (VI) orange to green.
Chlorine	Cl_2	Pale green	Blue litmus paper is turned red.
Ethene	C_2H_4	Colourless	Takes bromine's colour away. Burns to form carbon dioxide and water.
Methane	CH_2	Colourless	Burns with a blue flame, forming carbon dioxide and water.
Nitrogen	N_2	Colourless	Puts out a burning splint and does not react with lime water.
Nitrogen dioxide	NO_2	Brown	Forms an acidic and colourless solution when mixed with water.

*Apparatus, 124.

Table of Elements

Below is table of the elements you are most likely to deal with when learning about chemistry. They are listed along with some of their key properties.

Element	Symbol	Atomic No.*	A_r*	Valency*	Boiling point (°C)	Melting point (°C)
Aluminium	Al	13	27	3	2470	660
Argon	Ar	18	40	1	-186	-189
Barium	Ba	56	137	2	1640	714
Beryllium	Be	4	9	1, 2	2477	1280
Boron	B	5	11	1, 3	3930	2300
Bromine	Br	35	80	1, 5, 7	58.8	-7.2
Calcium	Ca	20	40	2	1487	850
Carbon (diamond)	C	6	12	4	Unknown	3750
Carbon (graphite)	C	6	12	4	4830	3730†
Chlorine	Cl	17	35.5	1, 7, 5	-34.7	-101
Chromium	Cr	24	52	3, 6	2482	1890
Copper	Cu	29	64	1, 2	2595	1083
Fluorine	F	9	19	1, 7	-188	-220
Gold	Au	79	197	1, 2, 3	2970	1063
Helium	He	2	4	1	-269	-270
Hydrogen	H	1	1	1	-252	-259
Iodine	I	53	127	1, 5, 7	184	114
Iron	Fe	26	56	2, 3	3000	1535
Lead	Pb	82	207	2, 4	1744	327
Lithium	Li	3	7	1	1330	180
Magnesium	Mg	12	24	2	1110	650
Manganese	Mn	25	55	2, 3, 4, 7	2100	1240
Mercury	Hg	80	201	1, 2	357	-38.9
Neon	Ne	10	20	1	-246	-249
Nickel	Ni	28	59	2	2730	1453
Nitrogen	N	7	14	3, 5	-196	-210
Oxygen	O	8	16	2	-183	-218
Phosphorus (white)	P	15	31	3, 5	280	44.2
Platinum	Pt	78	195	2, 4	4530	1769
Plutonium	Pu	94	242	3, 4, 5, 6	3240	640
Potassium	K	19	39	1	774	63.7
Silicon	Si	14	28	4	2360	1410
Silver	Ag	47	108	1	2210	961
Sodium	Na	11	23	1	890	97.8
Sulphur (monoclinic)	S	16	32	2, 4, 6	444	119
Tin	Sn	50	119	2, 4	1730	1540
Titanium	Ti	22	48	1, 2, 3, 4	3260	1675
Tungsten	W	74	184	4, 6	5930	3410
Uranium	U	92	238	3, 4, 5, 6	3820	1130
Xenon	Xe	54	131	1	-108	-112
Zinc	Zn	30	65	2	907	420

†Graphite *sublimes** at this temperature.

Chemistry who's who

The list below contains short biographies of a number of the most influential chemists.

Much of modern chemistry has developed from skills such as metalworking and simple recipes for medicines, dyes and other everyday things. Chemistry gets its name from the Arabic word, *al quemia* meaning alchemy. Alchemy was an early form of chemistry practised in the Middle East from Roman times, and later in Europe.

Among other things, alchemists believed they could make gold out of more common metals. Much of their work was surrounded by magic and superstition, but alchemists did make many useful discoveries and evolved techniques which paved the way for modern chemistry. Modern chemical practice is generally considered to date from the 17th century with the work of scientists such as Robert Boyle.

Amedeo Avogadro (1776-1856) Italian.
Trained as a lawyer then turned to physics and chemistry in his thirties. He was the first to point out that equal volumes of gas at the same temperature and pressure contain the same number of particles. This led to the realization that one mole of any substance contains the same number of particles, the *Avogadro number**.

Antoine Becquerel (1852-1908) French.
Came from a distinguished family of scientists and succeeded his father as professor of physics at a college in Paris in 1895. A year later, he found that a uranium salt placed on a wrapped photographic plate gave out invisible rays which made the plate blacken: these rays were *radiation**. In 1903 he shared a Nobel Prize with Marie and Pierre Curie (see below).

Neils Bohr (1885-1962) Danish.
Born in Copenhagen, he created the first modern theory of how the atom is constructed. He worked in England for a time before becoming Director of the Institute of Theoretical Physics in Copenhagen. In 1922, he won the Nobel Prize. Escaping Nazi Europe in 1943, he moved to England and worked on the Atomic bomb programme. He was actively anti-nuclear in later years.

Wallace Carothers (1896-1937) American.
He was the first chemist to make a synthetic fibre. He worked for a company called Du Pont and synthesized the synthetic rubber, Neoprene, marketed in 1932. He went on to produce nylon which had huge commercial success and is still widely used today. Carothers is considered the father of the plastics industry. He suffered from depression and committed suicide at the age of 41.

Henry Cavendish (1731-1810) British.
An eccentric recluse, Cavendish inherited a vast fortune which he used to finance his experiments. He devoted his life to science and was one of the first chemists to study gas reactions. One of his most important discoveries was that water was a compound and not an element.

Marie Curie (1867-1934) French.
Discovered the radioactive element radium and conducted pioneering work (with her husband Pierre) into radioactivity. She was considered to be a chemist and physicist of world standing despite living and working in a male-dominated world. She won Nobel Prizes, twice, once in 1903 and again in 1911. She died in 1934 from leukaemia caused by exposure to radioactive materials.

Robert Boyle (1627-91) Irish.
Came from the Irish aristocracy and is best known for his work with pressures and volumes of gases. His important Boyle's Law is illustrated opposite. His book, 'The Sceptical Chymist' rejected old ideas and insisted on scientific methods of experiment and observation. He also proposed the notion of simple elements which could be combined to form compounds.

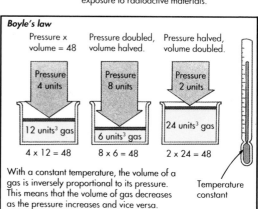

Boyle's law

Pressure x volume = 48

Pressure doubled, volume halved.

Pressure halved, volume doubled.

Pressure 4 units — 12 units³ gas — 4 x 12 = 48

Pressure 8 units — 6 units³ gas — 8 x 6 = 48

Pressure 2 units — 24 units³ gas — 2 x 24 = 48

With a constant temperature, the volume of a gas is inversely proportional to its pressure. This means that the volume of gas decreases as the pressure increases and vice versa.

Temperature constant

*Avogadro number, 92; Radiation, 112; Boyle's Law, 122.

John Dalton (1766-1844) British.
The son of a Quaker, Dalton spent most of his life in an isolated village in Cumbria working as a school teacher. Famous for his innovations on the subject of atomic theory, he was the first to suggest that molecules are made from atoms combined in simple ratios.

Michael Faraday (1791-1867) British.
Faraday was both a physicist and chemist. He discovered the compound benzene in 1825 and was the founder of the area of chemistry known as *electrochemistry**. It was through his discoveries that the modern battery was developed. He contributed greatly to the understanding of electricity and the electronic properties of certain solutions. He was a deeply religious man who despite gaining fame, lived in a simple, modest way.

Joseph Gay-Lussac (1778-1850) French.
Although he is most well-known for his experiments with gases, Gay-Lussac was also the first to use chemistry to prepare sodium and potassium, as well as isolating boron. A pioneering hot air balloonist, Gay-Lussac held the world altitude record of approximately 7500 metres for many years.

Fritz Haber (1868-1934) German.
The inventor of the *Haber Process** to manufacture ammonia on an industrial scale. His work is said to have prolonged the First World War by two years, as it enabled Germany to manufacture explosives long after natural supplies of ammonia-yielding compounds had been exhausted.

He was of Jewish ancestry and, although a fervent patriot, was hated by the Nazis. He fled to England in the early 1930's.

Dorothy Hodgkin (1910-) British.
The first chemist to use X-rays to find the exact structure of complex molecules. Hodgkin's successes include the mapping of penicillin, vitamin B$_{12}$ and insulin. Her work has had important applications for the pharmaceutical industry. She won the Nobel Prize for Chemistry in 1964.

Antoine Lavoisier (1743-1794) French.
Lavoisier was the first to apply the principle of conservation of mass to writing chemical equations. He also introduced principles for naming substances that are still in use today.

Lavoisier experimented with gases, demonstrating the properties of oxygen and showing that water is made up of oxygen and hydrogen. He criticised the scientific ideas of Marat, one of the leaders of the French Revolution, and was guillotined in 1794.

Dmitrii Mendeleev (1834-1907) Russian.
Mendeleev was one of 14 children and grew up in Siberia. At the age of 15 his mother took him to St Petersburg where he became a highly successful student, and later a researcher and lecturer at the University. He created the periodic table of elements in 1869.

Alfred Nobel (1833-1896) Swedish.
The son of an inventor. In 1842, Nobel's family moved to Russia where he gained a scientific education. He finally settled in Sweden in 1859, after living in Paris and Russia. Nobel invented dynamite in a highly dangerous process that severely maimed him, killed his brother and, in one explosion, took five lives. He died extremely rich and bestowed money to create the annual Nobel Prizes.

Linus Pauling (1901-) American.
Creator of the modern *covalent** theory of bonding. Pauling also showed that sickle cell disease could be traced to changes occuring in the structure of important molecules in a victim's blood. He has won two Nobel Prizes, one for chemistry in 1954 and the Peace Prize in 1962. He is a controversial but highly respected figure in the world of science, and undoubtedly one of the greatest chemists of the 20th Century.

Joseph Priestley (1733-1804) British.
Although he had no formal scientific training, Priestley constructed numerous experiments. In 1774, he discovered oxygen and eventually identified most of the common gases.

Priestley was a schoolteacher, writer and politician, whose radical views on the French Revolution were so unpopular that he emigrated to the United States.

Ernest Rutherford (1871-1937)
New Zealander.
Originally interested in the phenomenon that became known as radio waves, Rutherford worked with J.J. Thomson at Cambridge, succeeding him as Professor there. Rutherford detailed the structure of the atom and was the first person to split an atom. For his work in determining the different types of radiation particles, Rutherford won a Nobel Prize in 1908.

J.J. Thomson (1851-1940) British.
Became a Professor at Cambridge at the age of only 28. His pioneering experimental work led to the discovery of the electron. He also discovered that gases could be made to conduct electricity, so paving the way for radio, television and radar. For this latter research, Thomson was awarded a Nobel Prize in 1906.

*Electrochemistry, 122; Haber process, 100; Covalent, 77.

Glossary

This glossary defines some of the more common terms used in chemistry which are not fully defined in the main text. Any word in the text of an entry which has its own entry in the glossary is followed by a † sign.

Abrasive. A substance capable of rubbing or grinding down another substance. Sand can be described as an abrasive.

Abundance. The measure of how much of a substance exists. It is often expressed as a percentage. For example, silicon is the second most abundant element on earth.

Allotrope. An element that exists in more than one form. For example, diamond and graphite are both solid allotropes of the element carbon. Sulphur has five different allotropes.

Aqueous solution. A solution which has water as its *solvent**. For example, an aqueous solution of ammonia is produced by dissolving ammonia gas in water. An aqueous solution found in an equation is denoted by the state symbol (aq).

Bleach. A substance used to remove colour from a material or solution. Sunlight and oxygen act as bleaches. The most commonly used bleach is sodium chlorate (NaClO). It is formed when sodium hydroxide solution is reacted with chlorine. Household bleaches and cleaners frequently contain sodium chlorate.

Carbon-12. One of the three *isotopes** of the element, carbon, carbon-12 is used as a reference for the calculation of both *relative atomic mass** and the *mole**.

Crystal. A solid whose atoms are arranged in a definite geometric pattern. The edges of crystals are straight and the surfaces flat.

Decompose. To break down substances into other substances. For example, heat decomposes lead(II) nitrate into lead(II) oxide, nitrogen dioxide and oxygen, as shown in the equation below:

$$2Pb(NO_3)_2(s) \longrightarrow 2PbO(s) + 4NO_2(g) + O_2(g)$$

Density. The mass† of a substance divided by its volume† and stated in units of g/cm^3. A substance with a large mass occupying a small volume (such as lead) has a high density. Many gases, have a low mass occupying a large volume. They have a low density. Every substance has its own different density. This helps in identifying substances.

Effervescence. The escape of bubbles of gas from a liquid. A glass of lemonade is described as being effervescent.

Elastic. A solid which can have its shape changed by force, but which returns to its original shape when the force disappears or is removed. For example, rubber is elastic.

Electrochemistry. The branch of chemistry which deals with electrolysis and electricity related areas.

Energy of combustion. The amount of energy released when one mole of a substance burns completely. For example, the energy of combustion of methane is 890 kilojoules per mole.

Evaporation. The change in state of a substance from a liquid to a gas or vapour, at a temperature below the liquid's boiling point. Evaporation requires heat energy and occurs from the surface of the liquid.

Evolve. To form bubbles of a gas during a reaction and then to give off that gas. For example, carbon dioxide is evolved when methane is combusted.

Flammable. A substance which will burst into flames under the right conditions. Inflammable is another word for flammable. Non-flammable is the opposite of flammable.

Food web. A diagram to show how animals obtain energy from different sources. For example, a stickleback in a small pond may eat watersnails and tadpoles which themselves feed on pondweed and algae. A break in the web (for example, a wiping out of algae due to chemical pollution) can be disasterous to the whole web.

Geiger-Muller tube. Commonly known as a geiger counter, it is an instrument used to measure *radioactivity**. When a radioactive particle or ray enters the tube, an argon atom *ionizes**, releasing an electron. The electrons discharge and register as a series of clicks or meter readings.

General formula. A formula which accounts for any member of a particular *homologous series**. For example, the general formula of all *alkenes** is C_nH_{2n}. Ethene has two carbon atoms and twice as many hydrogen atoms as it does carbon atoms. Therefore it has a *chemical formula** of C_2H_4. Propene has three carbon atoms, and so its chemical formula is C_3H_6.

*Solvent, 114; Isotopes, 71; Relative atomic mass, 71; Mole, 92; Radioactivity, 112; Ionize, 76; Homologous series, 106; Alkenes, 107; Chemical formula, 67.

Heavy metals. Metals with a high density, such as lead, mercury and tungsten.

Hydroxide. A substance containing the ion, OH^-. The OH^- ion is negative and causes alkalinity. All alkalis contain OH^- ions. Most hydroxides, with the exceptions of ammonium, potassium, sodium and lithium, are insoluble.

Ignite. To start the process of *combustion**, usually with a spark. The **ignition temperature** of a substance is the lowest temperature at which that substance will combust.

Kelvin. A standard unit of temperature change, named after the scientist, Lord Kelvin. It has the symbol K. One unit Kelvin equals one degree Celsius.

Liquefaction. A change in state, from gas to liquid, of a substance that is a gas at room temperature. This is achieved by cooling and increasing pressure.

Mass. The amount of matter in a substance. Mass is measured in grams and kilograms.

Mineral. A material that occurs naturally but does not come from animals or plants. For example, metal ores, limestone and coal are all minerals.

Oxide. A compound formed by the combination of an element and oxygen only, such as calcium oxide (CaO).

Phosphates. *Salts** of phosphoric acid (H_3PO_4). They are used in fertilizers to replace the phosphorus used up by intensive farming.

Precipitate. An insoluble solid which separates from a solution during a chemical reaction. In the reaction below, lead(II) chloride is left as a precipitate.

$Pb(NO_3)_2$ + $2NaCl$ → $PbCl_2$ + $NaNO_3$
Lead(II)   Sodium   Lead(II)   Sodium
nitrate   chloride   chloride   nitrate

Promoter. Also called an **activator**, this increases the efficiency of a *catalyst**. For example, in the Haber process, the transition metal, molybdenum (Mo), increases the activity of the catalyst iron.

Proteins. A naturally-occurring *polymer** made from chains of *monomers** called **amino acids**. Proteins are used by living cells for growth and the repair of living tissue.

PTFE. An abbreviation for poly(tetrafluoroethene), PTFE is a polymer used as a non-stick, low friction coating on saucepans, frisbees and vehicle bearings.

Raw materials. A substance used at the start of a large-scale chemical process which is converted into a product required by industry. For example, sand, lead(II) oxide and calcium oxide are the raw materials needed to make lead glass.

Sediment. The solid which settles in a *suspension**. The speed at which the sediment collects can be used to determine the average size of the suspension particles.

Solvay process. A process which takes limestone ($CaCO_3(s)$) and brine ($2NaCl(aq)$) and converts them into sodium carbonate ($Na_2CO_3(aq)$ and calcium chloride $CaCl_2(aq)$). The process involves many stages but is a cheap way of producing the valuable alkali, sodium carbonate, from readily available resources.

Sublimation. The change of state from a solid to a gas without passing through the liquid state. For example, graphite sublimes at a temperature of 3730 °C.

Surface tension. The tendency of the surface of a liquid to act as if it was covered by a skin. This is due to the force of attraction between the surface molecules.

Synthesis. The formation of a substance from simpler substances. The term **synthetic** usually applies to an artificial or man-made substance.

Tarnish. To lose shine due to the formation of a dull surface layer. Many metals tarnish when left in contact with the air for a long period of time.

Volume. A measurement of the amount of space occupied by a substance. Volume is usually measured in cubic centimetres (cm^3).

Vulcanization. The process of heating raw natural rubber with sulphur. Vulcanized rubber is harder, tougher and less temperature sensitive than ordinary rubber.

Waves. When an object disturbs its immediate environment, the disturbance travels away from the source in the form of waves. Gamma ray radiation is a form of wave. Other types of wave include light and radio waves.

*Combustion, 74; Salts, 90; Catalyst, 99; Polymer, 108; Monomer, 108; Suspension, 114.

Laboratory apparatus

Equipment used in the laboratory is called **apparatus**. In exams and text books apparatus is usually drawn in a specific, two dimensional way. Below are some common pieces of apparatus.

Beaker

Used to hold liquids.

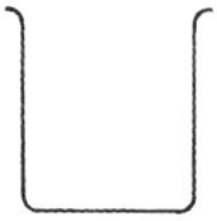

Beehive shelf

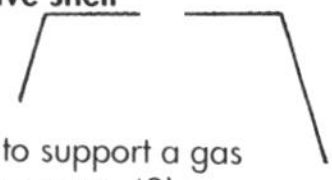

Used to support a gas jar (see page 43).

Buchner flask

Used when liquids are filtered by suction.

Buchner funnel

Used with Buchner flask.

Perforated plate on which filter paper is placed.

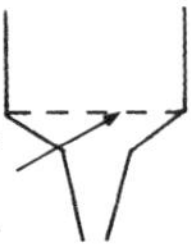

Burette

Used to add accurate volumes of liquid.

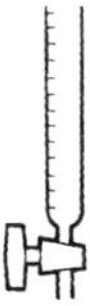

Conical flask

Used to hold liquids.

Crystallizing dish

Holds solutions evaporating into crystals (see page 27).

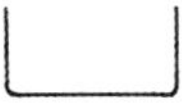

Flat-bottomed flask

Used to hold liquids which do not require heating.

Filter funnel

Used to separate solids from liquids.

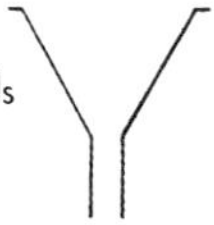

Gas jar

Used when collecting and storing gases.

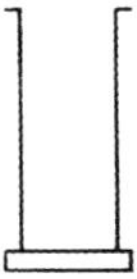

Gauze

Used to spread heat from a flame evenly over the base of an object being heated.

Heating apparatus

The method for supplying heat. This is usually a bunsen or spirit burner.

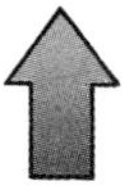

Liebig condenser

Used to condense *vapours** (see page 50).

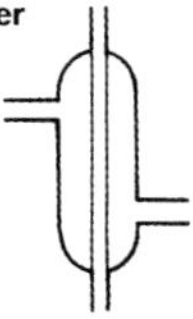

Measuring cylinder

Used to measure approximate volumes of a liquid.

Pipeclay triangle

Used to support objects on a tripod.

Pipette

Used to dispense an accurate volume of liquid.

Round-bottomed flask

Used for heating liquids evenly.

Spatula

Used to handle small amounts of a solid.

Tap funnel

Used to add a controlled volume of a liquid.

Thistle funnel

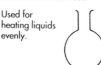

Used to add a liquid to a flask's contents.

Tripod

Used as a stand for flasks and beakers during heating.

  *Vapours, 114.

Drawing and labelling experiments

When writing the report of an experiment, you often have to include a diagram of the laboratory apparatus used to perform the experiment. This must be drawn accurately. It should also be clearly labelled. Most of the symbols for apparatus that you will use in experiments are shown opposite.

For example, the experiment to produce hydrogen in the laboratory (found on page 117) is shown here. The first picture shows a cutaway view of the experiment. The second picture shows a flat diagram drawn with eight common mistakes which you should avoid. The third picture is correctly drawn.

Preparation of hydrogen

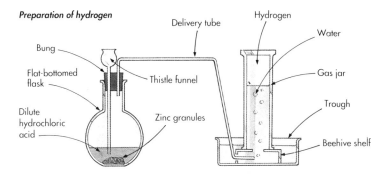

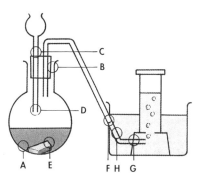

Wrongly drawn experiment

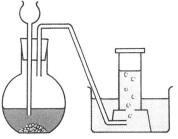

Correctly drawn experiment

A: The flask drawn is round-bottomed. It should be flat-bottomed.

B: The bung is not fitted as tightly as it would be in the laboratory. As a result, gas will escape from the flask.

C: The lines on the bung appear to cut through the stem of the thistle funnel.

D: The end of the thistle funnel should be submerged in the liquid, otherwise the gas formed from the reaction would escape up through the funnel's stem.

E: Although zinc is found in solid bars, the experiment requires zinc granules. Always pay attention to the exact requirements of an experiment.

F: The delivery tube looks as if it has broken through the side of the trough.

G: The beehive shelf is not correctly drawn. As a result, the tube looks as if it is breaking through the shelf.

H: The shaded area depicting water includes the end of the delivery tube. This tube is transporting the hydrogen gas into the gas jar standing on the beehive shelf. It would not be full of water.

Crystals

Crystals are solids with regular geometric shapes. They are formed from the regular arrangement of particles. Crystals have straight edges and flat surfaces called **planes**. They melt at a specific, measurable temperature. Sugar, sulphur and metals are examples of crystals.

A solid with the properties of a crystal is said to be **crystalline**. A substance without those properties is said to be **amorphous** or **vitreous**. Amorphous solids consist of a random arrangement of particles, which result in irregular geometric shapes. Amorphous solids also have no clearly defined melting point. When heated they soften gradually and slowly transform into a liquid state. Glass is an example of an amorphous solid.

Making crystals

The process of forming a crystal is called **crystallization**. There are a number of ways to form a crystal.

One common method involves *evaporating** the solvent from a saturated *solution**. The *solute** that remains behind forms the crystals. Copper sulphate is one type of crystal that can be made in this way.

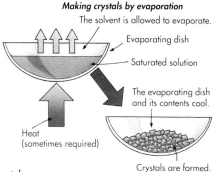

Making crystals by evaporation

The solvent is allowed to evaporate.

Evaporating dish

Saturated solution

The evaporating dish and its contents cool.

Heat (sometimes required)

Crystals are formed.

Using a seed crystal

Glass rod

Thread

Saturated solution

Seed crystal

*Solute** comes out of solution and attaches to seed crystal.

Large crystal is formed.

Mother liquor remains.

A second method uses a small crystal which is placed in a saturated solution of the same substance as the crystal. This crystal is called a **seed crystal**. It acts as a base upon which further crystals can grow. These new crystals will take the shape of the seed crystal. Sodium chloride, aluminium sulphate and potassium crystals can all be made in this way. The solution left after the crystallization process has been completed is called the **mother liquor**.

A practical crystallization process

A modified method of evaporation and crystallization is used to obtain sugar from sugar cane and sugar beet. The diagram opposite shows sugar beets being processed into raw sugar.

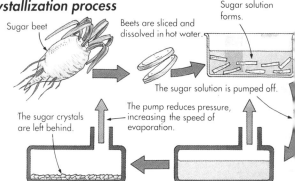

Sugar beet

Beets are sliced and dissolved in hot water.

Sugar solution forms.

The sugar solution is pumped off.

The pump reduces pressure, increasing the speed of evaporation.

The sugar crystals are left behind.

*Evaporating, 114; Saturated solution, 114; Solute, 114.

Shapes of crystals

The particles that make up a crystal can be arranged and bonded in a number of different ways. This means that crystals can come in a range of shapes and sizes. Below are six of the most common crystal shapes.

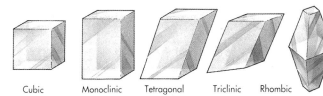

Cubic   Monoclinic   Tetragonal   Triclinic   Rhombic   Hexagonal

Crystal lattice

A crystal consists of millions of small particles packed in a repeating pattern. This structure is called a **crystal lattice**. The shape of a particular crystal depends on its lattice and how this lattice can be split.

A plane of particles along which a crystal can be split is called its **cleavage plane**. The cleavage plane is normally parallel to one of the faces of the crystal. When a crystal is split along its cleavage plane, a flat surface is left. The crystal would shatter if an attempt was made to split it along any other plane.

Split along cleavage plane

Not split along cleavage plane

Polymorphism

Some crystalline substances can exist in two or more different crystal shapes. This is called **polymorphism**. Changes between the types take place at the **transition temperature**.

Polymorphism in elements is called *allotropy**. Sulphur is an allotropic element with a transition temperature of 96°C. It has two stable forms of crystal, as shown in the diagram opposite.

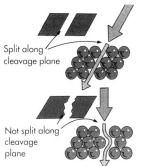

Rhombic sulphur

Monoclinic sulphur

Above transition temperature

Transition temperature 96°C

Below transition temperature

X-ray diffraction

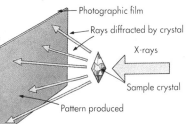

Photographic film

Rays diffracted by crystal

X-rays

Sample crystal

Pattern produced

The technique used to determine the lattice structure of a crystal is called **X-ray diffraction** or **X-ray crystallization**. X-rays are passed through a crystal. They are deflected through the crystal and form a **diffraction pattern**. This pattern is photographed and measured. The information obtained can then be used to work out the structure of the crystal.

Common acids, metal compounds and alloys

Common acids

Here is a list of acids you often come across in everyday life. They are listed together with the substances in which they are commonly found.

Vinegar	-	Acetic
Fruit	-	Ascorbic
Proteins	-	Amino-acids
Perspiration	-	Butyric
Disinfectants	-	Carbolic
Soda water	-	Carbonic
Lemons	-	Citric
Sour milk, cheese	-	Lactic
Linseed oil	-	Linolenic
Apples	-	Malic
Sorrel (a herb)	-	Oxalic
Batteries	-	Sulphuric
Tea, wine	-	Tannic
Grapes	-	Tartaric

Compounds of metals

Below is a list of common metallic compounds found in everyday life. Their common or household names are listed along with their chemical names.

Anaemia tablets	-	Iron (II) sulphate
Blackboard chalk	-	Calcium sulphate
Calamine	-	Zinc carbonate
Caustic soda	-	Sodium hydroxide
Chile saltpetre	-	Sodium nitrate
Blue vitriol	-	Copper sulphate
Epsom salts	-	Magnesium sulphate
Gypsum	-	Calcium sulphate
Plaster of Paris	-	Calcium sulphate
Saltpetre	-	Potassium nitrate
Rust	-	Iron oxide
Soap	-	Sodium stearate
Washing soda	-	Sodium carbonate
Zinc blend	-	Zinc sulphide

Common alloys

Alloy name	Approximate composition	Uses
Brass	Zinc (between 10% and 35%) copper (between 65% and 90%)	Decorative metal work.
Common bronze	Zinc 2%, tin 6%, copper 92%	Machinery and decorative work
Coinage bronze	Zinc 1%, tin 4%, copper 95%	Coins
Dentist's amalgam	Copper 30%, mercury 70%	Dental fillings
Duralumin	Magnesium 0.5%, copper 5%, manganese 0.5%, aluminium 95%	Aircraft frames
Coinage gold	Copper, 10%, gold 90%	Coins
Dental gold	Copper (between 14% and 28%), silver (between 14% and 28%), gold 58%	Dental fillings
Manganin	Nickel 1.5%, manganese 16%, copper 82.5%	Wire used for fuses and resistors.
Nichrome	Chromium 20%, nickel 80%	Wires used for fuses and resistors.
Pewter	Lead 20%, tin 80%	Utensils and decorative work
Coinage silver	Copper 10%, silver 90%	Coins
Solder	Tin 50%, lead 50%	Used to join metal objects together, such as wiring.
Stainless steel	Nickel (between 8% and 20%), chromium (between 10% and 20%), iron (between 60% and 80%)	Utensils, sinks
Tool steel	Chromium (between 2% and 4%), molybdenum (between 6% and 7%), iron (between 90% and 95%)	Tools including hammers, chisels and saws

ESSENTIAL
BIOLOGY

Rebecca Treays
with
Kris Scheinkonig and Peter Richardson

Illustrated by Sean Wilkinson and
Robert Walster
Additional illustrations by Aziz Khan, Ian Jackson and Chris Shields

Designed by Sharon Bennett
Additional designs by Diane Thistlethwaite

Consultants: Jonathan Cook and Sheila Martin
Series editor: Jane Chisholm

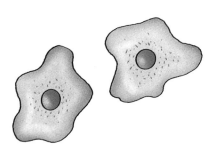

Contents

Using this section of the book

Essential Biology is a concise reference aid which clearly explains the key facts of biology. It is a useful companion to revision, containing the core knowledge needed for examinations. When revising, however, it is always important to check which syllabus you are studying, because different examining bodies require students to learn different material.

This section is arranged in chapters.

Each chapter covers one of the main topics of biology, providing simple yet detailed explanations of all the essential principles and facts. Particularly important words and equations are highlighted in **bold**. Words which are explained more fully on another page are printed in italics with an asterisk, like this: *respiration**. A footnote gives a reference to the page on which the explanation can be found.

The back of this section

The black and white pages at the back of this section provide practical information, such as units of measurement, and tables of indicators and food tests. It includes a guide to conducting experiments, setting up control experiments and recording results. You will also find a classification chart and biological keys.

A note on the illustrations

Many of the illustrations in this section, such as those of cells* and bacteria*, are simplified drawings of specimens as they would be seen under a microscope. A table at the back of this section gives their actual size and the magnification needed to see them.

What is biology?

Biology is the study of all living things, or **organisms**. All organisms, from the smallest to the largest, share certain common features.

●**Feeding**. All living things need food. Plants and animals feed in different ways. Plants make their own food in a process called photosynthesis (see page 148). Animals feed on other animals or plants.

A butterfly feeding

●**Respiration**. All living things get energy from food in a process called respiration (see page 136). Energy is needed for the **metabolism**. This is the general term for all the chemical reactions which occur in the body.

●**Excretion**. Metabolism produces some poisonous waste products which have to be removed. Getting rid of them is called excretion.

●**Growth**. All living things grow. Growth produces a permanent increase in size. Different organisms grow in different ways. Plants such as trees go on growing throughout their lives. Animals usually stop growing when they reach a certain age.

●**Movement**. All living things can move. Plant movement tends to be slow and difficult to see, such as the turning of leaves towards light. Animals usually move their whole bodies and can travel from one place to another. This form of movement is called **locomotion**.

●**Sensitivity**. All living things detect and respond to changes in their surroundings. Many organisms respond to light. Crocuses, for example, open their petals to the sun. Highly developed animals react much faster to light, closing their eyes or moving away if it is too bright.

●**Reproduction**. All living things produce new versions of themselves, called their **offspring**. This prevents populations dying out.

Structure of living things

All living things are made of one or more units called **cells**. Cells carry out all the chemical processes necessary for life. Each one is like a factory that makes products to repair its own machinery, and products for other factories. Each part of the cell, called an **organelle**, is like a different department doing its own job. Although different types of cells carry out different tasks within an organism, they all have the same basic structure.

Animal and plant cells

These diagrams show examples of a typical animal and plant cell. All cells share certain features: a nucleus, cytoplasm, and a cell membrane. Other features are common only to plant cells: a cell wall, a large vacuole and chloroplasts.

Typical animal cell

The **nucleus** is the 'control centre' of the cell, containing long thin threads called *chromosomes**. Chromosomes are made up of a complex chemical called *DNA** which directs all the activities of the cell.

Cytoplasm is a watery jelly-like solution in which all the chemical reactions of the cell (known as the metabolism) take place.

The **cell membrane** is a barrier between the cytoplasm and the cell's surroundings. It is **selectively-permeable**, which means that only certain substances can pass through it.

Typical plant cell

The large **vacuole** is a fluid-filled sac which holds water and the products of the cell's metabolism.

Chloroplasts are the structures that make plants green. They contain a green pigment called **chlorophyll** and are needed to make food in a process called *photosynthesis**.

The **cell wall** is a strong mesh made of tough fibres called **cellulose**. Its main function is to protect the plant cell and to help it keep its shape.

Nucleus

Cell membrane

Cytoplasm

Cells under the electron microscope

The diagrams above show cells seen through a *light microscope** which magnifies objects hundreds of times. By the 1950s a more advanced microscope, called the electron microscope, had enabled scientists to magnify objects thousands of times. This made it possible to study cells much more closely. New organelles were discovered in the cytoplasm and others were seen more clearly. More was understood about how cells worked.

Typical animal cell under an electron microscope

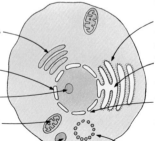

Parts seen more clearly:

The **golgi body** collects and distributes the cell's products in special sacs.

The **nuclear membrane** separates DNA from the cytoplasm.

The **nucleolus** makes ribosomes.

The **mitochondrion** is where *respiration** takes place.

Small impermanent vacuole

Parts seen for the first time:

Ribosomes help build up complex substances called *proteins**.

The **endoplasmic reticulum** transports materials around the cell.

The **nuclear pore** lets substances move between the cytoplasm and the nucleus.

The **centriole** is involved in *cell division**.

132 *Chromosome, 166; DNA, 135; Photosynthesis, 148; Light microscope, 177; Respiration 136; Protein 134; Cell division, 170.

Cells with special functions

Different types of cells are adapted to perform different functions. This is called **specialization**. Two examples of specialized cells in humans are given below.

Ciliated cells

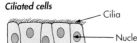

Ciliated cells are found in the nose and windpipe. On their surface they have thin strands of cytoplasm called **cilia** (sing. **cilium**). These beat to and fro causing a stream of liquid called mucus to carry dust and germs out of the body.

Pavement cells are flat and thin with a large surface area. This allows substances to pass through them very easily. They are ideal for lining tubes (such as *capillaries**) or air spaces (such as in the lungs) through which liquids and gases need to pass.

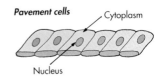

Pavement cells

Building with cells

Cells of the same type combine to form **tissue.** One of the simplest types of tissue is **epithelium**, which is made up of pavement cells. Other examples of tissues are blood and muscle.

Different types of tissue combine to make up **organs** such as the heart. The tissues in an organ work together to perform specific functions.

Organs are grouped together into **systems.** For example, the digestive system contains four organs: the stomach, intestine, liver and pancreas (see page 138).

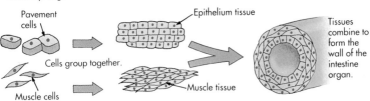

Pavement cells → Epithelium tissue

Cells group together.

Muscle cells → Muscle tissue

Tissues combine to form the wall of the intestine organ.

Diffusion

All substances are made up of particles called *molecules**. If a substance is in solution or in the form of a gas, the molecules of that substance will spread themselves out, until they are evenly spaced. Particles will always move from an area of high concentration, where there are many of them, into an area of low concentration, where there are fewer. This is called **diffusion.**

The difference in concentration between the two regions is called the **concentration gradient.** The steeper the concentration gradient (the bigger the difference in concentrations), the faster diffusion occurs.

When a potassium permanganate crystal is placed in a beaker of water its molecules diffuse until they are evenly spaced throughout the water.

Potassium permanganate crystal

Many substances get into and out of cells by diffusion. Waste materials which are highly concentrated inside the cell diffuse out of it. Raw materials which are more concentrated outside the cell diffuse into it.

---

*Capillary, 144; Molecule, 134.

Chemistry of life

A **molecule** is the smallest unit of a substance that can exist on its own. Each molecule consists of one or more tiny particles called **atoms.** The different types of atoms are called **elements.** The main elements in living things are carbon, hydrogen, nitrogen and oxygen. Most substances, however, are **compounds**, which means that their molecules are made up of different types of atoms.

Substances which contain carbon atoms are called **organic. Inorganic** substances contain no carbon.

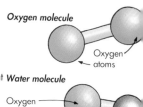

Oxygen molecule

Oxygen atoms

Water molecule

Oxygen atom

Hydrogen atoms

Organic substances

There are four main groups of organic molecules that make up and maintain the cells in all living things: proteins, carbohydrates, fats, and nucleic acids.

● **Proteins** are substances needed for growth and the repair of cells. They are made from atoms of carbon, hydrogen, oxygen, nitrogen and sulphur. Proteins are large molecules made up of smaller units called **amino acids.**

Part of a protein molecule

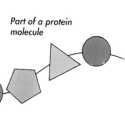

Amino acids

Plants make proteins from the products of *photosynthesis** and other molecules they get from the soil. Animals eat plant proteins and break them down into amino acids. They then rebuild the amino acids into animal proteins.

Enzymes are protein molecules which act as biological *catalysts**, speeding up chemical reactions in the body. Each enzyme attaches itself to one type of molecule, called the **substrate**, and builds it up or breaks it down into new molecules called **products**. The enzyme remains unchanged and is used again and again. Enzymes work best within a narrow range of temperature and *pH**.

How enzymes work

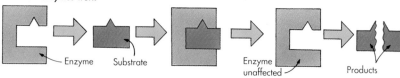

Enzyme   Substrate

Enzyme unaffected

Products

● **Carbohydrates** are an important source of energy. They are made up of carbon, hydrogen and oxygen.

One of the simplest carbohydrates is **glucose**, which is made by plants during photosynthesis. Animals get glucose through their diet. It is then broken down in *respiration** to release energy.

Animals and plants both store any glucose they do not immediately need. In plants, glucose molecules join together to form larger carbohydrate molecules called **starch.** In animals, glucose molecules combine to form **glycogen** molecules. Both starch and glycogen are reconverted to glucose when the organism needs energy.

*Cellulose** is a carbohydrate found in plant cell walls. It cannot be digested by mammals, but is important because it provides **roughage,** coarse material which helps food move through the gut.

*Photosynthesis, 148; Catalyst, 188; pH, 188; Respiration, 136; Cellulose, 132.

• **Fats** are an energy-rich store, respired after supplies of carbohydrate are exhausted. Mammals store some fat under the skin to help keep them warm. One fat molecule consists of three chains of chemicals, called **fatty acids**, attached to one molecule of **glycerol**.

• **Nucleic acids** are molecules found in the cell's nucleus. There are two types of nucleic acid. **Deoxyribonucleic acid (DNA)** is a large molecule twisted in a spiral staircase shape. The chemicals within the DNA molecule are arranged as a code, storing special *genetic** information. This is a series of instructions which directs all the activities of the cell (see page 166).

Ribonucleic acid (RNA) is a copy of part of the genetic information found in DNA. It carries genetic code from the nucleus to the cytoplasm, where it is used to build up proteins from amino acids.

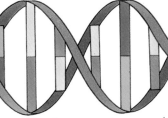

Part of DNA molecule
(Some of it is shown untwisted)

• **Vitamins** are organic compounds needed in the diet. Two of the most important vitamins for humans are vitamins C and D.

Vitamin C is needed for the growth and repair of tissue. Citrus fruit and green vegetables are good sources. Lack of vitamin C causes a disease called **scurvy** in which the skin and gums bleed.

Vitamin D is found in liver or is made by the action of sunlight on the skin. It helps the body absorb calcium, a mineral (see below) needed for strong bones and teeth. Without it, bones become weakened by a disease called **rickets.**

Inorganic substances

• **Water** makes up about 70% of living cells. It is vital to all organisms as the chemical reactions of the cell can only take place in solution. It is also important for carrying dissolved substances around the cell.

• **Minerals** are inorganic substances containing certain chemical elements essential to the health of all organisms. The table below shows the main elements which plants require from minerals.

Element	Use in plant
Nitrogen	Makes up part of proteins
Sulpher	Makes up part of proteins
Iron	Makes up part of the enzyme which makes *chlorophyll**
Magnesium	Makes up part of chlorophyll
Calcium	Helps glue cell walls together

A balanced diet

For a healthy diet humans need the right combination of proteins, carbohydrates, fats, vitamins, minerals and water. People who do not eat healthily become **malnourished.** When people eat too much the extra food is stored under their skin and they become **obese.** When people eat too little they lose weight, as their fat stores are broken down to provide energy. In severe cases fat stores are used up and the body breaks down essential protein tissues for energy.

*Genetic, 166; Chlorophyll, 132.

Energy from food

When food is burned its energy is set free as heat. Living things release energy from food, not through burning but by a complex chemical process called **respiration**. Respiration which uses oxygen is called **aerobic respiration**. Food, usually in the form of glucose, is broken down with oxygen, releasing energy and producing water and carbon dioxide.

Food + Oxygen → **Enzymes** → Energy + Carbon + Water dioxide

Some energy from respiration is set free as heat. The rest is stored in special molecules called **ATP** (adenosine triphosphate). When energy is needed ATP breaks down into **ADP** (adenosine diphosphate) releasing its stored energy.

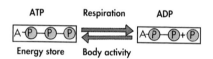

ATP   Respiration   ADP

A-P—P—P   A-P—P+P

Energy store   Body activity

Investigation to show that small animals take in oxygen for respiration

Method†
Set up the apparatus as shown. Also set up a control experiment excluding the woodlice. Leave both sets of apparatus for 60 minutes.

Result and conclusion
During respiration the volume of oxygen taken in is equal to the volume of carbon dioxide given out. This means that in normal circumstances the volume of gases in the tube would remain the same. However, in this experiment, the carbon dioxide produced is absorbed by the soda lime, so the volume of gas in the tube is reduced. The coloured water moves up the capillary tube to fill the space left by the removal of oxygen, showing that small animals take in oxygen.

Respirometer — Airtight bung — Rubber tubing — Closed screw clip — Capillary tube — Soda lime — Coloured water — Woodlice

Energy values

The amount of energy that can be released from a particular type of food is called its **energy value**. Different types of food have different energy values (see table below). Energy can be measured in calories. One **calorie** is the heat energy needed to raise the temperature of 1 gram of water through 1°C. These days however, scientists measure energy in **joules** (J) or **kilojoules** (kJ) (1000J). One calorie equals 4.2 joules.

1g of food	Energy value	Example of food source
Carbohydrate	16kJ	bread, sugar
Fat	39kJ	butter, corn oil
Protein	23kJ	meat, milk

Energy requirements

All organisms need energy to perform many of the essential functions of life, such as growth, transport and repair. The amount of energy required by an organism depends on how active it is. The table below shows the average daily energy requirements of humans with different levels of activity.

Person type	kJ/per day
Baby	3000
Teenage girl	9500
Teenage boy	11500
Pregnant woman	10000
Male office worker	11000
Manual labourer	15000

†For more about experiments and control experiments see page 182.

Investigation to find the amount of energy in a peanut

It is known that 4.2J (1 calorie) can heat 1g of water through 1°C. Therefore the energy value of a substance can be estimated when it is burned. The energy released is used to heat a known quantity of water.

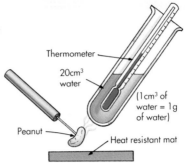

Thermometer

20cm³ water

(1cm³ of water = 1g of water)

Peanut

Heat resistant mat

Method
Put 20cm³ of water in a test tube and record its temperature. Weigh a peanut and set it alight. Hold it under the tube until it stops burning. Record any change in water temperature.

Result and conclusion
The energy released by the peanut in joules is the mass of water in grams x the rise in temperature in °C x 4.2.

To convert joules to kilojoules divide by 1000. The energy in 1 gram of peanut is the energy value of the whole nut divided by its original weight. This result is approximate as it can not measure all the heat given off, such as the heat lost to the air.

Respiration without oxygen

Many cells and organisms produce energy when there is no oxygen available. This is called **anaerobic respiration**. (Anaerobic means without oxygen.) It is less efficient than aerobic respiration because glucose is not broken down as completely. The products of anaerobic respiration vary according to the organism.

When animals respire anaerobically they release energy and produce a substance called lactic acid.

This process takes place in human body cells during hard exercise, when the muscles require lots of energy, but oxygen cannot reach them fast enough. Lactic acid is a mild poison and causes cramp. Immediately after exercise, it must be broken down into carbon dioxide and water using oxygen. The oxygen used is said to be 'repaying the oxygen debt'.

Yeast respires anaerobically producing carbon dioxide and alcohol. This is called **alcoholic fermentation** (see page 109).

Glucose ➡ Energy + Lactic acid

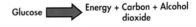

Glucose ➡ Energy + Carbon dioxide + Alcohol

Investigating the optimum temperature for fermentation

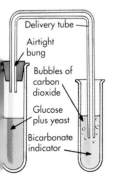

Delivery tube

Airtight bung

Bubbles of carbon dioxide

Glucose plus yeast

Bicarbonate indicator

Method
Set up the apparatus in water baths of temperatures ranging from 0°C to 40°C. After one hour count the bubbles of carbon dioxide produced in one minute at each temperature. This can be taken as a measure of the rate of fermentation. Repeat three times and find an average number of bubbles at each temperature. Plot the results as a graph.

Result and conclusion

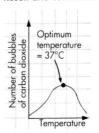

Optimum temperature = 37°C

Number of bubbles of carbon dioxide

Temperature

Breaking down food

As food passes through the body, large food molecules are broken down into smaller molecules tiny enough to diffuse into the blood. This is called **digestion.** Food is digested in two ways. It is broken down physically by chewing and churning, and chemically by the action of **digestive juices.** These juices contain enzymes, and are secreted by special organs, called **glands.**

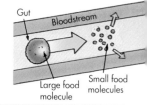

Gut

Bloodstream

Large food molecule

Small food molecules

The human digestive system

Food passes from the mouth into the gut or **alimentary canal,** a long tube running from the mouth to the anus.

The diagram below shows what happens to food and the digestive juices which act on it.

Food is chewed and mixed with **saliva** in the **mouth.**

The **liver** produces a fluid called **bile** which is stored in the gall bladder.

Gall bladder

The **small intestine** consists of the duodenum and the ileum.

Bile and pancreatic juice act on food in the **duodenum.**

The **ileum** produces juices which complete digestion. Digested foods are absorbed into the bloodstream.

Caecum (pl. **caeca**) - no function in humans

Appendix (pl. **appendixes**) no function in humans

Oesophagus (food passage)

Food is churned up with **gastric juices** in the **stomach.**

A muscular ring called the **pyloric sphincter** stops food leaving the stomach until it is properly mixed.

The **pancreas** produces **pancreatic juice.**

The **large intestine** consists of the colon and the rectum.

Undigested food passes into the **colon.** Water is absorbed into the bloodstream.

The **rectum** stores undigested food as **faeces.**

Strong muscle contractions in the rectum remove faeces through the **anus.**

Anal sphincter (muscular ring)

Enzyme and bile digestion

Digestive juice	Produced by	Digestive enzyme	Food acted on	Product
Saliva	Salivary glands in mouth	Amylase	Starch	Maltose
Gastric juice	Gastric glands in stomach wall	Pepsin	Protein	Peptides
Bile	Liver	Bile salts (not enzymes)	Fat	Fat droplets
Pancreatic juice	Pancreas	Amylase Trypsin Lipase	Starch Protein Fat	Maltose Peptides Fatty acids
Intestinal juice	Intestinal glands in small intestine	Maltase Peptidase	Maltose Peptides	Glucose Amino acids

How food moves through the gut

The gut is surrounded by circular and longitudinal muscles. While the longitudinal muscles relax, the circular muscles contract, pushing food along the gut. This is called **peristalsis**. The production of a slippery mucus makes food passage easier.

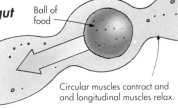

Ball of food

Circular muscles contract and and longitudinal muscles relax.

The ileum

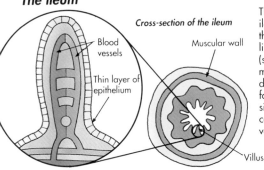

Cross-section of the ileum

Blood vessels

Thin layer of epithelium

Muscular wall

Villus

The surface area of the ileum is greatly increased by thousands of small finger-like projections called **villi** (sing. **villus**) This allows more efficient absorption of digested foods. Digested foods diffuse through the single layer of *epithelium* cells and pass into the blood vessels in the villi.

The liver

Absorbed foods are carried in the blood to the liver where they are 'processed' before they reach the rest of the body.
● Poisonous substances are made less harmful.
● Excess amino acids are broken down in a process called **deamination.** The part of the amino acid which contains

nitrogen is converted to a substance called **urea** and is excreted (see page 150). The remaining part of the amino acid is broken down or converted to glucose.
● Excess glucose is stored as *glycogen*
● Some vitamins and minerals are also stored.

Digestion in herbivores

Animals can be grouped according to their diet. **Carnivores** eat meat, **herbivores** eat plants, and **omnivores** eat both plants and meat.

The bulk of a herbivore's diet is made up of *cellulose**. Mammals are not able to digest cellulose but certain *bacteria** can. Herbivores have special adaptations so the bacteria can live inside their gut and do the job for them. Some herbivores, such as rabbits, have an enlarged appendix and caecum in which the bacteria live. The bacteria break down the cellulose for them, so it can be absorbed. In

other herbivores, such as cows, the bacteria are found in a special chamber in their stomach, called a **rumen.**

Herbivores' intestines are relatively long to allow more time for digestion and absorption.

Digestive system of the rabbit

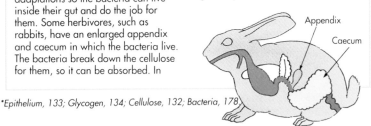

Appendix

Caecum

*Epithelium, 133; Glycogen, 134; Cellulose, 132; Bacteria, 178.

139

Teeth and food capture

Most *vertebrates** have teeth. Teeth are used for getting food into the mouth and for breaking it down mechanically by chewing. Compared with other organisms, mammals have very complex teeth.

There are four types, all with the same basic structure, which perform different tasks within the mouth. These four types of teeth (shown below) are adapted to suit the diets of different mammals.

The structure of a typical tooth

The part of the tooth that can be seen is called the **crown.**

The **pulp cavity** contains blood vessels and *nerves endings**.

Tough fibres between the jaw bone and cement keep the tooth in place and act as shock absorbers.

Jaw bone

The **enamel** is a hard layer surrounding the crown for biting and grinding.

Dentine is a bone-like substance that supports the tooth.

The **root** anchors the tooth in the jaw.

The tough layer which surrounds the root is called the **cement.**

Types of mammalian teeth

Incisors are chisel-shaped teeth used for biting off small pieces of food.

Canines are longer, more pointed teeth. They are used for piercing and killing prey, and tearing off larger pieces of food.

Molars and **premolars** are the cheek teeth. Both have broad bumpy surfaces for grinding food. Molars are bigger than premolars.

Human teeth

Humans develop 20 'milk' teeth in the first few years of life. By about the age of 12, milk teeth have fallen out, to be replaced by 32 permanent teeth.

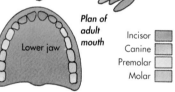

Plan of adult mouth

Lower jaw

Incisor	
Canine	
Premolar	
Molar	

Carnivore and herbivore teeth

● Carnivores have teeth adapted to killing their prey and eating meat.

Carnivore's skull

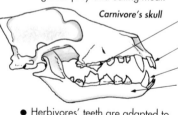

Carnassials are cheek teeth with elongated crowns. They slide past each other, like scissors, snipping small pieces of meat and scraping flesh off bones.

Incisors meet and grip for pulling small bits of food.

Extra long canines kill prey and tear its flesh.

The jaw bone moves up and down in a powerful biting action.

● Herbivores' teeth are adapted to a diet of plant food.

The lower jaw moves from side to side in a strong grinding action, to break down *cellulose** This action wears hard ridges of enamel in the cheek teeth, which act as grinding edges.

In place of canine teeth, herbivores have a gap called a **diastema** where food is kept when it is not being chewed.

Incisors on the lower jaw act with a hard pad on the top jaw to cut and pull up grass.

Herbivore's skull

*Vertebrate, 178; Nerve ending, 152; Cellulose, 132.

Tooth decay

*Bacteria** in the mouth feed on sugar left on the teeth and form a mixture called **plaque.** The bacteria release acids that dissolve the tooth's enamel and dentine, making **cavities** (holes) and causing slight toothache. Toothache worsens if bacterial decay reaches the pulp cavity.

If the root starts to decay, an abcess can form and pain will increase. The bacteria in plaque can also irritate the gums. The gums become red and inflamed and may bleed slightly when the teeth are brushed. This is called **periodontal disease.**

The stages of tooth decay

 1 2 3 4

Preventing tooth decay

A healthy diet without too much sugar and frequent teeth-cleaning can reduce the risk of tooth decay. Regular visits to the dentist can prevent decay spreading. The dentist can fill in any holes in the enamel with fillings before decay gets too serious. A mineral called fluoride is believed to strengthen the resistance of enamel to plaque. It can be taken as tablets or in toothpaste.

Feeding in non-vertebrates

Organisms without teeth have various different ways of taking in and digesting their food, using different parts of their bodies.

Bacteria and *fungi** secrete enzymes on to *organic** matter. The enzymes break down the organic matter externally and the digested food is then absorbed by the organism. Some organisms feed on dead organic matter. These are called **saprophytes.** Others feed on living organisms and are called **parasites.**

Fungi feeding on bread

*Amoebas** surround their food with their cytoplasm (see right). This forms a food vacuole into which enzymes are secreted and where digestion takes place. ▶

Food vacuole

Amoeba

Typical arrangement of insect mouthparts (grasshopper)

Mandibles grind up food.

Maxillae push food into mouth.

Labium protects other mouthparts.

◀ All insects have three basic mouthparts: the mandibles, the maxillae (sing. maxilla) and the labium (see opposite). The appearance of these mouthparts differs according to the insect's feeding methods. In mosquitoes, for example, the maxillae fit together into a **proboscis,** a long tube for sucking blood.

Mussels are **filter feeders.** They draw water into their shells and over special *gills** which filter out small food particles. Rows of beating *cilia** sweep food into the opening of the gut. ▶

*Bacteria, 178; Fungi, 178; Organic, 134; Amoeba, 178; Gill, 143; Cilia, 133.

141

Gaseous exchange

During respiration cells use up oxygen and produce carbon dioxide. Most organisms take the oxygen needed to respire from their external environment and release waste carbon dioxide back into it. The process by which these gases diffuse into and out of a body is called **gaseous exchange**.

Respiratory surfaces

The place where gaseous exchange occurs is called a **respiratory surface**. All respiratory surfaces must have:

● a permeable surface to allow diffusion;
● a moist surface to dissolve the gases (as they can only diffuse in solution);
● a means of receiving and removing a steady flow of gases;

● a means of transporting the gases to and from the cells.

In unicellular organisms, gases diffuse across the organism's entire surface, and move within it by diffusion. Larger organisms need specialized respiratory surfaces to exchange gases with their environment, and *transport systems** to carry the gases to and from the cells.

Gaseous exchange in humans

In humans the lungs are the main respiratory surface. They are found side-by-side in the **thorax** (chest cavity).

Together with the tubes that connect them to the outside of the body, they make up the **respiratory system**.

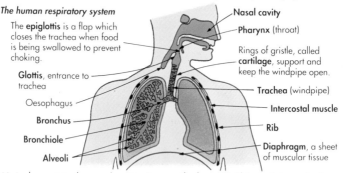

The human respiratory system

The **epiglottis** is a flap which closes the trachea when food is being swallowed to prevent choking.

Glottis, entrance to trachea

Oesophagus

Bronchus

Bronchiole

Alveoli

Nasal cavity

Pharynx (throat)

Rings of gristle, called **cartilage**, support and keep the windpipe open.

Trachea (windpipe)

Intercostal muscle

Rib

Diaphragm, a sheet of muscular tissue

Air is drawn into the nasal cavity via the nostrils. The air passes down to the pharynx and into the trachea via a small hole called the glottis. The trachea divides into two branches, the bronchi (sing. bronchus), which lead to the lungs. Within each lung, the bronchi divide into branches called bronchioles. Each bronchiole ends in a cluster of air sacs called alveoli (sing. alveolus). In the alveoli gases are exchanged between the air and the blood.

The alveoli

Blood flowing into the lungs has a low concentration of oxygen and a high concentration of carbon dioxide. The air filling the alveoli has a high concentration of oxygen and a low concentration of carbon dioxide. Oxygen and carbon dioxide diffuse across the thin walls of the alveoli and *capillaries**. Blood flows away from the lungs with more oxygen and less carbon dioxide than before gaseous exchange. Air leaves the lungs with more carbon dioxide and less oxygen.

The alveoli

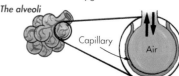

Capillary

Air

*Transport system, 144; Capillary, 144.

Ventilation of the lungs

The movement of air in and out of the lungs is called **ventilation**. It involves **inhalation**, which is breathing in, and **exhalation**, which is breathing out.

The **pleural cavity** is a fluid filled space which stops the lungs rubbing against the rib-cage during breathing.

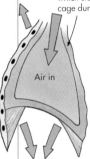

Air in

Inhalation

The intercostal muscles and diaphragm contract. The rib cage expands. The volume of the thorax increases lowering *air pressure** in the lungs. Air rushes into the lungs to equalize air pressures in and outside the body.

Air out

Exhalation

The intercostal muscles and diaphragm relax. The volume of the thorax decreases. Air pressure in the lungs becomes higher than outside the body. Air is expelled from the body until the pressures are equal.

Investigation to compare exhaled and inhaled air.

Method

Set up the apparatus and breathe in and out of the tube where indicated.

Result and conclusion

The limewater in tube B turns cloudy, showing that exhaled air contains enough carbon dioxide to turn limewater milky but inhaled air does not.

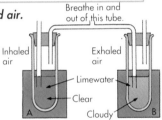

Breathe in and out of this tube.

Inhaled air

Exhaled air

Limewater

Clear

A

Cloudy

B

Respiratory surfaces in fish and insects

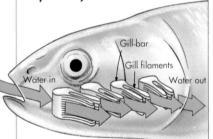

Gill-bar

Gill filaments

Water in

Water out

Fish use **gills** for gas exchange. Gills are made up of fine branches called **gill filaments** containing many blood vessels. As water flows over the gill filaments, oxygen diffuses into the blood, and carbon dioxide diffuses from the blood into the water.

Insects exchange gases through a network of tubes, called **tracheae** (sing. **trachea**), which extend to all parts of the insect. Each tube opens at the surface at a tiny pore called a **spiracle**. Air passes down the trachea. Oxygen diffuses through the tube walls into the cells, while carbon dioxide diffuses in the opposite direction.

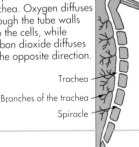

Trachea

Branches of the trachea

Spiracle

*Air pressure, 188.

Transport in animals

All organisms carry raw materials to their cells and remove waste products from them. Most unicellular organisms, such as *amoebas** transport substances by diffusion. Larger organisms require a **transport system**. The movement of materials using a transport system is called **mass flow**.

In mammals, mass flow is carried out by the **circulatory system**. This consists of the **blood**, a liquid which carries materials to and from the cells, the **heart** which pumps blood around the body, and **blood vessels** (**arteries**, **veins** and **capillaries**), tubes which carry the blood (see 'Blood vessels' table below).

The human circulatory system

Humans have a **double circulation.** This means that blood passes through the heart twice on its journey around the body. Blood is pumped to the lungs by the right side of the heart. It then returns to the left side of the heart, from where it is pumped around the rest of the body.

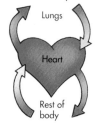

Lungs
Heart
Rest of body

Simplified human circulatory system

- Head and arms
- Pulmonary artery
- Pulmonary vein
- Vena cava
- Aorta
- Hepatic vein
- Hepatic artery
- Liver
- Hepatic portal vein
- Mesenteric artery
- Renal artery
- Renal vein
- Legs and abdomen

Lungs
Intestines
Kidneys

■ **Deoxygenated blood**
■ **Oxygenated blood**

As blood travels around the body, substances diffuse through the walls of the capillaries into a solution called **tissue fluid.** Body cells extract the materials they need from the tissue fluid and release waste products into it. The tissue fluid is then reabsorbed into the blood via the capillaries or the lymphatic system. The **lymphatic system** is a series of small **lymph tubes** which join to form larger ducts. These empty into the blood near the vena cava.

The composition of blood changes as different materials are exchanged between it and the different organs.

Capillary
Cells
Tissue fluid
Vein
Lymph tube
A capillary bed
Artery

Place in body	Composition of blood	
	Gains	Loses
All tissues except lungs	Carbon dioxide	Oxygen, dissolved foods
Lungs Ileum	Oxygen Dissolved food	Carbon dioxide
Liver	*Urea**	Glucose, vitamins, minerals
Kidney		Salts, water, urea

Blood vessels

Comparison	Artery	Vein	Capillary
Cross section	Muscle wall — Lumen		Thin *epithelium** wall
Wall structure	Thick and elastic	Thin	Very thin for easy diffusion
Valves	Heart only	Present	None
Oxygen content in blood	High	Low	Loses oxygen to cells
	(except in pulmonary vessels)		
Pulse	Strong near heart	None	None
Blood travel	Away from heart	Towards heart	From arteries to veins

*Amoeba, 178; Urea, 139; Epithelium, 133.

The heart

The heart is a muscular organ which, unlike other muscles, never tires. It consists of four chambers: two **atria** (sing. **atrium**) and two **ventricles.**

Cross section of the heart

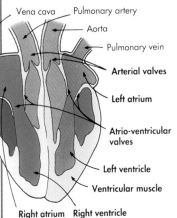

Vena cava — Pulmonary artery
— Aorta
— Pulmonary vein
— **Arterial valves**
— **Left atrium**
— **Atrio-ventricular valves**
— **Left ventricle**
— **Ventricular muscle**
Right atrium   Right ventricle

At rest, the heart pumps about 70 times a minute. During exercise, this rate increases because the cells need a more rapid supply of oxygen. Each pumping action involves two phases: the relaxation and then contraction of the ventricular muscle.

The ventricular muscles relax and blood flows from the atria into the ventricles. The arterial valves close to prevent blood flowing into the ventricles from the arteries.

Heart relaxes (left side only)

The ventriclular muscles contract and blood flows up the pulmonary artery and aorta. The atrio-ventricular valves close to stop blood being pushed into the atria.

Heart contracts (left side only)

Blood structure and function

Blood is a tissue made up of plasma, platelets and two types of cells: red blood cells and white blood cells.

Plasma is a watery liquid which transports dissolved food and waste. It also carries important proteins, such as enzymes and *hormones*.

Red blood cells are disc-shaped cells made in the *bone marrow*. They have no nucleus but contain a red pigment called **haemoglobin** which carries oxygen around the body. When red blood cells pass through the lungs, oxygen combines with haemoglobin to form **oxyhaemoglobin.** As the blood circulates around the body, oxyhaemoglobin breaks down and oxygen is released to the tissues. The haemoglobin returns to the lungs to pick up more oxygen.

White blood cells are large cells, important in body defence (see page 157).

Platelets are tiny cell fragments important in blood clotting.

Blood clotting

When blood from a cut comes into contact with the air, the platelets start off a complex series of steps which stop the blood flowing. This is called **clotting.** It prevents excess blood loss and stops *bacteria* entering the wound. In the final step, a blood protein called **fibrinogen** is turned into a mesh of clotting fibres called **fibrin.**

Oxygen collected at lungs
Haemoglobin ⇄ Oxyhaemoglobin
Oxygen released at tissues

Blood smear seen through a light microscope

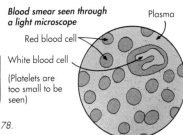

Plasma
Red blood cell
White blood cell
(Platelets are too small to be seen)

*Hormone, 154; Bone marrow, 158; Bacteria, 178.

145

Transport in plants

Plants transport water and minerals from their roots up to their leaves. Water is used in *photosynthesis** to make glucose. The minerals are used to build up complex chemicals, such as proteins.

These products are then transported to other parts of the plant, where the glucose is stored as starch or used in respiration, and the proteins are used for growth and the repair of tissue.

Vascular tissue

The tissue involved in transport is called **vascular tissue**. It is made up of two parts: xylem and phloem. **Xylem** carries water and minerals up the plant (see below). **Phloem** carries dissolved foods such as glucose around the plant. Food transport involves a complex process called **translocation**. It is not known exactly how translocation works, except that it requires energy. Transport that uses energy is called **active transport**.

Section of vascular tissue

Xylem vessels —

Cambium is a tissue separating xylem and phloem. It produces new xylem and phloem tissue.

Phloem vessels —

The diagrams below show the arrangement of vascular tissue in the roots and stems of plants. Xylem is coloured red, and phloem blue.

Cross section of stem

Cortex - tissue found inside stems and roots

Cross section of root

Cambium —
Cortex —
Root hair —

Water transport in plants

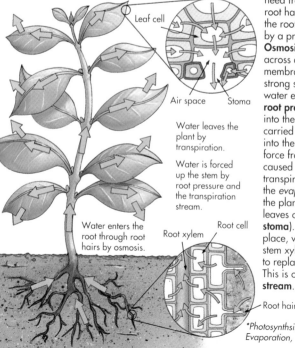

Leaf cell

Air space   Stoma

Water leaves the plant by transpiration.

Water is forced up the stem by root pressure and the transpiration stream.

Water enters the root through root hairs by osmosis.

Root cell   Root xylem

Root hair

Plants obtain the water they need from the soil. It enters the root hairs and passes through the root cells to the root xylem by a process called osmosis. **Osmosis** is the flow of water across a *selectively-permeable** membrane, from a weak to a strong solution. The pressure of water entering the root (called **root pressure**) pushes water up into the stem xylem. Water is carried up the stem xylem and into the leaves by a sucking force from above. This is caused by a process called transpiration. **Transpiration** is the *evaporation** of water out of the plant, through pores in the leaves called **stomata** (sing. **stoma**). As transpiration takes place, water is forced up the stem xylem and into the leaves, to replace the water that is lost. This is called the **transpiration stream**.

*Photosynthsis, 148; Selectively-permeable, 13 Evaporation, 188.

The rate of transpiration

The speed at which a plant loses water depends a lot on the conditions around it. The rate of transpiration of plants in different conditions can be measured using an apparatus called a potometer (see below).

Investigation to measure the rate of transpiration

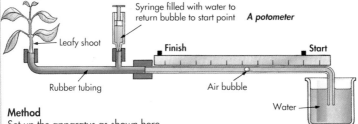

Leafy shoot

Syringe filled with water to return bubble to start point *A potometer*

Finish　　　**Start**

Rubber tubing　　　Air bubble

Water

Method
Set up the apparatus as shown here. Introduce an air bubble by lifting the capillary tube out of the water and touching the end with blotting paper. Replace it immediately. Time how long it takes for the air bubble to travel between the start and finish points. The faster the bubble travels, the faster transpiration is taking place. Repeat under different conditions of temperature, humidity, wind and light.

Result
The experiments show that the rate of transpiration increases with increased temperature, lower humidity (less water in air), stronger winds and more light.

Conclusion
A hot sunny day with dry winds would provide conditions for a high level of transpiration. High temperatures provide more heat energy, which enables more water to be evaporated. Low humidity leads to a large *concentration gradient**, which makes water vapour diffuse more quickly out of the leaves. Winds maintain the concentration gradient by blowing water vapour away from the leaf. Light conditions ensure the stomata are fully open.

Mineral uptake

Certain minerals enter the root along with the water. If these minerals are in a higher concentration in the soil than in the root, this happens by diffusion.

When there is a lower concentration of minerals in the soil than in the root, minerals are absorbed by a very complex process of active transport.

Plant support

Plant support is provided by a woody substance called **lignin** found in the walls of xylem vessels. However, before lignin has developed, new growth is supported by special cells, called **packing cells**. Water enters the packing cells by osmosis and inflates them, in the same way that air inflates a balloon. The cells are prevented from bursting by their strong cell walls. Packing cells in this condition are said to be **turgid**. If a plant is not getting enough water, the packing cells begin to shrink and become limp, or **flaccid**, and the plant wilts.

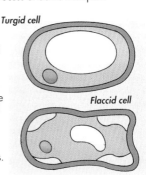

Turgid cell

Flaccid cell

Concentration gradient, 133.

How plants make food

Plants, like animals, need food to provide energy. Unlike animals, however, plants can make their own food by a chemical process called **photosynthesis.** In order for photosynthesis to take place, a plant needs light, water, carbon dioxide and the green pigment *chlorophyll**. Chlorophyll is found in the cell *organelles** called *chloroplasts**. This equation summarizes what happens.

Carbon dioxide + Water → (Sunlight and chlorophyll) Glucose + Oxygen

Chlorophyll absorbs light energy and transfers it into chemical energy. This energy is used in a chemical reaction which turns carbon dioxide and water into glucose and oxygen. The glucose is either stored as starch, or used for respiration. The oxygen, released as a by-product of photosynthesis, is very important because it provides the main source of oxygen for animal respiration.

Where photosynthesis takes place

Photosynthesis occurs in all the parts of a plant which contain chloroplasts. However the leaves are specially adapted for food production.

Surface of a leaf

The leaf is very thin so gases only have to diffuse over a short distance.

Large surface area to absorb sunlight

Veins made up of vascular tissue provide support and carry water into the leaf and food away from it.

Cross section through leaf

Palisade mesophyll cells are the main site of photosynthesis. They contain chloroplasts.

Chloroplasts

Spongy mesophyll cells are rounded cells, surrounded by air spaces, into and out of which gases diffuse. They carry out less photosynthesis than palisade cells, as they have fewer chloroplasts.

Upper epidermis

The **epidermis**, is a thin, protective layer of cells on both surfaces of the leaf. It is covered by a waxy substance called **cutin**, which prevents excess water loss.

Stoma allows gas exchange between leaf cells and air.

Lower epidermis

Testing for starch

The glucose made during photosynthesis is very quickly converted to starch. This means that the presence of starch in a plant can be used to show that photosynthesis has taken place.

1. Dip a leaf in boiling water to kill its cells and to stop any further chemical activity.

3. Place the leaf on a white tile and add iodine. A change of colour from orange/brown to blue/black shows the presence of starch.

2. Immerse the leaf in hot ethanol to remove the green chlorophyll pigment. Then wash the leaf in warm water to remove the ethanol. (Never heat ethanol over a naked flame; use a water bath.)

*Chlorophyll, 132; Organelle, 132; Chloroplast, 132.

Investigations to show the factors needed for photosynthesis

In an investigation to show the factors needed for photosynthesis, you need to use destarched leaves. This enables you to prove that any starch present has been produced by the experimental conditions. You can destarch a plant by keeping it in the dark for at least 12 hours.

Experimental conditions	Factor under investigation	Result of starch test	Conclusion
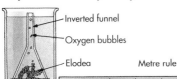 Leaf A — Leaf B (control) — Carbon dioxide absorbant — Water	Carbon dioxide	Leaf B contains starch, but Leaf A (which has been deprived of carbon dioxide) does not.	Carbon dioxide is needed to make starch.
Leaf A — Leaf B (control) — Dark mask with cross to let light in — Transparent mask	Light	In leaf A starch is only present in the area not covered by the mask. All leaf B contains starch.	Light is needed to make starch.
Variegated plant — Part A - contains chlorophyll — Part B (control) - no chlorophyll	Chlorophyll	Starch is present in green part of leaf (A) only.	Chlorophyll is needed to make starch.

Investigation to find the effect of light intensity on the rate of photosynthesis

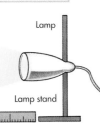

Inverted funnel
Oxygen bubbles
Elodea   Metre rule
Lamp
Lamp stand

Method
Set up the apparatus. Vary the light intensity by placing the lamp at different distances from the plant. At each distance count the number of oxygen bubbles released in one minute. This is used as a measure of the rate of photosynthesis. Repeat three times and calculate an average number of bubbles for each distance.
Result and conclusion
Record the results as a chart and use them to plot a line graph.

The graph shows that the greater the light intensity, the higher the rate of photosynthesis. Once the plant is photosynthesizing as fast as it can, increased light ceases to have an effect.

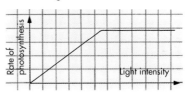

149

Removing waste

All living cells produce waste from the chemical reactions that take place in their cells. The removal of this metabolic waste is called **excretion**.

Plants produce relatively little waste because they have a less active metabolism than animals. Waste gases from photosynthesis and respiration are excreted through stomata. Other wastes are either stored in dead plant tissue, or kept in the leaves and removed when they drop off.

Animals have several different ways of removing waste. This table shows the main wastes excreted by humans.

Organ	Waste removed	Source
Lungs	Carbon dioxide	Respiration
	Water vapour	Respiration and excess in diet
Kidney	*Urea**	Waste amino acids
	Salts	Excess in diet
	Water	Excess in diet and respiration
Skin	Urea (in sweat)	Waste amino acids

The human kidneys

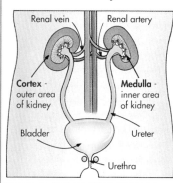

Renal vein   Renal artery

Cortex - outer area of kidney

Medulla - inner area of kidney

Bladder   Ureter

Urethra

Blood is filtered in the kidneys. Water and small molecules, including glucose, pass from the blood vessels into millions of tiny tubes called **nephrons**. As the filtered solution (the **filtrate**) passes through the nephron, useful products, such as water and glucose, are reabsorbed into the blood. The remaining waste solution is called **urine** and consists of salts, water and urea. Urine passes from the nephron into a tube called the **ureter**. The ureter carries urine to the **bladder** from where it is expelled from the body through a tube called the **urethra**.

The nephron

Each nephron consists of a cup-like structure called the **Bowman's capsule**. This is found in the cortex, and is connected to a narrow tube which runs into the medulla. After a complicated series of loops, this tube joins a **collecting duct** which leads to the ureter.

After the renal artery enters the kidney it splits into bunches of tiny capillaries called **glomeruli** (sing. **glomerulus**). High pressure in the glomeruli forces smaller molecules in the blood to filter into the Bowman's capsule. This filtrate passes into the tube and, as it travels towards the collecting duct, glucose and variable amounts of water and salts are reabsorbed into capillaries. The remaining filtrate (urine) passes into the collecting duct and 'clean' blood flows into the renal vein.

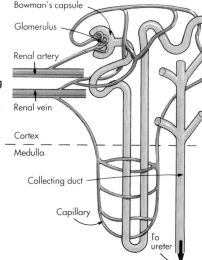

Bowman's capsule

Glomerulus

Renal artery

Renal vein

Cortex

Medulla

Collecting duct

Capillary

To ureter

Water potential and osmoregulation

Water potential is the pressure with which water molecules would travel by *osmosis** into another solution, if separated from it by a *selectively-permeable** membrane. The stronger the solution, the lower its water potential, because it contains fewer water molecules. It is important that the water potential of the blood and *tissue fluid** remains constant. If, for example, the water potential in tissue fluid were too low, water from surrounding cells would flow into it and the cells would die. The kidneys control the water potential of the body fluids by regulating the amount of water and dissolved substances that are reabsorbed in the blood from the nephron. This is called **osmoregulation**.

Temperature control

Keeping the body, and the chemicals inside it, in a stable condition is called **homeostasis**. Osmoregulation is one form of homeostasis. The control of body temperature is another. Part of the brain, called the *hypothalamus** detects temperature changes in the body and sends out messages, causing either heat-making or heat-losing actions (see table below). Many of these actions involve the skin.

Cross section through the skin

Hair   Sweat pore

The **epidermis** protects the skin. It consists of a waterproof layer of cells

Fat insulates the body.

Erector muscle

*Nerve cells** sensitive to pain, touch and temperature

Oil glands keep the hair and skin soft. This is very important in mammals that spend time in water.

Blood vessels

Sweat gland

Summary of temperature control functions

Body temperature rises		Body temperature falls
Action	Structure	Action
Relax so hairs lie flat and hot air cannot be trapped close to the skin.	Erector muscles	Contract so hairs stand up trapping a layer of air which is warmed by the body. This acts as insulation.
Produce sweat which *evaporates** out of the sweat pores, cooling the body.	Sweat glands	Cease to operate preventing heat loss from evaporation.
Widen so warm blood flows near the surface of skin, and heat is lost.	Blood vessels in dermis	Constrict so less blood flows near the surface minimizing heat loss.
Slows down because activity in the cells produces heat.	Metabolism	Speeds up, so more heat is produced.
Relax to slow down respiration.	Muscles	Contract involuntarily (shivering) increasing respiration rate.

Normal body temperature (37°C)

---

*Osmosis, 148; Selectively-permeable, 132; Tissue fluid, 144; Hypothalamus, 153; Nerve cell, 152; Evaporate (Evaporation), 188.

Sensitivity

In order to survive, all organisms react to changes in their internal and external environment. This is called **responding to stimuli** (sing. **stimulus**) or **sensitivity**. Complex animals respond in very specific ways to different stimuli. Their response is controlled by two systems - the nervous system and the endocrine system (see page 154). Both use the same basic mechanism shown below.

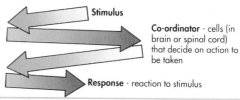

Receptor - a cell or group of cells, called **sensory cells**, sensitive to a particular stimulus

Stimulus

Co-ordinator - cells (in brain or spinal cord) that decide on action to be taken

Effector - part of body that produces the response

Response - reaction to stimulus

The nervous system

The **nervous system** consists of two parts: the **central nervous system** (**CNS**) and the **peripheral nervous system** (**PNS**). The CNS consists of the co-ordinators, the **brain** and the **spinal cord.** The PNS consists of **nerve cells** which connect the receptors and effectors to the CNS.

The nerve cells that make up the PNS and CNS are called **neurons.** Neurons carry special electrical messages, called **impulses,** around the body. Each neuron consists of a **cell body**, which contains the nucleus, and strands of cytoplasm called **dendrites** and **axons**. Dendrites carry impulses towards the cell body, and axons carry them away from it.

Different neurons have different structures and functions.

Sensory neurons carry impulses from receptors to the CNS.

Intermediate neurons in the CNS connect sensory and motor neurons.

Motor neurons carry impulses from the CNS to the effectors.

CNS

PNS

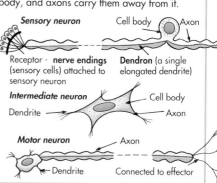

Sensory neuron   Cell body   Axon

Receptor - **nerve endings** (sensory cells) attached to sensory neuron

Dendron (a single elongated dendrite)

Intermediate neuron   Cell body

Dendrite   Axon

Motor neuron   Axon

Dendrite   Connected to effector

Voluntary and involuntary actions

There are two kinds of response which the nervous system controls: voluntary and involuntary actions.

Voluntary actions are those, such as walking across a room or pressing a door bell, which result from conscious activity in the brain. Nerve impulses reach the brain and are 'analyzed' before a response is decided.

Involuntary actions are actions over which the brain has no conscious control. These include reflex actions. A **reflex action** is the immediate response of the body to a stimulus, which occurs without conscious thought. Pulling away from a hot object is a reflex action. Most reflex actions are directed by the spinal cord. We only become aware of them when other impulses are sent to the brain to 'tell' it what is happening. The path which impulses travel along during a reflex action is called a **reflex arc.**

How a reflex arc works

1. Sharp pin touches nerve endings in foot.

2. Nerve endings send impulses down sensory neurons.

3. Impulses pass to intermediate neurons in spinal cord.

4. Impulses pass from the spinal cord to motor neurons (the brain is by-passed) and travel to the effector (in this case, the thigh muscles). Separate impulses are sent to brain, so that the person is aware an action is taking the place.

5. In response thigh muscles contract and the foot moves.

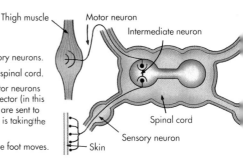

Thigh muscle · Motor neuron · Intermediate neuron · Spinal cord · Sensory neuron · Skin

The brain

Different areas of the brain are used for receiving and sending out impulses which control different functions.

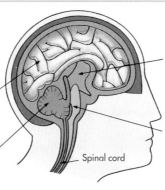

The **cerebrum** is the decision-making centre. It controls most physical and mental activities. Different areas of the cerebrum control all the various voluntary actions.

The **cerebellum** co-ordinates muscle movement and balance, as directed by the cerebrum.

Spinal cord

The **hypothalamus** controls involuntary actions. It is vital to *homeostasis**, maintaining body temperature and *water potential**.

The **medulla**, under the direction of the hypothalamus, controls some involuntary actions, such as heart rate.

The eye

The eye is a receptor which converts light energy into nerve impulses. These nerve impulses travel to the brain, where they are interpreted as images.

The **sclera** is a thick fibrous coating, known as the 'white' of the eye.

The **iris** is an opaque disc with a central hole, called the **pupil.** Muscle fibres in the iris relax and contract, altering pupil size and controlling the amount of light entering the eye.

Optic nerve

The **conjunctiva** protects the cornea.

The **cornea** is a transparent disc in the front part of the sclera. It bends light rays on to the lens as they enter the eye.

The **vitreous humour** is a jelly-like solution that gives the eye shape and protects the retina.

The **lens** is a transparent body. It focuses rays of light, so that they form an upside-down image on the retina. For more about lenses see page 23.

The **aqueous humour** is a watery liquid which carries food and oxygen to the lens.

Ciliary muscles relax and contract to alter lens shape for accurate focusing.

Rods and **cones** convert light stimuli into electrical impulses which travel along the optic nerve to the brain.

The **retina** is the innermost layer of tissue at the back of the eyeball. It contains millions of light-sensitive neurons called rods and cones.

*Homeostasis, 151; Water potential, 151.

Drugs and the nervous system

Drugs are substances which affect the nervous system. There are four groups of drugs which affect the body in different ways.

● **Sedatives** are drugs that slow down the brain. They have a calming effect and can induce sleep. Valium, barbiturates and alcohol are sedatives.

● **Stimulants** speed up the brain and make it more alert. Some stimulants are taken medically to relieve depression. Caffeine, nicotine and cocaine are stimulants.

● **Hallucinogens** cause hallucinations, visual images that are sensed but don't actually exist. Cannabis and LSD are hallucinogens.

● **Analgesics** are painkillers. They numb the part of the brain that senses pain. Aspirin, morphine and heroin are analgesics.

Drugs play an important part in modern medicine and, taken under medical advice, can be beneficial to ill people. However, all drugs are potentially dangerous. They can impair judgement and do long-term damage to the body cells. Many drugs are addictive; giving them up can cause painful withdrawal symptoms.

The endocrine system

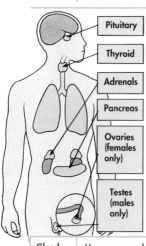

Pituitary

Thyroid

Adrenals

Pancreas

Ovaries (females only)

Testes (males only)

The **endocrine system** is responsible for changes which affect the whole body or take place over a long period of time. It consists of a collection of glands, called the **endocrine glands.** The main human glands are shown in the diagram opposite. All glands secrete useful substances. Digestive glands, for example, release enzymes to aid digestion (see page 138). The endocrine organs secrete **hormones.** These are chemical messages which, like nerve impulses, stimulate a response in different parts of the body. Nerve impulses travel to one particular part of the body, where a response is required. Hormones, however, are released into the blood stream and travel to every cell in the body. Different cells are sensitive to different hormones so, although every cell receives each hormone, only a limited number respond. The table below shows the effect different hormones have on the body.

Gland	Hormones produced	Effect of Hormone
Pituitary gland	Growth hormone	Controls growth of bones and muscles.
	Anti-diuretic hormone	Increases reabsorption of water in kidneys.
	Gonadotrophins	Controls development of ovaries and testes.
Thyroid gland	Thyroxine	Controls rate of metabolism and rate that glucose is used up in respiration.
Adrenal gland	Adrenaline	Prepares the body for emergencies: increases heart rate and rate and depth of breathing, raises blood sugar level so more glucose is available for respiration, diverts blood from gut to limbs.
Pancreas	Insulin	Converts excess glucose into *glycogen** in liver.
	Glucagon	Converts glycogen back to glucose in liver.
Ovaries	Oestrogen†	Controls ovulation and secondary sexual characteristics (see pages 161-162).
	Progesterone	Prepares the uterus lining for receiving an embryo (see page 161).
Testes	Testosterone	Controls sperm production and secondary sexual characteristics (see page 161).

*Glycogen, 134.   †Estrogen = US spelling

Hormones and homeostasis

Hormones play a very important part in *homeostasis** (maintaining the chemical balance of the body). For example, the hormones secreted by the pancreas keep the amount of glucose in the blood at a constant level.

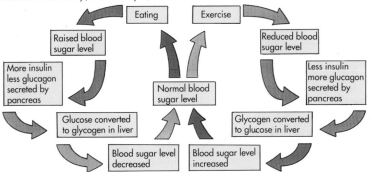

Plant sensitivity

Plants are less sensitive to their environment than animals and their responses are more limited. Most plant responses involve growth (see page 170) either away from or towards a stimulus. These responses are called **tropisms** and are controlled by plant hormones called **auxins**.

When the stimulus is light, the growth response is called **phototropism**. When the stimulus is gravity it is called **geotropism**. Growth towards a stimulus is called **positive tropism**, and away from it is called **negative tropism**. Roots and shoots respond to stimuli in different ways.

Stimulus	Shoot response	Root response
Light	Positive phototropism	No effect
Gravity	Negative geotropism	Positive geotropism

Phototropism

The tip of a shoot produces an auxin which has two important properties. It increases growth and moves away from light. This auxin diffuses down the shoot and gathers in cells furthest away from the light source, stimulating more rapid growth in these areas. The shoot then grows towards the light source.

Auxins gather away from light source.

Plant bends to light source.

Faster growth on darker side.

Light source

Geotropism

The shoot bends upwards.

Auxin from shoot gathers here and promotes growth.

Auxin from root gathers here and inhibits growth.

The tips of shoots and roots both produce auxins which are sensitive to gravity. The auxins diffuse in the direction of gravity (downwards), but have opposite effects. The auxin from the shoot increases growth but the auxin from the root slows it down. The effect of these auxins is seen in seedlings where the shoot always grows towards the surface and the root always grows into the soil.

The root bends downwards.

*Homeostasis, 151.

How the body fights disease

Disease is the disruption of the normal working of the body. There are many types of disease. Some are caused by *parasitic** organisms, called **pathogens**, which live in or off another living organism, damaging its cells. Other diseases not caused by another organism are often linked to diet, *genetic** defects, old age, or the intake of poisonous chemicals.

Pathogens

There are four main types of pathogen: viruses, bacteria, protoctists and fungi. (See 'Classification' pages 178-179.)
● **Viruses** are strands of DNA* surrounded by an envelope of protein. They invade cells and use their materials to feed and reproduce. This eventually kills the cell. Diseases caused by viruses include colds and influenza.

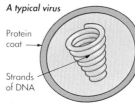
A typical virus
Protein coat
Strands of DNA

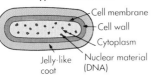
A typical bacterial cell
Cell membrane
Cell wall
Cytoplasm
Jelly-like coat
Nuclear material (DNA)

● **Pathogenic bacteria** cause disease because they produce poisonous waste products, called **toxins**. Unfortunately the human body, being warm with plenty of food, provides ideal conditions in which the bacteria can live and breed. Different types of bacteria cause different diseases, some of which are shown below.

Coccus (sphere shaped) - causes sore throats and gonorrhoea. →

Vibrio (bent rod shaped) - → causes cholera.

Bacillus (rod shaped) - causes typhoid and tuberculosis. →

Spirillum (spiral shaped) - → causes syphillis.

● **Protoctists** are unicellular organisms. They live in the body and deprive it of essential substances. They cause diseases such as malaria.

● **Pathogenic fungi** usually affect the outside rather than the inside of the body. They cause skin diseases such as ringworm and athlete's foot.

How disease spreads

Pathogens are **infectious**, which means they pass from one organism to another. This occurs in the following ways:

Droplet infection. When a person breathes out, sneezes or coughs, tiny drops of moisture shoot from his or her mouth. If the person is ill, these droplets may contain pathogens which can be breathed in by others, and can infect water and food. The common cold and influenza are spread like this.

Contaminated food and water. Food and water can be contaminated by *faeces** or contact with diseased organisms. If a drinking supply is contaminated, disease spreads very quickly through a community. Typhoid and cholera are spread in this way.

Vectors. Vectors are organisms that carry pathogens and pass them on to other organisms, often without catching the disease themselves. Certain mosquitoes, for example, carry the malaria virus and pass it on to humans.

A mosquito

Touch. Diseases which can be caught by physical contact with the pathogen are said to be **contagious**. Most human fungal diseases, such as athlete's foot and ringworm, and sexually transmitted diseases, such as syphilis, are contagious.

*Parasitic (Parasite), 141; Genetic, 166; DNA, 135; Faeces, 138.

Fighting disease

The skin is a very efficient barrier against pathogens. Even if it is cut, germs can only enter the body for a short time before *clotting** takes effect. The air passages, which are not protected by skin, are partly protected by mucus which traps pathogens, and by *ciliated cells** which sweep them out of the body. Acid in the stomach helps kill pathogens which enter the body in food and drink. If these defensive barriers fail, a second line of defence, involving *white blood cells**, is brought into operation. There are two types of white blood cells: phagocytes and lymphocytes.

Lymphocyte

Bacteria

Antibodies

Lymphocytes are made in swellings in the tubes of the *lymphatic system**, called **lymph nodes**. Lymphocytes produce chemicals called **antibodies**, which help phagocytes destroy pathogens or neutralize the poisons they produce. Any pathogen that stimulates production of an antibody is called an **antigen**. A new antibody is made for each new antigen that enters the body, but this takes time. Once the antigens have been destroyed, the antibodies remain in the circulation for a very short while. If, however, the same antigens enter the body again, the lymphocytes respond immediately and kill them before any illness develops. This is called **active immunity**.

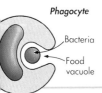

Phagocyte

Bacteria

Food vacuole

Phagocytes engulf bacteria and digest them in a special food vacuole. *Amoebas** also feed in this way.

Immunization

Active immunity can be artificially brought on by injecting a weakened form of an antigen into the body; not enough to cause the disease, but enough to make the lymphocytes produce antibodies against it. If that antigen enters the body any time after this, the body can respond immediately

and no illness will develop. This process is called **vaccination**; it protects us from diseases such as smallpox and polio.

Injecting antibodies after a disease has developed provides **passive immunity**. The pathogens are killed, but the immunity does not last.

AIDS

AIDS stands for **acquired immune deficiency syndrome**. It is a disease which damages the *immune system**, making the body vulnerable to infections. AIDS is caused by a virus called **human immunodeficiency virus** (HIV). The virus infects, and eventually inactivates the lymphocytes, the very cells which fight infection. HIV is passed on via blood, *semen** and *vaginal** fluids. The spread of this disease can be reduced by ensuring that only uninfected blood is used in transfusions, by using sterile syringes and by wearing a *condom** during *sexual intercourse**.

Smoking and ill health

Smoking involves the inhalation of over a thousand different chemicals, which form a thick black substance called **tar**. Tar can seriously damage the *respiratory system*,* and can cause or aggravate many diseases which infect the lungs, such as bronchitis and asthma. Cigarette smoke is also a **carcinogen**, which means it can cause *cancer**.

*Clotting, 145; Ciliated cell, 133; White blood cell, 145; Amoeba, 178; Lymphatic system, 144; Immune system, 188; Semen, 160; Vaginal, 160; Condom, 162; Sexual intercourse, 160; Respiratory system, 142; Cancer, 188.

Skeletons and movement in animals

Most animals require some means of supporting their bodies, to stop them collapsing. A **skeleton** is one kind of support. There are three basic types of skeleton in the animal kingdom.

Some animals, such as earthworms, are supported by liquid in their bodies. This is called a **hydrostatic** skeleton.

The bodies of animals such as insects and *crustaceans** are surrounded by a hard outer covering called an **exoskeleton.** This provides protection and a firm base for muscle attachment.

Many animals are supported by a hard frame inside the body, surrounded by muscles. This is called an **endoskeleton.**

The human endoskeleton

The human endoskeleton has other functions as well as support. It protects vital organs such as the brain, lungs and heart. It acts as a firm attachment for muscles, allowing movement, and is the site of blood cell production.

The skeleton is made of two tissues called **bone** and **cartilage.** The main components of bone are protein, and calcium which makes it strong. Cartilage is a softer tissue, found in between bones. It acts as a shock absorber, cushioning bones during movement. In the centre of bones there is a substance called **marrow.** Blood cells are made in the marrow.

Skull
Cranium
Upper jaw
Lower jaw

Shoulder
Collar bone
Shoulder blade

Breastbone

Ribs

Arm
Humerus
Radius
Ulna

Backbone
Vertebrae
(sing. **vertebra**)

Hip
Pelvis
Pubis

Leg
Femur
Fibula
Tibia

Joints

A **joint** is where two or more bones meet. There are four main types of joint in the human body. Most are movable and give the body flexibility.

- **Fixed joints** occur when bones are fused together by a protein called **collagen,** so no movement is allowed. The skull is made up of fixed joints.
- **Sliding joints** are those in which bones meet at flat surfaces and glide over each other. The wrist and ankle work in this way.
- **Hinge joints** work like any hinge, allowing movement in one plane only. Elbows and knees are hinge joints.
- **Ball and socket joints,** such as the hip and shoulder, give the greatest flexibility. A bone with a rounded head fits into a cup-like socket of another bone, allowing movement in any direction. Hinge joints and ball and socket joints are also called synovial joints (see opposite).

*Crustacean, 178.

Synovial joints

Synovial joints are lubricated by a fluid called **synovial fluid**, which reduces friction and allows smooth movement. They are joined together by inelastic fibres, called **ligaments**.

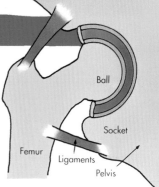

Hip joint

Cartilage

The **synovial capsule** is a bag containing synovial fluid.

Synovial membrane

Ball

Socket

Femur

Ligaments

Pelvis

Muscles and movement

All movement in the body is caused by muscles contracting (shortening).

Different kinds of muscle control different types of movement.

Type of muscle	Position in body	Action
Smooth muscle	Walls of intestine, iris*, blood vessels	Weak, slow contractions controlled involuntarily e.g. *peristalsis*. Muscles never tire.
Cardiac muscle	Heart only	Makes the heart beat by powerful involuntary action. Muscles never tire.
Skeletal muscle	Attached to skeleton	Move bones by powerful contractions controlled by will. Muscles tire easily.

Skeletal muscles

When skeletal muscles contract, they pull bones towards them. However, they cannot push. This means that another muscle is needed, on the other side of the bone, to return it to its original position. While one muscle contracts, an opposing muscle, called the **antagonist**, relaxes. Muscles that work in this way are called **antagonistic pairs**.

Muscles that bend or flex a joint are called **flexor muscles.** Those that work in the opposite direction to straighten it, are called **extensor muscles.** In the forearm, the flexor muscle is called the **biceps** and the extensor muscle is called the **triceps.**

Movement in the forearm

Shoulder blade

Flexor muscle (biceps) Contracts to bend arm

Extensor muscle (triceps) Contracts to straighten arm

Ulna (forms the elbow)

Strong fibres called **tendons** attach muscles to bone.

Radius

Fitness and health

Exercise is an important part of good health. Muscles are unusual in that they get stronger, and more of them are formed, the harder they are made to work. This is particularly important for cardiac muscles. Exercise increases the volume and strength of the heart so that it has to work less hard when at rest. Chest muscles also benefit from exercise and breathing is improved.

*Iris, 153; Peristalsis, 139.

Human reproduction

Sexual reproduction creates offspring by joining together a male and a female sex cell. In humans, a female sex cell, called an egg or **ovum** (pl. **ova**), joins a male sex cell, called a **sperm**. Sex cells are also called **gametes** and are made in organs called **gonads** (see below). The two cells are brought together by a process called **copulation**. Copulation may result in **fertilization**, the fusing of the nuclei of the two gametes.

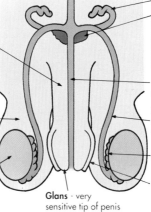

Sperm — Tail, Head, Nucleus

Ovum — Nucleus, Jelly-like coat, Cytoplasm, Membrane

Male reproductive organs

Penis - organ through which sperm are ejected. Consists of a soft tissue called **erectile tissue**, blood vessels and *nerve endings* *. Becomes erect and stiff during sexual excitement.

Scrotum - sac, hanging outside the body, in which testes are kept cool at the ideal temperature for sperm production.

Testis (pl. **testes**) (male gonad) - place where sperm are made once puberty is reached. It consists of many very small tubes called sperm tubules.

Seminal vesicle
Prostate gland
These secrete fluids which keep sperm alive. Sperm and fluids together are called **semen**.

Urethra * carries sperm out of the body.

Sperm duct - carries sperm from testes to urethra and penis.

Epididymis - coiled tube where sperm are stored.

Foreskin - protective covering of glans

Glans - very sensitive tip of penis

Female reproductive organs

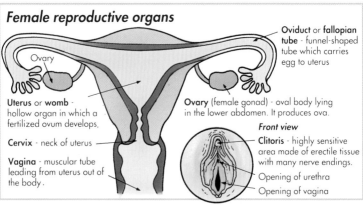

Oviduct or **fallopian tube** - funnel-shaped tube which carries egg to uterus

Ovary

Uterus or **womb** - hollow organ in which a fertilized ovum develops.

Cervix - neck of uterus

Vagina - muscular tube leading from uterus out of the body.

Ovary (female gonad) - oval body lying in the lower abdomen. It produces ova.

Front view

Clitoris - highly sensitive area made of erectile tissue with many nerve endings.

Opening of urethra

Opening of vagina

Copulation

Fertilization takes place within the woman's body when a sperm meets an ovum in the oviduct. Sperm enter the female during copulation (also called **sexual intercourse**) when an erect penis is inserted into the vagina. Movement of

the pelvis stimulates nerve endings in the penis. This sets off a *reflex action* * which results in semen being ejected into the vagina. This is called **ejaculation**. About 4cm³ of semen are ejaculated, containing about 300 million sperm.

*Urethra, 150; Nerve endings, 152; Reflex action, 152.

Fertilization

Sperm swim from the vagina to the oviducts. If they meet an ovum, fertilization can take place. One sperm head penetrates the ovum and the two nuclei fuse. This forms a *zygote**, the first cell of a new baby.

Sperm head

Ovum

The zygote travels to the uterus and becomes implanted in the uterus wall. After this happens it is called an **embryo**. The uterus has prepared for implantation by building up a thick lining, rich in blood vessels.

Pregnancy

The time between implantation and birth is called **pregnancy**, or **gestation**. In humans it lasts about 38 weeks. The growing embryo, also called a **fetus**, becomes surrounded by an **amniotic sac**, a bag containing watery liquid called **amniotic fluid**. This protects the

A baby about to be born

Placenta

Umbilical cord

Fetus

Amniotic fluid

Amniotic sac

embryo from knocks.

The embryo needs food and oxygen in order to grow. At first these come directly from the blood vessels in the uterus wall. After a few weeks, however, a special plate-shaped organ develops, called the **placenta**. Capillaries from the mother and fetus flow into the placenta and substances diffuse between them. The fetus receives food and oxygen from the mother's blood, and releases carbon dioxide and other waste matter into it. The baby is connected to the placenta by a cord, called the **umbilical cord**.

During the last few days of pregnancy, the baby moves so that its head is near the cervix. Finally the baby is squeezed out through the vagina by strong contractions of the muscles in the uterus. This is called **labour**.

Puberty

A baby is born with a full set of reproductive organs, called the **primary sexual characteristics**. However, these do not become active until puberty. **Puberty** is a series of body changes, stimulated by hormones from the

*pituitary gland** and sex organs, which make a person capable of reproducing. The new physical features brought about by puberty are called the **secondary sexual characteristics**. They are described in the table below.

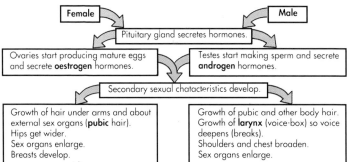

Female ⟶ Pituitary gland secretes hormones. ⟵ **Male**

| Ovaries start producing mature eggs and secrete **oestrogen** hormones. | Testes start making sperm and secrete **androgen** hormones. |

Secondary sexual characteristics develop.

| Growth of hair under arms and about external sex organs (**pubic** hair). Hips get wider. Sex organs enlarge. Breasts develop. | Growth of pubic and other body hair. Growth of **larynx** (voice-box) so voice deepens (breaks). Shoulders and chest broaden. Sex organs enlarge. |

*Zygote, 170; Pituitary gland, 154.

Ovulation and menstruation

At birth the ovaries contain many thousands of immature eggs. After the onset of puberty, one egg matures every 28 days and is released into the oviduct. This is called **ovulation** and is part of the **menstrual** (monthly) cycle. During the cycle the uterus prepares itself for implantation by a fertilized egg. It is controlled by hormones secreted by the pituitary gland and the ovaries.

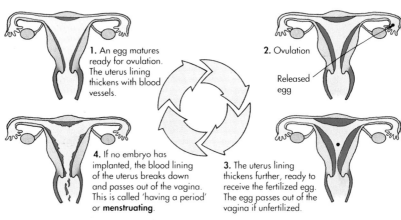

1. An egg matures ready for ovulation. The uterus lining thickens with blood vessels.

2. Ovulation

Released egg

4. If no embryo has implanted, the blood lining of the uterus breaks down and passes out of the vagina. This is called 'having a period' or **menstruating**.

3. The uterus lining thickens further, ready to receive the fertilized egg. The egg passes out of the vagina if unfertilized.

Contraception

Conception includes fertilization, and the implantation of an embryo in the uterus. **Contraception** is any device which prevent this. All methods of contraception achieve one of three things: they stop an egg being released, stop sperm reaching an egg, or stop an embryo from implanting in the uterus.

Method	How it works
Withdrawal	Penis is removed before ejaculation. Very unreliable as some sperm are released before ejaculation.
Diaphragm	A rubber cap that fits over cervix and stops semen entering uterus. Reliable if fitted correctly and used with sperm-killing cream.
Condom	A rubber sheath worn over penis which stops semen entering vagina. Reliable if used correctly.
Intrauterine device	Shaped metal and plastic device designed to fit into uterus which prevents a fertilized egg from implanting into the uterus. Reliable, but may cause heavier periods.
'The pill'	A pill that contains the chemicals found in pregnant women that prevent ovulation. A very reliable method.
Rhythm method	Limits intercourse to 'safe period', the days when fertilization cannot take place. Unreliable as periods are not always regular.
Sterilization	A permanent form of contraception. In men, sperm ducts are cut so sperm cannot leave testes. In women, oviducts are cut so eggs cannot reach the uterus.

Asexual reproduction

Asexual reproduction is a form of reproduction that involves only one parent and creates organisms that are *genetically** identical to their parent.

Single-celled organisms, such as *amoebas** and *bacteria**, reproduce asexually by dividing in two. This is called **binary fission**.

Binary fission in an amoeba

The nucleus starts to divide.

The nucleus splits in two, and the cytoplasm gathers around each nucleus.

The cytoplasm divides fully. Two separate but genetically identical cells are formed.

Some simple animals, such as *hydra**, reproduce by **budding**. This is a form of asexual reproduction that involves the growth of a new body out of the side of a parent body. Eventually the new body breaks off and a new individual is formed.

A hydra budding

Asexual reproduction in plants

In addition to reproducing sexually (see page 164), many plants have developed ways of reproducing asexually. This is called **vegetative reproduction**. Different plants use different methods of vegetative reproduction. Here are some examples.

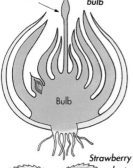

New shoot

Daffodil bulb

Bulb

Strawberry plant

Runner

Daffodil

Daffodils form **bulbs**, short stems surrounded by fleshy leaves filled with food. The food in the bulb makes possible the growth of several new shoots, which eventually grow into individual plants.

Strawberry

A stem, called a **runner**, grows out from the base of the parent plant and puts down roots. A new plant begins to grow at this point. At first the new plant is fed by the parent but, once it can live on its own, the runner rots away.

Potato plant

Food is stored in an underground stem which forms a swelling called a **tuber**. Each plant forms several tubers, each of which can give rise to a new plant.

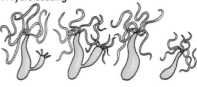

Potato plant

Tuber

Plant reproduction

All flowering plants reproduce sexually. The organs of sexual reproduction are contained in the flower. Most plants are **hermaphrodites**, which means that each flower has both male and female sex organs.

Longitudinal section through cherry blossom

Stamen - male reproductive part

The **anther** makes tiny grains called **pollen**, which contain male sex cells.

The **filament** holds up the anther.

Receptacle - expanded tip of stalk from which the flower grows. In some plants it produces a sugary liquid called **nectar**.

Petal

Carpel - female reproductive part

Stigma - top part of carpel with sticky surface to trap pollen.

The **style** joins the stigma to the ovary.

The **sepals** protect the flower when it is in bud.

The **ovary** contains the female sex cells, called ovules.

Ovule

Pollination

The first stage of sexual reproduction in flowering plants is **pollination**. This is the transfer of pollen from the stamen to the stigma.

When pollen is carried from the stamen to the stigma of the same plant, the process is called **self-pollination**. When pollen is carried to the stigma of another plant, it is called **cross-pollination**. Most plants have developed ways of avoiding self-pollination because it reduces genetic* variation (see page 168). Cross-pollination increases variety and can give rise to changes that help a species* survive.

Pollen can be carried from one plant to another by insects or by the wind. During insect pollination, an insect visiting a flower becomes dusted with pollen from the stamens. On visiting another flower, the pollen becomes attached to the sticky stigma. Wind pollination blows pollen from anthers to stigmas. If pollen grains land on a different species of plant they will not develop. Plants are closely adapted to the way in which they are pollinated; the table opposite shows the different features found in insect- and wind-pollinated plants.

Features of insect-pollinated flowers	Features of wind-pollinated flowers
Large brightly coloured petals	Very small petals
Scent	No scent
Nectar	No nectar
Large pollen grains with a rough surface to help them stick to the insect's body	Many small pollen grains with a smooth surface
Stigmas inside flower	Stigmas hanging outside flower

When a grain of pollen lands on a stigma, a tube, called a **pollen tube**, grows from the stigma down into the ovary. The male gametes* in the pollen pass down this tube and meet the ovule.

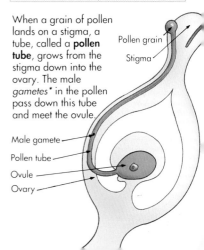

Pollen grain

Stigma

Male gamete

Pollen tube

Ovule

Ovary

Fertilization

During plant fertilization a male and female gamete fuse inside an ovary. This results in the formation of a **seed** which contains a plant embryo. The ovary ripens to form the **fruit** around the seed. After fertilization the plant no longer requires many of its flower parts, so they wither and die.

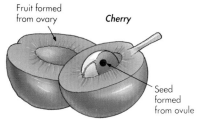

Fruit formed from ovary

Cherry

Seed formed from ovule

Seed dispersal

In order to prevent overcrowding and competition for space light and water, seeds and fruits are carried away from the parent plant. This is called **dispersal**. Plants are adapted to three main methods of dispersal: by wind, animal, or explosion.

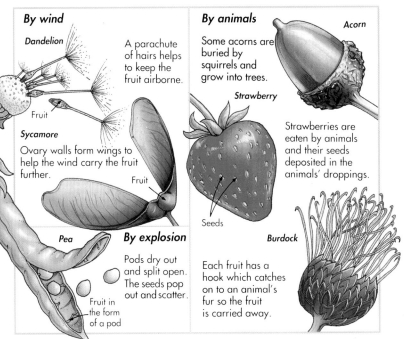

By wind

Dandelion

A parachute of hairs helps to keep the fruit airborne.

Fruit

Sycamore

Ovary walls form wings to help the wind carry the fruit further.

Fruit

Pea

Fruit in the form of a pod

By explosion

Pods dry out and split open. The seeds pop out and scatter.

By animals

Acorn

Some acorns are buried by squirrels and grow into trees.

Strawberry

Strawberries are eaten by animals and their seeds deposited in the animals' droppings.

Seeds

Burdock

Each fruit has a hook which catches on to an animal's fur so the fruit is carried away.

Germination

Germination is the growth of a new plant from a seed. Most seeds do not grow as soon as they are dispersed but stay **dormant** (their metabolism slows down) until the spring. In spring a seed will germinate if it has enough water, oxygen and warmth. Water is needed as a *medium** for the metabolism. Oxygen is needed for respiration, which breaks down food releasing energy for growth. Warmth activates plant enzymes, also necessary for respiration.

Chromosomes and genes

Chromosomes are long, thread-like structures found in the nuclei of all cells. They consist of one molecule of *DNA**, combined with special proteins. DNA is arranged in units called **genes**. Each gene carries **genetic information**. This is a set of coded instructions relating to the composition of a chemical, often an enzyme, which in turn controls the production of a characteristic (or part of it). Some characteristics are controlled by just one gene, such as height in pea plants. Others are controlled by several genes working together, such as hair colour in humans.

The total number of chromosomes in each cell is called the **diploid number** (except in sex cells - see next page). Chromosomes are arranged within the cell in pairs, called **homologous pairs**. Human cells have 46 chromosomes, arranged in 23 pairs.

At a specific position on a chromosome called a **locus** (pl. **loci**), homologous chromosome carry genes determining the same characteristic, or making the same chemical. For example, at locus A on a homologous pair, both chromosomes carry the gene for making eye colour.

Eye colour gene

Alleles

There are several different eye colour types. This is because each eye colour gene can contain one of several sets of instructions, making the eyes, for example, either brown or blue. Each alternative form that a gene can have is called an **allele**. An individual with identical alleles at a specific locus on homologous chromosomes is said to be **homozygous**. An individual with different alleles at a specific locus is said to be **heterozygous**.

2 pairs of homologous chromosomes

Allele for blue eyes

Allele for brown eyes

Homozygous condition   Heterozygous condition

Genotype and phenotype

The genetic information about a particular part of an organism is called its **genotype**. The appearance of the organism due to the presence of these genes is called the **phenotype**. The phenotype depends on the way that the alleles of the genotype interact with each other.

Alleles can be either dominant or recessive. A **dominant** allele always affects an individual's phenotype, even when it is part of a heterozygous pair of alleles. A **recessive** allele only affects the phenotype when it is part of a homozygous pair. It never affects the phenotype when it is part of a heterozygous pair. The table opposite shows examples of different types of genotypes and what effect they have.

B = dominant allele for brown eyes
b = recessive allele for blue eyes

Genotype	Phenotype	Description
BB	Brown eyes	Homozygous dominant
Bb	Brown eyes	Heterozgous
bb	Blue eyes	Homozygous recessive

Some alleles are **codominant**. This means that both alleles in a heterozygous pair affect the phenotype. An example of codominance is seen in the colour of some flowers, such as snapdragons.

R = red allele
r = white allele

Genotype	Phenotype	Description
Rr	Pink	Heterozygous codominant

Meiosis

The only cells in the human body which do not have 46 chromosomes are the *gametes** (*sperm** and *ova**), which contain only 23. This is called the **haploid number**.

During fertilization the nucleus of the sperm and the egg fuse and a **diploid cell** with 46 chromosomes is created. The 46 chromosomes arrange themselves in homologous pairs with a chromosome from each parent in every pair.

Haploid cells are created by a special sort of cell division called **meiosis** which occurs in the *reproductive organs**. One diploid cell divides to make four haploid cells, with half the number of chromosomes as the diploid cell.

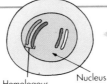

1. Chromosomes form short, fat strands and arrange themseves in homologous pairs. (Only two pairs of chromosomes are shown.)

Homologous pair — Nucleus

Replica —

Chromosome

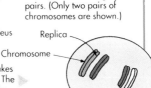

2. Each chromosome makes a replica (copy) of itself. The nuclear membrane breaks down.

3. Homologous pairs separate and move to opposite ends of the cell. The cell divides in two.

4. In each new cell, the chromosome and its replica move away from each other. (Only one new cell is shown.)

5. Each cell divides into two gametes, each containing half the number of chromosomes as the original cell. The nuclear membrane re-forms.

Patterns of inheritance

The study of inheritance is called **genetics**. In sexual reproduction, offspring inherit half their genetic instructions from each parent. If the genotype of each parent is known, it is possible to predict the various ways characteristics can be inherited. This is particularly easy to see in **single-factor inheritance**, where a characteristic is controlled by genes at a single locus.

There is, for example, a gene with two alleles that controls the ability to roll your tongue. One allele allows tongue rolling (**T**) and is dominant, so people that can tongue roll are either homozygous dominant (**TT**), or heterozygous (**Tt**). The gene preventing rolling (**t**) is recessive, so people who cannot tongue roll are homozygous recessive (**tt**).

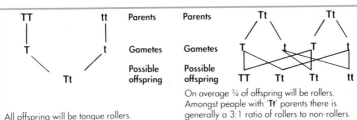

TT tt	Parents	Parents
T t	Gametes	Gametes
Tt	Possible offspring	Possible offspring
		TT Tt Tt tt

All offspring will be tongue rollers.

On average ¾ of offspring will be rollers. Amongst people with 'Tt' parents there is generally a 3:1 ratio of rollers to non-rollers.

*Gamete, 160; Sperm, 160; Ova (Ovum), 160; Reproductive organs, 160.

Variation

There is an enormous variety of living things. Not only are there millions of different *species**, but within each species no two individuals are exactly alike.

Differences between individuals of the same species are examples of **variation**. There are two types of variation: discontinuous and continuous.

Discontinuous variation

Discontinuous variation is the name given to characteristics which have a limited number of forms. For example, there are only four blood groups to which humans can belong: A, B, AO or AB. There are no intermediates. In the same way, people either can or cannot roll their tongues; there are no half-way stages.

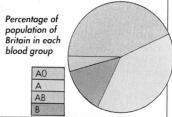

Percentage of population of Britain in each blood group

| AO |
| A |
| AB |
| B |

Continuous variation

Characteristics which show a range of values between two extremes are examples of **continuous variation**. Height shows continuous variation because when people are measured no specific groups emerge. The differences in height are gradual, ranging from very tall to very small. Weight also shows continuous variation.

The varying heights of people in a group can be shown as a *histogram** (see opposite). All characteristics showing continuous variation form histograms of roughly the same shape when presented in this way. Whatever the characteristic,

there are always fewer individuals at each end of the range, and more towards the middle where an average value is reached. If a line is drawn joining the tops of each bar, a bell-shaped curve is formed. This is called the **normal distribution curve**.

Normal distribution curve

Number of people (y-axis)

Height (x-axis)

Origins of variation

The main cause of variation in organisms that reproduce sexually is a process called **crossing over** which occurs in the early stages of *meiosis**. During crossing over the chromosomes, arranged in their *homologous pairs** randomly swop lengths of genetic code. This ensures that every *gamete** has a unique set of chromosomes. Therefore, when two gametes fuse during fertilization, an individual with a unique *genotype** is formed.

Variation is also caused by **mutation**, a permanent change in the genetic material of a cell. Some mutations are chance occurrences, but others are caused by radiation or chemicals. Most mutations upset the balance of chemicals within an organism and cause diseases, such as cystic fibrosis. Others can result in harmless defects, such as six toes. Occasionally mutations are helpful (see next page). Mutated genes can be inherited by offspring who in turn pass them on to subsequent generations.

Variation can also be produced by the environment. Variation of this type, however, is not genetic and cannot be inherited by offspring.

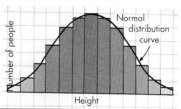

Crossing over

Homologous pair of chromosomes

*Species, 178; Gamete, 160; Histogram, 183; Meiosis, 167; Homologous pair, 166, Genotype, 166.

Evolution

Many scientists believe that organisms have changed over many millions of years, becoming more and more complex. This is called **evolution**. There are many different theories about how evolution works. The most widely accepted is Charles Darwin's theory of natural selection.

Natural selection

The theory of **natural selection** states that the individual organism best adapted to the environment will survive. It is based on the idea that most species produce more offspring than could possibly be supported by the environment. This inevitably leads to competition between individuals. Therefore, if a variation arises which better adapts an individual to the environment, that individual is more likely to survive. If this variation is caused by mutation, it will be inherited by the organism's offspring, who in turn are also more likely to survive. In this way species change and over millions of years new organisms arise.

If an existing species is separated into groups living in very different environments, the groups evolve independently of each other. This happens because different mutations suit different environments. Eventually the groups become so different that they cannot interbreed. In this way new species are formed.

Natural selection of the peppered moth

In 19th-century Britain, pollution altered the environment of the peppered moth. A light-coloured tree lichen*, which provided camouflage for the silvery form of the peppered moths, was killed by factory pollution, and the trees became blackened with smoke. As a result the silvery moths became easy prey to birds. A black form of the moth, which had arisen through mutation, now had an advantage. Their numbers gradually grew as the silvery moths disappeared.

Since the 1950s pollution levels have dropped and lichen is beginning to grow again. The population of the silvery form of the peppered moths is also increasing.

Evidence for evolution

Evidence for evolution can be found in fossils*. Scientists can work out how old fossils are by studying them and can arrange them in order according to age. Sometimes a sequence of fossils emerges which shows the gradual development of a species, from a simple organism to a more complex and better adapted one. Fossil records for the horse show such a development.

Evolutionary development of the horse from fossil evidence

Evidence for evolution is also seen in **homologous structures**. These are features, found in different species, that share a common underlying form. For example, the forelimbs of all vertebrates have a similar bone structure, although they all look very different and have different functions. One explanation for this is that the species all evolved from the same ancestor.

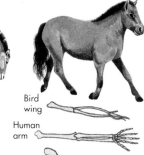

Bird wing

Human arm

Rabbit leg

*Lichen, 188; Fossil, 188.

Growth and life cycles

Growth is a permanent increase in the size or complexity of an organism. It involves a process called **synthesis**, during which new cytoplasm and cell parts are built up. Synthesis requires energy from food, and raw materials, such as amino acids.

Most multicellular animals and plants begin life as a single cell, called a **zygote**. This cell grows, taking in raw materials and making new cytoplasm and *organelles**. There is a limit, however, to how large a cell can grow.

To allow growth to continue, the cell divides to form new cells, which in turn, grow and divide. This type of cell division is called **mitosis**, and is the basis of all growth. While they are growing and developing, many organisms are called **embryos**.

As an embryo grows, groups of cells develop into *specialized** types of tissue performing different functions. This process is called **differentiation**. Once cells have become specialized, they do not usually divide any more.

Mitosis

1. Just before cell division, ▶ long and entangled chromosomes become short and fat.

2. The nuclear membrane around the nucleus disappears. Each chromosome makes an identical copy of itself. ▶

◀ **3**. The original chromosome and its copy move to opposite ends of the cell. The cell begins to divide in two.

◀ **4**. The cell divides completely. Two new cells are formed with the same number of chromosomes as the original cell. The nuclear membrane re-forms and chromosomes become long and thin again.

Measuring growth

There are three main ways of measuring growth: length, fresh mass and dry mass.
● **Length** is an easy, but not very accurate, measure of growth. It only shows upward growth and does not account for size increases in other directions.
● **Fresh mass** is a measure of the total mass of an organism. However, a measurement of fresh mass is inaccurate because it includes gains in mass which are not permanent, such as water intake.
● **Dry mass** is probably the most accurate means of measuring growth. Dry mass is found by heating an organism to just above 100°C until no further loss in weight occurs. This *evaporates** the water in the organism. The obvious disadvantage of this method is that it involves killing the organism. Therefore, in order to observe growth patterns in a particular *species**, several specimens kept in identical conditions have to be used.

Patterns of growth

The processes involved in growth are the same in all organisms, but different species grow in different ways. Uninterrupted growth in an organism is called **continuous growth**. Humans grow continuously, until they reach their full size at about the age of eighteen. Other organisms, such as insects, grow in spurts. This is called **discontinuous growth**. Insects periodically have to shed their hard *exoskeleton** to allow growth. This is called **moulting**. They can only grow in the time just after moulting before a new exoskeleton has hardened.

*Organelle, 132; Specialized, (Specialization), 133; Evaporates (Evaporation), 188; Species, 178; Exoskeleton, 158.

Development in humans

Humans grow continuously, but different parts of the body grow at different rates at different stages. The head, for example, grows very quickly in the womb, and at birth makes up one quarter of total body length. Head growth then slows down, while growth in other parts of the body speeds up. By adulthood, when growth stops, the head makes up only one eighth of body length. The diagram opposite shows how the proportions of the body change in human development.

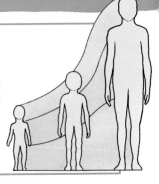

Development in insects

Many insects undergo a dramatic change in their body form in the course of their development. This is called **metamorphosis**. Metamorphosis can either be complete or incomplete.

During **incomplete metamorphosis** insects develop from a young form called a **nymph**. A nymph is similar in structure to the adult form, but lacks some of its features, such as wings and sexual organs, which develop as it reaches maturity.

During **complete metamorphosis** insects develop from a young form called a **larva** (pl. **larvae**) which does not resemble its adult form. A larva undergoes a complete change before it reaches maturity.

The stages in development of an organism from an embryo to sexual maturity is called its **life cycle**.

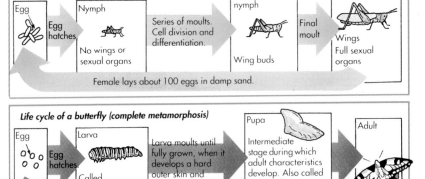

Life cycle of a locust (incomplete metamorphosis)

Egg — Egg hatches — Nymph / No wings or sexual organs — Series of moults. Cell division and differentiation. — Final nymph / Wing buds — Final moult — Adult / Wings / Full sexual organs

Female lays about 100 eggs in damp sand.

Life cycle of a butterfly (complete metamorphosis)

Egg — Egg hatches — Larva / Called a **caterpillar** — Larva moults until fully grown, when it develops a hard outer skin and becomes a pupa. — Pupa / Intermediate stage during which adult characteristics develop. Also called a **chrysalis**. — Adult

Female lays eggs on the leaves of plants.

Development in plants

Cell division in plants mainly takes place in the tip of the root and shoot (see page 155). These areas are called **meristems**. Plant cells also grow by taking in water and forming a large permanent vacuole.

Root of a young plant

Cells in this region are differentiating into specialized cells.

Cells in these regions are taking in water and expanding.

Cells in this region are dividing.

Ecology

Ecology is the study of the environment. It looks at the relationships between the **biotic** world (living organisms) and the **abiotic** (non-living) world they inhabit.

The particular place where an organism lives is called its **habitat**. The habitat of a trout , for example, is a river. The different types of organisms that share the same habitat make up a **community.**

Habitats and communities that interact to create a self-sustaining unit are called **ecosystems**. Small ecosystems interconnect to form larger ones.

Community living under a stone, makes up part of pond community

Pond community makes up part of woodland community

The Joshua tree

The abiotic features of an ecosystem, such as climate and soil composition, determine the organisms which live in it. Over millions of years organisms have evolved adaptations (see page 169) to suit a particular environment. For example, the Joshua tree has spiky leaves and a thick waxy skin made of *cutin**. These reduce water loss, so it can survive in hot dry deserts.

Ecological succession

Sometimes a habitat is cleared of its existing community. This happens, for example, in a forest after a fire. It gives the opportunity for new organisms to colonize the land. Over the years, different plant and animal communities succeed each other, as the habitat of the area changes. Eventually a community is established which will remain unchanged, as long as the abiotic factors are stable. This known as a **climax community.**

Fire destroys the existing community.

Grasses begin to grow, providing food for plant-eating animals. Plant-eating animals attract carnivorous animals to the area.

Animals supply the soil with nutrients so larger plants, shrubs and small trees can establish themselves.

Trees gradually replace shrubs and a forest develops, supporting many different animals and plants. This is the climax community.

172   *Cutin, 148.

Food chains

In an ecosystem all living things are linked by their dependence on each other for food. One *species** eats another, which in turn, is eaten by another species. This is called a **food chain.** Green plants begin any food chain because they are the only organisms that can make their own food. They are called **producers.** The food they produce provides **consumers** (all animals) with the energy they need to live. Energy is passed up the chain from plants to **primary consumers** (animals which eat plants) and from them to **secondary consumers** (animals which eat primary consumers). Secondary consumers provide energy for **tertiary consumers**, which eat secondary consumers.

All food chains also rely on **decomposers,** *saprophytic** organisms that feed on the dead remains of plants and animals. Saprophytes break down dead organic matter. This returns to the soil chemicals needed by plants to build up essential substances, such as proteins.

A food chain in a small lake

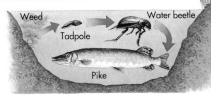

Weed · Tadpole · Water beetle · Pike

Trophic levels

A pyramid of biomass

Tertiary consumers - owls

Secondary consumers - shrews

Primary consumers - caterpillars

Producers - grasses and flowers

The position of an organism within a food chain is called its trophic level. The mass of all the organisms at a given trophic level is called the **biomass.** At each trophic level the organisms use up much of the energy they have obtained, so there is less energy to pass on to the level above. This means that at a high trophic level, fewer animals can be supported than at the level below it. This effect can be shown in a pyramid, which shows the relative biomass of each trophic level.

Food webs

Most ecosystems consist of several food chains that interlink to form complex **food webs.** This is because most animals eat more than one type of food.

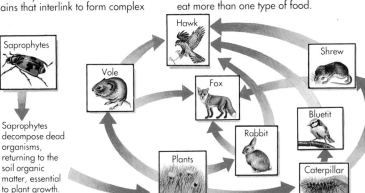

Saprophytes

Saprophytes decompose dead organisms, returning to the soil organic matter, essential to plant growth.

Hawk · Shrew · Vole · Fox · Bluetit · Rabbit · Plants · Caterpillar

**Species, 178; Saprohytic (Saprophyte), 141.*

Cycles in nature

Every ecosystem relies on the circulation of important substances between its *biotic** and *abiotic** environments.

Without this natural recycling of resources, essential elements would soon be used up.

The carbon cycle

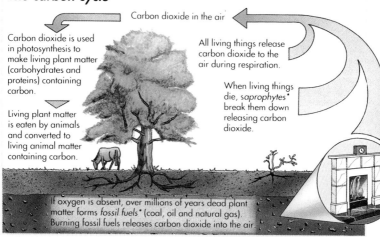

Carbon dioxide in the air

Carbon dioxide is used in photosynthesis to make living plant matter (carbohydrates and proteins) containing carbon.

Living plant matter is eaten by animals and converted to living animal matter containing carbon.

All living things release carbon dioxide to the air during respiration.

When living things die, *saprophytes** break them down releasing carbon dioxide.

If oxygen is absent, over millions of years dead plant matter forms *fossil fuels** (coal, oil and natural gas). Burning fossil fuels releases carbon dioxide into the air.

The nitrogen cycle

Plants take in *inorganic** nitrogen *compounds**, called **nitrates**, from the soil and use them to build up complex proteins. These plants are then eaten by animals, which convert plant protein into animal protein. When plants and animals die this nitrogenous matter is broken down by saprophytes and returned to the soil in the form of a nitrogen compound called **ammonia**. Ammonia also enters the soil through *urea**. Special *bacteria**, called

nitrifying bacteria, turn ammonia into minerals called **nitrites**, and then into nitrates. Nitrates are absorbed by plants and the cycle repeats itself.

Plants cannot take in nitrogen directly from the air, but there are some bacteria which can. They are called **nitrogen-fixing bacteria** and are found in the roots of some plants and in soil. They build nitrogen gas into nitrates. **Denitrifying bacteria** break down nitrates in the soil and release nitrogen to the air.

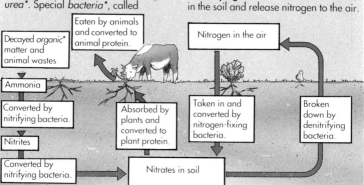

Eaten by animals and converted to animal protein.

Decayed *organic** matter and animal wastes.

Nitrogen in the air

Ammonia

Converted by nitrifying bacteria.

Absorbed by plants and converted to plant protein.

Taken in and converted by nitrogen-fixing bacteria.

Broken down by denitrifying bacteria.

Nitrites

Converted by nitrifying bacteria.

Nitrates in soil

*Biotic, 172; Abiotic, 172; Saprophyte, 141; Fossil fuel, 188; Inorganic, 134; Compound, 134; Bacteria, 178; Organic, 134.

The water cycle

The sun's heat *evaporates** water from the seas, the earth and from the leaves of plants. Water vapour *condenses** into droplets and forms clouds. Droplets collide and join together, forming larger droplets which fall as rain.

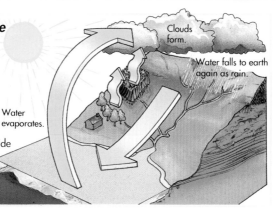

Clouds form.

Water falls to earth again as rain.

Water evaporates.

Upsetting the cycles

The natural cycles ensure that there is no waste in nature, and that the earth's resources are continually re-used. **Pollution**, however, puts into the environment materials that disrupt these cycles and threaten the balance of nature.

Acid rain

Smoke from factories and exhaust pipes contains sulphur and nitrogen oxides. These react with oxygen and water in the atmosphere to form acids which fall to earth as **acid rain** (see page 110). This interferes with the natural water cycle. The soil becomes acidic and vegetation is killed. The acid erodes stone and brick work, damaging buildings.

Chemical changes in the atmosphere turn toxic gases from power stations and car exhausts into acids.

Acid rain damages the environment.

The greenhouse effect

Carbon dioxide and some other gases in the atmosphere help keep the earth warm by trapping the sun's heat. This is called the **greenhouse effect** (see page 111).

Industrialization has led to more and more fossil fuels being burned. This means that more greenhouse gases are being released into the atmosphere. Ecologists do not know what effect that this will have, but many predict a rise in global temperatures which could result in large-scale changes in the earth's climate. This could have serious consequences for agriculture and many *habitats**.

The effect of fertilizers

Many farmers today ignore the natural nitrogen cycle and farm their fields intensively. This means that little dead organic matter (which supplies the soil with nitrates vital to healthy plant growth) is returned to the ground. To make up for this loss, farmers use chemical fertilizers. Fertilizers drain from the soil into streams and cause algae to grow unnaturally fast. In some cases algae can cover the whole surface of a stream. This prevents sunlight reaching the plants which live at the bottom of the stream, so they can no longer photosynthesize and eventually die. Complete stream *communities**, which rely on these plants, die too.

*Evaporates (Evaporation), 188; Condenses (Condensation), 188; Habitat, 172; Community, 172. 175

Conservation

Conservationists try to protect the environment from the effects of pollution. There are many different ways of doing this. Some governments pass laws that control pollution, and conservationists put pressure on politicians to introduce stricter regulations. In the end, however, conservation depends upon an awareness in everyone of how humans affect the environment.

Recycling

A compost heap

Much of the everyday waste that is thrown away could be recycled. Food wastes can be used to make compost and returned to the soil, supplying the soil with important minerals. Materials that do not decompose naturally, such as glass and plastics, can be broken down and used again. This not only reduces the amount of rubbish in rubbish dumps, but also slows down the rate at which the earth's resources are used up. Many local councils now provide recycling facilities.

Conservation of natural habitats

Gazelles are protected in East African nature reserves.

Many natural habitats are destroyed by human activities, such as farming, quarrying,and the clearance of land for new housing and roads. *Ecosystems** which have developed over hundreds of years are destroyed, and in some cases complete *species** can be wiped out. Conservationists want to minimize the number of habitats which are destroyed, and to create areas called **nature reserves**, in which wildlife can be protected. There are nature reserves all over the world which have saved species otherwise facing extinction.

Tropical rain forests

Tropical rain forests grow near the *equator** where there is an average yearly temperature of 27°C, and an average rainfall of between 40 and 100 cms per year. Rain forests are one of the oldest natural habitats on earth. They have existed and been developing for millions of years. Consequently an enormous wealth of animals and plants has evolved there, which is not found anywhere else in the world.

The rain forests are now under threat. They are being cut down for the economic benefit they provide for the often poorer countries in which they are found. This has long-term consequences. Many species are becoming extinct as their habitats are destroyed. This not only upsets larger ecosystems, but also destroys a potential source of new medicines, as many species in the rain forests produce unique chemicals. The global consequences of mass deforestation are not yet fully understood, but some ecologists believe that the world's climate will change as the forests' place in the carbon, oxygen and water cycles is upset.

Red-eyed tree frog

This is one of the species that is threatened by the destruction of the rain forests.

*Ecosystem, 172; Species, 178; Equator, 188.

The light microscope

When light travels through a **lens** (a piece of glass with curved surfaces), light rays are bent either towards or away from each other, depending on the shape of the lens. This is called **refraction** (see pages 170-171).

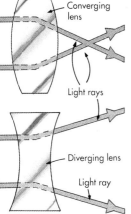

Converging lens

Light rays

Diverging lens

Light ray

Converging lenses have surfaces which curve outwards. Light rays passing through a converging lens bend inwards.

Diverging lenses have surfaces which curve inwards. Light rays passing through a diverging lens bend outwards.

How objects are magnified

An object can be seen when rays of light pass from it to the eye (see page 153). If a converging lens is placed in front of the eye, a magnified image of the object is seen. This is because the brain interprets the image the eye receives, as if light rays have travelled straight from the object, and have not been refracted by the lens.

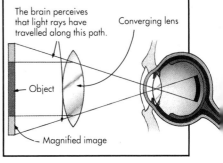

The brain perceives that light rays have travelled along this path.

Converging lens

Object

Magnified image

How a light microscope works

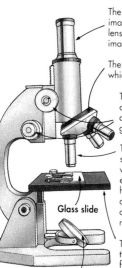

Glass slide

The **eye-piece lens** magnifies the image received by the objective lens (see below), creating the image you see.

The **nose piece** is a rotating plate which holds the objective lenses.

The **focusing knobs** allow you to change the distance between the objective lens and the specimen, to get the image in focus.

The **objective lens** magnifies the specimen, producing the image which is in turn magnified by the eye-piece lens. Some microscopes have three objective lenses with different magnifications. You can choose which one you want by rotating the nose piece.

The **stage** is the base on to which the glass slide and specimen are fixed.

The illumination system is the means by which light is passed through the specimen. In simple microscopes this is a mirror which reflects light up through the specimen.

A light microscope consists of two or more compound lenses fixed into a tube. **Compound lenses** are made up of two different types of glass which prevent the image from looking blurred.

The specimen to be examined is placed on the glass slide on the stage. It must be thin enough to allow light to pass through it, otherwise it will be invisible. To look at a thicker object, it is first necessary to cut it into thin slices. Light rays can then pass through the object, through the lenses and up to the eye. Each lens has a **magnification value** which tells you how many times bigger it makes an object appear. To find the total magnification of a microscope multiply the value of each lens being used.

Classification

To make organisms easier to study, biologists divide them into groups with similar characteristics. This is called **classification**.

Modern classification is based on a system devised in 1735 by the Swedish botanist Carl von Linné (also known as Linnaeus). Organisms are classified into groups and subgroups. The largest group is called a **kingdom**. As the groups get smaller, the organisms belonging to them have more in common. One of the smallest groups is called a **species**. Organisms of the same species are very alike and can breed together.

The list below shows the main groups in classification, using the example of a human. Scientists usually give names in Latin so that biologists all over the world can follow a single system. However the chart below uses English names, where they exist. Every organism is given two names. The second name comes from the species it belongs to and the first from the **genus** (the next largest group). This is called the **binomial** system. The biological name for a human is *Homo sapiens*.

Kingdom	Animal
Phylum (pl. **phyla**)	Chordate
Class	Mammal
Order	Primate
Family	Hominidae
Genus (pl. **genera**)	Homo
Species	sapiens

It is not possible to classify all specimens. Some, such as viruses, do not fit into any group. **Viruses** consist of *nucleic acid** within a protein coat. They can only 'live' and reproduce when living in and off other cells. Therefore biologists do not classify them as organisms, although they show many of the characteristics of living things.

The chart opposite shows some of the main groups in classification.

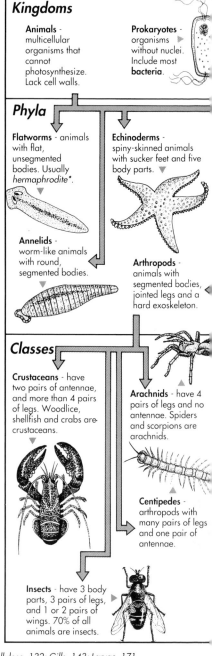

Kingdoms

Animals - multicellular organisms that cannot photosynthesize. Lack cell walls.

Prokaryotes - organisms without nuclei. Include most **bacteria**.

Phyla

Flatworms - animals with flat, unsegmented bodies. Usually *hermaphrodite**.

Echinoderms - spiny-skinned animals with sucker feet and five body parts.

Annelids - worm-like animals with round, segmented bodies.

Arthropods - animals with segmented bodies, jointed legs and a hard exoskeleton.

Classes

Crustaceans - have two pairs of antennae, and more than 4 pairs of legs. Woodlice, shellfish and crabs are crustaceans.

Arachnids - have 4 pairs of legs and no antennae. Spiders and scorpions are arachnids.

Centipedes - arthropods with many pairs of legs and one pair of antennae.

Insects - have 3 body parts, 3 pairs of legs, and 1 or 2 pairs of wings. 70% of all animals are insects.

Protoctists - simple organisms with nuclei, often unicellular. Some show characteristics of both plants and animals. Include **amoebas**.

Fungi - organisms which cannot photosynthesize. They have cell walls, which do not contain *cellulose**.

Plants - multicellular organisms capable of photosynthesis.

Molluscs - soft-bodied animals with shells.

Bryophytes - plants with simple stems, leaves and undeveloped roots. They include mosses.

Conifers - cone-bearing plants which produce seeds but without flowers or fruits.

Cnidarians - aquatic animals with tentacles, and only one body opening. They include **hydra**.

Ferns - plants with well-developed leaves, stems and roots. They do not produce seeds.

Chordates (vertebrates) - animals with backbones.

Angiosperms - seed-bearing plants that produce flowers. Most plants belong to this phylum.

Fish - have scales and fins, breathe with *gills**, and live in water. They are **cold-blooded** (their body temperature is determined by their surroundings).

Reptiles - cold-blooded with dry scaly skins. They lay soft-shelled eggs on land. They include snakes and lizards.

Amphibians - cold-blooded animals with soft skins. They live both on land and in water. *Larvae** have gills, and adults have lungs. Frogs and newts are amphibians.

Monocotyledons - angiosperms with narrow leaves.

Birds - animals covered with feathers. They have wings, lay hard-shelled eggs and are **warm-blooded**. This means they can control their body temperature internally.

Mammals - warm-blooded vertebrates, covered with hair. They produce milk for their young.

Dicotyledons - angiosperms with broad leaves.

179

Biological keys

The identification of different organisms is an important part of many biological investigations. There are many books with accurate illustrations that can be used but, in the case of organisms that look very alike, it is easy to make mistakes. To get round this, many biologists use special **biological keys**. This is a method of identification which highlights the differences between organisms and isolates the features of a specimen that separate it from others of a similar species. The diagram opposite shows a **branching key** for the identification of species collected from leaf litter (decaying plant matter which consists mainly of leaves). At each branch there is a choice between two or more characteristics, and the collector asks "Has the specimen got...". Each answer leads on to another set of characteristics until the specimen is identified.

The key shown is for the organisms found in a specific habitat. Keys for more general use are more complex with many more branches. These days, however, the use of computer programs can make identification a much quicker and easier process.

The simplest type of key is one where you are given a choice of only two statements. These are called **dichotomous keys**. Dichotomous keys can be presented as pairs of numbered statements and instructions. Use the key given below to identify the organisms shown on the right.

A branching key

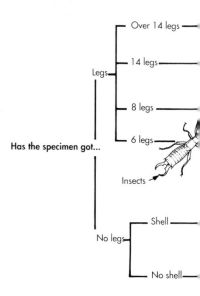

Has the specimen got...

1.	Animal with 6 jointed legs	Go to **4**
	Animals with no legs	Go to **2**
2.	Body divides into segments	Go to **3**
	Body has no segments	Flatworm
3.	Suckers at front and back end	Leech
	Long tail	Hoverfly larva
4.	Has 2 tails	Stonefly nymph
	Has 3 tails	Go to **5**
5.	Tails are 'paddle-like'	Damselfly nymph
	Tails are 'feathery'	Mayfly nymph

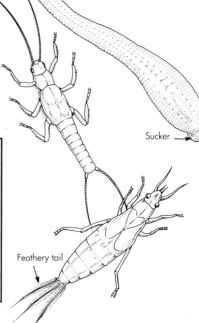

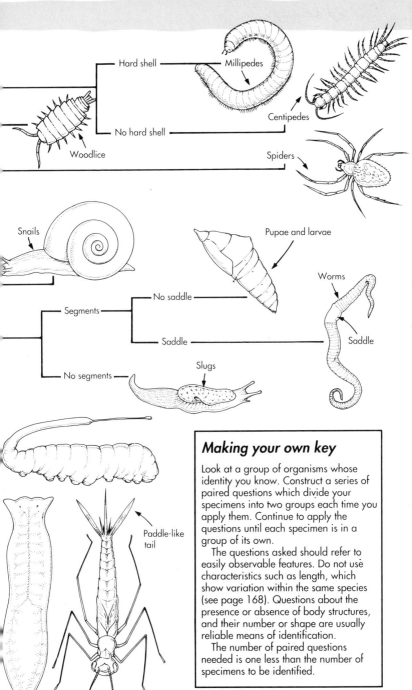

Hard shell ——— Millipedes

Centipedes

Woodlice

No hard shell

Spiders

Snails

Pupae and larvae

Worms

Segments

No saddle

Saddle

Saddle

No segments

Slugs

Paddle-like tail

Making your own key

Look at a group of organisms whose identity you know. Construct a series of paired questions which divide your specimens into two groups each time you apply them. Continue to apply the questions until each specimen is in a group of its own.

The questions asked should refer to easily observable features. Do not use characteristics such as length, which show variation within the same species (see page 168). Questions about the presence or absence of body structures, and their number or shape are usually reliable means of identification.

The number of paired questions needed is one less than the number of specimens to be identified.

Experiments

Scientists often suggest an explanation for why or how something happens. This is called a **hypothesis** (pl. **hypotheses**). Experiments are designed to test whether or not a hypothesis is correct. In the example below, an experiment has been designed to test the hypothesis that greater light intensity increases the rate of photosynthesis.

How to design an experiment

Firstly, it is essential to understand what is to be observed or measured. This is called the **dependent variable** and, in this case, is the rate of photosynthesis (measured by the number of bubbles of oxygen given off). The factor in the experiment which is being deliberately changed, in this example, light intensity, is called the **independent variable**. Set up apparatus so you can vary the light intensity and measure the bubbles of oxygen given off by a photosynthesizing plant (see page 149).

For this experiment to be 'fair', all other factors, such as temperature and humidity, must remain the same. In this way it can be shown that it is only light intensity that is affecting the result. The factors that must not change are known as **fixed variables**.

Control experiments

When the effect of the independent variable cannot be measured using only one experiment, a **control experiment** is needed. This is performed in identical conditions to the main experiment, except that the independent variable is not applied. Only by comparing the two sets of results can the effect of the independent variable be seen. For examples of control experiments see page 149.

Processing results

The way the results of an experiment are processed is very important. Well processed results show up patterns and relationships which make reaching a conclusion easier. Different ways of recording different sets of results are described below.

Line-graphs

Line-graphs visually represent the link between two sets of results, such as temperature and the rate of yeast fermentation (see page 137), showing how one changes in relation to the other.

How to plot a graph
• The x-axis is the horizontal axis. It is used to plot the independent variable (in this case, temperature).
• The y-axis is the vertical axis. It is used to plot the dependent variable (in this case, the rate of fermentation, measured by the number of bubbles of carbon dioxide released in one minute).
• Label each axis and include the unit in which it is measured (e.g. temperature in °C).
• Mark the scale of each axis and show its value. Use equal divisions along the whole axis. It is not necessary to use the same scale on both the x- and y- axis.
• Plot the points on your graph using a fine pencil. Points should be marked using a cross, or a dot within a circle ⊙
• Connect the points using a smooth curve or a straight line which is as close to as many of the points as possible. This is called the **best fit line**.

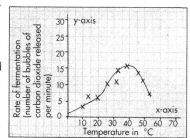

Pie charts

Pie charts represent different quantities as sectors of a circle. For example, on page 168, a pie chart is used to represent the percentage of population in Britain in each blood group.

How to construct a pie chart
The angle at the centre of a circle is 360°. This represents 100%. To find out how to draw other percentages (x) follow the formula given below:

$$360 \times \frac{x}{100} = \text{angle of circle}$$

This pie chart shows the main substances that make up the human body. The angle of the sector that represents water is calculated in the following way:

$$360 \times \frac{65}{100} = 234°$$

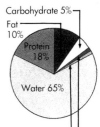

Carbohydrate 5%
Fat 10%
Protein 18%
Water 65%
Other organic substances 1%
Inorganic substances 1%

Bar charts

Bar charts make a visual comparison between several sets of results. They are used when one value is not numerical. In this example, the bar chart shows the percentage of carbohydrate in different types of chocolate.

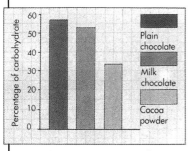

Plain chocolate
Milk chocolate
Cocoa powder

How to draw a bar chart
• Plot the non-numerical value (type of chocolate) on the x-axis, giving spaces of equal width to each value.
• Plot the numerical value (percentage of carbohydrate) on the y-axis.
• Plot the results by drawing bars of different heights. The bars must not touch. Each bar can be a different colour or shading.
• Label the chart or use a key.

Histograms

Histograms show the number of times certain values appear within a set of data. This example shows the number of individuals of a particular height within a group of 16 year old girls.

How to draw a histogram
• On the x-axis plot the value against which the set of data is being measured, in this case, height. Draw a scale dividing the axis into bars of equal width, each representing a range of heights.
• On the y-axis plot the number of

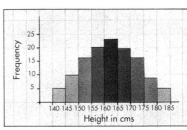

individuals in the set that fall into each range of heights.
• Plot the results. Unlike bar charts, the bars on histograms are touching.

Writing up a conclusion

A conclusion is the interpretation of the results of an experiment. It should state whether or not the results support the original hypothesis.

Indicators and tests

Many experiments and biological explorations require the identification of different substances. There are special tests which help to do this. Many of these tests use **indicators**, substances which show up the presence of another substance.

Food tests

All foods are made up of different combinations of carbohydrates, proteins, and fats (see pages 134-135). There are some basic ways in which foods can be tested to reveal the substances of which they are made (see below). Some of the solutions used could be dangerous, so wear goggles where indicated, and always wash spills with plenty of water.

- **Tests for carbohydrates**

Some carbohydrates are more complex than others. Carbohydrates of different complexities require different tests.

Simple carbohydrates, such as glucose, are tested using **Benedict's solution** in the following way:
Mash the food, then dissolve it in water.
Put a little in a test tube.
Add Benedict's solution until the solution turns blue.
Gently heat the solution in a water bath until it boils. Wear goggles for this part of the test.
A colour change to green, orange or red indicates that the food contains simple carbohydrates.

Some more complex carbohydrates, such as sucrose, do not cause a colour change when tested with Benedict's. Therefore to test for their presence they must first be broken down:
Mash the food, then dissolve it in water.
Put a little in a test tube.
Add hydrochloric acid and boil for ten minutes. Let it cool, then add a little **bicarbonate solution**.
Perform a Benedict's test as above.
Starch is tested using **iodine**:
Add drops of brown iodine solution to the food. A change to a blue/black colour shows starch is present.
(See page 148 for how to perform a starch test on a leaf.)

- **Test for protein**

The protein test described here is called the **biuret test**. You must wear goggles when performing this test.
Mash the food, then dissolve it in water.
Put a little in a test tube.
Add a little biuret solution. A mauve colour shows the presence of protein.

- **Test for fat**

Mash the food, then dissolve it in alcohol.
Put a little in a test tube.
Pour the alcohol into another test tube and add water.
If a milky white liquid forms, it means that fat is present.

Tests for gases

- **Carbon dioxide**

Bubble the gas through purple **bicarbonate indicator**.
A colour change to yellow indicates that the bubbles are carbon dioxide.
A similar test can be done using **limewater**. Carbon dioxide turns the clear limewater solution cloudy.

- **Oxygen**

Collect the gas in an inverted test tube.
If the gas is oxygen, it will relight a glowing splint.

pH tests

pH* tests show whether a solution is acidic or alkaline (see page 89). Two different methods are shown below.

- **Litmus paper**

Red litmus paper turns blue if dipped in an alkaline solution.
Blue litmus paper turns red if dipped in an acidic solution.

- **Universal indicator and the pH chart**

The **pH chart** is a range of colours, each with a corresponding number. Low pH values (1-6) are acidic, 7 is neutral and high pH values (8-13) are alkaline.
Dip the indicator paper in the solution. Remove it and observe any colour change. Match the colour to one of the colours on a pH chart.

Measurements and units

Quantity	Unit of measurement	Symbol	Relationship between units
Mass	Kilogram Gram	Kg g	1g = $^1/_{1000}$th of a kilogram
Length	Metre Centimetre Millimetre Micrometre	m cm mm μm	1cm = $^1/_{100}$th of a metre 1mm = $^1/_{1000}$th of a metre 1μm = $^1/_{1\,000\,000}$th of a metre
Area	Square metre	m²	
Volume	Cubic metre Cubic decimetre Cubic centimetre	m³ dm³ cm³	1dm³ = $^1/_{1000}$th of a cubic metre 1cm³ = $^1/_{1000}$th of a cubic decimetre
Energy	Joule Kilojoule	J kJ	1kJ = 1000J
Temperature	Degree Celsius	°C	
Time	Second Minute	s min	1 min = 60 seconds

Index notation

Index notation is a simple method of writing very large and very small numbers. For example 10,000,000 is written 10^7, and 0.0000001 is written 10^{-7}. The number written above the ten is the same as the number of zeros.

Relative sizes

Typical organisms		Length or height in metres		Magnification needed to see organisms clearly
Redwood tree Beech tree		10^3 10^2 10^1 1 10^{-1} 10^{-2} 10^{-3}	Seen by the human eye	None
Unicellular algae Buttercup				
Animal cells		10^{-4} 10^{-5} 10^{-6}	Seen through a light microscope	Between × 10^1 and × 10^3
Bacteria Viruses		10^{-7} 10^{-8} 10^{-9} 10^{-10}	Seen through an electron microscope	Between × 10^3 and × 10^6

Advances in biology

The time line below lists some of the most important biological discoveries. It also gives brief biographies of some of the scientists whose work has made a significant contribution to the study of biology.

1615 **William Harvey** (1578-1637), an English physician, discovered blood circulation.

1665 **Robert Hooke** (1635-1703), an English inventor of scientific devices, produced the first *compound lens** for a microscope. This enabled him to observe that thin sections of cork were made up of angular spaces which he called 'cells'.

1680 **Anton van Leeuwenhoek** (1632-1723), a Dutch microscopist, observed blood capillaries, red blood cells, bacteria and pond microbes. He made his own lenses for his microscopes.

1750 **Carl von Linné** (1707-1778), also known as **Linnaeus**, was a Swedish biologist. He proposed a system for the classification of organisms which is still used today (see pages 178-179).

1796 **Edward Jenner** (1749-1823), an English physician, discovered a new procedure to inoculate individuals from disease. He prevented people from catching the fatal smallpox disease by injecting them with cowpox, a mild form of the smallpox virus developed by cows.

1840 **Jakob Schleiden** (1804-1881), a German botanist and a skilled microscopist, observed cells in all plant structures and accurately described many of their properties.

Claude Bernard (1813-1878) was a French medical experimenter. His work revealed the importance of *homeostasis**, the role of the pancreas in digestion, the way oxygen is carried round the body, and how involuntary actions are controlled.

1858 **Charles Darwin** (1809-1882), a British naturalist, published his theory of evolution (see page 169).

Gregor Mendel (1822-1884), an Austrian monk, discovered the basic laws of inheritance through his experiments with pea plants. He deduced that hereditary elements determine the characteristics of offspring.

1875 **Louis Pasteur** (1822-1895), a French chemist, showed that microbes cause fermentation and disease. The German bacteriologist, **Robert Koch** (1843-1910), also contributed much to this field.

1928 **Alexander Fleming** (1881-1955), a Scottish bacteriologist discovered penicillin, a mould that kills bacteria.

Karl von Frisch (1886-1982), an Austrian biologist, pioneered the practise of 'in the field' experiments for studying animals. His studies of honey bees showed that they use a complex system for transmitting information.

1945 The American geneticists, **George Beadle** (1903-1989) and **Edward Tatum** (1909-), concluded that one gene controlled the production of one enzyme.

1950 The electron microscope revealed more clearly the structure of the cell.

1953 **James Watson** (1928-), an American biochemist, and **Francis Crick** (1916-), a British molecular biologist, co-discovered the structure of DNA.

Louis Leakey (1903-1972) and **Mary Leakey** (1913-) were a British husband and wife team whose archaeological findings showed that humans had evolved in Africa earlier than was previously believed.

Rachel Carson (1907-1964) was an American biologist whose book *The Silent Spring* popularized and raised awareness of ecological matters.

*Compound lens, 177; Homeostasis, 151.

The development of life on earth

Scientists believe that the earth formed about 4,500 Ma (million years) ago. The study of fossils suggests that primitive life, such as unicellular protoctists, first appeared on the earth about 3500 Ma ago, when the earth was covered with water. About 1000 Ma ago multicellular life appeared, and 700 Ma ago more complex organisms, such as jellyfish and molluscs, had developed.

As the earth's surface changed and land appeared, organisms developed which could live out of water and breathe through lungs. About two million years ago an organism appeared that walked upright. This organism has been given the name *Homo erectus*, and is thought to be one of the ancestors of humans (*Homo sapiens*).

This chart shows when different organisms first appeared on earth. The dates are only approximate.

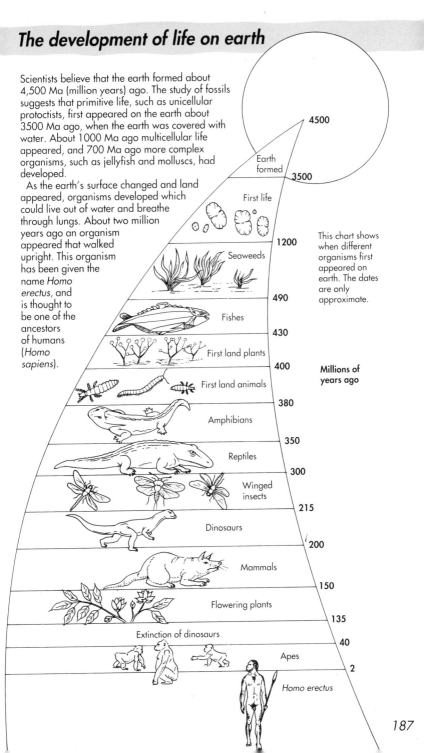

4500

Earth formed

3500

First life

1200

Seaweeds

490

Fishes

430

First land plants

400

Millions of years ago

First land animals

380

Amphibians

350

Reptiles

300

Winged insects

215

Dinosaurs

200

Mammals

150

Flowering plants

135

Extinction of dinosaurs

40

Apes

2

Homo erectus

187

Glossary

The glossary defines some of the more difficult terms which are used in the text but are not fully explained.

Air pressure. The earth is surrounded by a layer of gases which make up air. The weight of air above any part of the earth is called air pressure. Air pressure increases when air is compressed into a smaller volume, and decreases when it is expanded into a larger volume.

Cancer. A disease caused by a disorder in cell growth. Cells continue to grow and divide after they should have stopped. This results in a lump of cells, called a **tumour**, which can invade and destroy the healthy tissue surrounding it. Cancer cells may spread to other parts of the body via the bloodstream or the lymphatic system, causing more extensive tissue damage.

Catalyst. A substance which increases the rate at which a chemical reaction takes place, without undergoing any permanent change itself.

Condensation. The change of a vapour or gas into a liquid, normally caused by cooling. The vapour or gas loses some of its energy.

Equator. An imaginary line that circles the centre of the earth from east to west.

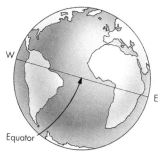

Evaporation. The change in state of a substance from a liquid to a gas or vapour, at a temperature below the liquid's boiling point. Evaporation requires heat energy.

A fossil of a shell

Fossil. The remains or traces of an organism that lived millions of years ago. Fossils are formed in exceptional circumstances when, instead of decaying, dead organisms become buried in mud and sediment. Over millions of years they are hardened into rock. In general, it is only the hard parts of the organisms, such as wood, bones or shells, that are preserved.

Fossil fuels. The general term for coal, oil and natural gas. Fossil fuels are formed over millions of years by the bodies of dead organisms which are compressed under the earth's surface.

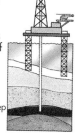

Oil rigs recover oil from deep below the earth's surface.

Immune system. The name given to the body's internal defences against disease.

Lichen. A combination of two organisms, a fungus and an alga, that live off each other. The alga photosynthesizes and provides food for the fungus. The fungus protects the alga. Lichens grow in many places, including on tree trunks, over old walls, on the ground and on exposed rocks.

Medium. An environment in which other substances exist, or certain phenomena take place. For example, water is the medium for the chemical reactions which take place in the body.

pH. The acidity or alkalinity of a solution. Acidity and alkalinity depend upon how the hydrogen atoms within a solution behave chemically. The pH of a solution can tested using universal indicator and a pH chart (see page 184).

Index

First published in 1992 by Usborne Publishing
Ltd, 83-85 Saffron Hill, London EC1N 8RT,
England.

The name Usborne and the device ᵜ are
trade marks of Usborne Publishing Ltd.
Printed in Spain.